Silent Partners

Kristy —
To someone who saw
this in its raw form!
Thanks for all your help!
Best wishes

SILENT PARTNERS

Michael Ting

iUniverse, Inc.
New York Lincoln Shanghai

Silent Partners

Copyright © 2006 by Michael Ting

All rights reserved. No part of this book may be used or reproduced by any means, graphic, electronic, or mechanical, including photocopying, recording, taping or by any information storage retrieval system without the written permission of the publisher except in the case of brief quotations embodied in critical articles and reviews.

iUniverse books may be ordered through booksellers or by contacting:

iUniverse
2021 Pine Lake Road, Suite 100
Lincoln, NE 68512
www.iuniverse.com
1-800-Authors (1-800-288-4677)

This is a work of fiction. All of the characters, names, incidents, organizations and dialogue in this novel are either the products of the author's imagination or are used fictitiously.

ISBN-13: 978-0-595-38245-3 (pbk)
ISBN-13: 978-0-595-82614-8 (ebk)
ISBN-10: 0-595-38245-2 (pbk)
ISBN-10: 0-595-82614-8 (ebk)

Printed in the United States of America

PROLOGUE

▼

The vacuum seal wrapped around the black binder was airtight. It had been tested repeatedly to ensure that the contents would stay intact indefinitely. He held it in his hands and estimated that there might be about two hundred pages inside. It would weigh twice as much once he was in the water.

The boat rested calmly on the glassy surface of the western Caribbean. He placed the binder inside the black metal box and sealed it. The box had been specifically designed to withstand long periods in water: it was rust-resistant and lined with a military-strength seal to prevent leakage.

He had traveled about twenty miles off the Yucatan's eastern coast. The Chinchorro Banks was a thirty-mile stretch of reef between Cozumel and Belize, with close to one hundred and twenty recorded shipwrecks in the vicinity. He checked his compass. His wreck was no further than two hundred yards to the south. It was still early, and he was alone. The live-aboard dive boats which frequented the area throughout the day would be arriving soon, so he had to get moving. He ran his hand over his shiny, bald head and felt the first signs of sun exposure on his scalp. He had shaved his hair off just the day before and hadn't yet grown accustomed to it.

He quickly strapped on his gear and walked over to the edge of the deck, where he gently lowered the metal box into the water. He held onto the end of the yellow rope that was tethered to the box. He slightly inflated his BCD, the vest which divers wear to control their buoyancy level in the water. His weight belt contained only a fraction of the weight he normally wore while diving, since he knew the weight of the metal box would cause him to sink like a rock. Holding the rope tightly, he dropped into the open water.

Immediately, he felt the weight of the box pulling him down. He grasped the rope with both hands while kicking to control his rate of descent. At about twenty-five feet, he began making his way south along the reef. He passed by several wrecks, ranging from cargo ships to Spanish galleons.

And then he saw it. About thirty feet in length, the small vessel lay on its side. It had been down there for some thirty years, and parts of it showed the wear of decades of neglect. Despite the discoloration from years of sunlight and seawater, it appeared intact. Still feeling the weight of the box, he slowly made his way around the boat, searching for the opening to the galley. Pulling the rope toward him until his hands were firmly around the box, he negotiated his way through the doorway, careful not to brush the top of the frame with his tank. He found the small compartment against the far wall, as expected, and gently placed the box inside. Sliding the four-inch dagger from the sheath wrapped around his leg, in a single motion he slashed through the rope, which he coiled and secured inside his vest. With one quick look around, he exited the sunken boat and began slowly ascending to the surface. The whole operation had taken twenty-three minutes, two and a half short of what he had targeted.

On the surface, the sun was shining brightly by this time, and he could make out the small shape of a distant boat approaching, likely recreational divers. He started the engine and turned south, toward Belize.

Back in Ambergris Caye, the Plantation Suite at Victoria House was just what he had expected: a sitting room with light wood furniture and white cushions, as well as a full bar and kitchen. Double French doors opened onto a veranda overlooking the crystal clear waters. It was exquisite, but he knew he could not stay.

He rummaged through the dressers and desk drawers until he found two brass keys. He held them up to examine the serial numbers closely before shoving them into his pocket.

He left the suite and walked to the reception area. A young black man behind the counter smiled and handed him the bill. He paid in cash and bid the young man farewell.

"Thank you for staying with us, Mr. Phillips," the young man said in a Caribbean accent.

He had spent the last eighteen years of his life answering to names that were not his own. It had become as natural to him as breathing.

He nodded back to the desk clerk and stepped out onto the paved path of Coconut Drive. He glanced in both directions and casually began the one and a half mile walk to the airstrip.

Chapter 1

▼

At the opening bell, Ensight, Inc. was trading at fifteen and a half, down from eighteen and three-quarters at the close from the day before. All this, despite the NASDAQ being up by more than thirty points. The company had missed its second quarter earnings estimate by more than twenty cents per share. Ensight's new CEO, brought in after her predecessor's tragic death, had completed her first full quarter, and the results were atrocious. Although the new CEO made the best attempt to allay the concerns of investors, they remained disillusioned. They wanted growth, the same growth the company had shown in the late 90s.

Ensight, Inc. was a financial software firm, specializing in finding solutions for financial advisors and community banks to better facilitate their back-office operations, such as accounting, reporting, billing, and so on. The burst of the Internet bubble and the industry consolidation that followed dried up the demand for such solutions. Ensight needed an infusion of innovation to recover and revitalize.

In contrast, Maguire Solutions was the newest Wall Street darling, competing with the likes of Google and eBay. The Chicago-based company had completed three acquisitions in the last eighteen months, each deal valued at close to a billion dollars. On this same day, Maguire's stock was up fourteen points on news that the company's second quarter earnings announcement was going to blow the doors off the estimate.

The strategy and finance teams at Maguire had been looking covertly at Ensight for the last year. As each fiscal quarter passed, the idea of acquiring Ensight became more tempting. The think tank at Maguire knew it could keep

Ensight running by purchasing it and, in a year or less, enjoy the rewards of its expected rebound in the marketplace.

The CEO of Maguire had first approached his counterpart at Ensight in June about a deal, only two months after she replaced the old chief. The meeting lasted less than one hour. The Ensight CEO assured the Maguire executives and the rest of the world that she had a plan to turn the company around. But after some significant client attrition over the next three months and a failure to reorganize the company structure, Ensight's board grew impatient and recommended that it begin entertaining potential suitors, while it could still command a respectable price tag in the market.

Not far from Ensight's offices in San Francisco, the man sat on the edge of his bed in his hotel room at the Hotel Vitale. It was 6:45 AM, and he had been awake for nearly two hours. As he rapidly packed his bags, he could hear the television faintly in the background. The two analysts on CNBC's morning business news agreed that Ensight needed a kick in the pants and debated the fair value of its assets. He laughed lightly to himself as he listened to these two people speculate about Ensight's future, hearing them talk about what a few select people had known for quite some time.

He stepped toward the door in his hotel room and looked in the mirror on the wall. He tied his ponytail tightly and checked the rest of his appearance. He smiled and exited the room.

Chapter 2

▼

"Thirty-four, please."

"Certainly," replied the man in a brown UPS uniform.

Amber was breathing heavily as she entered through the elevator doors. The delivery man stood at the front corner of the elevator, eyes forward, inches from the button panel. From the corner of his eye, he couldn't help noticing the constant tapping of Amber's sling-backs on the floor, while she simultaneously twirled her fingers in her hair. Playing with her hair was a nervous habit that she had adopted at an early age. She would continue doing it until her fingers were completely entangled in her hair. Then she would make a game of reversing the process until her fingers were free again. When she was young, it gave her something to do when her parents were arguing in the next room.

The delivery man glanced over his shoulder, and Amber stopped her tapping.

"Sorry about that," she said with a nervous laugh, untangling her fingers from her hair.

He smiled back. At that moment, the elevator doors opened on the twentieth floor. As he exited, Amber assumed his position in front of the button panel. She hit the button to the thirty-fourth floor over and over, whispering to herself, in the hopes that the elevator would respond to the urgency of her request.

She had been combing the building in search of Marty for over thirty minutes. She tried contacting him on his Blackberry but knew immediately that he would never respond. All officers in the company were required to carry the electronic leashes on their belts. During the last eight months, accessibility had become a key objective established by the executive team. However, thirty years at Ensight,

Inc. had earned Marty Callahan some liberties, the most prized of which was the right to be unavailable at times.

Amber watched the red digital numerals change as the elevator gradually ascended. Thirty-two, thirty-three...She moved to the midpoint of the two doors. The numbers on the display finally read *34*. The doors were not open more than six inches before Amber squeezed her way between them. As she walked quickly down the hallway toward the main conference room, she caught a blurred glimpse of the offices lining the perimeter of the executive floor. All were unoccupied, their lights off, chairs pushed in, and desks neatly organized.

All the executives were in the main conference room. The rumor within the privileged areas of the company was that Maguire was making a bid to acquire Ensight. Today the officers of Ensight were meeting with their counterparts at Maguire to discuss terms of the deal. Generally, Marty would never be invited to such a meeting, much to his relief. But Ensight's CEO, Kaitlyn McBride, insisted that he attend this meeting. The companies were planning to discuss staff integration and the inevitable cuts to the Ensight workforce. As senior vice president of human resources, Marty had to be present.

Amber approached the large oak doors of the main conference room, Gandalf, a reference to the Tolkien epic, *The Lord of the Rings*. Naming conference rooms after literary characters was a remnant of the dot-com days, a way to appeal to Ensight's young, Internet-savvy customer base. These days it was just a stupid name whose context was lost on most visitors.

From beneath the doors, it was evident that the lights were off, a clear indicator of a presentation in progress. She cracked open one of the doors, and a beam of light stretched the length of the room, immediately prompting all of the attendees to turn toward the source of the interruption.

At the far end of the long mahogany table sat Kaitlyn McBride. She leaned forward in her leather, high-backed chair and held up one hand toward the presenter.

"Hang on a second, Dick." The CFO immediately stopped his presentation. "Yes, Miss Wakefield?" she asked.

"I need to steal Marty for a quick moment if that's OK," Amber practically whispered. She hated interrupting these meetings.

Kaitlyn looked over at Marty, who was stirring in his seat, no doubt pulling himself out of the nap he had been enjoying ever since the lights went down. "Go ahead, Marty. We can fill you in later."

"Thank you," Marty replied, trying hard to mask his elation. He turned towards the Maguire team. "Excuse me for stepping out like this."

They all turned back toward the screen hung on the wall, where an enlarged graph illustrated one of Ensight's key metrics. He would not be missed.

"Go ahead, Dick," Kaitlyn said.

As Marty rose to his feet and headed toward the door, he winked at Amber, who shook her head in playful disapproval.

Dick continued with his presentation. "So, as you can see, we had a 31 percent increase in…" The door closed quickly behind Marty.

"Thank you for that," said Marty, placing his hand gently on Amber's shoulder. "No officer in this company has an assistant who can get him out of a meeting like you can."

"Well, Marty, I wish that was the only reason today."

"Ah, man, are you going to tell me that I'm actually going to have some work to do?" There was that wink again.

"Marty, be serious." Amber wasn't smiling this time.

Marty's smile faded quickly. He knew when to stop with Amber. Despite the fact that he was much higher in the company than Amber, he always made the effort to avoid testing her, much more so at least than he would with either of his ex-wives.

"OK, I'm sorry. What's the problem?"

"Guess." She raised her eyebrows in a way that let him know that she was offering him only one guess.

He read it instantly. "You're kidding me." Amber shook her head slowly. She held out a FedEx envelope to his face. He stared at it as if it carried some communicable disease.

Taking the envelope from her, he pulled out a single sheet of paper and read, his lips slightly moving.

"Well, I guess I can't hide from them any longer," he said.

For the last three months, the Internal Revenue Service (IRS) had been calling Marty about some W-2 forms the company had filed on behalf of its employees during the last tax year. The IRS had been asking him to assist them in reconciling some of the employees' records. To date, the details had been vague, and Marty was not about to ask for more information, fearing that any curiosity on his part would be interpreted as implicit cooperation. Marty was sixty-three years old, on a one-way trip toward retirement. His white hair was distinctive, but sparse. Unfortunately, while his hair was thin, the rest of him was not. He had been on cruise control for the last seven months, coincidentally around the time Kaitlyn McBride took the helm at Ensight after the death of Bill Raleigh, the former CEO and Marty's best friend. Marty was fond of Kaitlyn but lacked the energy to keep up with his much younger superior. The last thing he wanted was to enter into any obligation that might have even a remote chance of prolonging his stay at Ensight. But the IRS was clearly onto him. He had run out of excuses. He couldn't hold them off any longer.

He handed the letter back to Amber. "It says they're going to be here tomorrow at eight o'clock AM. Can you book a conference room for us?"

"Sure, no problem. Do you want me to call them to confirm?"

"I don't think that's necessary, Amber. They'll be here bright and early tomorrow whether it's convenient for us or not." He glanced down at his watch. Four thirty. "I'm going for the day."

"Do you want to grab a drink or dinner or something tonight?" Amber called out to him as he turned to leave.

"Probably not tonight, dear." Standing nearly six inches taller, Marty looked into her large hazel eyes. When she looked upwards, they took on a playful manner. Her nose turned slightly upwards, which was always a source of self-consciousness. Only a handful of people knew that she had surgery to correct a deviated septum just before her freshman year. She looked stunning today, with her dirty blonde hair cascading down her shoulders. Her blouse was powder blue, and the top two buttons were undone, a hint of white lace visible from his vantage point. It left just enough to the wandering eye of a twice-divorced, soon-to-be retiree.

"Are you sure?" She cracked a sensuous smile that didn't reveal her near perfect teeth. Harmless flirting, she called it.

Marty looked away, trying feebly to hide his embarrassment but playing the game right back. "I've got to work tomorrow," he teased. At that, he delivered a final wink.

Amber smiled again and rolled her eyes. "See ya tomorrow, Marty."

He waved good-bye over his shoulder and walked toward the elevator.

Chapter 3

"Mr. Callahan, I presume?"

"That's right. Please, call me Marty." Marty extended his hand.

"I'm Bruce Fox, IRS Wage and Investment Division," he said, reaching across the conference table to shake Marty's hand. They exchanged business cards and laid them face up on the table.

"This is Amber Wakefield, my assistant." Amber stepped forward and extended her hand.

"Miss Wakefield." Fox shook her hand and nodded, noting her features.

Fox was flanked by two men on either side of him, both of whom wore bland-colored suits with striped ties.

"This is David Stemple and Charlie Wood." The two men held their hands out.

"Gentlemen," Marty said as he shook their hands. Amber parroted her boss's actions.

Everyone sat down at the table simultaneously.

Fox spoke first, being sure to dictate the pace of the meeting. "Well, now that introductions are out of the way, I want to thank you, Mr. Calla—uh, Marty, for meeting with us. I realize we aren't exactly the type of visitors you wish to roll out the fine pastries for."

The three IRS men laughed. Marty sat expressionless. *Can we get through this, please?* he thought to himself.

Fox continued, "Anyway, as we've mentioned in our numerous letters to you over the last few months, we've come across some irregularities related to documents Ensight has furnished to the IRS on behalf of its employees."

"Irregularities?" Marty asked. "Can you be more specific?"

"'Inconsistencies' is probably the more appropriate term to characterize this situation," Stemple interjected.

Marty sat forward in his chair, his stomach pinned against the table's edge and his elbows resting firmly on the tabletop. "With all due respect, I appreciate your attempt at being tactful here, but can we cut to the chase? We have over ten thousand employees worldwide. If one of our employees is involved in any type of impropriety, then we have no reason not to cooperate with you. Tell me what's going on."

Fox mirrored Marty's posture. "It seems that one of your employees, for whom we have received a W-2 for the past three years, has not filed a Form 1040 for those same periods."

"You're saying that we have an employee who has possibly been evading taxes for the last three years?"

"That's what the early indications tell us," replied Fox. His two lieutenants nodded in agreement.

"Well, isn't that an issue between the IRS and this individual? After all, Ensight fulfilled its obligation. We're not responsible for enforcing the tax law for the IRS, are we?" Marty grinned smugly. He then turned quickly to Amber. "We're not, are we, Amber?"

Amber shook her head while looking down, obviously embarrassed by her boss's sarcastic behavior.

Fox stroked the gray goatee on his chin. "Generally speaking, Marty, you are correct. It is an issue to be resolved directly with the individual. However, we've attempted to contact this individual to no avail. Over the last several months, we've mailed him three separate letters marked as urgent to the address printed on his W-2, and we have yet to receive a response." Marty's smile faded. "Furthermore," Fox continued, "we've never had any of the letters returned to us, which would indicate that the address is valid."

"Well, naturally, we'll do whatever we can to help you," Marty said. "But I have to wonder how unique this situation really is. I mean, there's got to be more than a handful of people in this country who skip out on filing their tax returns. Do you go after all of them with the same vigor?"

Fox smiled. "I'd love to say we do, Marty. But you're right; we can't catch all of them."

Amber was becoming more intrigued. "Mr. Fox, may I ask what was so special about this particular case?"

Fox and his two lieutenants sat up simultaneously, each starting to respond to this beautiful woman's question. But Fox spoke first, practically standing on the tongues of the other two.

"I was waiting for you to ask that question, Miss Wakefield," he said with a wide grin.

Amber raised her left eyebrow and tilted her head slightly, as if to say, "Well?"

Fox caught himself looking at Amber's chest and fantasizing. He cleared his throat. "This particular individual grossed nearly two million dollars in total wages during that three-year period."

Marty let out a loud obnoxious cough in an effort to redirect Fox's focus to the topic and away from Amber's breasts. "Al Capone evaded taxes and made a hell of a lot more money than that. Look how long it took to catch him."

Charlie Wood finally spoke. "Al Capone buried his income in a host of business fronts. He made damn sure to hide from the government. The person we are investigating here is not making any effort to hide. He is blatantly and openly defying his obligation."

Marty gazed at the young man quizzically. *Jesus, did this Boy Scout just read me an excerpt from the citizen's rulebook?*

"Besides, what's your point?" Fox asked.

"My point is simple. There are probably tons of people out there whose income is a lot more than a half million a year, and I'm sure a not-so-insignificant number of these big fish are 'defying their obligations,' if not fudging them a little. I'm just curious as to why you guys are so intent on pinning this one down." Marty could be relentless at times, to the point of being annoying for no other reason but that.

Fox sat back in his chair and sighed, doing nothing to mask his frustration. "Marty, I promise you something. As we get further into the details of this case, all your questions will be answered."

The two men stared at each from across the table for a long minute. Finally, Marty smiled and nodded. "Then let's get on with it."

* * * *

The men had removed their suit jackets and hung them over their seat backs. David Stemple took his briefcase from beneath the table and removed a brown-marbled accordion file. He began to take pages out and lay them neatly on the table. Marty took the liberty of picking up the pages in arbitrary order and scanning them. "Harper Phillips," he said quietly. He handed the page to Amber. "Does that name ring a bell?"

Amber read the name closely as if seeing it might have a different effect than hearing it. She shook her head slowly. "I can pull up the personnel files and check."

"Yes, why don't you go do that, dear," said Marty.

"I'll be right back." The men watched her leave.

After a few moments, Amber returned carrying a laptop computer, which she set on the table. As the machine booted, Marty continued to peruse the numerous documents: W-2s, 1099s from a number of brokerages, credit card statements, bank statements, all with red marks and notes transcribed in the margins.

The room was silent except for the rhythmic clatter of Amber's fingernails as she typed a series of commands.

"Here we go," she said. "This is the company-wide personnel database with the records of all employees—salaries, bonuses, performance reviews, resumes, W-2s, W-4s, stock options, 401(k) information. Everything you need to know." Continuing to type as she talked, Amber entered *Phillips* in the search field. *62 results.* She filled in the first name field: *Harper* and immediately got one result. She highlighted the name on the screen and double-clicked. A number of colored boxes appeared onscreen, each labeled with a specific section of the employee's file.

Marty leaned to the side to get a better view of the computer. Fox and the two others had made their way to the other side of the table, where they huddled around Amber and focused on the screen "OK, first things first," Marty said, his interest piqued. "What office does this Harper Phillips work in?"

Amber navigated the cursor to the orange box labeled *Basic Information*, and clicked once on it. The screen immediately displayed details of the employee's personal data and position in the company. Harper Phillips was a security engineer in the information systems department.

"Hey, what do you know, he works in this office," Amber noted by pointing to the field marked *TITLE/DEPARTMENT*. The men moved in closer to get a better look.

"How many people work in this office?" Fox inquired.

"I think at last count, it was about four hundred and thirty-five. That includes temps and contractors," Amber replied. "It's hard to keep track, since this is the global headquarters, and we've always got people from the other offices transferring here or out on extended assignments."

"Can we tell what floor he's on?" Wood asked.

"Right here," Amber said as she pointed to the field marked *LOCATION* on the screen.

"Ninth floor," Stemple read.

"Can we pay him a visit?" Fox asked with eyebrows raised.

Amber turned to Marty, who was scratching his head. "I feel a little strange pointing out one of our employees to the IRS. Is there another way to do this without making it look like his own company ratted him out?"

"We feel like we've tried everything we can," Fox explained, while counting off his fingers. "We've tried letters, even phone calls to his home, and we've never had a reply."

"Amber, can we try calling him at his desk?" Marty asked.

"Sure," Amber replied, reaching for the phone in the middle of the conference table and dialing the numbers she read on the computer screen. The men in the room waited intently as she listened. She shook her head at them. "Voice mail."

"Marty," Fox started. He cracked a smile, as if he and Marty had been friends for years.

Marty looked down at his shoes for an answer. Without looking up, he nodded ever so slightly.

Fox and his men grabbed their coats and followed Marty and Amber out of the conference room.

Chapter 4

▼

As the elevator descended to the ninth floor, no one spoke. Fox tried some small talk to relieve the guilt that was obviously scrawled across Marty's face. When the elevator doors opened, the group immediately smelled the stench of what could only be the floor housing the information systems department. It was a blend of perspiration and aging food buried deep in the overflowing trash receptacles. The IRS visitors held their hands to their noses as they stepped onto the floor.

The hallway was lined with cardboard boxes labeled Sun, Cisco Systems, and a few other common brand names. Amber was walking in front of the group, holding an oversized sheet of paper that depicted the seating chart for the building.

"What cube number is he in, Amber?" Marty called out from the rear of the pack.

"Seventy-nine," Amber said as she read the chart.

"Here's sixty-eight." Stemple pointed to the cube they were passing.

"It must be one of those against the window." Amber gestured with her chin.

They proceeded toward the window, where one could see a clear view of the San Francisco Bay. As they walked along the sequentially numbered cubicles along the window, they each counted to themselves, even Marty. Seventy-six, seventy-seven, seventy-eight, seventy-ni—. They all looked around simultaneously, all equally puzzled.

"Where's seventy-nine?" Fox asked.

"The desks just end here with seventy-eight," Wood noted. "There is no seventy-nine."

Amber pulled out her cell phone. "Hang on, I probably don't have the most updated seating chart. I'll call the facilities manager really quickly." She hit two digits on her phone and held it up to her face like a walkie-talkie. Finally, a beep sounded, followed by a deep voice.

"Hey, Amber, you pinged me?" said the voice on the other end.

"Hey, Max. Question for you."

"Yeah, go." Max's voice was a baritone. He was obviously eating something crunchy, probably potato chips, or some snack which should never be eaten before ten o'clock in the morning.

"I've got the seating chart in front of me, and I was wondering…" Amber began.

"Which version?" Max clearly didn't have time to spare, away from his noshing.

"Um, I don't know. How do I figure that out?"

Max sighed through the speaker. "It's on the bottom, right-hand corner. It has four characters."

Amber scanned the sheet. Stemple stepped forward and pointed out the four numbers to her, as if she needed help. She read the numbers into the phone.

"Hang on," Max sighed. After a beat, he returned. "OK, I've got it in front of me. What's your question?"

"Well, we were trying to find cubicle number seventy-nine on the ninth floor. We can't seem to find it. It runs only to number seventy-eight."

Again, the line was silent for a few seconds until Max returned. "You're right. I see that, too. Some guy named Harper Phillips sits there. Never heard of him."

"I assume I'm looking at the most recent version, since I picked it off the intranet," Amber said.

"You should be. Hang on a sec, let me pull the original chart." Another few seconds passed. "Hmm, that's odd."

"What's that?"

"There is no cubicle seventy-nine on the master version," Max reported. He sounded a little bit more alert.

There was a long silence on both ends. Amber ended the call, as they all attempted to answer the rushing river of questions flowing through each of their minds. Amber, who had clearly assumed leadership for this expedition, walked quickly toward the hallway leading to the kitchen. Walking in the opposite direction was one of the residents of the ninth floor, whom it was clear that Amber knew well.

"Sanjay, how are you today?" she said as she waved down the hall. Sanjay Mehta was one of the more seasoned IT professionals at Ensight. He was also Amber's backdoor key. Everyone who was anyone in the company had a backdoor key, someone who could shortcut any request without having to go through all the usual protocol. Password resets, new equipment, software and memory upgrades—whatever you needed, the backdoor key could get it done.

"I'm very well, Miss Wakefield," replied Sanjay with a thick Indian accent. "What brings you to the dark bowels of the ninth floor?"

"I'm looking for someone who supposedly works on this floor. His name is Harper Phillips. Do you know him?"

Sanjay cocked his head back and frowned. "I've never heard of any such person. What department does he work in?"

"Well, according to the personnel database, he works here, in security."

"Not possible. I know everyone in security, as well as everyone on this floor. There is no one by that name here. The personnel database is probably false. You know how faulty these systems can be," he laughed.

"I'm sure you're right. Thanks, Sanjay." Amber smiled and placed her hand gently on his arm. "I'll talk to you soon."

"My pleasure, Miss Wakefield," he said, blushing. As she walked away, Sanjay looked around to see if any of his IT buddies had caught a glimpse of the affectionate contact he had just made with the coveted Miss Amber Wakefield. But no such luck. Damn, no witnesses.

"What did Mr. Mehta have to say?" Marty asked as Amber was walking toward them.

"He's never heard of Harper Phillips."

Four hours later, the search for Harper Phillips had progressed no further than it had since eight o'clock that morning.

"This is the part of my job I love," said Sean Hillard, a twentysomething IT worker. Sean had a shaved head, piercings in his nose and eyebrow, and four tattoos on both arms. He rode his skateboard to work each day and graduated in the top ten of his class at MIT. "It's like I'm in the CIA and someone has just asked me to infiltrate the top secret files of an enemy's defense system."

"Not quite, Sean," Amber said. Sean was accessing Harper Phillips's personal folders on the network. He adeptly typed commands to bypass the password of the authorized user.

"Dude, this guy doesn't work very hard," Sean said as he read a series of rows on his terminal screen.

"Why do you say that?" Fox asked.

"Well, only about 3 percent of his storage drive is occupied right now. Let's take a look at his e-mail account." He continued to type furiously.

The screen pulled up an inbox of a Microsoft Outlook window. A series of messages were listed, all in bold type, indicating that they had not been opened or read.

"Well, it looks like he definitely gets e-mail, so the account is valid," Stemple noted.

"Not necessarily," Amber said, pointing the tip of her pen to the *From* column. "All these messages came from the company. These are all internal memos posted to the *All Employees* distribution group."

"Nice catch, Lois Lane," Sean remarked.

"Go to his Sent Items box," Amber said with a suspicious tone. She already had a feeling what they would find there, but she had to be sure. As her fingers got lost in her blond tresses, she watch as Sean clicked on the *Sent Items* box. Nothing. The message in italics read *No items to display in this folder.*

Fox stared intently at the air in front of him. It was as if he was performing some extensive calculation in his head. "Mr. Stemple," he started, as he turned to his assistant, "call the commissioner's office. Tell them we need some help out here."

Chapter 5

▼

He stepped out of the red taxicab and walked toward the large glass doors of the Conrad Hotel. The humidity in the evening air was thick, and he took a deep breath as the taxicab drove away. A tall Chinese man, wearing a white uniform, manned the door.

"Good evening, sir," he said with a courteous nod.

The man with the tight dark ponytail nodded back with a slight smile.

"Checking in this evening, sir?" the doorman asked reaching for the suit bag and the computer case slung over the man's shoulder.

The man grabbed the bags in protest. "I've got it."

"Very well. Enjoy your stay, sir."

The man entered the lobby, a grand foyer with pristine marble floors and a large center table. He walked to the reception desk, where a very attractive young woman stood, smiling at nothing in particular.

"Good evening, sir," she said as he approached. "Checking in this evening?"

"Yes. The reservation is under Phillips. Harper Phillips."

The receptionist typed his name gently on the keyboard, still smiling. "Yes, Mr. Phillips, it says you'll be with us for two nights. Is that correct?"

"That is correct."

"You are in Room 5803. Do you need any assistance with your luggage?" she asked with a slight tilt of her head.

"No, thank you. I'm fine," he said.

She smiled again and nodded. "Very well, then. Here is your key. The elevators are to your right. Enjoy your stay, Mr. Phillips."

"Thank you. I will."

He entered the room. The bedside table lamp was dimly lit, creating a warm ambience. He walked to the window and slid back the curtains, revealing the bright lights and bustling activity of a Hong Kong evening. From high on the hill, the room's view offered a glimpse at a city that barely slept. He pressed his forehead against the window as he watched the cars below, all moving like fireflies against the dark street. The chambermaid had already turned down the bed, and had laid a single purple orchid on the pillow. He picked up the flower and held it against the lamp so that the light shining through the translucent petals evoked a calm beauty. Then he squeezed the orchid in his palm and tossed the remains into the garbage can. He was not here to enjoy himself. He had to get to work. His employer in Washington would be expecting to see some progress soon.

He ordered a room-service dinner of ginger chicken and rice, his usual fare during his visits to Hong Kong. As he sat down to eat, he reached into his computer bag and pulled out a laptop PC, no thicker than a dinner plate. Portability was key to his work. As the laptop booted, he swallowed a mouthful of chicken and rice and took off the rubber band holding his ponytail in place. Turning to the PC, he typed a few keystrokes, and the screen illuminated. The corporate logo for Ensight, Inc. appeared prominently, and in italicized letters the words *Personnel Database*. He quickly logged in, entering the ID and password which were exclusively reserved for system administrators within the company. As with any security-conscious organization, Ensight had developed an algorithm that would automatically change the password every three calendar days. It was more than mere luck that he had found a way around this obstacle.

His access to the company's system opened a world of opportunity for him to manipulate virtually any record in that database. He had often toyed with the idea of screwing around with the compensation records of some of the company's executives. But in the end, that would have been cruel. His sliver of moral fiber reminded him that the motives of his profession were selfish, not spiteful. After all, he didn't know any of those people, and therefore had no issues with them.

Creating the record for Harper Phillips three years ago had been a simple task, particularly since he had been equipped with step-by-step procedures from the manual. Someone had done a fine job writing it. He had given himself a title, assigned a fictitious cubicle number, and given himself a salary. He had also granted Phillips 10,000 options to purchase the company's stock at a strike price of three dollars each—a modest number of options considering the gigantic option pool. The options were merely a drop in the bucket to the company, and a small windfall for himself for all his effort.

As the lights from the Hong Kong evening shone brightly, he pulled up the account for Harper Phillips from the personnel database. He immediately noted that someone had been viewing the account recently. He ran down the system's audit report, which displayed various views of the most recent user. There was an inordinate amount of attention paid to the area of taxes and compensation. He wondered who was so curious. The user name was *awakefield*. He had never met Amber but knew exactly who she was and what her role was at Ensight. She and anyone else looking at the file would have certainly learned by now that something was not right.

He sat back in his chair and let out a deep breath. He stared at the floor, his eyes darting back and forth from the laptop screen to the carpet. So the pursuit had begun. He had thought he would have more time, as he had taken great care to hover quietly beneath the company's radar. But he had been advised that his activities would eventually reach a level that could no longer go undetected. It was time to get moving.

He picked up his cell phone and punched a few digits. He fiddled with the diamond stud in his left earlobe as he waited.

"Good evening, Singapore Airlines reservations, how can I help you?"

"Yes, I'd like to book a flight leaving Hong Kong tomorrow morning to Singapore." He hoped he still had time.

Chapter 6

▼

It had been two weeks since the IRS visitors had left the doors of Ensight, determined to continue their investigation into a man named Harper Phillips. Marty told Amber that he would assume the task of ensuring that Ensight removed this mysterious employee from its database, since he would have to explain to the executive team how something like this could have occurred and gone undetected for so long. Fox had requested that they not purge the records completely but store them in the archives. It was really the only information they had on this guy, so they had to keep a firm grasp on it.

Amber had spent most of the last seventy-two hours trying to answer the same questions all of them had been asking since Bruce Fox and his men had left their building. Only hours after Fox's team had left, Amber paid a visit to the guys in the mailroom. As she entered, they all dropped whatever fat-filled snack they happened to be eating and tried to look presentable. She asked about any mail sent by the company to Harper Phillips at his home address she had pulled from the personnel database. The mailroom team combed through their sorting system, which consisted of cardboard boxes divided by colored tabs and labeled with Post-its. Of twenty-five pieces of correspondence sent to Phillips's address, not one had been returned for having an invalid address.

Returning to her desk, Amber wondered whether she should have disclosed to the IRS that the integrity of the data in the personnel database was fair, at best. Several months before, during a weekend upgrade routine, about a third of the database had been inadvertently purged. One of the engineers decided to take a shortcut and overwrote some of the information stored in the database. He was later fired, but that did not offer any consolation to those who had to work around the clock to re-enter the data, much of it manually. At the time, no one had reviewed the entries for accuracy. And when the new personnel database was scheduled to launch, the data was simply transferred to the new platform. A review of the data was scheduled, but Ensight's internal system was low on the list of priorities, particularly compared to those aimed at improving customer products. So, the personnel data was really only as accurate as those who had entered it.

Amber launched her Internet browser and quickly typed the URL for MapQuest. She entered the address she wanted, and the screen immediately displayed a map. Harper Phillips's house was only ten minutes away from the office by cab. Marty was out of the office today, playing a leisurely eighteen at the Olympic Club. He would not be returning until tomorrow, late in the morning. Amber locked her PC, grabbed her coat, and walked to the elevators.

The San Francisco afternoon was sunny, with a gentle breeze from the bay. As usual, the area south of Market Street was filled with a lunchtime crowd and a number of others playing hooky, no doubt. Amber walked to the corner of Spear Street and waved down a yellow taxicab approaching from the opposite direction. She gave the address to the driver as she slammed the door. He pulled out a street map, a clear sign that this was not a familiar address. She explained that it was a few blocks east of Washington Square Park in North Beach.

The apartment was located on a narrow alley, wide enough to fit only one car at a time. She walked down the alley looking at the numbers, some of which were concealed by overgrown ivy and spider webs. The house was located toward the end of the alley, a bottom-floor flat in a two-story building. The white paint was badly chipped, and clearly it had been quite some time since someone had bothered to sweep the rickety steps leading up to the front door. The curtains at the one window were drawn. Hardly what one would expect to be the residence of a six-figure salary-earner.

As she approached the house, she detected the residual scent of day-old trash. Evidently the city's trash collectors had been on the street not long before. However, the house she was looking at did not have any receptacles in front like the rest of the homes. Amber gently knocked on the door, but there was no answer. Noticing that the door had a mail slot halfway down, she bent down and flipped open the brass door covering the slot. As she peered through, she could see a small mountain of paper and envelopes piled on the dusty hardwood floor. As she leaned toward the side of the slot, trying to get a peripheral view of the apartment, she nearly bumped her forehead on the door at the sudden sound of a woman's disapproving voice.

"Can I help you with something?"

Amber whipped around to see a woman at the bottom of the steps, her hands on her hips. The woman was probably in her early forties, dressed practically but certainly not fashionably.

"Uh, I was looking for the gentleman who lives here," Amber said, with her voice trembling.

The woman stared at Amber suspiciously. "May I ask why? Or better yet, who the hell you are?"

"Well, I work with him," replied Amber.

"With whom?" the woman pressed on.

"Harper Phillips. This is his home, isn't it?"

The woman's eyes softened for a moment. "You work with him, you say?"

"That's right," Amber said confidently.

"And when was the last time you spoke with him?" The woman seemed to be testing Amber.

"Well, to be honest, I don't actually know him personally. We just work in the same company." Amber decided not to fall into the trap. "Excuse me, ma'am, but might I ask who you are?"

"No, you may not," the woman darted back. *OK, that was quick and painless,* Amber thought to herself. "But I'll tell you anyway. I'm his daughter, Priscilla."

"Well, it's a pleasure to meet you. My name is Amber Wakefield," she said, reaching out her hand. Priscilla ignored the gesture.

"So, what exactly do you need?" Priscilla asked impatiently.

"I need to talk to Mr. Phillips for a moment. Or perhaps you can give him a message for me?"

Priscilla straightened her neck so her head moved back. "Are you out of your mind? My father has been dead for nearly three years. The only way either of us is getting a message to him is through some divine miracle."

Amber stood motionless, and for a moment, didn't breathe. "Dead, you say?" Her voice was shaking again.

"That's right," Priscilla said. "I've been meaning to come by here to clean this place up, but every time I get to the front steps, I just..." She held the back of her hand to her mouth and looked down, obviously restraining her emotions in front of this stranger.

"I...I'm terribly sorry, Miss Phillips. I had no idea." Amber regretted coming here at all.

"How's that? Are you new to the firm?"

Amber was totally dumbfounded. *What was she talking about? The firm?* She decided not to raise any more suspicions in this poor grieving woman's mind. "Yes, just joined a few weeks ago. Which would explain why I didn't know him personally." *Phew. Don't dig yourself any deeper,* she told herself.

"It's like I told the other lawyers in the firm. Just give me some time, and I'll deal with all of his insurance stuff and clean up his files, et cetera," Priscilla explained, her voice shaking.

"Of course, please take your time. I completely understand," Amber said. *The other lawyers in the firm? Wasn't this guy an engineer of some sort?*

"Are you a lawyer as well?" Priscilla was starting to open up a bit.

Amber raised an eyebrow. "No, you see, I work in human res—" Again with the lawyers. "Excuse me, did you say lawyer?"

"That's right," said Priscilla. Amber's confusion was clearly painted on her face. Priscilla noticed. "Why does that surprise you? Jackson Winthrop is, after all, a law firm, is it not?"

Amber's head was spinning. She needed to get off this ride—fast. She nodded slowly. "Why, yes, of course it's a law firm. I guess I'm just still a little taken aback by the news of your father."

"Well, I don't know much about his work. We didn't exactly have what you would call a close, loving relationship," Priscilla explained. "Anyway, like I told the others, I'll be in touch soon."

"Thank you, Miss Phillips. And again, please accept my condolences." Amber held out her hand again. This time, Priscilla shook it.

"Thank you," Priscilla replied, looking away.

As Amber walked hurriedly toward the end of the alley in search of a taxicab, she stopped to turn around. Priscilla stood in front of the house, staring at it intently, ever so still. After a few seconds, the daughter of Mr. Harper Phillips turned and walked toward the opposite end of the alley. Perhaps she might return again in a few months, but maybe not.

Amber returned to the office just after two o'clock that afternoon. As she walked out of the elevator doors and toward her desk, she saw Marty standing in his office, the glass door closed. He was on speakerphone. Donning a golf shirt and casual pants, he was talking while flipping through papers on his desk. He looked up for a moment and saw her walking toward him. He motioned for her to wait. It was a private conversation. Probably his ex-wife. At least one of them.

After a few minutes, Marty emerged from his office and walked to Amber's desk.

"Welcome back. Long lunch?" he asked playfully.

"Oh, yeah. An old girlfriend from college is in town just for the day. You know how girls can talk forever," she said, trying to smile. She hated lying and she had told nothing but them for the last two hours.

"Is she married?" Marty joked.

"Marty," Amber said with a disapproving tone. "I didn't think you were coming to the office today."

"Neither did I until I got a call on my personal cell on the fifteenth hole. Jamie told me that Kaitlyn was calling an emergency exec meeting at 2:30." Jamie was Kaitlyn's assistant. Marty said all this while holding his cell phone between his fingers like he was ready to hurl it across the floor.

"What's the emergency?" Amber asked, suddenly concerned about everything around her.

Marty took his Titleist hat off and scratched his head. "I think some developments are unfolding on the Maguire deal."

"Good or bad developments?"

Marty shrugged. "I don't know, but in my experience, good news doesn't warrant an emergency meeting."

Amber nodded slowly.

"I won't be coming back to my office after the meeting, so I'll see you tomorrow, all right?" He gave her a light squeeze on her shoulder.

"OK, Marty," she said, and gently patted his hand.

He left and walked toward the elevator. Once he was out of sight, she immediately turned back toward her computer terminal and pulled up her Internet browser again. She did a Google search for the words Jackson Winthrop. The search returned one result. She clicked on the URL. The home page to the firm's Web site appeared on the screen. She clicked on the section labeled *About Us*, in which there was a brief but stale summary of the firm's history. The firm specialized in representing high-tech businesses, entrepreneurs, and some offshore businesses. It also represented its clients in merger and acquisition deals. As she scanned the list of prominent clients, she came across one that sounded awfully familiar—Bartlett Enterprises. She had heard of them before but couldn't quite place the name at the moment.

With her fingers getting lost in her hair, she skimmed through the press releases, but there was no mention of the death of a lawyer named Harper Phillips. That absence of an announcement wasn't uncommon, however, since most companies wouldn't publicize that information unless the employee was a high-profile person, recognizable to the public. She noted that the firm had an office on Bush Street, in the middle of the San Francisco's financial district, as well as offices around the world.

She wanted to write down the local phone number of the firm and opened her desk drawer to pull out a notepad. As she turned to write down the number, her elbow knocked over the bottle of Evian which she always kept at her desk, spilling it onto her keyboard.

"Oh, shit," she said loudly, looking for something to mop up the water. She walked to the kitchen to get some paper towels, cursing as she walked down the hallway.

At that moment, Marty walked briskly out of the elevator doors and toward his office. He had obviously forgotten something for the meeting, probably a writing instrument of some kind. As he walked out of his office again and back toward the elevator, he passed by Amber's desk, then stopped and backpedaled slowly. He took a close look at the large letters that read *Jackson Winthrop, LLP* on her computer screen. His eyes grew big, a dozen questions swirling in his mind. His heart began beating quickly. After standing in front of her desk for what seemed like an hour, Marty slowly turned back toward the elevators to return to the exec meeting. He would deal with this later.

Chapter 7

The fall humidity in Washington DC was brutal. Bruce Fox had returned two days earlier from his visit to San Francisco. He and his two protégés had spent the entire return trip reviewing their notes from their meeting with the people at Ensight, Inc. As he walked through the National Mall toward the Reflecting Pool, he thought about Marty Callahan and especially about Amber Wakefield. He had fantasized about her most of the trip back, and he was sure Stemple and Wood had done the same. He wondered whether she would try to perform any independent research, but he hoped that she would simply forget about it and be happy that her involvement was now over.

The foot of the Lincoln Memorial was bustling with activity as usual—families, foreign tourists, school field trips. Fox made his way through the crowd and began ascending the steps toward Honest Abe. He barely heard a voice call out to him.

"Mr. Fox?"

Fox turned toward the voice. A young man in his late twenties, maybe early thirties, stood halfway up the steps. He wore khakis, a white shirt, and a blue blazer. No tie.

"Yes, I'm Bruce Fox," replied Fox, lightly patting beads of sweat from his forehead.

"It's a pleasure to meet you, Mr. Fox. I'm Thomas Blake. We spoke on the phone a couple of weeks ago." The young man thrust his hand out. Fox reached out reluctantly. "Why don't we get out of the sun and talk somewhere."

They descended the steps and walked toward the shaded path running the length of the Reflecting Pool.

Blake began talking as if they were old friends. "So, how was San Francisco?"

"Fine. A little windy." Fox was clearly not comfortable discussing details with this person. "Listen, I thought I was supposed to meet the deputy director here today. Where is he?"

"That's where I'm taking you now. He preferred to meet in a more casual setting, away from the office. I hope that's OK."

Fox nodded slowly as the two men continued walking along the tree-lined path toward the Washington Monument.

* * * *

"Harry Lang," the man said reaching out his hand. "It's a pleasure to meet you, Bruce."

Harrison W. Lang was the deputy director of the Federal Bureau of Investigation. At fifty-two, he was lightly balding but in excellent physical shape, no doubt the result of his five days in the gym each week.

"Likewise," Fox replied as the two men shook hands. Blake stood a few feet away, smiling. The men began strolling through the sandy paths of the Mall, toward the Smithsonian.

The meeting between Lang and Fox had been scheduled long before Fox and his men visited Ensight in San Francisco. Only Fox had been officially notified about the meeting just forty-eight hours earlier. Following his meeting with the people at Ensight, he and his two assistants had returned to their rooms at the Embarcadero Hyatt. As he entered his room, his cellular phone began ringing. He was needed in Washington by the FBI.

"I suppose we may have caught you off guard by scheduling this meeting on such short notice."

"Well, it's not highly unusual. I've worked pretty closely with you guys on several occasions," Fox explained. "Of course, I've never had to meet with anyone at your level. You didn't mention in your message what this was all about."

Lang turned toward the young man who had escorted Fox. "Tom, would you mind giving us a moment?"

Blake, who was still smiling, nodded. "Of course," he replied. Then he began walking in the opposite direction, with no destination in particular. As soon as he was out of earshot, Lang turned quickly to Fox.

"Bruce, people are asking questions. I don't know what to tell them."

"Will you please relax? Your panic is understandable, but it's also obvious. Besides, I thought we all had agreed that we would keep our contact to a minimum. What the hell are you doing sending your little minions to escort me around?" Fox was wearing a pair of dark sunglasses, but he was clearly looking at Lang.

"Oh, it just adds somewhat to the credibility. When I'm seen around this town by myself, it looks odd—unless I'm on the way to the airport. But forget about that. We haven't heard from you in several days. Minimal communication does not mean no communication. Are we clear on that?" Lang stood tall, an obvious attempt at intimidation. But Fox had seen the act before.

"You can unclench, Harry. It's not going to work on me," Fox said with an annoyed smirk. "No single person is running the show here. Remember?"

"Well, it certainly doesn't feel that way," Lang said, almost pouting.

"Why are you all getting your panties in a twist? We agreed that my first trip out there was simply to plant the seed, to make it known that an investigation had begun. Did that change at some point?"

"Not at all. We just need to control the level of attention we attract on this. Foxy, I don't need to tell you that a heap of man-hours went into this. Precision is the key here."

"Are you worried about Callahan?" Fox asked.

Lang shrugged. "Shouldn't we be? The guy's a loose cannon."

"He's also clueless, Harry. The scouting report on him was dead-on. He's got his eyes on retirement and wealth. He's got a fat pension awaiting him, not to mention however much we promised him. We just need to keep a close eye on him."

Lang nodded. "Did you meet with him alone?"

"No, Stemple and Wood were with me. You knew that."

"I mean, did you meet anyone else from Ensight?"

"Oh. Well, not exactly. I mean, Callahan's assistant was there," Fox began. Lang began to say something, but Fox held his hand up. "But she's harmless. Just a smiling little sorority chick with a pretty face and a cute ass."

"I wish I could share your peace of mind," said Lang.

"You can. Just trust me, Harry. And you can send that same message to the rest of our friends."

Lang leaned closer, as if they should be concerned that their conversation might be overheard among the hundreds of people walking through the Mall. "Hopefully, you'll be able to tell them yourself. And soon."

"I'm sure Harper is smiling down on us right now," Fox replied.

"Don't you mean smiling up at us?"

The two men laughed, turned their backs to one another, and walked in opposite directions.

On Saturday, Marty Callahan arrived at Dulles International Airport at a few minutes past four o'clock in the afternoon. He caught a taxicab and instructed the driver to take him to the St. Regis Hotel. The rest of the Committee, as they generically named themselves, had arrived at the agreed-upon destination hours before. They forgave his tardiness, largely because he had the greatest distance to travel, but mostly because he added the least value to their efforts.

It had begun almost three years ago. The plan was quite simple—at least it had appeared that way. The suicide death of Harper Phillips had come as a shock to all of them. Few of them actually felt much remorse, but the death stunned them nonetheless. After all, there was unfinished business among them. Harper had been dead for nearly three years already. In retrospect, they would have thought longer about giving Harper as much latitude as they had to look out for their collective interests.

Marty entered the St. Regis and proceeded through the decorative lobby toward the elevators. He knocked twice on the doors of the Royal Suite. The door opened, and Bruce Fox stood in the entry, wearing a navy blue knit shirt and khaki pants.

"Marty, long time no see," he said sarcastically, holding his hand out.

"Bruce," Marty replied, nodding. With the exception of Fox, he had met the members of the Committee only a few times before.

As he entered the suite, with its French-style sofas and polished tables, he immediately felt like an outsider. Here he was, a city-college boy, fraternizing with these Ivy League MBA types. He wondered whether the others in the room were thinking the same thing. Seated around the room were the three others who comprised the Committee. Harry Lang, the deputy director of the FBI, sat in a large chair with floral patterns. He had removed his tie and unbuttoned the top two buttons on his shirt. He had a smug, crooked smile on his face. Terence Hammond sat on one end of a large sofa, sipping a miniature bottle of Pellegrino, managing to get most of it in his mouth, while the remainder dribbled down the front of his shirt. His thin-rimmed glasses balanced precariously on the bridge of his nose. An ebony-colored cane rested against the armrest beside him. He was the illustration of human fragility, but his colleagues knew better. He was seventy-two years old, a forty-year veteran of the Central Intelligence Agency, who had since retired. He spent most of his career focused on domestic terrorism, and as a result, had become a friend to at least one person in every dark corridor from

Langley to Capitol Hill. Standing by the window, smoking his pipe and not seeming to notice Marty, was Dennis Fitch. His flattop haircut was the same one he had worn since his days at Princeton in the late sixties, though the tints of gray had become more abundant in the past six years. A venture capitalist who had elected to temporarily retire after the economic downturn, Fitch had a keen eye for unexploited investment opportunities. During the 90s, he had made plenty of his friends and clients extremely rich, though none wealthier than himself. He wore a scowl as he looked out at the view.

After a few minutes of impersonal pleasantries, Harry Lang finally spoke. "All right, gentlemen, let's begin." The five men sat down in the parlor of the Royal Suite.

"So, where is our good friend these days?" asked Hammond, shoveling a fistful of mixed nuts into his mouth.

Lang slowly leaned forward in his chair and took a sip from his water glass. "Our guys at the Bureau have been tracking him since he left San Francisco. So far, he's been pretty predictable. But it looks like he's on the move."

The others waited for him to add color to this nondescript account of their subject's actions.

Lang continued. "He stopped over in Hong Kong for a night—or rather eleven hours. Apparently, he had been scheduled to stay for a couple of nights, according to the hotel records." He paused to grab a handful of sunflower seeds from the bowl on the side table.

"Where did he go?" Hammond asked, clearing the phlegm from his throat.

"We believe he's on his way to Singapore," Lang answered.

"You *believe* he's on his way to Singapore?" It was Fitch, the grouch, asking the question.

"Calm yourself, Denny. Our confidence is high. We're not going to lose him, but we need to keep a safe distance, or else this whole thing will explode in our faces." Lang took another sip of water. "Relax. I've got total jurisdiction over this investigation, which means that my agents out there follow my lead. They look where I tell them to look. They piss when I tell them to piss."

"But they're not idiots," offered the old man, Hammond. "They're highly trained and smarter than any of us, so their natural intuition and ability could entice them to get ahead of us." He dabbed his mouth with a napkin. "It almost happened once already. Our man took his sweet old time in San Francisco and almost got caught, which would have been disastrous. It certainly made Harry's boys feel like they were gaining momentum on their investigation."

Fitch pointed a finger at Hammond, then at Lang, while pacing in front of the window. "Stop the charade. And stop calling this an investigation. We all know it's a crock of shit. How did you find this sleazeball? Have your guys even seen this fella?"

Lang shook his head. "They're tracking his whereabouts through his credit card activity and bank account withdrawals. That always leaves them a step behind. Any other leads come directly from me. And as for how I found him, let's just say that after thirty years tracking down the most skilled identity thieves in the world, you eventually make some friends."

"Friends? You've never met the guy in person," Fitch reminded him.

"That's in all of our best interests," Lang replied.

"And how do you know that your *friend* isn't going to take off with whatever he finds? How do we know that he's making any progress?"

"Because I'm the one feeding him the account numbers of the banks around the world. After each withdrawal, he's depositing the funds into an offshore account which I set up, and I'm monitoring it every day with the help of our in-house auditor here." He slapped Fox on the back. Unamused, Fox ran his hand over his goatee.

"It's not rocket science, gentlemen," Lang continued. "After he gets the account numbers, we monitor the accounts for activity. The moment we see the withdrawal, we know that he's been there. By the time my men see that activity, he's long gone. How many times do I have to explain this to you?"

Fitch continued to look skeptical. "Denny, so far our man has stuck to his end of the agreement," Lang went on. "He's hit two accounts: one in Buenos Aires and one in Sao Paolo. And of course, you all know now about his recent visit to HSBC in Hong Kong. It's all been deposited into the offshore account."

"I don't like it, Harry," Fitch said. *The skeptic as usual*, Lang thought.

He put his hand on Fitch's shoulder. "Denny, relax. If he does try to screw us, I'll turn this thing around on him so fast, he won't know what hit him. The Bureau has been trying to catch up to this guy for three years, and we were finally close. Really close. That's when I stepped in and took over the investigation. So, in his eyes, if it wasn't for me, he'd be in jail. But I offered him this deal, and the guy's got a big chunk of change waiting for him at the finish line, so my guess is he's going to do what we ask."

Lang took a moment for effect, to be sure Fitch and the others were paying attention. Then he continued. "We're totally safe on this one. After all, I'm not telling him how to do it or when to make his next move. He's the professional, not me. That's why I chose him. It's also why he and I agreed to minimize communication with one another until the job is finished. It's too dangerous. The less we know about how he's going about it, the better. I know it's a leap of faith, but you will be patient, Denny. You have no other choice."

Fitch stopped pacing the room. He was digesting Lang's words.

"You're running a real three-ring circus, aren't you?" Hammond said.

Fitch sat down on the sofa. "Listen, I don't care about the intricacies of your arrangement with this guy. And I don't give a shit how long a leash you give him. Just as long as you don't let go. This is your guy, Harry. You found him. You hired him. It's on your head if this thing goes to hell."

"I'll take that under advisement, Denny," Lang replied, stone-faced.

Hammond sat up slowly, securing the glasses on his nose. "But don't extend the leash too long. I'm not as young as all of you. I'd like to see this thing wrapped up before I die, if you don't mind." They all laughed, except for Fitch.

"Laugh it up, old man. But I've had just about enough of this bullshit." Fitch's face was crimson. "I've got twenty-five million dollars tied up in the name of some goddamn phony corporation, and no way to touch it. All thanks to that prick Phillips."

It was Fox's turn to speak. "We've all got a lot of money tied up there, Denny. Not just you. And I might remind you that there are a number of other people out there who want their money back as well. And not the type of folks we wish to make enemies out of."

"Well, none of you seem to be that concerned that we may never see it again. For Christ's sake, the money is spread across dozens of bank accounts around the world. It's going to take forever and a day to collect it all."

"We're concerned, Denny. Trust me. Why the hell else do you think we're going through all these motions?" Fox was standing now.

Fitch wasn't listening. He just continued his tirade as if he hadn't been interrupted. "Leave it to Harper to fuck this thing up. And now we've pinned our hopes on some faceless guy who we're praying will lead us to our money."

"I'd like to remind you that we all gave our consent to allow Harper to set up the corporation. Including you." Fox pointed his finger at Fitch. "We agreed to keep our names off the bank accounts, so that we could protect our anonymity. Christ, were you there when we set this whole thing up?"

"Let's keep our voices down, gentlemen," Hammond said.

Lang lowered his tone. "Oh, and Denny, one more thing. We're the ones leading this so-called 'faceless' guy to our money. Not the other way around. Get that part right."

"I wish I could have had a crack at that son-of-a-bitch Phillips before he decided to blow his head off." Fitch was almost smiling.

Marty sat silent throughout the meeting. The temptation to tell them about what he had seen on Amber's computer screen a couple of days earlier came and went. He could not endanger her. These men were not kidding around. He wondered, as he had done on many other occasions, whether he had made the right decision to affiliate himself with them. As the other men feuded over who had more vested in the operation, Marty looked out the window as dusk began to fall over the nation's capital. He needed a martini.

Chapter 8

▼

He walked into the hotel bathroom and wiped the steam from the large mirror with his palm. He hunched forward and placed his hands on the edge of the counter. He looked at himself as if he were examining a stranger. The definition in his physique had suffered terribly, he noticed, as he pinched the sides of his abdomen. Short stubbles of blond hair were beginning to grow back on his once-shaved head. He had shaved it off a year ago and had found that having a low-maintenance hairdo was high-maintenance work.

He tried to recount the number of people he had encountered in the last several months, all of whom would know him by the name of Harper Phillips if they ever saw him again. He picked up a can of shaving cream from the counter and sprayed a mound in his hand. As he applied it to his five-day-old beard, he realized for the first time in months how far he'd come since assuming the name of Harper Phillips a year ago.

The shower felt good, particularly since he hadn't taken one since arriving in Singapore. He had arrived there two days before, checked into his room, eaten a quick dinner in the hotel coffee shop, and then gone to bed. He exited the shower and wrapped a thick white towel around his waist. He picked up one of the soap bars in the glass tray on the counter. As he unwrapped the soap, with its Four Seasons Hotel logo, he overheard the sound of the television just outside the bathroom. It was Tuesday morning in Singapore, and he had been up since six o'clock, the latest he had slept in about three months. He walked around the room, enjoying the soft carpet beneath his bare feet. He sat on the foot of the bed and fixed his gaze on the screen. The show was CNN's *International Edition*. In the upper left corner next to the female anchor was an image of a fingerprint, with the words *Identity Theft* in bright red. The story centered on a man just outside Houston, Texas, who had become a victim of what the reporter deemed the fastest growing crime in the country, and arguably in the world. He watched intently as the identity-theft victim told his story.

The victim was Hispanic, in his mid-forties, and had recently become a citizen of the United States. He had opened a hardware store, enrolled his two young children in elementary school, and just purchased his first home. An entrepreneur. A family man. The American Dream in real life. But eight months later he was suckered into an e-mail phishing scam, a common tactic employed by fraudsters to lure potential victims into revealing personal data. Jorge Luis Escoboza wept as he described the horror of having his loan rescinded, his store vandalized, and his children mocked—all the result of someone else's doing.

As the segment continued with some expert advice and insights from some guy at the Federal Trade Commission, the man shivered as the draft from the hotel room's air conditioner tickled his still damp body. He shut off the television and glanced at the clock. It was time to move.

Orchard Road, the main thoroughfare of Singapore's commercial district, was buzzing with buses, taxis, cars, motorcycles, and pedestrians. He was exhausted as he stood in the sun, but his adrenaline was running high.

He approached the front doors of the Development Bank of Singapore at the Plaza Singapura. He silently quizzed himself on the account details. He had memorized most of the information necessary to access the safe deposit box issued to Mr. Harper Phillips but had spent the last eighteen hours rehearsing his delivery. It could not sound as if though it was a perfunctory delivery of a script.

He breathed a sigh of relief as the woman in charge of administering access to the safe deposit vault accepted the information without hesitation.

"Please follow me, Mr. Phillips," she said, leading him toward the vault. He detected a slight British accent in her voice.

They passed through the large steel doors and made their way past dozens of rows of metal boxes. They arrived at a box at the end of the row.

"Do you have your key with you?" the young woman asked.

He reached into his pocket and pulled out one of the small brass keys he had picked up in Belize months before.

"Please insert your key into the slot on the right-hand side."

He slowly inserted the key, trying his best to project the image that he had done this a dozen times. As he inserted the key, she did the same on the opposite side. At that moment, they simultaneously turned their keys. He felt the beads of sweat on his forehead rapidly evaporating. The woman opened the small metal door to the compartment, turned to him, smiled, and walked away, leaving him there alone.

The box slid easily from its compartment. He looked around as if someone were spying on him—the natural paranoia that accompanied this type of work. As he lifted the lid to the box, he prepared himself. It would be filled with junk, or worse, it would be empty. He cracked a smile as he looked in. Bills. U.S. dollar bills. All crisp. All one hundreds and packaged in even stacks. He picked up one brick of bills bound by a rubber band and fanned them as people did in the movies. He estimated that he held about twenty thousand dollars in his hand. Another gush of adrenaline flooded his body as he took a quick inventory. Fifty stacks. A million bucks!

"Christ Almighty!" His voice echoed. He hushed himself.

This was his payment for completing his first task back in the Caribbean. It was also a down payment for the future. He quickly emptied the contents of the box into his backpack but not before reaching into his pocket and pulling out the other brass key he had found in the desk drawer in Belize. He placed the key inside the deposit box and slid it back into the vault.

On his way out of the vault, he smiled and nodded at the woman who had just unwittingly given him the largest single payday of his life. On his way out, he stopped at the counter and handed the teller a withdrawal slip. After tucking the withdrawn cash into his backpack, he exited the bank into the humidity of the Singapore afternoon. He would be checking out of the Four Seasons in a few hours.

Two Caucasian men entered the Development Bank of Singapore at about a quarter past two o'clock in the afternoon. They were both casually dressed, one in black gabardine pants with a white button-down oxford shirt and the other in blue jeans and a gray knit shirt. They were accompanied by an Asian man wearing a dark suit, a shiny badge hanging from his breast pocket. Behind them were four uniformed police officers, all the same height with the same haircut. They walked to the nearest counter and whispered something to the teller. After more whispering and pointing around the bank, the older-looking American proceeded to the rear of the bank where the safe deposit boxes were housed, while his young partner continued to interrogate other bank staff.

"Yes, may I help you, gentlemen?" asked the woman near the safe deposit boxes. There was a hint of a British accent.

The Asian man in the dark suit displayed a badge and introduced himself as Detective something-or-other. He introduced the man with him as a federal investigator from the United States, who was working with local police to find a man named Harper Phillips, an American. The American pulled out a badge and displayed it to the woman, who quickly glanced down at it, not exactly sure what she was looking at.

The more seasoned of the two Americans told her that according to Mr. Phillips's credit card record, he had checked into the Four Seasons Hotel the night before. However, he had checked out about an hour ago. The woman explained that a man by that name had been in the bank earlier that day and had accessed his security deposit box. He had a backpack with him. She didn't see him leave. The American cursed loudly, clearly offending the woman and the rest of the customers in the bank.

He walked across the floor to his younger partner. "Call the boss. Now. Wake him up at home if you have to."

After a few seconds, his partner handed him the cell phone.

"Sir, it's Griffin." He listened. "Yes, I know it's late, but this is important. We're at the bank in Singapore." He looked down and put his hand on the back of his neck. "We just missed our guy." A muffled sound could be heard through the phone.

"A couple hundred thousand from a savings account," Griffin said. He was clearly answering his boss's questions. He listened some more.

"U.S. dollars, sir," he continued. "And the contents of a safe deposit box. Whatever happened to be in there." Another pause. "We don't know what was in there, sir."

After listening to the deputy director berate him and his partner for another minute, Special Agent Griffin hung up.

It was nearly midnight on the East Coast. Harry Lang placed the telephone back on the kitchen counter, trying to restore his calm following his performance. He walked down the hallway of his Georgetown home and into the family room, where his wife lay across the sofa in her pajamas, her eyes fixed on the movie-of-the-week playing on the television. He sat down next to her and put his arm around her. She nestled up to him and rested her head on his chest. He leaned back, took a sip from his glass of Macallan 15, and smiled.

Chapter 9

Her alarm clock had been buzzing for nearly two minutes before she awoke from her sleep. Amber had gone to bed only four hours before, but she felt like it had been twenty minutes. She took a quick glance around her room, decorated in the wooden rustic furniture she had bought as a set when she first moved in. Consistent with her daily routine, she grabbed the remote control, which was buried beneath her pillow, and turned on the television located on the opposite side of the room. She enjoyed the background noise while she ran the shower. She lived on the bottom floor of a Victorian in Pacific Heights, built in the early 1900s, so the hot water was slow to get going.

She was somewhat ashamed that she had spent the better part of the weekend mapping out possibilities about her latest obsession, Harper Phillips. She had never seen him, had never met him, and had never even heard his voice. Yet, for some inexplicable reason, she wanted to know more. Her senior class poll in high school had named her "Biggest Gossip." She had not disappointed them. But besides that, she was terribly bored in her job. After the launch of the new personnel database, there weren't any projects for her to work on, at least none that appealed to her. Her boss had lost all interest in his own career and had even less interest in helping Amber to advance hers. She had a few close friends in the city, but most of them lived on the East Coast, while the others were married and driving SUVs to daycares and soccer practices. Her mother, an early-onset Alzheimer's sufferer, lived back East in the New England community where Amber had grown up. Her father had left them when she was eight and died six years later of lung cancer. She and her mother never spoke of him.

Amber hadn't shared with Marty anything related to her encounter with Priscilla Phillips, Jackson Winthrop, or Harper Phillips's death. Besides, she was certain he would not care. There was no way he would miss her today or this week, for that matter. He was on vacation for the week, visiting family and old friends in Boston.

She paced back and forth in her bedroom brushing her teeth and wearing the boxers and tank top she slept in. The local news was on TV, which seemed odd to her. Normally, at this time, she would hear the familiar voices of Matt Lauer and the *Today* gang. Interruptions occurred only if there was breaking news of some kind, like an earthquake or a chemical spill on one of the freeways.

She walked into the bathroom and placed her hand beneath the running water in the shower. Still cool. She walked back out to the bedroom and caught a glimpse of the television reporter standing in front of a park that was roped off with yellow police tape. Amber turned up the volume. The reporter repeated the story. A woman had been found murdered along a jogging path near Golden Gate Park. Amber winced as a police sergeant described the condition of the body—a single gunshot wound to the head. She turned back toward the bathroom to check on the water temperature, still eyeing the television. And she suddenly stopped, not able to move, as if her feet had been pinned to the hardwood floor by a nail gun. A sketch of a woman's face appeared on the screen with no name beneath it.

"Oh, my God," Amber said, holding her hand to her gaping mouth, still full of toothpaste foam.

It was the woman she had met only days earlier, Priscilla Phillips. A police detective explained that there were no suspects as of yet and no positive identification of the victim, making it impossible for police to contact any family members.

Amber stood motionless, her hand still covering her mouth. With her toothbrush sticking out of her mouth, she walked to the phone on her nightstand and began to dial 911. She would tell them that the unidentified woman murdered in the park was Priscilla Phillips. But something made her stop as she played the scenario in her head. Someone from the police department, probably the detective in charge of the case, would call her back—or worse, visit her personally. He would ask how she knew this information. He would ask her where she was on the night and time of the murder. He would ask how she knew the victim. She immediately hung up the phone and backed away.

The steam from the hot water had clouded the bathroom mirror. Her shower was ready.

Amber boarded the bus on Fillmore Street. It was a usual Monday morning, and the fog was clearing quickly. The somber faces with damp hair waited at the bus stop, holding their cups of coffee and probably wondering why this past weekend seemed shorter than the weekend before. She found a spot to stand toward the rear of the bus and stared out the window at the passing buildings, convincing herself that she was doing the right thing by not calling the police. After all, she didn't know Priscilla. They weren't friends. They barely qualified as acquaintances. It was none of her business. *Stay out of it*, she silently mouthed to herself. The bus arrived at the corner of Mission and Spear Streets, where she disembarked and headed toward the entrance of the Ensight offices.

Marty's office was dark, his desk neatly organized, or at least as neatly as he liked it to be. Knowing him as she did, Amber thought he had probably taken a late flight in from his East Coast vacation and would be taking his time getting to the office. She sat down at her desk and logged on to the company network. On any other day, she would have filtered through all the pointless memos that usually got distributed on Monday mornings, announcements about temporary system downtime or the birth of someone's fourth kid. But today, she would read them, all of them, word for word. She needed something to keep her mind occupied and distracted from Priscilla Phillips. Amber intently read an e-mail from an administrator in the finance group announcing that one of the accountants had just given birth to twins on Sunday afternoon. Mom, Dad, and babies were all doing well.

She gingerly took a sip of her hot coffee and burned her tongue at the sound of her desk phone. The caller ID display said *Operator*, which usually meant that someone from the outside who didn't know her direct extension was trying to reach her through the company's main switchboard.

"This is Amber Wakefield," she said politely into the receiver, her eyes welling up with tears from the burning sensation in her mouth.

"Miss Wakefield?" She didn't recognize the male voice on the other end.

"Yes."

The line went dead. She replaced the receiver and stood up from her desk in the cube. She looked around. At that moment, her PC made a pinging sound, indicating that a new message had arrived in her inbox. She sat back down. The new message did not contain a subject. It was being sent from an anonymous e-mail address. Just a bunch of letters and numbers preceding the @ symbol. She leaned forward to read it.

Amber, need to talk to you. Can't communicate over e-mail or phone. 411 about H. P. Will be in front of AT&T Park at noon. Will find you.

She closed the message quickly and looked at the small clock on her desk. It was 9:15. What did it all mean? *411 about H. P.* She thought for a few seconds, and her heart skipped a beat. *411.* Information. *H. P.* Harper. Why was someone tying her to Harper Phillips? She wound her fingers through her hair and cursed herself for having gone to his house that day, for being so damn curious, for talking to Priscilla. She thought about just ignoring the message, but she knew that whoever had sent it would find her. They obviously knew where she worked and probably knew what she looked like. She had to talk to someone. She had to tell Marty. Let him talk to those guys at the IRS. She just needed to remove herself from this mess.

She stepped into Marty's empty office and closed the door. She dialed his cell phone digits from the phone on his desk. She tried several times, but there was no answer. After about an hour, she tried again. The phone rang four times, and she was preparing to leave a message when someone picked up.

"Amber?" Marty asked through a slightly static-filled connection.

She exhaled loudly. "Oh, Marty, thank God you picked up. Where are you right now?"

"I'm in Boston. At the airport, waiting for my flight. What is it, dear?"

"Marty, do you remember Harper Phillips?" Her voice was quivering.

"Who?"

"Harper Phillips," she said, this time louder. "He was the man who the IRS was looking for a few weeks ago. Remember?"

"Oh, right, right, right," he said. "What about him?"

"I found out some stuff about him, which I think you should know."

"Please don't tell me that those IRS guys are asking you more questions. I thought we told them that this was their investigation and that we couldn't help them anymore," he said in an irritated tone.

"No, it's not that, Marty. I haven't heard from them since our meeting. I think there is something not quite right about this whole situation."

Marty was silent on the other end for a moment. "Let me guess. My little Nancy Drew over there did some poking around."

"It's frightening how well you know me."

"So, what did you find out?"

"Well, let's just say that the Harper Phillips who is supposedly employed by Ensight is not exactly real."

"I think we already knew that, didn't we?" he asked, sounding rushed. "Obviously, someone is running around with this guy's information. This sounds more like a problem for whoever this poor Phillips fella is."

"Doubtful."

"I beg your pardon?" Marty's tone was serious.

"Marty, he died nearly three years ago. Don't ask me how I found out."

"Don't worry, I don't think I want to know," he said with a light laugh.

"Good. There's one other thing," she began before he interrupted.

"Dear, unfortunately, they're boarding my flight right now." He spoke louder to drown the background noise. "Can we talk about this when I'm back in the office tomorrow morning?"

"I suppose," she said.

"Amber, listen to me. This is not our problem. Let the authorities deal with this matter. You've done enough." She could tell by his heavy breathing that he was rushing. "We don't know who Harper Phillips is. Either one of them. We don't know why he killed himself. It has nothing to do with you, me, or the company. So, don't worry yourself. None of us are going to get into any trouble over this. I'll make sure of that."

It was silent on the other end. Amber held the receiver to her ear and stared forward, her gaze fixated on no specific object.

"Amber, you there?" he called out.

She snapped out of it momentarily. "Yes, I heard you, Marty."

"We'll talk tomorrow, OK? Try to get out of the office early and get a drink for yourself." More static on the line. "Have one for me too."

"See you tomorrow," she replied. The line went dead.

Amber replaced the receiver and walked to the large window in Marty's office. As she looked out on to the bay, she could feel small goose bumps developing on her arms. Something just didn't feel right. Something in his tone. Then it struck her. *How the hell did he know that Harper Phillips killed himself?* She certainly never said anything. In fact, she didn't even know how he had died.

She walked back to her desk. There were eight more e-mail messages in her inbox, which had arrived while she was in Marty's office. More stuff from the IT team about system upgrades. The last message was from that same anonymous address as before, again with no subject. She opened it quickly.

Please meet by the Willie Mays statue in the main plaza at the ballpark. Don't talk to Callahan until we meet. Please come alone.

She couldn't believe what was happening. What had she gotten herself into? Better yet, how would she get herself out? Her stomach turned over at the thought of someone following her, knowing how to contact her, aware that she knew more than she probably should. She sat at her desk and debated with herself. She would call the police and simply explain the situation—explain that she had stumbled upon some information and that she was now afraid for her safety. Of course. The police would protect her.

She ran her fingers through her hair and pulled it back behind her shoulders. She stretched out the scenario further. She envisioned two men in suits sitting in an unmarked van across the street from the office building, equipped with headphones and state-of-the-art surveillance gear. She had seen it on television and in the movies dozens of times. They would be listening to her phone conversation with the police. They would nab her on her way out of the office and toss her off the Bay Bridge in a sack tied to cement blocks. Or worse, they would visit her home and pour gasoline on the wooden front steps. Then they would light a match, and…

"Amber?" The voice caused her to scream out loud. She looked up. It was Carlos, the young mail clerk. The sound of the scream just about hurled his slender frame into the credenza behind him.

She put her hand out to break his fall. "Carlos, I am so sorry. You startled me."

He held his hand to his heart. "Sorry, I'll try wearing a cowbell around my neck next time." He bent down and collected the dozens of envelopes that he had dropped on the floor. He sorted through them and handed a large FedEx envelope to her. "This one's for your boss. It actually came last week, and for some reason those potheads downstairs put it in the wrong pile. Sorry about that. I hope it's not urgent."

She took it from him. "Thanks," she said, holding it by her fingertips in an attempt to assess its contents.

"No problem. Go easy on the espressos, huh?" He laughed as he walked away.

She examined the package. It was from a travel agency in Los Angeles, one she had never heard of. Generally, Marty booked all his travel—business and personal—through the corporate travel service. Before this day, she would have thought that perhaps he was planning another "preretirement vacation," as he liked to call it, and was simply abiding by Kaitlyn's recent mandate that the company's resources not be permitted for personal use. But at that moment, she didn't feel like she knew Marty as well as she had thought.

She opened the package and pulled out a single sheet of paper, which was marked *ITINERARY* across the top. She felt a sense of relief when she noticed the dates on the schedule. It showed Marty's flight and hotel information for his trip during the past week. Obviously he didn't need it anymore. She was about to put it through the shredder when she read it more closely. There was a single round-trip flight to Dulles International Airport listed, but nothing else. *Washington?* Didn't Marty say he was in Boston? She sank into her chair as her heart sank in her chest. Then as she thought about her earlier phone conversation with him that morning, she suddenly felt a strange emotion. It wasn't anger and it wasn't fear. She realized it was sadness. Marty had been a trusted mentor, confidante, and friend to her for almost five years. But today, he was a liar, a deceiver, and a stranger.

Amber glanced at her watch. 11:25. She knew that meeting the stranger at their rendezvous destination was risky. She had no idea what that risk was, but the physical danger was not what concerned her the most. She worried about learning more information that might make her even more of an object of curiosity to those watching. But unfortunately, the "Biggest Gossip" deep inside of her controlled the rational thinking portion of her brain. She picked up her sunglasses and purse and walked to the elevators.

The gates at AT&T Park had just opened, and the crowd had begun filing in. There was an unmistakable buzz in the air as the Giants were hosting the Dodgers. Amber made her way down King Street, riding the wave of black and orange clad fans. The statue in the plaza was surrounded by a myriad of characters—program vendors, ticket scalpers, screaming parents, pickpockets. She took a circular route to the statue, hoping to remain inconspicuous, all the while staring at the faces of the people passing by her. She didn't have the first clue of who she was looking for, but she hoped that something might catch her eye. She walked past one of the program vendors, a man in his fifties, with a potbelly and a shaggy gray beard. He wore a large black cowboy hat with the Giants logo on the front.

"Programs! Get your programs here!" he called out to the crowd.

As she passed, he held a program in front of her.

"No, thanks," she said, waving it off.

"Take it, Amber," he insisted, his eyes looking over her head.

She took hold of the program and continued walking, her heart beating out of her torso. She opened the program to the first page. In large black marker, the words were handwritten: *Meet me in MoMo's. I'm at the bar.* She looked around, certain that every one of the forty-one thousand people around her were looking over her shoulder.

She crossed the street against the light, one of only a few people walking in the direction away from the ballpark, and proceeded up King Street toward MoMo's. The front of the restaurant was packed with people enjoying their libations before the first pitch. She walked up the steps and pushed her way through the crowd and into the bar area. She glanced up and down the bar, again not certain as to what she was looking for. At the end of the bar, she noticed a man in a charcoal suit with no tie, sitting by himself and drinking what appeared to be an iced tea. His dark hair was cut close, and his face was nicely tanned, a stark contrast to his white shirt. A fish out of water in the most literal sense. Despite her nervousness, she felt the blanket of safety provided by the crowd, and before she realized it, she was standing at the end of the bar.

"Thanks for coming. I realize it must have seemed sort of sketchy. Sorry about the cryptic messages," he said, taking a sip from his glass. "Can I get you anything?"

She shook her head no. "Who are you?" she asked pointedly. She had told herself that the appearance of confidence and an unwavering demeanor might shroud the overwhelming panic in her stomach.

"Does the name Harper Phillips mean anything to you?" She hesitated for a moment, which answered his question.

"I guess it has to at this point, doesn't it?" she replied. "Believe me, if I could turn the clock back and never have heard that name, I would love it."

"I'm sure you would. I feel the same way."

"You didn't answer my first question." She took a look around the bar to see if anyone was paying attention to them. Not a soul. A synchronized chant of "Let's go, Giants!" broke out.

"I'm not a cop, if that's what you're thinking," he said a bit louder with a smile, an attempt to soften his face. For the first time since she had approached the bar, she noted his blue eyes.

"I didn't ask who you were *not*, I asked who you were," she said, growing impatient.

He sighed deeply. "My name is Jack. Jack Bennett. I'm with the Bureau, or the FBI rather. At least I used to be."

"So, when you said you weren't a cop, you weren't exactly being truthful." She ordered an ice water from the bartender, and then turned to Bennett. "Did you say 'used to be'?"

He nodded. "I was let go not too long ago." She raised her eyebrows, an indicator for him to continue his explanation. "I was based out here on the West Coast for about fifteen years. But I spent most of the last three years with the Bureau, spearheading its efforts to crack down on the growing number of identity-theft cases." He took a long sip of his iced tea until there were only a few cubes left in the glass. She noticed the absence of a wedding band on his left hand.

"So you're probably aware that someone is walking around with Harper Phillips's name," she said. She wasn't going to pretend she didn't know anything.

He nodded again. "I was assigned to the investigation during my time there. We started out by tracking fraud cases. You know, someone gets hold of a Social Security number, invents a name and an address, and then goes around opening up credit card accounts and bank accounts. Then we began to focus on true identity theft. People who get hold of all the vital information on a real person, then begin running up a tab or committing crime in that person's name. In this age of technology and Internet commerce, it's relatively easy to stay under the radar and faceless."

Amber bit her lip, waiting for this guy to pull out an overhead projector with a statistical graph. *Thanks for the presentation*, she said to herself. "I guess that's how you came across Harper Phillips."

"Right. Mr. Phillips's credit history was impeccable, for the most part. Then suddenly, it fell apart in a matter of a few months. His credit card issuers wrote down a total of two and a half million dollars in his name. So we immediately put him on our watch list." He could tell that he had her attention.

"I guess you're also aware of the fact that someone claiming to be Harper Phillips is listed as an employee at Ensight," Amber said. "We've been paying him a moderate salary and everything. We never knew. Whoever this person is, he's good."

Jack nodded again. "They usually are. They're normally two steps ahead of their pursuers. My team and I just couldn't make much headway at the outset."

"Is that why you were fired?" she asked.

"No, that's not it," he said, shaking his head. "Of course, that's what they'll have you believe. The truth is that I really don't know why I was axed. They just told me that my position had been eliminated." He shrugged his shoulders and ordered another iced tea.

She began to speak, but he beat her to it. "It was strange timing, though. As you'd expect, it didn't take us long at all to learn that Harper Phillips was actually dead." He leaned in closer. She didn't back away. His aftershave was intoxicating.

"We started to look in closer and found some offshore bank accounts in his name. We felt like we were generating some real momentum when the deputy director dropped the bomb on me. Harry Lang, that fucker." She was staring at him.

"Sorry," he said. "He told me he wasn't happy with how things were going and that he was going to take over the investigation. I found it strange because the Phillips case was only one of a few dozen I was working on. In fact, I had made quite a bit of progress on most of the others. But for some reason, he singled this one case out. A week later, I was packing my desk."

Amber took a moment to digest everything he had said. "I'm sorry to hear that things didn't work out for you. And I'll admit, it doesn't sound fair. But I have to ask what all this has to do with me."

"During our investigation, or at least the part I was involved in, we only got as close as our subject allowed us to. These impostors, they like to play little cat-and-mouse games. All of this guy's activities were pretty much aligned with the typical profile of an ID thief—credit card fraud, passing bad checks, that sort of thing. The last thing I learned about this guy before I was fired was that he managed to get on the payroll of your company. I never got to find out how or why." They both watched as the patrons at MoMo's began pouring out, in the direction of the ballpark.

"I suppose that's where I come in?" Amber asked. Bennett nodded one last time. "But I don't quite understand," she continued. "Why do you care, anyway? It's not your problem anymore."

"Because something is not right. There's a reason why he chose Ensight. You said yourself that he gave himself only a moderate salary. Why not go for the whole pot of gold? There's something about your company that interested him. And I'm guessing it's something that's not written in any public filing. There's something there that might help to explain why I don't have a job right now."

Amber looked at her glass of ice water, which had been sitting on the bar, its beads of condensation beginning to run down the glass. "Listen, Mr. Bennett, I'm sorry about what happened to you. I truly am. And I wish I could help. But I'm just not comfortable getting involved in this. Besides, I get the feeling that whatever I could do to assist you wouldn't exactly be on the up and up." She slung her purse over her shoulder and pulled her sunglasses off the top of her head.

"Fair enough, Amber." He reached into his suit pocket and pulled out a card. "Here's my contact information, in case you change your mind. Or if you just want to talk." He smiled again, and she had to look away quickly.

She held out her hand. "It was nice meeting you, Mr. Bennett. Good luck to you."

He shook her hand. "Likewise."

She walked out of the bar and put her sunglasses on to fend off the glare. Before descending the steps, she turned back around. Through the large open doors, she could see that only about ten people remained standing around the bar. At the end, there were two glasses sitting on the bar. The barstool was empty.

She crossed King Street and walked toward the grassy field outside the ballpark entrance. As she walked past the giant brick wall of the stadium, she could faintly hear the sound of the national anthem on the other side.

Chapter 10

The Wednesday morning edition of the *San Francisco Chronicle* ran a two-page story about the woman who had recently been found murdered in the park. Since the victim had no identification, the police still hadn't been able to learn her name. A small fanny pack was found on her, containing a few dollar bills mixed with some receipts, some lint, and chewing gum. Among the receipts was one from a local pizza delivery service. The police had questioned the pizza place and were told that a delivery had been made a week before. The pizza place had recorded the address but unfortunately had no name for the person who placed the order and said the woman had paid in cash. The police had discovered that the house was located on a narrow street in the Sunset District. The front door was open, but when the investigators entered, they found only an empty house. Either the victim was a minimalist in the purest sense, or someone had gutted the place. The case would likely go down as unsolved, with an unidentified victim. The news story then went on to discuss safeguards for walking or jogging alone at night.

Marty Callahan sat at his desk with the newspaper spread in front of him. He had been in the office since 6:20 that morning. His coffee cup was still full, but the coffee was now cold. He read the article twice, the first time in disbelief, the second in anger. The police detectives had described the gunshot wound to the victim's head as "very clean, almost professional—hardly the work of street thugs." Marty had seen Priscilla Phillips's picture before. He looked at the sketch of the victim. It was her. No mistake. Marty tried his best to dismiss her death as a remote coincidence, but he somehow felt connected. He had called Bruce Fox but had not yet been able to reach him.

The name *Priscilla Phillips* had come up only once during his meetings with the Committee. It was more of an incidental mention when Lang and the others began asking about Harper's relatives and other personal interests. But her name never again surfaced. When he first met the Committee, Marty would never have suspected that any foul play would be the result of their doing. These were businessmen, not mobsters. But his most recent meeting in DC forced him to consider just how desperate and vengeful these men had become. He realized that they would be willing to bulldoze over anything or any person standing in their way. And that included anyone who knew or might eventually learn about the nature of their affiliation with the dead Harper Phillips.

He breathed deeply, as something in his chest felt heavy. He lifted his head and slowly looked up. Amber stood in the doorway. She looked beautiful with her hair in an updo, and she wore a light-colored pants suit. But he didn't have the energy to gawk and fantasize as he would have on any other day.

"Good morning and welcome back. I didn't expect to see you here so early," she said, only slightly smiling. Her eyes were red, an obvious sign of fatigue.

"I was about to say the same thing to you."

"Well, I didn't get much done yesterday, so I thought I'd get an early start today." *What a lie*, she told herself.

It was easy to see that he was preoccupied. "Is everything OK?" she asked.

"Oh, sure," he said. "I'm just a little jet-lagged."

She wanted so badly to walk up to his desk and swipe the contents onto the floor. She wanted to shake a finger in his face and tell him that she didn't trust him. She wanted to demand that he tell her what he knew or else she would call Bruce Fox. But seeing Marty at his desk, looking defeated and much older, she couldn't do it. But she wouldn't let her guard down, either. She would bring it up to him later.

"How was the weather in Boston?" she asked. She had read the Boston weather reports for the week before.

"It was a little muggy. It rained a couple of days." Apparently, Marty had studied those same reports before returning to the office.

She glanced at his desk and noticed the newspaper article on his desk. She saw the portrait of Priscilla. "Isn't that awful?"

He shook his head slowly. "Senseless is the word." There was remorse in his tone.

"Right."

He continued to look at the page. "You sounded pretty concerned when we spoke on the phone the other day."

She looked at him intently.

"Something you want to talk about?" He looked up at her, and for a brief moment, the two of them stared at each other, almost as if they both knew what the other was thinking.

Amber shook her head. "It can wait. I'll leave you alone. You look like you have a lot on your mind right now." She started to back out of the office.

"Thanks, Amber," he said, and managed to smile.

Amber returned to her desk and began her daily routine of reading her morning e-mail. She had thought a lot about Jack Bennett since their meeting at MoMo's. He had not tried to reach her since, and a part of her felt disappointed. She reached into her purse and fished out his card. Even the printed letters on his card were bold and chiseled. She wondered whether he was thinking about her too. Probably not. Her last relationship had been over a year ago and had ended with her significant other moving in with an American Airlines flight attendant. She hadn't dated much since then, and her cheater radar was on constantly. It probably explained why she and Marty got along so well. They understood each other, or at least they used to.

She looked into Marty's office and saw that he was still sitting at his desk. She recalled some of the details from her meeting with Jack. He had written to her in one of his e-mails that she should not talk to Marty Callahan. It didn't occur to her to ask during their conversation, but at this moment, there was no doubt in her mind that Marty was not as uninterested in the Harper Phillips case as he had originally pretended. Apparently, Jack must already have known that. It would be easier to call him and ask what Marty's involvement was in this whole deal. She convinced herself that that would be her primary motive for calling him, and not her superficial attraction to him. Picking up her cell phone, she walked into a conference room, closed the door, and dialed the digits.

"Hello?" It was Jack's voice. She remembered it distinctly.

"Hello, Mr. Bennett?"

"Yes, who's this?"

"It's Amber Wakefield." Her voice was quivering.

"Amber, hi. I'm glad you called. I was just about to call you," he said. "And please, call me Jack."

She spoke quietly as she felt a fluttering in her stomach. "All right. Why were you going to call me?" She didn't want to miss the opportunity to learn the answer to that question.

"I'm sure you recognized the police sketch of the woman who was recently murdered in Golden Gate Park. Priscilla Phillips, right?"

"Yes. How did you…" she began.

"There's something I need to share with you, Amber," he said. "I don't want to do this over the phone. Can you meet me in Justin Herman Plaza in thirty minutes? In front of the fountain?"

She hesitated before speaking. "Sure. There's something I need to talk to you about as well."

At that moment, the line went dead. Jack apparently had no intention to chit-chat.

Amber arrived at Justin Herman Plaza at nine o'clock, amidst a fleet of trucks and vans, with metal poles and tarps visible from the backs of the vehicles. A stage was being constructed in the plaza for a free concert that afternoon. She walked toward the fountain where a few people sat, drinking their morning coffees and smoking cigarettes—no doubt procrastinators who were dreading the start of their workday. A group of pigeons were pecking at the ground for scraps left over from the night before.

She looked around her anxiously. Jack wasn't there yet. There was a loud screeching sound from a hot microphone near the stage, prompting her to turn around. She almost fell into Jack as she turned.

"Good morning," he said, breaking her fall by bracing her arms. His hands were strong. He stood about a head taller. He wasn't in a suit today—only navy Adidas warm-up pants and a gray sweatshirt. He carried a black backpack over his shoulder.

"Morning, Jack." She felt her cheeks suddenly get warm. "What, no scavenger hunt with little 'meet me here, meet me there' letters?"

"Not today," he said, showing his perfect teeth.

They sat down on one of the ledges. Amber picked up where they had left off earlier.

"So, you knew her?" she asked.

"Yes," he said, nodding and looking at the ground. "When I began investigating this case, I learned immediately that Harper had a daughter. I met with her several times over a short period. But she wasn't close to him, so she didn't have much to share." The music from a local radio station broadcasting from a van across the plaza began playing at a deafening volume.

"Nonetheless," he went on, "as the next of kin, I figured she might be able to help me get my hands on any confidential or personal information about him.

She had contacted his law firm, and they told her that she could pick up his personal items at her leisure." He shrugged his shoulders and looked down, seeming almost remorseful. "But I guess she never got around to it."

"Why are you telling me all this?" Amber asked, a cautious tone obvious in her voice.

"Well, I'm sure you've seen the reports on her murder investigation. No one has any idea who this woman was. Her house was empty; she had no identification on her and no friends or family to speak of. In other words, no one would know this woman if she showed up on their front doorstep."

Jack gazed in the direction of the stage being erected across the plaza. "I was so close. I just wish there someone who could," he paused, searching for the right words.

"Who could what?" Amber asked.

He continued to stare into space for a moment. "Finish what she started, in a manner of speaking." His voice trailed off, as his eyes slowly shifter in her direction.

After a few seconds, a sarcastic smile came to her face. "Wait a minute. I think I get it now. I'm a woman, she's a woman. You want me to pick up where she left off. That's it, isn't it?" she asked, her eyes directly on his. He looked back at her without saying anything. "Are you out of your goddamn mind?" she said loud enough for the whole plaza to hear, but the thundering music in the background drowned her voice.

"Well, if you change your mind," he began.

She cut him off. "Will you please stop saying that? I'm not going to change my mind. You're on your own, Mr. Bennett. I'm not helping you."

"Then why did you agree to meet me here? Why did you call me first this morning?"

"It doesn't matter now. Besides, they'll eventually find out who she is. They have dental records and stuff like that," she said confidently, trying to steer him away from his question, when in truth she had no idea what she was talking about.

Jack moved forward so that his nose was nearly touching the top of her head. "Look, I can't be sure about who killed her. But I can tell you that if they want to keep her identity concealed, they will figure out a way."

She tried to look away, but couldn't.

He leaned in closer and spoke quietly into her ear. "Amber, whoever killed Priscilla did it because they were afraid that she might learn something about her father. It's something that apparently is very important to these people. So you can refuse to help me, but you should keep in mind that you know an awful lot about Harper Phillips. It doesn't matter how you got the information or whether you want to pretend you never knew it. Sooner or later, someone is going to realize that you know more than you should." He said all these words in what appeared to be a single breath. "After all, I did."

"If you're trying to intimidate me, it's not going to work," she replied, not believing a word of what she had just said.

"Fine," he said, exasperated. "Good luck, Amber." He turned, shaking his head, and began walking toward the Embarcadero, the wide, tree-lined avenue which ran adjacent to the bay.

After a few steps, he turned to face her. "By the way, are you aware that your boss was in Washington last week?"

She nodded.

"Do you have any idea why he was there?"

She looked at him but said nothing.

"What a shame." He threw his backpack over his shoulder and walked away.

She didn't notice the man sitting at a small table on the opposite side of the plaza. He sipped his coffee slowly, and the Chinese symbol tattooed on his neck pulsated as he swallowed. He watched Amber Wakefield and Jack Bennett talk, and while he couldn't actually hear them, the conversation appeared contentious, much more so than the first time he had watched them from the opposite end of the bar at MoMo's.

As he watched Amber standing alone in the plaza, he held his cell phone to his ear and listened.

"Yeah," said the voice on the other end.

"It's Watts." He put his finger in his free ear to block the music coming from the plaza.

He tapped his foot to the rhythm of the music as he waited.

"Yeah, what do you got?" demanded the voice on the other end.

"They just met again. It was a much shorter meeting than the one near the ballpark the other day. Neither of them looked very happy with the other," Watts said.

"Keep an eye on her." The voice on the other end told him.

"What about Callahan?"

"Don't worry about old Marty. He's been pretty predictable so far."

"What if he talks to her?" Watts asked.

"Then I'll take care of it."

Watts smiled at this. It sounded so sinister and cold-blooded. Just what he liked.

"She's moving," Watts said, as Amber began walking out of the plaza, back in the direction of her office. "I'll be in touch soon." The line went dead.

Across the country, Harry Lang leaned back in his leather chair and turned to look out the window. The Washington sky was gray. He picked up his cell phone again and punched one button.

"Bruce, it's me," he said into the phone. "Get everyone together. One hour from now."

"What about Callahan?" Fox asked.

"We don't need him for this meeting."

Chapter 11

He eagerly accepted the hot towel from the flight attendant and wiped his face and the back of his neck. It felt so refreshing. He untied his ponytail and ruffled his hands through his hair. He removed his diamond earring and cleaned it so it sparkled brightly. He sat in a row by himself while pondering his latest discovery, as disappointing as it was. He was flying from Athens, his favorite destination. He could get lost there. He sat back and tried to relax, an exercise in futility.

According to his employer in Washington, there were six bank accounts in Europe, all under the name of Harper Phillips, each containing large balances according to the statements. He had calculated the total to be around ten million dollars. He was well aware that he was being tailed. His only mandate from his employer was to stay ahead of his FBI pursuers. The agreement was simple. If he was caught, he was on his own, and there would be no payday for him.

He had followed virtually the same routine for each bank. Once his boss in Washington supplied him with the account numbers, he would run through a series of steps. Before visiting the bank to make the withdrawal, he would call to check the actual balance. Most of the activity details were available either through Web access or by touch-tone telephone. Therefore, the transactions were reported in near real-time or on a next-day basis at the latest. He had cautioned himself that there was nothing more suspicious than someone who requested a withdrawal and didn't know the balance of his own account, so he went to great lengths not to deviate from his process.

While he knew that a physical trip to the bank was unnecessary to withdraw the funds, he enjoyed the adrenaline rush of impersonating an actual person.

Plus, he was a travel junkie and took every opportunity to frolic in a foreign locale.

After leaving Hong Kong, he was scheduled to go to Singapore. But at the last moment he decided to throw his FBI pursuers a curve by changing his flight to Sydney, Australia. He knew that the men in Washington who had hired him would not be happy about that move. But he had fallen behind during his trip from San Francisco to Hong Kong, and the G-men had come close to catching up to him on a couple of occasions. He needed to create some distance, but he would make sure to keep them in the game. At some point, he would backtrack and hit the Singapore account.

He had arrived in Paris early on a Tuesday morning, having come from London, where he cleaned out both the Barclays and Lloyds accounts—a total of one and a half million pounds. Upon arriving in France, he took the train to Lyon to the main branch of the Credit Lyonnais Bank. As usual, he had called the night before to confirm the balance in that account—five and a half million euros. But to his surprise and disappointment, he would never see that money.

He contemplated the possibilities while the aircraft ascended to its cruising altitude. It had been over eight hours since he had left the French bank's doors, having learned that the bundle of cash waiting for him was not in the account as he had thought. When he reviewed a transaction statement that one of the bank employees furnished to him, it indicated that the funds had been withdrawn that morning. Someone had been there before him.

After learning about the Credit Lyonnais account, he immediately began checking with the next bank he planned to hit, Deutsche Bank. The call yielded the same result. The account balance was now at zero. However, it was not this fact that startled him. He learned that the account had been depleted that afternoon. Whoever took the money was moving quickly, almost as if they were competing in a race or some type of scavenger hunt.

He considered aborting. He would take whatever he had earned thus far and go underground for a while. But the reward to him for completing the whole operation was an enormous amount of money, and he wasn't willing to leave it on the table. *Son of a bitch.* Someone was beating him at his own game. *Did someone know about him? Was someone following him? Or was someone just screwing with him?* He couldn't help but feel a sense of admiration for whoever it was.

He wondered what he would tell his boss in Washington. He knew how powerful his employer was, and his head began to throb at the thought of disappointing him. He felt the sweat on his forehead and quickly unfastened his seatbelt.

He walked quickly to the lavatory at the rear of the cabin and vomited into the toilet.

The meeting among the Committee members, minus Callahan, took place in an apartment across the river in Arlington in a small, furnished two-bedroom apartment that Lang and his wife had owned for twenty years. The former tenants had recently vacated, and it was currently unoccupied.

Lang quickly briefed them on the details of the latest status update from his agents. He explained that their boy was moving quickly. There were eyewitnesses at three hotels and four banks who testified to Lang's men that a man named Harper Phillips had visited their establishments. The surveillance reports showed that according to the recent bank records of Harper Phillips, the accounts in London, Lyon, Frankfurt, and Barcelona had all been emptied, as had the account in Singapore, and of course, the one in Hong Kong. Everything was going according to plan, and in fact, it was all happening much faster than any of them had anticipated.

The meeting broke shortly after three o'clock. After Fitch and Hammond left the apartment, Lang sat down on the sofa and leaned his head back. He scratched his head with both sets of fingers.

"What's on your mind?" Fox asked, noticing Lang's behavior.

Lang let out a sigh. "Bruce, when was the last time you checked the account in Curaçao?"

Fox shrugged and stuck his bottom lip out. "I don't know. Yesterday, maybe."

"Well, I think we have a problem."

Fox sat down next to him. "Let's hear it."

"I didn't want to bring it up earlier, especially in front of Fitch. He would shit if he heard this. And that old fart Hammond would probably have a stroke right here on this nice Oriental rug." Lang rubbed his eyes, which were already bloodshot.

"Tell me."

Lang stood and walked to the window. "According to the statements, a total of ten million dollars has been withdrawn from all of Harper's accounts around the world."

"And?" Fox urged, stroking his goatee.

"The balance in the Curaçao account is four and a half million." Lang waited while his partner performed the calculations in his head.

"Well, where's the rest of it?"

Lang shook his head slowly to indicate that he had already asked that question a dozen times.

Fox stood. "You think that son of a bitch is playing with us?"

"Well," Lang began but Fox interrupted him.

"Why the hell would he do that? Doesn't he realize what he's risking?"

"Bruce," Lang said, but Fox kept mumbling expletives. "Bruce, shut the hell up and listen for a second, will you?"

"What?"

"Believe me, I've walked through a hundred scenarios already. At first, I thought the same thing you were thinking—that our trusted friend was screwing us. After all, what else could it be, right?" Lang was setting up his delivery.

"Jesus Christ, stop with the dramatic introduction, Harry. If this guy is fucking around with us, then let's send a team out there to track his ass down and slit his throat!"

Lang swallowed the little bit of saliva left in his mouth. "Sorry, I'll stop sugar-coating this." He paused for a few seconds, struggling to find the words. "I don't think our guy is cheating us out of anything."

Fox picked up a file folder from the table. "What are you keeping from us? You just reassured us that everything was on track. Now you're telling me that we're missing close to six mil. And yet, you're willing to give this asshole the benefit of the doubt?"

"We don't know that he withdrew the funds, Bruce."

"Well, someone pulled the money out. It didn't just happen by itself!" Fox's face was turning red.

"That's correct. *Someone* did take the money."

Fox looked at him, perplexed.

"Bruce, come sit down. Let me show you something," Lang said, taking the file folder and opening it.

Fox sat down next to him. Lang spread the papers across the coffee table. "Now, my agents out there sniffed our guy's trail and according to this, he arrived in France on Tuesday at noon. Judging by the transaction report for the account, a total of five and a half million euros was withdrawn that morning at 9:15." Lang pointed to a line on the page. Fox scratched his head.

"Are you seeing it yet, Bruce?" Lang continued

Fox shook his head. "Am I seeing what?"

"The money was taken out more than three hours before our guy showed up at the bank. Someone else got there before he did."

Fox stared at the page, fighting to hold his composure. But his face suddenly softened. "Wait a minute, that doesn't prove anything. We all know that you don't have to go into a bank to make a withdrawal. He could have done it electronically that morning."

"That's true. But take a look at this." Lang pulled out another sheet. "This is the authorization that the bank furnished to my agents. See here?" He pointed to the bottom of the page. "It was signed for by Harper Phillips."

Fox shrugged. "It doesn't prove anything. Your guys out there probably got his arrival time wrong. He probably changed his itinerary at the last moment and arrived a day earlier."

Lang could tell that he was going to have to sell his partner on this. He found another sheet and put it in front of Fox. "This one here is another signed authorization from another bank. Take a close look. Same day. Also signed for, but the time stamp says 9:34 in the morning."

Fox stared at the page and read the bank name off the top. "Barclays," he whispered to himself.

"Now Bruce, are you going to tell me that the same guy made a withdrawal in London, and then twenty minutes later he showed up in Lyon?"

Fox put his hand over his forehead, while he looked at the rug beneath his feet. "I can't believe this. How could you let this happen, Harry?"

"This wasn't part of the plan."

"But you promised us that you had this thing ironclad."

"What do you want me to say?" said Lang. "Believe me, I've gone over this thing a million times in the hopes that I may have missed something or gotten the dates mixed up. But unfortunately, I keep coming to the same conclusion."

"I don't have to believe you, Harry. Just fix it." Fox stood without looking at Lang and walked out of the apartment, slamming the door behind him.

Lang took a long sip from his glass, followed by a deep breath. He despised the notion that someone—anyone—could be beating him at his own game. He felt a surge of heat rising in his body, and in a single motion, he turned around and threw the glass against the fireplace, creating an exploding shower of crystal and ice.

Chapter 12

▼

Carrying a cup of coffee, Amber walked down the Embarcadero, then up Mission toward Spear. She spent the walk reassuring herself that she had done the right thing in rejecting Jack's request, all the while oblivious to the stranger with the tattoo who had been pacing her all morning. Despite it all, she couldn't help but experience the heartache of knowing that Priscilla's death would go unsolved.

She arrived at her desk and noticed that Marty wasn't in his office. It didn't matter now anyway. She wouldn't approach him. She would put it behind her. She reached into her Rolodex and pulled out Jack's business card. She held it in her hand for a moment. *What a jerk.* She ripped the card in half, then into quarters. She threw the scraps into the trash can beneath her desk. During all of her huffing and puffing, she didn't notice the manila envelope on her desk. It hadn't been there when she had left her desk that morning.

She opened the envelope and felt around inside. She immediately recognized what felt like a compact disc, accompanied by papers. The CD had no label or writing on it. The pages were business-style letters addressed to Priscilla. Amber looked at the letterhead: *Jackson Winthrop, LLP*. She immediately closed the envelope and looked around her cube. Everyone around her was busily tapping away at their keyboards.

Amber inserted the CD into her disk drive. The whirring sound of the CD reader complemented the monotonous buzzing of the fluorescent lights above her. There was one file on the disk, an Excel spreadsheet. She opened the document and watched the animated sands pour through the rotating hourglass. The spreadsheet was plain, with no title, just a list of names and numbers. There were a dozen names on the list with amounts ranging from ten million to fifty million.

What the hell was this? Twirling her hair, she browsed the list of names, which were obviously not sorted in any logical order. She didn't recognize any of them. T. Hammond. D. Fitch. And then, there it was: M. Callahan. And the number written next to his name? Ten million. She gazed at the spreadsheet, and at that moment, despite all of the names and digits on the sheet, only one name existed within her field of vision.

"Marty," she murmured to herself.

Knock, knock.

She spun around quickly. It was Marty tapping the wall of her cubicle.

"Sorry, dear, didn't mean to startle you."

"Oh, you didn't startle me. I'm just a little anxious this morning," she said, doing her best to collect the pages on her desk and stuff them back into the large envelope.

"What are you working on?" he asked, nodding toward her monitor, the contents of which were illegible from his distance.

She instinctively poked at a number of buttons on her keyboard until she found the sleep button. Her screen saver of black Labrador puppies immediately came up. "Nothing important." She grabbed the envelope and folded it in half.

"Lunch?" he asked.

"What about it?"

"Let me take you to lunch. It's been a while since we've spent time together." Marty had that paternal look on his face.

She looked around her desk, as if some excuse not to go would make itself visible.

"Well?"

"Kind of early for lunch, isn't it?"

"We'll make it a long one. How does that sound?"

"OK," she replied, trying to maintain an atmosphere of normalcy. She tried to smile. "Can you give me five minutes to freshen up?"

"Absolutely. I'll meet you downstairs in the lobby." He turned and walked toward the elevators.

Amber stuffed the folded envelope into a desk drawer and locked it. She stood up and walked toward the ladies room.

They walked down the street and into Boulevard, a common destination for entertaining business clients and other VIPs. Marty was a regular there, so the waiter knew to bring him a Ketel One martini before he had dropped his napkin into his lap, and for Amber, a Diet Coke. For the next ninety minutes, they covered every topic under the sun, from family to education to the war on terrorism. Marty updated her on the status of his most recent divorce. He still had an amicable relationship with Cindy, his latest ex. But that didn't stop Cindy from unleashing her pack of legal pit bulls on him.

They talked about the company and the status of the Maguire acquisition. At one point, he suggested to Amber that she take some time off. She still had all eighteen days of vacation left for the year. She told him that she would think about it.

After about thirty minutes of boring chitchat, Marty asked her about Harper Phillips. She hadn't forgotten about their conversation on the phone, just before Marty had to board his plane.

"It was nothing important. Just forget about it," she told him.

"Well, you sounded like you had a lot to tell me at the time." He took a bite of one of the olives from his second martini. "Is there something you want to tell me now?"

"Should I be asking you that question?" She was tired of answering other people's questions.

"What is that supposed to mean?"

"Marty, I realize that your knowledge about Harper Phillips extends beyond that meeting we had with the IRS." She looked at her boss, who was gazing out the window. "If you were involved with him or you know something about his death, I promise not to say anything. I just don't want to find myself getting a subpoena one day as a result of my association with you. What you do is your own business."

Marty bowed his head. He was embarrassed, disappointed that she had developed such a polluted image of him. He nodded slowly. "You're right. That wasn't the first time I had heard his name."

She looked away. He put his hand on her arm. "But I swear on the Bible, Amber. I had nothing to do with his death. I didn't know the man, never met him." His eyes were soft and relaxed, practically begging her to believe him.

"Then how do you know about him?"

"It's better that you don't know that. At least now right now."

"I want to believe you, Marty. You have no idea how much I want to believe you." He could always tell when Amber was being sincere, as she was this time. "It's just that ever since those IRS men came to our offices, nothing has been normal. Information keeps popping up, some of it the product of my own nosiness, I'll admit."

"You mean like finding out that the real Harper was dead?" he asked.

She nodded. "And then discovering that his daughter had been murdered in the park."

Until now, Marty had no inkling that she knew about Priscilla, or even who she was. "How do you know that?"

"I recognized her face when they flashed the picture of the anonymous woman. I had met her when I tried to visit Harper Phillips at his house. I'm guessing that her death wasn't entirely random, either."

It occurred to him at that moment that Amber had immersed herself much deeper than he had originally suspected. "Her death was a shock to me as well. But I never knew her," he said.

She studied Marty, and his body language signaled that he was telling the truth.

He leaned in closer. "Amber, honey. Do me a favor. Do yourself a favor. Take that vacation we just talked about. Get away for a while. Take your mind off this stuff."

She wondered whether he was offering his advice or a warning. "Have I gotten myself into trouble here, Marty?" She suddenly felt comfortable talking to him, as though she was chatting with the old Marty again.

"No, not at all," he said, shaking his head emphatically. "It's just not worth your while to get involved in this anymore. It's not fair to you." He was tempted to tell her the truth—that it wasn't her time or effort that concerned him, but her safety. He decided that there was no need to scare her. If she really was in danger, there wasn't much either of them could do to protect her.

"Thanks, Marty. That's sweet of you. I was starting to worry that I had lost you. You've been acting so strange lately." *Should I tell him about Jack Bennett? Should I ask him what he was doing in DC? No. He was right. No need to get any more involved.*

"I've noticed the same about you." He smiled at her and winked, which made her giggle. "So, are you going to take that vacation, or do I need to drop you onto an island from a plane?"

She smiled. "The vacation starts next week. I'll need the company jet," she said playfully.

"Nice try. Even I don't get to use that thing. Will you settle for a ride to the airport in the company limo?"

"I guess." She stuck her fork into her salad, which had been sitting untouched for the last fifteen minutes.

They laughed together and spent the remainder of the lunch discussing who was sleeping with whom in the office and who was lucky to still have a job with the company. Both felt as though an enormous weight had been lifted from them. But each knew that they hadn't told the other everything.

A man seated at the restaurant bar sipped coffee slowly. He didn't face them, and they certainly didn't see him. He wore a gray turtleneck sweater, which covered the tattoo on his neck. After Marty and Amber left the restaurant, the man stepped down from his barstool and walked to the restroom. In front of the door to the men's room, a young Hispanic busboy stood wearing an apron. His instructions had been simple: to deliver the basket of bread to the pretty young woman sitting with the gray-haired gentleman at the table by the window. The busboy handed the basket to the man, and in return, accepted a crisp one hundred dollar bill, which he folded and placed into his pocket. *Cheap labor.* The man patted the youngster on his back, and the busboy walked toward the dining room.

The man took the remaining piece of bread in the basket and put it into his mouth. He turned the basket over and removed the tiny black recording device attached to the bottom. He placed the device into his pocket and walked toward the front doors. With the scent of seawater crossing his path, the wind from the bay felt good as he went outside. As he walked toward the nearby piers, he chewed the bread with an open mouth while tapping digits into his cell phone.

Chapter 13

Bruce Fox and Harry Lang spent the remainder of the week combing through the bank statements and surveillance reports of Harper Phillips. They were able to reconcile all of the deposits into the Curaçao account by matching them to the withdrawals from various accounts around the world. There were a number of withdrawals that didn't have corresponding deposits into the Curaçao account. They concluded that those were the ones this stranger had gotten his hands on.

Lang was relieved that Fox had calmed down since their recent discovery, yet he felt nauseated at the thought that it was not his hired man who had cleaned out those accounts. Nonetheless, he was able to regain his focus.

"It has to be someone who knew Harper," he told Fox.

"Probably," Fox acknowledged.

"Or someone who is just trying to piss me off."

"Harry, as many people as there are out there who would like to take a shot at you, I think you're being paranoid. You've been playing this one pretty close to the vest. I don't know how many of them know to push this particular button."

Lang thought for a moment, and a slight smile crept across his face. "Except for one."

"Who are you talking about?"

"My good friend and protégé. Jack Bennett."

"I think he would take exception to either of those terms. Besides, do you really think he could pull this off?"

"Listen, Jack Bennett may represent everything that I loathe. Good looks, charm, no wife."

"Hair?" Fox said, unable to resist taking a potshot.

"Shut up," Lang said. "I was going to say that despite all that, he is good at what he does. He's smart, determined, and instinctive. That's enough in this line of work."

"Well, you always did say that he was a hell of an investigator."

"He still is. And that scares the shit out of me." It was clear that Lang was starting to convince himself that he was onto something. "Think about it, Bruce. He knows I'm working on the Harper Phillips case. Hell, I fired him at the height of his investigation." Lang shook his head. "He knows just as many people as I do, maybe more. And therefore, he's totally capable of bypassing most security measures. He'd relish the notion of screwing up the official investigation, even if it's just to make me look like a jackass in front of the director and the rest of the Bureau."

"So you think that Jack Bennett hired someone just to dick with you? Sounds kind of petty."

Lang looked at him and shrugged. "My career has taught me that there is nothing in this world completely outside the realm of possibility. And I work in a world where your career path is exclusively defined by your reputation."

"Fine. So, how do we make absolutely certain about your theory?" Fox asked, his tone filled with doubt. "Why don't we just give Watts the green light to take care of him?"

"No way. Watts is trigger-happy. He won't be subtle about it. Anyway, if Bennett is behind all this, then he's also the only person who can lead us to our money. We need to keep our eyes on the prize."

"Great. So, how would you prefer to do it? Shall we send him a Hallmark card and politely ask him if he's conspiring to embarrass the deputy director of the FBI?" Fox's sarcasm never played well with Lang.

"No, smart-ass. We may not be able to get to Jack, but we can get near him."

"How?"

"What's the name of Callahan's little assistant?"

Fox shook his head in protest. "Not Amber!"

Lang looked at him disgustedly. "Oh, will you please stop saying her name like she's your goddamn niece or something?"

"But why her?"

"Jack obviously thinks that she can help him. Plus, I'm sure he's got a little thing for her. If we can't stop him, then we need to slow him down at least. Just enough so that he doesn't gain any more momentum."

"What if he just stops as a result and disappears? Then we're screwed."

Lang shook his head. "I know him. He'll keep trying. After all, he didn't stop after we did Priscilla Phillips."

"Let's not talk about that. That was all you. Don't drag us into your dirty world."

"Sorry. Look, I need to slow Jack down and get a reading on him. I can't do that if he's bouncing around. If I can chop down whatever tree he's currently barking up, then at least we can gain some ground on him."

He placed his hand on Fox's shoulder. "Bruce, I need you to stand behind me on this one. Do you want to be the one to tell that hothead Fitch that we're being outplayed? It won't just be me he'll want to strangle."

"I don't take well to blackmail tactics, Harry."

"But they are effective, wouldn't you say?" Lang smiled back.

Fox sneered. "I'm guessing that you've already conceived a plan for this?"

Lang nodded. "I talked to Watts yesterday. He played back the tape for me. It sounds like Miss Wakefield is planning to take a vacation next week. We can make sure it's a permanent one." Lang's smile was sinister. "What do you say?"

After a few seconds, Fox slowly nodded.

The weekend went by much faster than Amber had anticipated. She felt relaxed for once, and took her mind off her problems by hanging out on Saturday night with a few friends. She even surrendered to temptation by smoking a couple of cigarettes, something that occurred only when she was in the company of girlfriends and wine. She kept the matches as a reminder that she was still able and entitled to have a good time once in a while.

According to the meteorology reports, the temperature in Kauai was eighty-seven degrees Fahrenheit. Amber made her reservations to stay at the Hyatt resort on Poipu Beach only thirty minutes after her lunch with Marty. She hadn't taken a vacation—a real vacation—in nearly thirteen months, so she was eager to accept Marty's offer for time off. Besides, he wasn't planning to be in the office much anyway. He was flying to Chicago to meet with Kaitlyn and the other executive staff members on Wednesday to talk with the Maguire folks.

Amber made arrangements for the company limousine service to pick her up at the office on Monday afternoon at 1:30 and take her to San Francisco International Airport. Her flight was scheduled for three o'clock. At one o'clock, Marty called her into his office. She walked in to see that a black rollaway suitcase was sitting beside his desk. He explained that Kaitlyn had just called and asked that he come out to Chicago immediately, rather than wait until Wednesday. The next flight was out of Oakland at 2:45 that afternoon. He needed to use the limousine service; the one she had reserved for her ride to the airport, which meant that it probably wouldn't be back before 2:30, much too late for her to make her flight. The other vehicles in the limo service's fleet had been booked long before, so she was out of luck. She acted disappointed, simply to make him feel bad. But since the limo service was intended for business use, it was hard to justify her Hawaiian vacation over his trip to meet Kaitlyn and the others to discuss the biggest deal in the company's history. She would take a taxi and expense it to the company, she told herself.

"I'll make it up to you," he said before leaving with his bags.

"Can I get that in writing?" she jokingly asked as he entered the elevator.

Back in her office, she pulled out a phone book from her cabinet and flipped through the Yellow Pages for a taxi service. After making a reservation with the taxi company, she walked to the break room to wash her coffee cup. As she walked down the hallway, she heard the faint sound of an explosion. Probably a car backfire. Although it was less than likely, considering how audible it was from twelve floors up. Apparently, the rest of the people on the floor thought the same thing, because in a matter of seconds, every occupant on the floor was pinned against the north window.

Amber weaved her way between the bodies to get to a front row view. On the street below, she could see a billow of black smoke starting to spread across the eastbound lane. It was impossible to see anything through the thick smoke, but suddenly her stomach felt uneasy. She pushed herself away from the window and ran to the elevators, with a number of other employees racing behind her.

She arrived at the lobby level and pushed open the glass doors at the entrance. She ran around the corner, able to smell the odor of burning rubber and fuel. There were a number of people running in different directions, all trying to distance themselves from the expanding smoke plume. As she walked closer, she could make out the blurry image of the likely source of the inferno. A black Lincoln Town Car. A limousine. *Oh God.* She felt her eyes watering but wasn't immediately sure if it was the intense heat and smoke causing her to well up, or something else. She tried to approach the vehicle, but the heat was unbearable.

She stayed at the scene, as did dozens of other rubbernecking drivers and pedestrians. The intersection in front of the Ensight offices was entirely gridlocked. However, a fire truck and an ambulance miraculously managed to make their way to the scene after about eight minutes. They were able to extinguish the flames quickly, but it took a while for the smoke to clear from the street level.

Despite the police's efforts to keep the crowd at a distance, the officers couldn't keep the onlookers from seeing through the blown-out windows of the charred limousine. The force of the explosion left virtually no remains of its occupants. Amid the blurry cloud of smoke in the front seat, all that was left was a man's shoe, probably that of the chauffeur. The back seat was still filled with smoke, but the charred scraps of clothing left no doubt that someone else had perished.

Amber turned away and walked in the opposite direction, holding her hand to her mouth and nose, trying to stifle her nausea and grief. As she walked across the street, dodging pieces of burned metal, she stepped on a piece of black plastic with an object dangling from it. Bending down to pick it up, she recognized it as a plastic handle of some sort. The letters engraved on it said *Samsonite*. It was a suitcase handle. The object hanging from the handle was a luggage tag, and some of the inscription was still legible. She read the letters: *M RT N CAL AH N*. She dropped the suitcase handle on the ground and ran away, sobbing uncontrollably.

"Watts! You dumb motherfucker! What the hell were you thinking?" Lang yelled into his phone.

Watts held the receiver two inches from his ear.

"I told you to be subtle about it, and you go and plant a bomb in a limo and detonate the thing in the middle of downtown San Francisco!"

"Hey, what difference does it make how it's done?"

"Well, you missed an important detail, you imbecile! You were supposed to take out the girl. Not Callahan."

"Look, I had this whole thing mapped out. She was the one who was supposed to take that limo. Not him. Something must have changed at the last minute."

"Do you think so, you dumb asshole?" Lang asked. "Now what are we supposed to do?"

"I can still take care of the girl," Watts said, breathing heavily into the phone.

"No! Forget about it, you sadistic cocksucker. Just get your fat ass back here. Now! You've done enough. She's not an idiot like you. By now, she knows that the bomb was meant for her. You won't find her now." Lang slammed the phone down.

Lang stood in front of the large window to his office. Amber Wakefield was probably crying in some corner, regretting that she'd never have the opportunity to see her boss and friend again. He grinned. She would get her opportunity soon. Very soon. He would make sure of it.

Chapter 14

The offices of Ensight, Inc. were quiet on Tuesday morning. Kaitlyn McBride and her executive team had taken a red-eye flight from Chicago upon hearing the tragic news of Marty Callahan's death on Monday afternoon. Kaitlyn sent out a company-wide e-mail and voice mail, eulogizing Marty and expressing condolences to his family and gratitude for his countless contributions and years of service to the company. The company's intranet site posted a photograph of Marty at the last year's Christmas party. The caption read, *Martin Callahan: Faithful Friend, Inspiring Mentor, Dedicated Professional.* The following pages were filled with quotes from fellow employees, memorializing him in their own personal ways. The funeral service was scheduled for the coming Friday at Grace Cathedral on Nob Hill.

Amber remained absent from the office, a surprise to no one. Her fondness for Marty was no secret. She sat in her apartment, still in the clothes she had slept in. Seated on her bed, she watched the local news, which recounted the awful events of the previous day, complete with graphic images of the incinerated limo. Crumpled pieces of Kleenex tissues littered her bed and the floor around it. Her eyes felt heavy and sore from the endless flood of tears she had wept during the last twenty hours. She had awakened several times during the night, certain that she had dreamed the entire thing. But the awful visual images reminded her that it was all too real.

Her phone had been ringing constantly that morning. Friends and fellow employees were leaving her messages, checking in on her. All of them knew how close she had been to Marty. But she didn't feel much like talking to anyone. Finally she got off her bed and walked to the kitchen to get some water. She picked up her phone and dialed the number to access her voice mail. Eleven messages. She decided to listen to them, to give her something to do, if nothing else.

The first four messages were from friends at the company. The fifth message was from Jack. He said nothing except for "I'm sorry." For a brief moment, she thought about their last meeting in Justin Herman Plaza—how abruptly it had ended, how rude she had been to him. The details of the meeting were still vivid. She recalled the last thing he had said to her—something about not knowing why Marty was in Washington. He knew something that she did not. At the time, it had seemed like nothing. But now, for some reason, that remark seemed to be a premonition of sorts. She glanced at the caller ID display which showed the most recent callers and dialed Jack's number. He answered after half a ring.

"Amber, it's nice to hear from you," he said, trying to respect the fragility of the situation. "I don't know what to say. I'm so sorry about Marty."

"Thanks." She wished Jack was standing there with her.

"How are you doing?" he asked, doing his best to not upset her. "It was a horrible accident."

"Why do the papers and the TV news keep referring to it as an 'accident'? You and I both know that it was no accident. They murdered my friend." She placed her hand over the mouthpiece and sobbed into the back of her hand.

"I know." He waited before asking his next question. "What can I do for you?"

"Considering the circumstances, I feel you're the only person who can help. I'm certainly not going to share with anyone else the history of the last few weeks."

"How can *I* help?"

"You probably didn't know that I was scheduled to be in that limo."

"What?"

"That's right. I had arranged for it to drive me to the airport, but at the last moment, Marty needed it for a business trip." Her voice drifted away.

"Are you saying someone is trying to kill you?"

"Well, didn't you tell me that at some point, someone would realize that I knew too much?"

He sighed. "I guess I did. So, where shall we start?"

"I need to know about Marty's involvement with Harper Phillips," she said. She wasn't crying anymore.

They met at an antiques store in Ghirardelli Square and sat on a bench in the courtyard. For the next hour, Jack poured over the details of his investigation into Harper Phillips. As it turned out, he knew little about Marty or his connection to Harper, much to Amber's disappointment. Instead, he dominated most of the conversation with remarks aimed at the man who had abruptly put an end to his career with the FBI, Harry Lang.

He recounted that it had been almost a year ago when he had seen Marty and Lang drinking brandies and smoking Montecristos in the lounge of a Virginia country club. Harry had introduced Marty as an old college friend. Two other men were with them, but they didn't say much. One was an older guy with a name he couldn't remember. The other was a mean-looking bastard named Finch or Fitch. They had all just finished a round on the golf course. At the time, he thought it was odd that someone like Marty, a simple middle manager of a West Coast tech company, would be allowed to step onto the finely manicured fairways of the Hidden Creek Country Club, let alone drink and smoke in the clubhouse. But he had dismissed it at the time, particularly because he wanted nothing to do with Lang or his cronies.

He had never thought about that event again until, in the midst of his investigation, he was browsing through Harper Phillips's address book and found Marty's name. Amber didn't hear much of what else Jack had to say. She was fixated on something he had just told her. A name. *Fitch.* She distinctly recalled seeing that name on the list stored on the CD that Priscilla had given her—the one from her father's files. The same CD that Amber had read at work. *The CD she had forgotten to take out of her disk drive when she left for her lunch with Marty,* she thought to herself.

"Oh, my God," she muttered.

"What is it?"

"I need to get back to my office." She stood up and threw her purse over her shoulder.

"Now?"

"Right now." She started to walk down the steps with Jack close behind her.

They jumped into a taxi and told the driver to take them to her office. They arrived there in less than ten minutes. The block in front of the Ensight offices, the place where the explosion had taken place the day before, was taped off by a yellow banner. They burst through the lobby doors and sprinted to the elevators, ignoring the security guard who was pleading for them to slow down.

"Are you going to fill me in on what the hell we're doing here?" Jack asked.

"Just wait down here for me. I'll be two minutes." She entered the elevator and the door closed.

As she exited the elevator onto her floor, she was immediately inundated with hugs and expressions of regret from her coworkers. Finally extricating herself, she made a beeline to her desk and hit the eject button to her CD-ROM drive. It was empty. She wasn't surprised. She was certain that whoever had taken that disc was also responsible for Marty's death.

She walked back toward the elevators, dodging more well-wishers. On her way, she walked past Marty's office. The door was closed and the lights were off. His desk was still the way he had left it. Outside the door were flowers, balloons, cards, and teddy bears. She fought back the urge to begin weeping and stepped into the elevator.

Jack was waiting by the guard desk, his arms folded.

"Let's go," she said, gripping his arm and pulling him out the door.

"Tell me what's going on." He was past the point of impatience.

"There was a CD in my computer," she started.

"What CD?"

"I received it last week at my desk. It arrived while I was with you in the plaza." Her eyes shifted from side to side, as she tried to put together the sequence of events that day.

"Who sent it to you?"

"I have no idea. But I think it was Priscilla."

"Why didn't you tell me this earlier, Amber?" he asked.

"I didn't trust you. I was scared, OK? Can you understand that?"

He appeared satisfied that her skepticism about him was fading slightly.

"It was in your computer, you say?"

"Yes." She was walking at a brisk pace down Spear Street. "Someone stole it from my drive. I left it in there last Wednesday. It was the last time I was in the office."

"Who do you think took it?" he asked.

"How the hell should I know? You're the detective." She was walking faster, but she didn't seem to have a destination. "All I know is that it's gone, and Marty's dead. I'm not a big believer in coincidences."

"Tell me what was on the CD," he said in a demanding voice.

She didn't care much for his tone. After all, she owed him nothing. "Names, numbers," she recalled. "It looked like some sort of payroll sheet."

Jack stared at the ground, studying her words. "Well, they obviously know that the CD fell into your hands. We need to get you some protection. I have friends at the Bureau who can—"

"No, wait. I don't have it anymore," she said, her tone calming. "Someone took it. So, they have what they want. Why would they come after me?"

"Amber, CDs can be copied. They are not valuable in themselves. It's what you saw on the CD that put you in peril. No one can undo that." He said this with certainty.

A few seconds passed. She took a deep breath. "I guess my vacation just ended."

Chapter 15

It was six-fifteen on Thursday evening. Amber walked down Market Street, dodging the oncoming foot traffic, primarily led by folks punching out for the day. It was the evening leading up to the long Labor Day weekend, and most people would be knocking off early, if they hadn't taken the day off altogether. Jack had outlined the plan for her in meticulous detail, so she knew precisely what she was looking for.

She reached the intersection of Market and Bush, and gazed at the black skyscraper on the opposite corner, which housed the law firm Jackson Winthrop, LLP. Amber entered through the large revolving doors and walked through the lobby. As she passed the security desk on her way to the elevator, the guard smiled and nodded, then turned quickly back to the sports section. The Giants were in the hunt for the pennant, so policing the building would have to wait.

Today, Amber was wearing her homeliest outfit, a plain brown cardigan sweater over an even plainer white knit shirt. She had a ratty backpack over her shoulder and wore jeans, the same ones she had worn the weekend before when she went out on the town with her friends. They still carried a faint odor of cigarette smoke, which added to the image she was trying to project. On her feet were sneakers with no socks. She hoped to present the ideal picture of someone who didn't care about her appearance. Her rubber soles squeaked and echoed on the marble floor as she exited the elevator doors and continued toward the main reception area of Jackson Winthrop. She had rehearsed everything a dozen times during the last twenty four hours.

Two attractive receptionists sat behind a large, mahogany desk. "Yes, may I help you?" asked one of them. The other was chatting into her headset on what was obviously a social call.

"Yes. I'm here to respond to a number of letters you've all written to me. My father used to work here." She handed the letters to the receptionist, who flipped through them. They looked official enough. "I'm not really sure who I'm supposed to talk to."

"Oh, gosh," said the young receptionist, handing the letters back to Amber. "I'm afraid that most of the people in this office have left for the long weekend."

"No. Please don't tell me that." Amber did her best to act disappointed. "Are you sure there is *no one* who can help me?"

"I'm afraid not. I've been here only a few weeks, so I'm not terribly familiar with who does what here. Maybe you could come by tomorrow or on Tuesday. I'm sure someone can help you then."

Amber sighed deeply. "I guess. It's just that…it's taken me almost three years to find the strength to come by here. It's just too painful."

The receptionist was clearly not following, as Amber noticed immediately.

"You see, my father passed away a few years ago. Tragically, I might add. I've been receiving these letters from your firm requesting that I come by here to collect his personal effects and all that. I guess I've been stalling."

The receptionist's eyes looked sad. Her response was sincere, and for a moment, Amber felt guilty about taking advantage of this young girl's emotions. In the meantime, the other receptionist had put her headset down and was pushing her chair in. "See you later, Gina. Have a great long weekend." After the other receptionist had left through the doors, Amber continued. "But I understand if there is nothing you can do to help me. I'll try to come back later. Maybe in a couple more years."

She turned to leave with her head down, pulling a tissue from her purse and dabbing her cheeks, enough so that Gina could see. She walked slowly.

"Wait," Gina called out. Amber stopped and slowly turned around to face her. "I don't want you to have to come back. It sounds like you've been through enough."

Amber smiled a little. Her high school drama teacher would have been so proud. She walked back toward the desk. Gina came out from behind her post. "What was your father's name?"

"Harper. Harper Phillips."

Gina began walking down the hall. "Follow me. If it was that long ago, then all of his stuff is probably locked in the storage area. And you're in luck. I'm training to be the office manager, so I have a set of keys to the storage room."

Thank God, Amber thought. That was a stroke of good fortune which neither she nor Jack had counted on. Unfortunately for Jackson Winthrop, she thought, they had hired a receptionist who was far too trusting. How ironic for a law firm.

They walked down the back stairwell to the next floor. It was deserted and only the emergency lights were on. They finally arrived at a large door with a brass plate fixed on the wall next to it. It read *Storage*. Gina fiddled with her keys until she found the right one. She opened the door and flipped a switch, and the fluorescent tubes above illuminated the large room, about the equivalent of three two-car garages. There were shelves from floor to ceiling, all stacked with file boxes, old computer equipment, and miscellaneous junk.

Amber followed Gina closely down the rows of shelves, with Gina looking at the labels affixed to the edges of the shelves. They were alphabetized as far as Amber could tell. Halfway down the row marked "P," Gina stopped.

"Here it is. Phillips."

There were three boxes, unlabeled except for the name, and covered in dust.

"I'll leave you here to go through his things. I'm not supposed to leave the reception area unattended."

But it's OK to leave the storage area unattended? Amber asked herself. Gina was clearly an eager kid who obeyed rules before using logic. Amber remembered being that way when she first started working, too.

"I'll be back in about thirty minutes. Is that enough time?" Gina asked.

Amber had no idea how long she needed. "That should be fine, Gina."

As Gina walked to the door, she turned. "I'm sorry, I didn't catch your name."

Amber smiled. "It's Priscilla. Priscilla Phillips."

"Nice to meet you, Priscilla. And…I'm sorry about your father."

"Thank you. You're very sweet."

And with that, Amber was left alone in the cold, quiet storage room.

She thumbed through the contents of the boxes, capturing images of as much information as she could with the miniature digital camera that Jack had given her. The camera was one of the many surveillance toys he had acquired over the years. She quickly scanned Harper's personnel files, where his compensation records were kept, along with performance reports and internal memos. Her pulse was racing madly. She'd never done anything like this before. She wasn't a spy. She had heard of classmates in school who would sneak their way into the teacher's office and steal copies of tests. At the time, she had stayed clear of those people. But that was child's play compared to what she was doing now.

In one of the boxes, the folders were neatly organized with labeled tabs and color codes. She speculated that they were probably contracts until she came across one of the tabs, labeled in handwriting. It read *Ensight*. It wasn't terribly thick. There were a number of pages with the law firm's letterhead on it, mostly copies of invoices. The bills were made out to a company called Bartlett Enterprises. As far as she could tell, the invoices said nothing more than SERVICES RENDERED. She positioned the camera and looked through the viewfinder to begin capturing whatever was in there. She didn't have a guess as to why it might be interesting, but she also knew that she didn't have time to stand there and pontificate about it. She was able to snap a few pictures before she heard a noise near the door. She stopped and listened. The noise was a rattling, like a shopping cart. It became louder. Or rather, closer.

She replaced the camera in her backpack and stepped toward the end of the aisle, peering around the corner to get a better view of the door. The light in the doorway darkened. A shadow. She walked briskly toward the back of the storage room, the rubber soles of her sneakers silent against the carpet below her.

She searched frantically for a way out, but there was only one door to the room. Against the opposite wall, there were a dozen black office cabinets, each about six and a half feet high and three feet wide. At the end of the aisle marked "R," she could see that the double doors of one of the cabinets were slightly ajar, and she could see that the bottom section of the cabinet was empty. She made her way toward it, slowing down to glance toward the doorway, which was partially visible between the boxes on the shelves. Through the doorway emerged a large black garbage can on wheels, with cleaning products and brooms dangling from its sides. Behind it was a tall man in gray coveralls. It was just the janitor. *Phew*. She released her breath, which she had been holding for the last minute. She watched him plug the cord of the industrial strength vacuum cleaner into the wall outlet and hit the button. The vacuum began humming.

She was just about to return to her research when she noticed that the janitor had stopped pushing the vacuum, although it was still running. He had his back turned to her. From her view, he was doing something with his hands, like he was rotating the sides of a Rubik's cube. As he turned around, she saw something thin protruding outward. She was no expert on cleaning instruments, but she knew enough to recognize that the dark object in the janitor's hand was no feather duster. In a second, she could see the black tip of the silencer in full view. Her eyes grew big, and she stopped breathing again. She could feel the perspiration dripping beneath her sweater. *Fight through it,* she said to herself. She turned around and slid her way back down an aisle toward the open cabinet. She crawled into the bottom compartment, like a magician's assistant performing an illusion. As she pulled the door closed, it squeaked, and she was sure she was done for. But apparently, the noise of the vacuum cleaner drowned it out.

She peered through a slit in the cabinet door. It provided a somewhat obstructed view of the aisle where she had just been. She could see that Harper's boxes and files were just as she had left them. She should have put them away, but there wasn't enough time to think. The man slowly approached the aisle, while Amber carefully retreated toward the back corner of the cabinet, until there was no room to move. The stranger, with his pistol poised, bent down in front of the open boxes. She could see that his neck bore an unsightly black tattoo—a Chinese character of some sort. He took a look through some of the papers, and then stood up, his gun still pointed while he glanced around the room. He had a smile on his face. "Nosy little bitch," he said out loud.

He turned slowly. "Am-ber?" he called out above the noise of the vacuum, like someone yelling out the name of a lost dog.

She was breathing again, albeit irregularly. The cabinet felt like an incinerator. Her eyes began to tear from the heat and the numbness developing in her legs. He was out of her field of vision, but she could smell his cheap cologne close by.

"Amber, darlin'? Are you in here?" His voice was fading, indicating that he was walking farther toward the rear of the storage room.

She heard him opening and closing cabinet doors. "Well, you're not in heeeere!" he would say obnoxiously. "Ooh, you are a slippery little whore, aren't you?"

She couldn't quite pinpoint his location, but she knew she had to make her move fast. She had a straight line to the exit, but she needed to take that file with her. There wouldn't be a second chance. She shifted her position a bit and stopped as she rolled over something under her buttocks. She reached behind her and pulled out a book of matches—the same matches she had kept from her night out the previous weekend.

The man with the tattoo was still slamming doors, but he definitely sounded closer now. "Listen, honey, I'm sorry about old Marty. Wrong place, wrong time. You know how that goes." He laughed loudly.

She bit her lip to avoid shouting an obscenity his way. *Asshole.* She closed her eyes and thought for a split second, which was all the time she needed. From her angle, she could see a computer monitor on one of the shelves. The lights in the room provided a blurry reflection from the screen, allowing her to see his figure.

She could see that he had ducked into one of the aisles, his gun still drawn. At that moment, she crawled out of the cabinet, ignoring the immense pain in her legs and back.

With the vacuum still purring loudly, she ran to the middle of the "P" aisle and began pulling boxes from the shelves and piling them, one atop another. After stacking three large boxes, she pulled herself up to the top box, giving herself a bird's-eye view of the room. She could see him looking under tables and shelves, but he did not look up. This was her chance. Her only chance. She pulled a piece of newspaper that was lining the top shelf and twisted it into a torch. She lit a match and held it to the paper. The paper began burning quickly, so she held it up as high and as close to the smoke detector as she could reach. After about five seconds, a bell began to sound, and a second later, the sprinkler nozzle dropped down from the ceiling and began dousing the room.

"What the…" the man said, trying to cover himself while the sprinkler showered him.

The flame touched her hand, and she shrieked in pain. He heard her this time. The flaming page fell to the ground but had extinguished itself before hitting the carpet.

"Who's there?" he called out, still unable to see her. "Is that you, Amber?"

Amber negotiated her way down from her makeshift ladder, but it was beginning to get slippery. Unfortunately, she hadn't thought about how to get down when she concocted this scheme. As the water continued to rain upon her, she placed her foot on the edge of the middle box. It slipped out from under her, and she came crashing down to the floor, along with all three boxes. One of them slammed against her leg and she screamed out loud again. He followed the scream.

As she lay on her back, she could see his feet under the bottom shelf. He was running down the aisle adjacent to her. He was one aisle away. She crawled along the floor, toward Harper's files. She searched frantically for the Ensight folder, but it was nowhere to be found. She was running out of time. She pulled herself up, but her leg was throbbing. Ignoring her pain, she hobbled toward the door, all the while searching for the file. When she arrived at the end of the aisle, she heard a voice.

"Looking for this?" He held up the folder in one hand, while his pistol was aimed directly at her with the other. Eye level. She pushed off her bruised leg and made a quick step to the exit. The bullet ricocheted off the metal shelf, inches from her ear. It made a ringing sound that stayed with her for a few seconds. She nearly slipped on the floor as she wrapped her hand around the doorframe and slung herself out of the storage room, dodging another bullet which found the middle of the door.

As she ran down the hallway, she heard him calling behind her. The puncturing sound of the silencer forced her to instinctively weave in her path. Another bullet pierced the wall just in front of her just as she threw her body against the steel emergency exit door.

She ran down the stairwell without looking back, skipping steps and jumping landings. With each jump, she felt as though someone had clubbed her in the leg. As she descended, she pulled out her cell phone, dropping it down the steps at one point. She found Jack's number in the phone's log of recent calls and tried calling him, but her phone could not pick up a signal in the closed building. Nine floors later, she burst into the lobby, her clothes soaked in water and sweat. She limped past the security guard's desk, which was abandoned. The guard was standing by the elevators with Gina, both of them pointing and shrugging. They were busy trying to determine the origin of the alarm.

As she stumbled out onto Market Street, she slowed down to a walk. Not surprisingly, her haggard appearance did not attract any attention, particularly since she was walking through a group of homeless people who were loitering on the corner. In less than a minute, she heard the sirens screaming down Market Street. The fire trucks pulled up to the entrance, inviting those in the immediate vicinity to gravitate toward the commotion. At that moment, Amber made her way in the opposite direction toward the Embarcadero Center. She pulled out her cell phone and dialed Jack's number again.

Chapter 16

▼

Jack pulled up to the back of the Embarcadero Four building, where Amber was standing in a dark corner, her hair still damp from the fire sprinkler. She ran to his black Range Rover and jumped into the passenger seat.

"What the hell happened?" he asked.

"Just go. Please." Her voice quivered terribly.

"Go where?"

"Anywhere, damn it! I don't care." She looked out the window, and then quickly ducked low in the seat to avoid being seen.

He flipped the car around and drove calmly so as not to attract any unwelcome attention.

"What are you looking for? What the hell happened in there?" She said nothing. He listened to Amber try to recover her breath and calm herself down. She began crying hysterically.

"Amber, talk to me," he pressed on.

"They followed me. They tried to kill me," she said through her sobs.

"What are you talking about? Who tried to kill you?" He felt silly asking the question, since he knew exactly who she was referring to.

"Who do you think?"

"Did you get a good look at the person?"

"Vaguely. He was dressed as the building janitor. He had a hat, so I didn't get a close look at his face." She pulled the visor down and began examining herself in the mirror.

"I assume that fire alarm was your work back there," he said.

She nodded. "I needed a diversion. It was the only way to get out of there."

They pulled into a public parking lot across Market Street. Jack killed the engine. "So, what did you find?"

She glared at him. "I'm fine. Thanks for asking." *Insensitive son of a bitch.*

"Sorry, you're right. Are you OK?"

"I hurt my leg, but it's not broken." She rolled up her pant leg and lightly patted her left tibia with her hand.

"They were probably just trying to scare you."

"Really? And I suppose he meant to just miss my head with the very real bullets from his gun?"

"The important thing is that you're not seriously hurt." He put his hand on her shoulder, and for the first time in many days, she felt safe.

"Well, now that we're sure you're OK, is it all right if I ask whether you found anything interesting in there?"

"I found a file labeled *Ensight*."

"Excellent. So, it wasn't a total bust."

She turned to him, her eyes disappointed.

"You didn't get it, did you?"

She shook her head and looked down. "I tried, but he picked it up while I was scrambling to get out of there."

"Well, you can't go home tonight. That's for sure. Whoever was in there knows that you're snooping around. That's enough to make you a target."

The words were chilling to her. "I'm not staying at your place, if that's what you're thinking."

"No. We'll stay in a hotel."

She glared at him suspiciously.

"Don't worry," he said. "Separate rooms."

They pulled into a small motel on Van Ness. Jack parked the car and went into the registration office. He returned a few minutes later, carrying two keys. They walked up to the second floor, and he gave her a key.

"You're on the end. I'm three doors down." He watched her walk away from him. "Get some rest for tomorrow."

"Why? What happens tomorrow?" Her eyelids were sagging from mental and physical exhaustion.

"We need to get you out of town."

They said good night and retired to their rooms. Amber peeled off her clothes and ran a hot shower. The water stung the scrape on her leg. She stood in the shower for the next twenty minutes, piecing together the events of the last several weeks. It was clear that someone was trying to kill her, but she still didn't know why. After all, with all the knowledge she had about Harper Phillips, there was nothing she considered to be of any value.

Wrapped in a large towel, she opened the bathroom door and was surprised to find the room completely dark. She could have sworn the lights were on when she entered the bathroom. But, then again, in the midst of everything that had occurred, she might have turned them off without thinking. Except for the dim light from the street shining through the curtain, the room was completely dark. She felt her way around the bed to the lamp on the nightstand, looking out the window. It was strange that the motel lights above the walkway outside were not on, either.

As she neared the nightstand, she tripped over one of the wheels attached to the bed frame. She shrieked in pain and fell to the floor, gripping her pinky toe. She crawled against the bed, wincing in agony, and heard a faint noise in the corner of the room. It sounded like a floorboard creaking. She looked around but could see nothing. She found the lamp and was about to turn the switch when she heard it again. When she looked up again, her heart skipped a beat at the sight of a man's silhouette in the window. At first, she thought she was hallucinating. Until the figure moved. Could he see her in the dark? She sat still, her eyes peering just above the top of the mattress.

It wasn't obvious whether the figure was inside or outside, but the subtle sound of something being turned on eliminated any doubts for her. It resembled the noise of a camera being powered up. The man turned sideways and she could see the lens attached to his head. She wasn't a surveillance equipment guru, but she knew what night vision goggles looked like. It was just a matter of time before he would see her. With the wall to her back, there was no avenue for escape. She tightened the towel around her body and closed her eyes tightly.

She could hear him kicking her shoes across the floor, then picking up her clothes and dropping them on the bed.

"Aw, you didn't have to take your clothes off for me." The voice was the same one who had called out to her in the storage room at the law office. He was laughing and clearly taking his time.

She had already dodged one attempt on her life, which ended in Marty's death, and then another attempt at the law office only a couple of hours before. She couldn't escape death a third time. Her luck had never been that good. She kept her eyes closed and recited a prayer. In the midst of her thoughts, she didn't hear the door open. But suddenly she heard her pursuer scream in agony. Jack had flipped on the lights, blinding the intruder through his goggles. As he twisted backwards, disoriented, his trigger finger sent a bullet into the bed's headboard. Jack pounced on the attacker like a cheetah on its prey. He had the man on his stomach, with his arms pinned behind his back in a firm hold.

"Go, Amber! Go!" Jack yelled, while wrestling with the assailant, who was writhing in pain.

Amber leapt up from behind the bed and ran out the door, clad in only a towel and no shoes. Her footsteps could be heard slapping against the concrete outside, quickly fading.

Once she was out of the room and out of earshot, Jack released his grip slightly.

"OK, that's enough. Get the hell off me, Jack," the man demanded.

Jack removed his knee from the middle of the man's back and stood up. "C'mon, Watts. I thought you were tougher than that." He held his hand out and helped Watts off the ground. Watts slapped his hand away.

"Dammit, did you have to try to break my arm?" Watts was dusting himself off, while massaging his arm.

"Stop being a baby. I didn't hurt you that badly."

Watts sneered at him.

"By the way, you came pretty close to hitting her back at the law office there. Can you take it easy, please?"

"She's a swift little tomcat, isn't she?" Watts said with admiration.

"You don't know the half of it."

"That little smoke alarm thing she pulled back there. Even I was impressed." Watts gathered his goggles off the floor and replaced his gun in its holster. "Is she just as skilled in the sack?"

"How the hell would I know?" Jack asked, wishing that he actually had the answer to that question.

"Oh, come on, pretty boy. Are you telling me you haven't gotten in her pants?" Watts asked, continuing to rub his elbow.

"This is business, you big ogre. Not a singles cruise," Jack said. Watts chuckled.

Jack put his hand on Watts's back and led him to the door. "You better get out of here. Take the back stairs. I'll tell her that you got away during our struggle."

When they got to the doorway, Watts stopped to face Jack. "Aren't you forgetting something?"

Jack frowned in bewilderment, but eventually his shoulders dropped in disappointment as he realized what Watts was referring to. He was hoping Watts wouldn't remember. "OK, but not in the nose. And tell me when it's coming."

Watts grinned widely in anticipation. "Don't fret, Casanova. I won't break that beautiful mug of yours. Incoming!" And with that, he cocked his arm back and drove his fist into Jack's right eye.

Jack jerked his head back and screamed in pain, certain that the balled-up hand had actually exited through the back of his skull.

"That'll leave a mark," Watts said, laughing and rubbing his knuckles.

"You were supposed to tell me when it was coming, you dumb son of a bitch," Jack shot back. His eye was already turning red.

"Oops, my bad," Watts replied, smiling widely.

"Now get the hell out of here before she decides to come back."

Watts patted Jack on the back and walked out of the room and calmly down the back steps.

Amber slipped on the sweatpants and sweater that Jack had retrieved from his car. She returned to the room carrying a bucket with ice he had filled from the dispenser down the hall. She wrapped some of the ice in a hand towel and held it against his eye.

"I think the swelling is going down."

He backed away. "Ouch! Don't press so hard." He gently pulled her hand away.

"Sorry." She sat down on the bed next to him. "Tell me, how did he get away? You looked like you had a pretty good stranglehold on him when I ran out of there."

Jack shrugged. "I don't know. I thought I had him pinned, but he was able to free himself and get a lucky shot in." He touched his hand to his eye. "And a solid one at that."

"And he still had time to go to the other side of the room and grab his gun before leaving?"

Jesus Christ, was this woman a police interrogator? "Uh, no," he stammered. "I mean, yes. I suppose the punch to my eye dazed me for a few seconds. I guess that was enough time for him."

She seemed satisfied for the moment. He exhaled, grateful that the inquisition was temporarily over.

"It was the same guy. I recognized his obnoxious voice."

"I didn't pay attention to his voice," he said, trying to direct her attention back toward his wounded eye.

"I still can't believe he found me. I was way ahead of him when I left the law office. How do you suppose he caught up to me so quickly?"

Jack shrugged. Unfortunately, he hadn't anticipated that question, despite it being obvious. Associating himself with that meathead Watts had made him dumber. "Who knows? It's not important now anyway. You're safe, and that's all that matters."

"Thanks to you," she said, her eyes sparkling. She leaned over and kissed him on his cheek.

He backed away slightly. "What was that for?"

"For saving my life."

They turned toward one another. Amber's hand was tickled by the light stubble on Jack's cheek. Her breathing quickened, and for a moment, she forgot about everything. About Harper Phillips. About Marty. Simultaneously, each moved toward the other and they kissed. Amber felt the blood rush out of her head and her body went limp. He put his hand on the nape of her neck and pressed his lips against hers, sensing her response.

They fell back onto the bed. Amber pressed against him as his warm hands ran against her bare back, and continued to explore her body. She tilted her head back as she felt his breath against her neck. It was the most vulnerable she had felt in a long while, but she didn't want it to stop. After all, she had no idea when she would have that feeling again.

Chapter 17

Harry Lang sat in his office with the door closed. It was Saturday evening, and he knew there would be no one around to disturb him. Although his wife had gone to Connecticut for the weekend to visit her sick mother, an empty house carried a number of its own distractions.

He had not heard from Watts in a week and hadn't been able to reach him. Lang began to worry. He had instructed Watts to return to Washington immediately following the botched job on the young woman named Amber Wakefield. Lang couldn't afford any more missteps. The precision with which his plan had been designed was already beginning to show signs of weakness.

The sun had gone to bed five hours before, and his dim desk lamp and the moonlight were the only sources of light in the office. He didn't hear his office door open and became aware of his visitor only when a shadow darkened the light on his desk. He glanced up in shock.

"Jesus Christ! Art, you scared the hell out of me."

Arthur Lassiter stood in front of Lang's desk. At six foot five, he was a statue of a man, which served him well as director of the FBI. He was dressed in a tuxedo, his bow tie undone and hanging around his neck. His cheeks were rosy and his eyes tired, a clear sign that he had enjoyed more than a few brandies that evening. An All-American defensive end at Ohio State University and a Marine Corps veteran, Lassiter had a natural instinct for honing in on his target, a quality that prepared him well for his future duties with the Bureau. He was fifty-six, and as he described it, in the prime of his life and career.

"Sorry, Harry. I saw the light under your door, so I thought I'd stop in to see what you could possibly be working on during a Saturday night." He sat down in the leather chair in front of the desk and crossed his legs.

"Just a little housekeeping. What are you doing here?"

Lassiter reached into his jacket pocket and pulled out a cigar. He clipped the tip and placed it in his mouth. As he was about to light it, he pulled it out of his mouth and held it up to Lang.

"You don't mind, do you? My wife won't let me smoke these in the house." he said.

Lang shook his head. Lassiter took a puff and held the smoke in his mouth for a second before exhaling.

"How was the president's dinner this evening?" asked Lang, trying to steer the conversation toward its end in hope that Lassiter would leave soon.

"Same old thing. A bunch of people who happened to have an extra ten grand in their pocket to pay for a dinner," Lassiter replied, a condescending tone obvious in his voice. He took another pull from his cigar.

"Well, I suppose that's why they call it fund-raising, wouldn't you say?"

"Oh, bullshit. Only a small handful of those people could give a rat's turd about the president's campaign. For them, their ten thousand is an admission ticket into the 'Who's Who of America Fair.'"

"How is our commander in chief?"

"Same old windbag. He spent forty-five minutes at the podium tonight justifying his reasons for flip-flopping on the Patriot Act. Needless to say, there were some mixed reactions from the audience."

"I take it that you have no plans to vote for him next November?"

Lassiter shook his forefinger playfully at Lang. "Careful, Deputy Director Lang. You know better than to ask someone in my position about his partisan views."

"Who's listening?"

"You are. That's who. Harry, in four years of college football and fifteen years in the Corps, I was trained to put my trust in any man who wore the same uniform as I did. But twenty years in this place, and this town in particular, has taught me to trust no one. Especially those with whom you share a common goal. The world is fraught with backstabbers, my good friend." He smiled widely.

Lang swallowed hard. "You never did tell me what *you're* doing here on a Saturday evening."

"I come here every single day. Even if it's just for an hour or so. No such thing as weekends or holidays for me." Lassiter spoke through a thick cloud of smoke. "You remember that, son, if you ever have plans to sit in my chair one day."

Lang hated it when Lassiter referred to him as 'son.' He wasn't that much younger, albeit his experience paled in comparison to that of his superior. Lassiter was always trying to sell Lang on the benefits of the director's position, almost as if he was grooming him for it. He probably pretended to be mentoring a dozen other men in the Bureau. Lassiter loved creating competition among his underlings.

They sat across from each other, neither saying a word for what seemed like a couple of minutes. Neither had much respect for the other, and they both knew it. The silence broke when Lassiter glanced down at Lang's desk. "Ah, I see you're reviewing the identity-theft reports. That's good to see. Any idea on when I might get an update on where we are on all of that?"

"Well, as you know, I had to assume ownership for this portion of the investigation as a result of the lead agent's termination." Lang was trying to keep the discussion vague. "So, it's taking me a bit longer than expected to pick up where he left off."

"I see. What was that fella's name again? Jack Benton? Or Barrett?"

"Bennett, sir. Jack Bennett is his name."

"That's it. What the hell happened there anyway? I'm still not exactly clear on the circumstances of his termination." Lassiter's cigar had burned out, and he was chewing on the soggy nub. It was disgusting to look at, Lang thought.

"It just wasn't moving as quickly as I would have preferred."

"Well, let's hope you can light a fire under it."

"I plan to," said Lang, praying that he would find the door soon.

"That's a nice lighter you got there," Lang said, noticing for the first time the platinum lighter in Lassiter's palm. It had his initials etched into the surface. Much too cheesy for his taste, but Lang saw it as a timely digression.

Lassiter held it up. "Oh, you like that, do you? Yeah, it was a gift from a defense company I used to sit on the board of. Me and another fella on the board were the only two who got lighters as gifts. You've probably heard of him. Denny Fitch."

Lang knew he couldn't feign ignorance, considering Fitch's prominence in the financial community. "Oh, sure. Dennis Fitch. The venture capitalist. Not a bad person to have as a friend."

Lassiter waved his paw at Lang. "Ah, don't kid yourself. Denny fell ass backwards into his fortune. Got lucky with some high-stakes bets and insider information during the dot-com carnival days. He's not the investment genius the media makes him out to be."

No shit, Lang thought.

"In fact, I ran into him tonight at the president's dinner."

Lang's heart stopped for a split second. "Is that right?" he asked, desperately trying to mask the nervous tremble in his voice.

"Yeah, I'll tell you something. When that son of a bitch gets enough scotch in him, he'll talk your goddamn ear off. Believe me, you don't want to share any secrets with that windbag. I swear to you, if he's got three of a kind, the whole table would know." Lassiter laughed heartily.

"Well, I'll try to keep that in mind. Thanks for the advice." Lang stood up, hoping his boss would interpret that as the end of their conversation.

Lassiter apparently picked up on the clue. "Well, I'm not going to take any more of your time." He got up from his chair and, with the soaked cigar still in his mouth, he held his hand out to his deputy director.

"You have a good one, Harry."

Lang shook his hand. "Likewise."

Lassiter exited the office and closed the door behind him. Lang sat down again in his chair and leaned back, his fingers interlocked under his chin. *Trust no one. Especially those with whom you share a common goal.* The words were echoing loudly in Lang's head. He wondered and worried about what, if anything, that gum-flapping moron Fitch had told Lassiter. He needed to find Watts. He had a new job for him.

CHAPTER 18

Amber awoke with the bright light of the San Francisco morning sun beaming through the window. Her eyes still closed, she pulled the pillow over her head, not quite ready to acknowledge the start of the day. She was naked beneath the covers, and her clothes were on the floor beside her. She slid her hand across the bed and felt the cold flatness of an empty sheet. She popped up quickly and looked around, squinting through the sunlight. She glanced at the clock on the nightstand. 10:15. She hadn't slept that late since she was in college. And that had been during spring break in Panama City.

She wrapped the sheet around her and walked to the window. The motel parking lot below was empty, with the exception of two cars, neither of which was Jack's. The towel that held Jack's ice pack from the night before was on the dresser. It was still slightly damp and stained with blood from his wound.

It was Friday. Marty's memorial service was scheduled for noon. She had no idea where Jack could have gone, or why he hadn't bothered to wake her before leaving. She felt a bit nervous about going to the funeral alone, but she couldn't be absent. Despite the elation she had felt during the last ten hours with Jack, the thought of Marty's empty office, the image of the smoldering limousine, and most of all, the memory of his smile immediately saddened her.

She needed to get back to her apartment to clean up and change her clothes, but she knew it was too dangerous to go there alone. Where the hell was Jack? She picked up her phone and dialed his cell phone. No answer. She got dressed and made her way down the hall to the other room where she had nearly been killed the night before. The door was unlocked. When she entered, the stark reminders of the previous night's events came rushing back. Her clothes were still strewn across the floor. The bullet hole in the headboard sent a cold sensation up her spine. She gathered her clothes and her backpack and left the room. She walked outside and down the steps to the motel office. A middle-aged Pakistani man sat behind the desk. He explained that he had just arrived on duty and hadn't seen anyone come in or leave the parking lot.

Amber walked around the corner and flagged a taxicab to take her to her apartment. They turned on to Lombard Street, where she asked the driver to stop at the Wells Fargo Bank ATM, since she realized that she didn't have any cash to pay him. As she stood at the teller machine, she leaned in and checked herself in the small, round mirror on the panel, behind which the bank's surveillance camera was housed. She didn't look as bad as she thought she would, considering the erratic ride she had been on during the last twenty-four hours. The bags under her eyes were heavy, but other than that, nothing looked too ghastly.

The cabdriver honked, urging Amber to pick up the pace. She took her money from the cash dispenser and was about to walk away when something in the small mirror abruptly caught her attention. She focused her eyes and saw a black Range Rover parked across the street. *Jack?* A man wearing a black leather jacket and sunglasses walked toward the car. But it wasn't Jack. He was far too big to be Jack. He balanced his coffee cup on the roof of the Rover and took his jacket off. He was wearing a tank top underneath, the tiny type that bodybuilders wear in the gym. When he turned to get into the car, Amber noticed a small black object on his neck. The tattoo. *My God, what had he done to Jack?* She froze, remaining with her back turned to the street. She would wait until the Range Rover drove away. Moments later, she saw Jack walking out of the same shop, also carrying coffee and a bag of pastries. He walked to the car and handed the pastries to the tattooed man. They exchanged a few words and laughed like they were old fraternity brothers. Amber thought she was going to vomit.

Honk! The cabdriver was growing impatient. The sound of the horn prompted both men to glance across the street in her direction. She watched them through the reflection of the ATM mirror. She could have sworn that they were studying her. She was about to sprint into the bank parking lot when they both got into the Range Rover and drove away.

She exhaled. When she turned around to get into her cab, she saw it almost half a block down Lombard, in search of the next fare. The Range Rover had turned the corner onto Van Ness, and she stood alone. She cursed Jack and then herself for being so damn naïve. Sleeping with the enemy. How utterly stupid could she be? He had been using her. She should have trusted her initial instincts when she refused to help him. She wondered why he hadn't simply cut her throat while she slept. Obviously, he needed to keep her alive. But for what, she hadn't the slightest idea. And she was afraid to find out. She needed time to collect herself and think. But she couldn't afford to be by herself. It was too dangerous. She glanced at her watch. Ten minutes past eleven. She needed to get to the funeral. As shameful as it sounded in her head, the memorial service would be the perfect venue to hide herself. According to the announcement she read in the paper, there were estimated to be four hundred family, friends, and colleagues in attendance.

She couldn't take the risk of going back to her apartment. He would surely be waiting for her once he learned that she was no longer in the motel room. She waved down another cab and told the driver to take her to the church.

"Goddamn it, Jack!" Watts barked. He stalked around the motel room, kicking the sheets and towels across the floor.

"She was fast asleep when I left this morning. I imagined she would panic a little but not take off on her own. She knows how much danger she's supposedly in."

"So, now what?"

"She needs me. She has no one else to turn to."

"Maybe we should call it off. Let's take a step back and strategize." For the first time, Watts sounded unsure.

"I'll find her. She's scared. She'll slip up at some point," Jack said confidently.

"But you're leaving today to fly to…" Watts began.

"I'll find her," Jack cut in.

At that moment, Watts's cell phone began chirping. He picked up.

"Yeah." His face turned serious. He nodded in response to whatever was being said to him over the phone. Jack watched his expression. "Sorry about the screw up with the girl." More listening. "Fine." He ended the call.

Jack looked at him for a couple of seconds. "Lang?"

Watts nodded.

"Is he badgering you because you didn't come back to Washington like he asked?"

Watts shook his head. "Nope. In fact, he's giving me a chance to make up for my *error* with Amber." He said the word 'error' while holding up quotation marks with his fingers.

"What is it?"

"He wants me to pay a visit to Dennis Fitch."

The two men smiled at each other.

"Well, then I suppose we should get to the airport. Looks like we both have flights to catch," said Jack. They left the room and drove out of the motel parking lot.

Chapter 19

The front steps of Grace Cathedral were filled with people clad in the dark tints of mourning. They whispered in small groups, some exchanging embraces of condolence. The faint sound of hymns played from inside.

Amber walked slowly up the steps, her eyes darting from side to side behind her sunglasses. In her jeans and sweater, she certainly didn't blend in with the rest of the attendees, who were all dressed more respectably and appropriately for the occasion. Her heart swelled at the sight of so many people who had come to pay their respects. If there was any silver lining to Marty's death, it was that it brought together such a broad community of friends and loved ones. On her path toward the large front doors, she kept her head down to avoid being recognized by any of her coworkers, nearly all of whom seemed to be in attendance.

She entered the church, a pleasant draft blowing through the foyer. As she slid laterally across the back wall, she could see all of the members of the Ensight executive committee assembled toward the front of the church, none more noticeable than Kaitlyn McBride, who seemed to be commanding attention as usual, dressed in a perfectly pressed black suit. Probably Armani. Even in grief, she could look powerful and elegant.

Amber decided to stand in the rear corner, near the exit. She watched the scores of people enter and walk down the aisle. At the front, the altar was nestled in a sea of flowers. The absence of a casket was all too evident, and in a way, a disturbing reminder of the cold, extinguishing force of the explosion that had taken Marty's life. In its stead, there was a massive wreath consisting of the most diverse bouquet of flowers she had seen in a long while. It was obnoxious looking, almost tacky, which was appropriate, considering it was for Marty.

Although her view was partially obstructed, she noticed on the left side of the altar, there were three large black-and-white photographs of Marty balanced on easels. One showed him skiing in Vail: Marty, the sportsman. Another pictured him sitting behind his desk at Ensight: Marty, the professional. And still another showed him at a Christmas party dressed as Santa Claus: Marty, the character. In all of the photos, he was alone.

The service was beautiful. A video was played on a large screen, celebrating Marty's life to the background melody of his favorite musicians, Nat King Cole, Tony Bennett, and of course, Sinatra. The images on the screen showed Marty in his younger years, the first time most of the attendees, including Amber, had ever seen him at that age. He was handsome before he gained his stomach and his eyesight went to hell. By the end of the montage, there was barely a dry eye in the house. Amber put her hands to her mouth as she cried silently.

Both of his ex-wives delivered heartfelt eulogies. It was clear that despite their differences as spouses, each of them loved Marty for many of the same reasons his friends loved him. After a few other college friends spoke, the pulpit was cleared for Kaitlyn McBride. She stood at the microphone as if she was addressing a shareholder meeting. But despite the business demeanor, her words were soft and touching. She praised Marty for his professionalism and his dedication, not so much to the company but to his personal relationships. For a short moment, Amber thought that Kaitlyn was referring specifically to her relationship with Marty. At one point, Kaitlyn paused, obviously overcome by her emotions. It was the first time her employees had ever seen that side of her—and most likely the last.

During the eulogy, Amber couldn't resist the urge to glance around the church to take in the beauty of the architecture and the attention to grand detail. When she glanced back toward the altar, she did a double take when her eyes caught the sight of Bruce Fox in the back row. He was looking back in her direction at the time, and the two nodded toward one another in silent acknowledgement. An older man whom she had never seen sat next to him, his eyes forward. She found it strange that the IRS would be in attendance.

At the conclusion of the service, the crowd proceeded out of the building and spilled out onto the front steps. For the same reason she had stood in the back of the church, Amber decided to bypass the receiving line. Besides, she had little confidence in her ability to contain her emotions. She also wanted to find Fox, but he was nowhere in sight. She made her way to the steps facing California Street and began walking down the street when a woman's voice called her from behind. It was Kaitlyn. In all her time at Ensight, Amber had spoken with Kaitlyn only a handful of times, not excluding the run-ins in the elevator or the ladies room.

"Amber, wait," she called out, excusing herself from the Ensight groupies around her.

Amber stopped. "That was a beautiful eulogy."

"Thanks. I was a little nervous." Kaitlyn's eyes performed a quick examination of Amber's choice of attire.

"You? Nervous?" Amber asked.

"Yes. You sound surprised."

"I guess I never envisioned you getting nervous. You always seem so confident."

"Oh no. Don't let the exterior fool you." Kaitlyn gently placed her hand on Amber's arm. "Listen, I've been intending to talk to you, but I haven't seen you in the office lately."

"I know. I'm sorry, but I haven't felt very well, if you can't tell," she said, holding her arms out in an attempt to explain her appearance.

"Relax, I didn't mean that as a criticism. I just meant that you should take however much time you need. I know how close you and Marty were. I'm very sorry."

"Thank you, Kaitlyn. That certainly means a lot."

"Amber, I realize this isn't the most appropriate forum, but I wanted you to know that Marty's vacancy, for lack of a better term, opens up an opportunity for you."

Amber frowned, unappreciative of Kaitlyn's implication that Marty's tragic death should be viewed as a career boost. "Kaitlyn, I don't think…" she began.

Kaitlyn immediately held up both hands in defense. "No disrespect to Marty, of course. I just meant that I hope you won't allow this tragedy to influence you to do anything hasty."

"You mean like quitting?"

"Exactly. I, myself, have always thought highly of you. The endorsements from Marty have been nothing short of glowing, and I've had the chance to observe the way you handle yourself in the company. You'd make an outstanding executive assistant."

"For you?"

Kaitlyn nodded.

"What about Jamie?"

"Oh, Jamie's fantastic. But I need someone a little more experienced who can help me on larger projects."

"Thanks again, but…"

"I'll tell you what," Kaitlyn stopped her. "We don't need to make any decisions now. I'm leaving for Europe tomorrow on business, but I'll be back in a week. Let's have lunch together. But think about what I said. Deal?"

"Deal. Thank you."

Kaitlyn smiled and walked down the steps, where a car was waiting for her. Amber watched the car drive away. She had no idea that Kaitlyn had been considering her for a position. It would be a wonderful opportunity. After all, Kaitlyn was right. There was no reason to allow Marty's death to be an excuse to give up on her future career.

Amber didn't attend the wake at the Nob Hill flat where Marty's second wife, Cynthia, lived. She felt terrible about missing it. But she knew that somewhere above, Marty was looking down on her. He would understand. She imagined people there talking about Marty as if they were roasting him rather than remembering him. It was the way he would have preferred it, anyway.

The area around Nob Hill was bustling with tourists. A large wedding party was arriving at the Mark Hopkins Hotel down the street, and a number of photographers stood by the entrance. Probably a celebrity couple, Amber thought. She walked down the hill toward Union Square, where she knew she could get lost in the crowd. She believed she was probably safer in the company of others, even if they were strangers. She also knew that she needed to buy some new clothes. Her apartment was still dangerous to her, not to mention the fact that she couldn't stand to be in those dirty clothes anymore. She bought two outfits at Macy's and a warm-up suit from The Gap. All cash.

Packages in hand, Amber crossed the park and entered the Grand Hyatt. She used her corporate card for a room on the eighth floor. She deadbolted the door and was about to get into the shower when her cell phone rang. She instinctively answered it. The display read *Caller ID Blocked*, and she knew right away that she had made a mistake.

"Amber. You're there," said a relieved voice.

The sound of Jack talking made her blood hot. She remained silent.

"Amber? Can you hear me?"

She held the phone for a second, resisting the urge to slam it down. "Yes. I'm here, Jack."

"What the hell happened to you? I went to get coffee for us this morning, and when I got back to the motel room, you were gone." He sounded almost convincing.

She was about to let him have it—to let him know that she had seen him with that guy who had tried to kill her. That she was on to him. That she was calling the police. But something stopped her. "You didn't tell me where you were going. I didn't have the whole morning to hunt around for you. Besides, I had a funeral to attend."

"I know. I would have gone with you. I went there looking for you afterwards, but you apparently had already gone." He almost sounded pathetic enough to feel sorry for.

"I didn't need an escort, thanks. It was a funeral, not a prom."

"Fine. Point taken. I was just worried. That's all."

Yeah, right. Worried that you'd lost your chance to set me up again, she thought. "I'm fine."

"Look, I've just come across some interesting information from a source abroad. I think it could help us. I'm going to Bern on Sunday. You should come with me."

"Bern?"

"It's in Switzerland."

Thanks for the geography lesson, jerk. "Switzerland? Are you crazy? I'm not going across the world with you."

"Well, you can't stay in the city, Amber. If you've forgotten the events of the last day, allow me to remind you that someone is trying to get to you. They've made three attempts on you in the last two weeks. Two of those attempts occurred within a few hours of one another. You're nowhere close to being out of the woods. This city ain't that big, sweetheart."

It was bad enough that this lying crook was trying to entrap her, but his condescension was unbearable. "Jack, I'll take my chances. I'm not going to embark on a globe-trotting adventure. If someone is after me, I'd much rather they do it in my own backyard rather than a foreign country. And please don't call me sweetheart. What we did last night does not give you license to use cheesy terms of endearment on me."

"Jesus, why so hostile today? I thought last night meant something."

"I just got back from the funeral of a friend who was murdered. So, you'll forgive me if I don't reminisce about what was merely a moment of adolescent behavior." It hurt her to say this. Until she had seen him getting into that Range Rover that morning, she thought there might actually be something there. *Stupid girl*, she said to herself.

"Suit yourself. I can't force you to go with me. But do me a favor. Don't run off like that again. Make sure you are somewhere I can find you in case of an emergency."

"You're the hotshot FBI agent. I'm sure you'll find me if you have to."

She hung up without another word. Her phone rang several times more during the next hour, but she didn't pick it up.

Amber sat in her hotel room that night, nestled under a blanket on her sofa. She hadn't eaten all day but was not about to leave or order room service. She opened a bottle of water and ate a Toblerone bar from the mini refrigerator. The television was on, but she wasn't watching. Despite the sounds of voices in the hallway and hotel doors slamming, she still felt somewhat protected, though not as safe as she had felt with Jack. Knowing what she knew now, it sounded ridiculous to her. But in some strange way, she wished that she hadn't seen him that morning. Until then, she had felt secure, complete, loved.

She considered calling her mother on the East Coast. But her mother's condition was worsening, and Amber didn't want to upset her. It was also one o'clock in the morning in Providence, and the sound of the phone ringing at that hour would probably give the poor woman a heart attack.

She considered her predicament. Its face had changed once again. Each day, she seemed to find herself in a new and different type of danger. She laughed out loud. It was all she could do to keep from screaming. It was as if she was living the role of a character in a movie thriller. As much as she distrusted Jack, he was correct about one thing. She couldn't stay in the city. She had no idea when he would come back or when the tattooed man would visit her again. There was only one way to make sure Jack wasn't following her. She would have to follow him.

It was late on a Friday night, so she knew that no one would be at the travel agency. But fortunately she had the cell phone number of one of the agents, named Sheila, who had made many last-minute flight reservations for Marty over the past few years. She called Sheila, who happened to be at home, and instructed her to book two separate flights—one which departed from San Francisco to London, and another which departed from Oakland and arrived in Miami. The total for the two fares was seven thousand dollars, which the agent charged to the corporate account. Amber had read many stories in which this diversion tactic was used. She was sure that someone would be tracking her, so perhaps creating two routes would confuse them.

Amber fell asleep on the sofa with the television on. She awoke shortly after six o'clock the next morning. She had been asleep for nearly three hours. She pulled her Palm Pilot from her backpack and searched the numbers in the company's emergency phone tree. At the top was Kaitlyn's cell phone number. Almost nobody ever called her on her cell phone unless the office building was on fire. After several rings, Kaitlyn finally answered.

"Kaitlyn McBride," she said quietly.

"Hi Kaitlyn? It's Amber Wakefield."

"Amber, hi," she replied, clearing her throat.

"I apologize for calling you so early."

"No, don't be silly. What can I do for you?" she asked.

"I've given a lot of thought to what you said to me yesterday afternoon following Marty's memorial service."

"Well, I'm happy to hear that. But couldn't this have waited until next week?"

"Actually, no," Amber said. "I wasn't sure what time you were leaving for Europe today, so I wanted to catch you before then."

"I see."

"Kaitlyn, I was hoping that you might let me accompany you to Europe. It might give me an opportunity to observe. Call it an audition of sorts."

"That's an interesting idea." Kaitlyn sounded a bit more alert now. "I actually had considered it yesterday, but I didn't want to seem too pushy. It didn't look like you were much in the mood."

"Yeah, I'm sorry about that. I am very interested. I guess I needed some time to relax and think it over."

After a beat, Kaitlyn responded, "Amber, I'd be delighted if you'd join me. We're scheduled to leave at nine o'clock."

"Sounds great. And I presume we're taking the corporate jet?"

"Yes. We'll be flying into Milan. We can spend the time on the plane talking. I'll brief you on the pending projects I'll need your help on."

Amber's excitement perked up at the thought of going to Italy. She had been there only once, and that was to Rome. But she needed to keep her mind focused. "Looking forward to it."

"I'll meet you at the airport at 7:30. Does that work?"

"Absolutely. And thanks for the opportunity, Kaitlyn."

"You're welcome, Amber. I think this is going to work out wonderfully for both of us."

They hung up. Amber sat back and took a deep breath. She wasn't exactly sure what she was doing. All she knew was that she couldn't remain idle. She picked up her phone again and dialed Sheila's number. This time, Sheila sounded less than enthusiastic to hear from her.

"It's awfully early, Amber. You sure are calling in a lot of favors suddenly," she said through an obvious yawn.

"Sheila, I apologize for this, but I need one more thing from you."

"Ye-es," she said jokingly.

"Do you have a way to get your hands on European train schedules?"

"Sure. Which cities?"

"Milan to Bern," Amber replied.

"Milan to Bern? You just made flights to London and Miami. What's going on?"

"I'm not sure," she said quietly.

"Excuse me?"

"Nothing. I'm just planning last-minute travel for a number of execs at the company."

"All in your name?"

"Sheila, please," Amber pleaded. She didn't need the questions.

"Sorry. I don't envy you, honey. When do you need this by?"

Amber paused. "Well…"

"Never mind, I get it. Fax number, please?"

Amber called out the digits to the hotel's fax, reading them off a piece of hotel stationery.

"It's coming over in five minutes."

"Thanks, Sheila."

"You owe me, Amber."

Amber nodded. "You have no idea."

Chapter 20

The Gulfstream 5 jet touched down in the predawn hours on Sunday, awaking Amber from her slumber. She had slept during the final four hours of the flight. Before that, she sat with Kaitlyn, who brought her up to speed on the purpose of the trip—a periodic visit to major European customers. Their first customer meeting was scheduled for Tuesday morning. Kaitlyn generally preferred to fly during the weekend so that she could relax and shop before she had to start thinking about business. She rattled off a number of administrative tasks for Amber to perform in preparation for their meetings. Under other circumstances, Amber might have felt misled. After all, Kaitlyn had told her that she needed an experienced person to manage some larger projects and that the paper pushing would be left to Jamie. But Amber knew that she was not on this trip for business or career building. She was a stowaway hitching a ride to Europe, so she was readily acquiescent.

Milan was pretty much the way Kaitlyn had described it to her on the way over. It didn't have the character and romance of Rome or Florence, but it was still Italy. They checked into their rooms at the Westin Palace, located in Piazza della Repubblica, about a mile from the center of the city. Kaitlyn invited Amber to visit a couple of boutiques that usually opened their doors to her on Sunday mornings for a personal shopping spree. Amber declined, claiming that she felt the onset of a migraine headache, which wasn't a complete lie as it turned out. They agreed to meet Tuesday morning in the lobby.

Amber entered her room and dropped her bags onto the bed. She showered and changed her clothes. She put on a sweatshirt and warm-up pants. With her Nike running shoes and black Abercrombie cap, she was the epitomized illustration of an American tourist. She put the train schedule and a jacket into her old backpack, and as she did, she felt a small object in the front pocket. She reached in. The camera. The one she had used to photograph the files from the Jackson Winthrop offices. She had completely forgotten about it, what with all the commotion in the motel room and the chance sighting of Jack and the tattooed man the next morning. She placed the camera back into the backpack. She figured that it would come in handy later.

It was still dark outside when she walked out of the hotel's front doors. To her surprise, a short queue of taxicabs was waiting in front, the drivers standing outside while smoking cigarettes and chatting in Italian. As they saw her approaching, they all walked to their respective cars and opened the passenger doors. The chances of them getting a fare at that hour were generally slim, particularly with an attractive female tourist. She walked to the first cab in the line and got in. The driver got into his side, but not before turning to his peers and shouting out some triumphant macho Italian phrase, to which they all jeered back in unison.

He dropped her off in front of the train station, which was close by. Unfortunately, she hadn't exchanged any of her U.S. currency, so she dropped a hundred dollar bill on the front seat and stepped out of the cab. She told him to keep the change. He didn't respond, either because he didn't understand her English or he had no intention of offering to break the C-note.

Amber had studied the train schedules pretty closely, so she knew that the train to Bern was scheduled to leave at five o'clock. After exchanging some dollars for euros and Swiss francs, she bought her ticket, walked to the platform, and boarded the train. The train station had quite a few people at that hour, which surprised her. But it was probably better on second thought, considering her desire to remain inconspicuous. She found a seat in a relatively empty car. There was a young couple sitting in the rear, kissing and whispering to each other. She quickly fell asleep, the monotonous sound of the running train playing a soothing lullaby in her ear.

Penetrating the deafening silence, her own coughing broke her out of her slumber. She had been asleep for nearly two and a half hours. When she focused her eyes, she saw three young men across the aisle, passing a lighter around, each firing up a cigarette. They were speaking French and laughing loudly. They looked like university students on vacation. Amber hadn't noticed the smoking section symbol when she first entered the car. For some reason, she had no problem smoking with friends while drinking, but when she wasn't a participant, it made her feel sick. She tried to tolerate the smoke, but she felt the nausea coming on rapidly. She picked up her backpack and walked toward the door, in search of a nonsmoking car. She walked through two more cars and finally saw the picture of a cigarette with a bright red slash across it. She felt her breathing begin to ease again.

The car was a bit more crowded than the smoking car, but there were still plenty of vacant seats. She settled on one toward the back and was about to take her seat when the train jolted slightly. She fell forward onto the seat. When she turned, she saw that a man had bumped into her. The movement of the train had thrown him into her as he was coming through the doors. He was holding a briefcase, the contents of which had spilled into the aisle.

"*Mi scusi*," he said, holding up his hand. He knelt down to pick up his papers.

Amber jumped into the aisle and began helping him. "Excuse me. Are you all right?"

"Yes, it is OK," he replied in an Italian accent.

She helped gather the papers together and watched him stuff them back into his briefcase, far from the order they were originally in. As Amber picked up the last of the pages from the train floor, she was suddenly stopped by what she saw. The embossed letterhead on one of the pages had a familiar name on it: Bartlett Enterprises. It was the same as the name of the company she had seen in one of Harper Phillips's files in the Jackson Winthrop storage room. The logo was plain and generic. She passed the pages to the man with a slightly trembling hand.

"*Grazie*," he said, accepting the loose papers from her and depositing them in his briefcase.

She fixed her gaze on him. Her paranoia was running on overdrive, and she was certain that she was being followed again. This was too weird. Her intense stare must have made him uncomfortable because he quickly closed his briefcase and found the door at the opposite end of the car. He turned to look at her one last time before going through the door. She sat awake for the remainder of the trip, flinching at the sound of every person who entered through the doors behind her.

The train arrived in Bern a little past 10:30. Amber stepped onto the platform and immediately began swiveling her head in search of the Italian man who had bumped into her on the train. He was nowhere to be seen, and she felt worried. There was nothing more unnerving, she thought, than trying to elude someone whom she couldn't see. She walked along the platform, merging into the crowd, when she finally saw the man walking down the ramp toward the main area of the train station. He was walking quickly, and not once did he turn to look around. It didn't make sense, Amber thought, that someone following her would be walking in front of her. Her anxiety began to wane as she walked past the ticket kiosks and saw him riding up the escalator to the street level. Perhaps he wasn't following her after all, and she was allowing her imagination to send up red flags in her mind. But she needed confirmation.

She climbed the stairs, keeping a safe distance behind the man. He crossed the street and headed in the direction of the Kornhausplatz, the main plaza of the western Old Town. She walked on the opposite side of the street, along Marktgasse, eyeing him as he moved briskly down the covered walkways lined with shops and cafes. At one point, he stopped at an intersection to wait for the passing tram to turn in front of him. He turned in her direction, and she stepped behind a tour group, pretending to listen to the guide explain the history of the Zytglogge, a massive clock tower in the center of the town. When she turned back around, the man was gone.

She continued east down the Kramgasse, weaving between the countless tables and chairs on the elevated path that characteristically flanked the three main streets of old Bern. Halfway down the street, she spotted him. He suddenly disappeared into an alley, as if one of the sixteenth-century stone buildings had swallowed him whole. She crossed the street and jogged to the same alley she had seen him enter. She stood against the wall and peered around the corner. The symmetry of the arches hanging over the alley characterized the artistic workmanship of the European architects of the past. Despite the graffiti—a sign of a new, rebellious generation emerging—the sight was still impressive. She walked slowly down the corridor, which led into a wide, open plaza, the Munsterplatz. The cobblestones on the ground were partially darkened by the jagged shadow of the Gothic cathedral hovering ominously over the east side of the plaza.

She stood among a group of Japanese tourists, all eagerly snapping pictures of the structure's ornate details. She found herself studying the carvings on the façade, only to remind herself why she was there. Spinning around in search of the man she had been tailing, she caught sight of him entering through a set of double gates behind the cathedral. Trying to behave as casually as possible, she proceeded through the gates, which opened into a large, square platform decorated with tall trees and lined with benches. Beyond the walls on the far side, more tourists posed for pictures with the backdrop of the green hills and red roofed houses. The rushing sound of the Aare River below complemented the buzz of conversations occurring among the old, retired men playing chess in the center of the platform. In the corners of the plaza, young punk rockers with shaved heads and Mohawks smoked joints and rambled in the local German dialect.

Amber put her sunglasses on and began walking around the perimeter of the platform. She took out the camera from her pack and pretended to take pictures of the cathedral. As she walked along the wall parallel to the river, she saw the Italian man standing on the opposite side against the wall of the cathedral. He was talking to another man, who had his back turned to Amber. The man had a crew cut and wore a black leather jacket with jeans. His clothing lacked the panache of European style which was so prevalent among men in that region. He dressed more like a New Yorker.

Amber tried to blend into the sea of tourists, occasionally glancing in the direction of the two men. After a few minutes, she watched as they embraced and shook hands, much like long-lost friends would. She moved in closer and stood behind a large oak tree. In the dark shade, it would be impossible for anyone to spot her even if she was standing out in the open. Nevertheless, she felt her nerves rattling inside her. Never in a million years would she have guessed she would do this sort of thing. Following people around the world. Deceiving others. But she had a real reason to believe that she was in danger.

The tall, crew-cut guy stepped away and began walking toward the gates. He turned in the direction of the river, and Amber immediately studied his face. Behind his sunglasses, it was difficult to pick up any features other than his gleaming teeth. With a quick glance around the platform, he walked out of the gates. Amber walked at a rapid pace through the platform, ignoring the catcalls and whistles from the local dope dealers and their customers. When she passed through the gates, she looked to her right and saw the Italian courier quickly rounding a corner behind a building. It would be impossible for her to catch up to him now. In the opposite direction, she noticed that the other man was crossing the plaza diagonally. She began walking in his direction when he suddenly disappeared behind a row of tour buses. She picked up her pace, but when she reached the last bus, he was nowhere to be seen.

The giant clock face on the Zytglogge tower read a quarter until noon. Amber continued walking back toward the train station. The next train was scheduled to leave Bern in an hour. For the first time in two days, her body began to feel the true signs of fatigue. The muscles in her calves were throbbing. She needed to rest. Frustrated and exhausted, Amber entered through the glass revolving doors of Jack's Brasserie in the Hotel Schweizerhof, located directly across the street from the train station. *Jack's*, she said aloud to herself as she read the name on the front window. *Sick irony.*

It was a relatively large place, brightly lit with hardwood floors. The age of the restaurant was clearly engraved on the small, rectangular brass plaques affixed to the wooden railings around the room. The plaques carried the notable names of past visitors—Peter Ustinov, David Niven, Ella Fitzgerald—reminders of the rich history of the hotel and the city. The wait staff dressed in the traditional uniforms of white shirts with black neckties, and black pants or skirts. White, shin-length aprons hung around their waists. Amber felt disappointed that she couldn't enjoy it more. She ordered an espresso, and as she sat there, her eyes darted around the place, particularly toward the door. She looked behind her at the kitchen, identifying the nearest exit, in the event that she had to leave quickly and inconspicuously. Ever the optimist, she watched through the large window facing the street, hoping she would get another shot at seeing the man with the crew-cut.

After a few minutes, two elderly couples entered the café. They looked like tourists with their oversized video cameras and maps in hand. They walked in Amber's direction and settled at a table near hers. They asked to borrow one of the chairs at her table. She smiled and removed her backpack from one of the chairs so that they could move it to their table. As she did, the miniature camera dropped out of the pack. She had forgotten to close the front pocket. She whispered a curse while she bent down to pick it up. She dusted it off and was about to put it back into the backpack when it occurred to her that she had never bothered to look at the pictures she had taken in the Jackson Winthrop offices. She didn't have any notions about what she might find, or what to look for. But it *was* Jack's camera. It had been his idea to take photos of the files. So, clearly, there was something significant in those files that he was hoping to capture. Perhaps the pictures she had taken would provide some information to explain who Jack Bennett really was and what exactly she was running away from.

As she began scrolling through the LCD screen on the camera, Amber worried that her amateur photography skills might have compromised some of the quality of the photos, rendering them useless. But to her surprise, the forgiving magic of digital photography had produced images that were crystal clear. Apparently she had managed to capture only a few shots of some pages in the file marked *Ensight* before the big meathead janitor with the tattoo began zinging bullets at her. She zoomed in on one of the images, and although it tended to slightly distort the printed letters on the file, the page was still legible. She recalled capturing pictures of invoices made out to the company named Bartlett Enterprises. As she squinted to read, it appeared that the invoices were for trustee services. What did grab her attention were the amounts of the invoices. They ranged from ten thousand dollars to ten million dollars. *Ten million dollars?* The rest of the invoices were illegible or had been cut off.

She started to turn the camera off when she noticed the counter in the corner of the display screen. It indicated that there were ten pictures on the memory card, even though there were only three pictures from her covert mission at the law office. She decided to scroll through the rest of the images. The first few were pictures of herself—one coming out of her apartment and one coming home in the evening. The last one was her sitting on her sofa in her own living room, taken from outside her front window. It sent a chill up her spine. The dates on them were all before her first meeting with Jack near the ballpark.

She continued to look through the other pictures. There was nothing very interesting, other than some shots of the Ensight office building. It was only when she arrived at the start of the reel that an uneasy sensation began to roil in her stomach. It was a picture of Jack, sitting off the stern of a boat. He wore sunglasses on top of his head and was holding a bottle of Belikin Beer in his hand. He was smiling widely, surrounded by three other men, all of them sitting on the back of the boat. On either side of him were two others with their arms around him. Unfortunately, the photo captured only their shoulders but no faces. She scanned down toward the lower portion of the picture. In large, blue cursive letters was the name of the boat: *NICOLETTE*.

She sat back as her espresso went cold. She began to remember the details of her visit to Jackson Winthrop. Why would an invoice to Bartlett be included in a file marked Ensight? Just at that moment, the sunlight that had been streaming through the large window in the front disappeared as a person suddenly approached her table. She slowly raised her head.

"Yes, may I help you?" she asked the stranger, though she recognized the Italian.

"I sorry. My Inglese is not so good." He waved his hand to emphasize his point.

She watched him as he pulled out a chair across from her and sat down at the small table.

He continued, "It is OK that I sit? I wish to ask a question to you."

Amber nodded slowly, her body numb. "Yes, it's OK. What do you wish to ask me?" She was speaking slowly, since it was clear he was having trouble understanding her.

"For why do you follow me?"

"Excuse me?"

"I see you on the train. I drop my papers before you."

"Oh, yes," she said, attempting to act like her memory had just been restored. "But I'm not following you."

"What is your purpose to come to Bern?" His eyes looked scared. She actually felt sorry for him.

"I'm just a tourist."

"You are on holiday?"

"Yes. That's right. Why do you think I'm following you?"

He reached into his jacket and pulled out a handkerchief, which he used to dab his forehead.

"I see you under Zytglogge, as I cross the street. Then behind the cathedral, again I see you."

Amber was about to deny it again, but it was quite obvious that he could not be convinced.

"I apologize if I've caused any concern to you. You are correct. I was following you. But only because I couldn't help but notice something when you dropped your papers on the train. Do you work for Bartlett Enterprises?" she asked.

He shook his head. "No. I deliver documents only. I do not remember how to say in Inglese. I am carrier?"

Amber thought for a moment, and then realized what he meant. "Courier. You're a courier."

He nodded eagerly like he just won at a game of charades. "Yes, yes. I am courier."

"And the man I saw you with behind the cathedral? He hired you?"

"Si, Signor Phillips." He wiped his forehead again.

"Phillips?" she asked, leaning forward. "Harper Phillips?"

"Si, signorina." He nodded enthusiastically.

"What did you deliver to him?" she pressed on.

He shrugged. "I do not deliver nothing to him. He pay me to deliver document."

"So he gave you some documents at the cathedral? He is paying you to deliver documents to someone else?"

"Si."

"What's in the documents?" She didn't exactly know where she was going with this, but she had run out of ideas.

"Oh, I do not know this. I only deliver. I do not look."

Amber looked across the table. She wondered why Jack had wanted her to come to Bern—perhaps to take her out of the picture completely. No one would ever know that she was missing. At that thought, she stood up from the table.

"I'm going now. I apologize for worrying you. I didn't mean to scare you." She reached out her hand. "*Mi dispiace,*" she said, faintly recalling the basics from her Italian language class in high school.

He smiled at her, shaking her hand. "Ciao, signorina."

"Good-bye." She walked out of the brasserie in the direction of the train station.

She walked quickly, doing her best to immerse herself into the crowd of train travelers. If anyone was going to take a shot at her, they'd have to put some magic spin on the bullet to get it around all the people who served as a human protective bubble. She was about to climb the ramp to the platform when she suddenly stopped. Back at the brasserie, she had allowed herself to become so lost in her own thoughts that she had temporarily abandoned logic. The conversation didn't make sense. How could her Italian acquaintance have claimed that he was hired only to deliver documents for the man who called himself Harper Phillips? The page with the Bartlett Enterprises letterhead was already in his possession when she collided with him on the train. *Before* the two men met behind the cathedral. There must have been something in those documents that might offer some explanation to her.

She turned against the flow of foot traffic and began heading back toward the brasserie. Before she realized it, she was running, her backpack strapped to both shoulders. Her mind was telling her to stop and go back to Milan, but her feet kept pushing her body forward like a racehorse. When she arrived at the front door of Jack's, her breath short, she slouched dejectedly at the sight of an empty table where she had been sitting. She walked in and approached one of the waitresses.

"Pardon me," she asked one of the young ladies. "The man who was sitting at that table with me a little while ago. Do you know which way he went?"

The young woman, her hair in a tight bun, nodded. "Yes. He is still here. He went to the toilet," she said, pointing toward a small door next to the kitchen. "It is through the hotel lobby and up the stairs."

Amber let out a breath of relief. "Oh, thank God."

She walked through the doors, which led into the main lobby. She crossed the marble floor and proceeded up the stairs. When she reached the first landing, she had to jump out of the way of one of the hotel's uniformed staff members running in the opposite direction. She watched him as he nearly slipped on the lobby floor, and then raced out the glass doors to the street. Turning back around, she placed her hand on the brass handrail and felt stickiness on her hands when she pulled it away. She wiped her hands against her sweatshirt, and immediately saw the unmistakable dark hue. It was blood.

She turned around, intent on running out of the hotel, when she heard violent coughing coming from up the stairs. She ran up the steps to the first floor, and as she turned the corner toward the restrooms, she ran straight into the Italian courier. He instinctively grasped her shoulders and looked into her eyes.

"You're here," she said. "I have to ask you about the papers you spilled on the train."

He continued to stare at her, but said nothing.

"Did you hear what I said to you?" she asked.

"Signorina," he whispered, slurring his words. He pulled away slowly, and Amber felt dampness on the front of her sweatshirt where he had been pressed up against her. More blood. She tried to scream, but no sound came out. She held her hands to her mouth as his knees buckled and he fell hard onto the deep red carpet.

She dropped to her knees and held his head up. She unbuttoned his shirt and saw that the wound in his chest was about two inches wide. She couldn't ascertain how deep it was because the rushing river of blood flowing out of the gash was flooding the cavity.

He pulled her down closer to his face. She couldn't bear to look at him.

"Signorina, *per favore*," he started to say, and then began coughing blood. "Take this from me." He handed her a large white envelope with nothing written or printed on the front.

"What is this? Where's Harper Phillips?" she said quietly but intensely, holding the envelope.

His eyes grew large, inhabited more by terror than pain. Slowly, they surrendered into a relaxed, almost serene state. She pleaded for him to answer her, but there was no reply. After a few more seconds, he stopped blinking.

"Please no. No," she repeated. He was gone.

Amber pulled her hands from under his head and gently laid him down. She took off the sweatshirt she was wearing, and pulled out the jacket from her backpack and put it on, zipping it up to her neck. She considered tossing the soiled sweatshirt into a trashcan in the ladies room, but thought better of it. Instead, she rolled it up and placed it into her pack. She stood up to leave, stopping briefly to look at the Italian courier lying dead in the hallway. He could have been mugged by a group of seedy teens. Or perhaps he was engaged in a drug deal of some kind. *In the hallway of a classy European hotel like this one? Not likely*, she surmised. She came up with a half-dozen possible scenarios, but in the end, she knew how he died. She just wasn't sure why. She glanced down at the envelope in her hand and knew that the answer to that question very likely lay within. She folded the envelope and placed it in the front pocket of her backpack. She closed it and then, with her body shaking almost uncontrollably, she managed to walk quickly down the stairs and out of the hotel lobby doors. She needed to get to the train station.

Chapter 21

▼

The sounds of silver dollars dropping into metal slot machine trays and the shouts of triumphant rollers at the craps tables were like symphonic music to Dennis Fitch. It was the sound of winning. And he loved it. He had been sitting for three hours at the same blackjack table at the MGM Grand Hotel and Casino for three hours. The tall cylinders of black and pink chips stacked in front of him were indicators that he wasn't about to go anywhere soon.

He was in Las Vegas to watch the big title fight. Second row seats, right behind Denzel and Costner. It was six-thirty, and his face was red and hot from the seven whiskey sours he had already drunk. It was the end of the shoe, and the dealer began shuffling. Fitch's eyes explored the casino, slowing down enough to soak in the sights of the voluptuous cocktail waitresses as well as the throngs of bachelorette parties giggling and gyrating across the floor.

He waved to the shift manager, who was pacing the tables. Fitch had become a recognizable face over the years at a number of casinos in the desert city. One of the cocktail waitresses arrived at his table and placed a napkin in front of him, but no drink. There was handwriting on the paper, and he rubbed his eyes to read it. Then he crumpled the napkin and looked around him. There was nothing but a sea of moving bodies, and it made him dizzy.

He tossed his cards onto the felt and collected his chips. He ricocheted off slot machines and fellow patrons, many of who were now working their way toward the arena. Once outside the front doors, the Las Vegas evening heat choked him. He coughed loudly, looking from side to side. He finally took note of the white Suburban with its lights off parked in the fire lane. He nodded to whoever was on the other side of the black tinted glass. Walking to the Suburban, he climbed into the backseat and tilted his head back

From the driver's seat, Bruce Fox turned around. "Didn't I tell you to take it easy on the booze tonight?"

"What the hell are you doing here, Foxy?" Fitch leaned forward and put his hands on the back of Fox's seat. "Am I not entitled to have some fun?"

Fox handed him a cup of hot coffee. "Here, drink this."

Fitch read his eyes and knew right away. "Something's wrong, isn't it?" He took a sip of the coffee.

"Things are coming apart."

"Enough so that I have to forgo a championship bout that I've been wanting to see for months?"

"We all need to be better about maintaining a low profile."

"So, I guess that means no sitting beside Hollywood celebs at prize fights?"

"Denny, you need to start being more careful. You can't be letting your guard down, and you certainly can't be seen talking in public to people like Art Lassiter. Lang's got all sorts of reservations about you. Frankly, he doesn't care for you much, in case that wasn't obvious."

"Well, you can tell him the feeling is mutual," Fitch said with a light chuckle.

"Listen to me," Fox began, his body almost completely turned around to face Fitch. "You need to play nice, Denny. At this point, we're all after the same thing. If we don't recover that money soon…"

"I know, I know," Fitch interrupted. He noted the doubt in Fox's expression. "Bruce, you don't have to worry. I know how volatile a situation this is, but you need to keep Harry on a leash."

"I will. I promise. We just need to watch ourselves. Don't let on that you know anything I tell you. Harry trusts me more than he trusts you. For what particular reason, I don't know. Perhaps because he knows that I'll worry about the details he's too lazy or stupid to worry about."

"Such as?" Fitch probed.

"Harry suspects that someone else out there is competing with his guy to access Harper's accounts."

"How?" Fitch was beginning to sober.

"He found some unusual patterns in the transaction statements."

"Damn."

"My sentiments precisely." Fox looked out the window at the bright lights. Then he turned back to Fitch. "But don't worry about that now. I'm handling that part. You just worry about the file."

Fitch's brow furrowed. "What are you talking about?"

"The file, Denny. You should have received it yesterday." Fox could see the empty look in Fitch's eyes. "The one from Switzerland," he reminded him.

"The articles of incorporation for Bartlett?"

Fox nodded.

"I never got it," Fitch told him.

Fox leaned in closer and spoke in a softer tone. "You should have received a file from the Italian courier agency. It was supposed to come from Bern, Switzerland."

"Well, I never got it."

"Shit." Fox's eyes darted sideways, searching for an explanation.

"You're telling me that the articles of incorporation for Bartlett are floating around somewhere, and we have no idea where?"

"This is bad."

"Bad? It's catastrophic. Our names are listed as principals of the corporation. It's the only documented record of our affiliation with Bartlett."

"I'm aware of that, Denny," Fox shot back.

"I thought the documents were safely housed in that bank in Switzerland. Why did we decide to move them now?"

"It's the deal with Maguire Solutions," Fox began to explain.

"The Ensight acquisition?"

"Yes." Fox took a quick look out the window to see if anyone was watching. "Maguire is planning to start its due diligence on Ensight soon. They've hired an independent firm to conduct an audit on the company's financials, as well as examine its affiliates and subsidiaries."

"Of which Bartlett is one," Fitch added, completing the thought.

Fox nodded. "Are you getting it now?"

"Sure. They start digging into Bartlett's business. They discover its purpose. The floodgates open. I get it."

"You forgot the most important detail of all. When those floodgates open, we're going to get trapped in the rushing water. You, me, Harry. All of us."

"Shouldn't we have seen this coming?"

"We did. We just didn't expect it to come this soon." Both men sighed deeply.

Fitch nodded in acknowledgment. "What do we tell Harry?"

"We tell him exactly what he wants to hear." Fox turned around and started the engine. "That you received the file and it's well concealed. He entrusted this part of the plan to us, so we just need to convince him that we're taking care of it."

"And where shall I say that it's hidden?"

Fox shook his head. "Don't worry about that. If he wanted to know, he would have had it sent to himself. He won't ask."

"You make sure of that, Bruce." Fitch looked out the window again.

Fox stared into the rearview mirror. "Trust me," he said, smiling.

Fitch smirked, unamused. "And what do you plan to do?"

"Find the documents."

At that, the Suburban slowly rolled away from the curb and turned onto the strip.

Parked in a black Nissan Pathfinder, Watts sat in the driver's seat, watching the white Suburban pull away. Leaving a good three car lengths between them, he followed the Suburban, dialing Lang's private number.

"Hey, it's Watts. I missed him again, sir. There were just too many people around."

"Where is he headed now?" Lang asked.

"Looks like the airport. He's with Mr. Fox."

"You don't say."

"I can still take care of him."

"No, Watts. If he's with Fox, then I have a better idea."

Chapter 22

Amber arrived back in Milan just before seven o'clock. Her attempts to sleep on the train proved fruitless, as the sound of her rapidly pounding heart kept her awake. She was able to wash away most of the blood which had stained her hands, but was unable to ward off the urge to vomit three times during the process. She had never before watched another human being take his last breath, let alone hold his head while he did it.

She arrived in her room and took a thirty-minute shower. She wished that she could have washed off more than the blood and sweat. She wanted to rinse away the memory of what she had just witnessed. Following the shower, she put on a bathrobe and sat in the large armchair against the wall. The envelope that the Italian courier had handed to her was sitting on the desk. The shades of dried blood on it had turned a brownish rust color. As she stared at it, she felt the sensation of nausea coming on again.

Her hair still damp from the shower, she walked to the desk and picked up the envelope, then returned to the chair, emptying the contents onto the coffee table. The envelope contained a short stack of papers, the first of which bore the Bartlett Enterprises letterhead, an all-too-familiar logo by this time. The letter was addressed to no one in particular and was not signed by anyone. In a plain courier font, it simply read:

```
Per your request, attached is the original Dutch version
of the company's Articles of Incorporation. An English
version has been enclosed for your convenience.
```

Amber flipped to the next page. The smudges on the text indicated that the document had been hand typed and that what she was holding was not a photocopy. She read the first few pages but realized quickly that it contained nothing telling, particularly because it was written primarily in standardized legal jargon and provided few details. Lacking the energy to read the entire document word for word, she fanned the pages with her thumb, hoping that something interesting might leap out at her. But to her disappointment, the only page that seemed noteworthy was the last page. It contained a list of names, under a heading that read *Principals of the Corporation*.

There were only three names listed: D. Fitch, H. Phillips, and B. Fox. She recognized all of the names, as they were on the list housed on the CD that Priscilla had sent to her weeks before. But it was the third name that forced her to pause. B. Fox. She hadn't thought about Bruce Fox since Marty's funeral, but looking at his name now, she realized that the nightmare she had been living for the last few weeks had begun only after Fox had brought the Harper Phillips investigation to them.

At that moment, she heard the faint sound of a bell ringing from the direction of the elevators. She walked slowly to the door and put her ear to it, hoping to judge the proximity of whoever happened to exit the elevator. She hit the light switch and the room immediately went dark. She stood in the corner in silence. Soon enough, the brushing sound of shoes on the thick carpet in the hallway became more audible. She closed her eyes and made her best attempt to hold her position against the wall. The rap on the door was soft.

"Amber?" It was a woman's voice. "Are you in there?"

Amber remained still, watching the lighted area beneath the door.

"It's Kaitlyn. Are you OK?"

Amber exhaled and leaned the back of her head against the wall in relief. She walked to the door and slowly opened it, with the brass latch still hooked.

"Kaitlyn, hi."

"Sorry, were you sleeping?" Kaitlyn asked, noting the darkness behind Amber.

"Uh, yeah. Trying to rest a bit."

"Well, I wanted to check on you, since I haven't heard from you since we checked in."

Amber unlatched the door and opened it wider.

"Feeling a little better. Thanks for checking." She rubbed her eyes, playing the role of the jet-lagged traveler.

"How about some dinner? I'm assuming you haven't eaten yet."

"Actually, I'm not that hungry," Amber began, but then reconsidered. "On second thought, sure, why not? Dinner would be nice." She needed the distraction and a drink to settle her nerves.

"Excellent. I hope you don't mind, but I was thinking we'd eat downstairs, here at the hotel. We have an early start tomorrow morning, and I'd rather not stray too far from here, if that's OK."

"That's fine with me."

"I promise I'll spoil you with a fabulous meal before we leave Milan. You won't be disappointed."

"I'm sure I won't," Amber replied.

"I'll give you a few minutes to get cleaned up. Downstairs in ten minutes?"

"Make it fifteen."

Kaitlyn smiled and nodded.

As Kaitlyn walked away toward the elevators, Amber scrambled around the room, collecting the Bartlett documents and shoving them into the desk drawer. She stopped at the door and turned to face the room. She walked to the desk and took out the documents, placing them into the safe located in the closet. A man had been brutally murdered for them, so clearly someone wanted them. Although she knew it was dangerous for her to have them in her possession now, she also knew that she could not simply get rid of them. For some strange reason, it reminded her of the childhood game of Hot Potato, and at that moment, she felt a burning sensation in her palms.

The two women sat at a corner table in a tan leather booth at the Casanova Grill. The dinner and the accompanying wine were delightful. The food had a Mediterranean flavor, and Amber felt relaxed as she and Kaitlyn discussed anything unrelated to business. She felt privileged to be sitting alone at a table with the person who Fortune magazine had voted as one of the fifty most powerful women in business. It was refreshing to be once again in the company of familiar people—people who represented the normal world to her. Until then, Amber had felt that she was wandering aimlessly in someone else's universe among total strangers, with no familiar face in sight.

According to the conversation, Kaitlyn had been divorced before she married her current husband. Kaitlyn shared photos of her dogs and one of her and her husband vacationing in Bora Bora. Amber reciprocated with some of her own episodes from her disastrous romantic history. She felt like a member of an elite social circle as Kaitlyn revealed a little-known fact that she had participated in the

1980 Olympic trials for the biathlon. She admitted that she still kept up with cross-country skiing, but the rifle shooting was a thing of the past.

After a bottle and a half of some three hundred dollar Bordeaux that Amber couldn't recall the name of, the conversation shifted to Marty. Kaitlyn admitted not knowing him well on a personal level, and Amber was happy to fill in the gaps for her. She shared some lighthearted anecdotes about him, many of which dated back to the days before Kaitlyn's arrival at Ensight. As the wine continued to flow, Kaitlyn became quick to offer her opinions on some of her own lieutenants on the executive committee as well as certain members of the board. They laughed together for the next two hours, like two gossipy high school friends catching up at a reunion.

At a quarter of eleven, they rose from their seats, despite the countless attempts by the restaurant staff to shuffle them out earlier. As they walked through the lobby, Kaitlyn offered a nightcap in the lounge. Amber declined the invitation, as the effects of sleeplessness had begun to take their toll on her. They hugged each other and exchanged light cheek kisses. Amber entered the elevator, leaning against the wall for support. Her head felt light from the wine, and for a moment she nearly forgot her room number. It was only when she reached the door to her room that she realized she didn't have her key in her possession. In fact, she couldn't recall bringing the key with her when she had left the room for dinner earlier.

Amber stepped back out of the elevator when it stopped at the lobby. As she approached the front desk to request a key, she did her best to feign the appearance of sobriety, although the glaze in her eyes made it somewhat of a challenge. After receiving her key, she headed back in the direction of the elevators, but not before noticing Kaitlyn sitting in the lounge, sipping a small glass of dessert wine. Seated next to her was a man in his fifties, whose gray hair and thin-rimmed eyeglasses exuded an air of confidence that complemented Kaitlyn's presence nicely. Amber took a few steps forward to join them but changed her course when she saw the two lean toward one another and kiss. According to the pictures she had been shown at dinner, this man was not Kaitlyn's husband. It was a brief kiss but clearly more passionate than the typical European greeting. Relieved at having avoided an embarrassing situation, Amber quickly made her way back to the elevator and up to her room.

The light on the nightstand was on when she entered her room, and the bed was turned down. Other than that, everything else appeared to be undisturbed. Instinctively, she opened the safe and found the Bartlett documents inside, precisely as she recalled leaving them. She brushed her teeth and crawled under the covers, her head propped up by the large sham on the bed. From her jacket pocket, she pulled out the steak knife she had stealthily removed from the restaurant and slid it beneath her pillow. Her paranoia had become all too real in the form of an innocent dead Italian courier. She was through putting her faith in something more divine. She turned the television on and watched a local music channel, leaving the lights on and combating her body's persistent pleas for much-needed sleep. In ten minutes, her eyes closed, and she drifted off.

The next three days consisted of meetings, slide presentations, lunches and dinners, endless handshakes, and business card exchanges. It was a complete, about-face transition from her job as an administrative assistant in human resources. She was tempted several times to approach Kaitlyn and inquire about the man in the lounge but reconsidered the idea each time. Kaitlyn McBride was one of the most powerful and respected people in the business community, and Amber was not about to cast a dark cloud over that image by asking questions, despite her own suspicions.

On Thursday evening, Amber approached the front desk after a dinner with the last of the customers on their agenda. She had left Kaitlyn and the others at the restaurant as they enjoyed what would probably be a long night of cocktails and more business talk. She was happy to have made it through the marathon week, but she did not feel the same elation about returning to San Francisco. Uncertain peril awaited her there, and she had no roadmap to avoid it. The clerk at the desk handed her an envelope with her name printed on the front. He told her that it had been left for her that afternoon.

She entered the elevator car alone, and as she rode up, she opened the unsealed envelope. Inside, a single sheet of paper on the hotel's stationery was meticulously folded in half. The handwriting was neat and, in block letters, it read:

> GO BACK TO SAN FRANCISCO, LEAVE THE DOCUMENTS AT THE FRONT DESK IN A PLAIN LARGE ENVELOPE, AND LABEL IT ROOM 0. YOU WON'T BE HARMED. IF YOU FAIL TO COMPLY, YOU WILL FIND YOURSELF IN FAR GREATER TROUBLE.

Amber gripped the note tightly until her knuckles were white. Her hands were shaking uncontrollably, and she dropped them to her sides. She closed her eyes tightly and searched her mind in the darkness. Someone was watching her, and they were close. But they were offering her an out. Whether they were being genuine or not, she was more than happy to leave the documents behind. She just didn't want to be around when whoever it was came for them. A sense of excitement passed through her body. As vague as the message was, it was a way to remove herself from the situation. It was the first promising sign that there was light at the end of this gloomy tunnel, and she was intent on mustering every ounce of strength to tighten her grasp on that hope. Sure, it was optimistic. Maybe even naïve. But it was all she could do to stay focused on her primary objective, which was to stay alive. Despite all of this, she felt uneasy about the threat of *far greater trouble*.

She held the note in her quivering hand and felt something else in the envelope, which she held in her other hand. Inside were two photographs, each printed on Polaroid film. As she looked closer, she recognized that the first image was of her and the Italian courier talking at the Hotel Schweizerhof brasserie in Bern. The second was of her walking down the stairs of the hotel, the legs of the dead courier clearly visible poking out from behind the wall to the restrooms. Whoever was watching must have been only steps away from her, hidden in one of the rooms on that floor, when she had discovered the dying man. She figured out the tactic immediately. *Blackmail.* She had been seen by so many that day talking with the courier. On the train. In the brasserie. There were potential witnesses everywhere. And with the coveted documents now in her possession, it would be a slam dunk to pin the murder on her. It was frighteningly clear to her now that the whole encounter on the train had been a setup. She needed to get rid of those papers. It didn't matter to her anymore *why* they were so valuable.

The elevator doors opened, and a young couple stood there as Amber stepped out. She screamed loudly as she collided with them. They looked at her in astonishment as she walked quickly toward her room. The room was dark when she entered. She opened the door wide so that the light from the hallway illuminated the room. She stood in the doorway, motionless. Someone had visited her room while she was away, and by the looks of things, it was not the chambermaid. Her suitcase was on her bed, wide open. She saw articles of her clothing tossed around the room. She walked into the bathroom and found her cosmetics splattered across the counter and in the bathtub. She ran out of the bathroom toward the door but stopped when she noticed the open door to the safe. Her shoulders dropped as she approached it, knowing full well what to expect. Along with her passport and a few traveler's checks, the only other missing item was the file containing the Bartlett documents.

Amber ran back to the elevators and rode down to the lobby. She approached the front desk, pushing aside an elderly couple who was checking in.

"Someone has been in my room," she told the desk clerk.

"Signorina?" he asked, confused.

"Someone has been in my room," she repeated, this time her voice a few octaves higher. "They broke in. They stole some items."

The manager on duty stepped to the desk and patted the young clerk on the shoulder, prompting him to step aside. He recognized her, largely due to her association with Kaitlyn.

"What is the problem, signorina?" he asked politely.

"For the third time, someone has broken into my room," she said sternly, suppressing her urge to shout.

The manager smiled, feigning a calmness that he hoped would comfort the guests and hotel staff who were standing in the vicinity.

"Signorina, do you mean your husband?"

She looked at him quizzically. "Excuse me?"

"Yes, your husband arrived and asked to go to your room." He smiled widely, so proud that he had abetted the plan for a romantic rendezvous between a loving couple.

"My husband?" she asked.

"Si, signorina. We received a call this morning from your room, requesting that we permit your husband to enter the room when he arrived today. Was it not you who called?"

"I don't understand this. There must have been a mistake."

It was becoming clear to the manager that the hotel had been deceived. The butterflies that had inhabited Amber's stomach for the last ten minutes seemed to have undergone a metamorphosis, as she now felt what could have been fruit bats frantically searching for a dark corner within her. "What did this man look like? How long ago was he here?" she persisted.

"I don't remember his appearance very well. But his hair was short, like a military man. His name was Phillips, I believe."

"Of course it was," she said, shaking her head in disbelief.

"He left only minutes ago," he explained. He craned his neck to get a look around Amber, and pointed. "There. He is getting into that taxicab out there."

Amber swung around and, through the doors, saw a man opening the door to the taxicab. He stopped and turned around slowly, almost in the way one would do to taunt another. Behind his dark sunglasses, it was impossible to determine where he was looking, but it was clear that he wasn't looking at her. The smile was unmistakable. She knew him. It was the man who had been speaking with the courier earlier. At that moment, the man closed the door to the taxicab, and it sped away. When she burst through the doors of the entrance, she looked in the direction where the taxicab had gone and could barely make out the rear of the car, but the image of him through the back window was all too clear.

She considered jumping into the next taxicab and pursuing him, but in the end, she decided that he was too far ahead. She had no idea where he was going, and she had no idea what she would do to him if she caught up to him. What was worse, she had no idea what he might do to her. A dense, weighty sensation of panic set in. They had taken her passport, probably to delay her exit from the country. They could strike at any point. She couldn't afford to move alone. What had become an all-too-familiar feeling, solitude, was once again her most threatening nemesis.

She walked back into the hotel, deflecting the stares of all in the lobby who had just stood witness to her tantrum at the front desk and her sprint out the front doors in a manner most uncharacteristic of the average sane person. The hotel manager was now standing in front of the desk, his arms folded, with a look of disdain painted across his face.

As the vivid image of the open safe door flashed through Amber's head, she felt a faint draft and clutched her arms around her body. The words *far greater trouble* resonated in her brain, as she considered the possibility that whoever had taken those documents was not the same person who left the note. After all, it didn't make sense that someone would leave a threatening note telling her to leave the documents but then break into her room anyway. There was only one way to find out. She walked to the concierge and asked for a large white envelope. With the hotel's logo in the corner, it wasn't exactly plain as the instructions had demanded, but it would serve its purpose. From the top of the reception desk, she grabbed one of the complimentary newspapers reserved for guests and placed it inside the envelope. She wrote the words *Room 0* on the front and left it with the clerk.

Amber walked back through the lobby and found a seat in the corner of the lounge with a clear view of the front desk. She leaned back in one of the large, ornate chairs and waited.

CHAPTER 23

Harry Lang sat patiently sipping a cup of coffee, spiked with a couple of shots of brandy. It had been weeks since he had spoken with the other members of the Committee. The train station in DC was alive with scores of people moving in all directions. He watched as Dennis Fitch and Bruce Fox walked toward him from opposite directions. Fitch had been instructed by Fox to keep his lips tight about their conversation in Las Vegas. *He'll interpret your silence as an acknowledgment of his authority*, Fox had said.

"Gentlemen," Lang said, as they approached his table. "Welcome."

The two men nodded, but only Fox spoke. "Harry."

Lang held his hands out. "Please, have a seat." He waved the waitress over. "What are you guys drinking?"

"Coffee," Fox replied.

"Denny?" Lang asked, a giant grin stretching his cheeks. Fitch shook his head. "Nothing."

"Tell me, how was the big fight?" Lang asked, staring directly at Fitch.

"I missed it, unfortunately."

"Aw, that's a shame." Lang was smiling widely.

Fitch shot a look toward Fox, who could almost feel the steam reflecting off the venture capitalist's head.

"Harry, that's enough," Fox said, trying to stop the situation from reaching a boiling point.

"Where's Terry?" Fitch asked, doing his part to change the topic.

"Old man Hammond is in Langley. It's the holiday season, and the terror alert is orange. The Homeland Security boys have asked the old guy to help analyze some of their recent intelligence data."

"So what's this all about?" Fox asked.

"Jack Bennett was seen in Italy. Milan, to be exact."

"Seen by whom?"

"Does it matter?" Lang shot back.

"Well, I think you should consider the source. There are folks out there who will tell you whatever you want to hear."

Lang leaned forward and pinned his eyes on Fox. "Are you one of those folks, Bruce?"

"Don't start that. I'm just telling you to take whatever you hear with a grain of salt."

"What was Jack doing out there?" Fitch asked.

"Funny you should ask that," Lang replied. "He was seen at the Westin, coincidentally the same hotel where Foxy's little friend Amber Wakefield was staying."

"What? How the…" Fox began.

"I don't know. I told you Bennett was up to something." Lang noticed the uneasiness between the other two.

Fitch's eyes shifted toward Fox, who was staring at the table.

"Bruce," Lang said, as Fox turned slowly toward him. "The documents. Are they safe?"

Fox turned to Fitch, who continued to look at the deputy director, until he realized that this was his question to answer. He nodded slowly. "Yes. I got them. They're safe."

Lang breathed a sigh of relief and sat back in his chair. He pulled a flask from his coat pocket and poured a few drops of brandy into his coffee cup.

"And the money?" Fitch pressed on.

"I'm sensing by your tone that Mr. Fox here has filled you in on our discovery." Lang glanced toward Fox.

"He had a right to know, Harry."

Lang looked at both of them but didn't offer a reply. "Don't worry about the money. I'm handling it."

"No, no, no," Fitch insisted. "From this point on, everything is out in the open. When we started this thing, we all had an equal stake and an equal say. Somewhere along the line, the weight shifted toward you. It's time to balance things out again."

Lang smiled. "Fair enough. What do you want to know?"

"Well, for starters, how the hell does something like this occur? You told us you had a handle on this."

"I do."

Fitch raised a skeptical eyebrow.

"I'm telling the truth. That's all I can do. Whether you believe me or not is your problem."

"And why are you so hung up on Jack Bennett as the guy behind it all?"

"Why not? Look, Bruce and I have gone through this repeatedly. Jack knows all the right people to get him the information he needs. More importantly, he hates me. I fired his ass, and he wants me to pay for it. It's simple, really."

"To extinguish any doubt, can't you use some of your FBI muscle to inquire with the bank in France about who accessed that account last? The account was considered pretty exclusive, so they probably remember most of the people who come in and out of their doors." Fitch had obviously done some thinking about the situation.

"There is no way in hell that I'm going to launch an investigation with the bank, using the FBI. You don't think that'll reach Lassiter's desk in a minute? It would blow the whole thing wide open. I've got to do this without the involvement of the Bureau."

"Don't you mean *we*?" Fitch reminded him.

Lang rolled his eyes, then offered a quick smirk toward his partners. "Of course."

Fox poured a packet of sugar into his coffee, which had been sitting in front of him for nearly five minutes. "So, why are we here, Harry? And why are we meeting in a train station?"

"It's public." Lang tipped his coffee cup into his mouth until it was upside down. He placed it back in the saucer and cleared his throat. "My buddies at the SEC tell me that Maguire Solutions is stepping up the due diligence on Ensight."

"What do you mean 'stepping up'?" Fox asked.

"Accelerating. Moving up on the agenda," Lang replied with a sarcastic tone.

"When?"

"The first of next month."

"That's two weeks from now."

"I'm impressed, Bruce. Did the IRS teach you how to read a calendar on the job, or is it a prerequisite?"

"You know, you can kiss my…," Fox said, rising from his seat, but Fitch placed his hand on Fox's arm and pulled him back down into his chair.

"What are you working up a sweat for, Foxy? They won't find anything we don't want them to see."

Fox and Fitch looked toward one another, although their eyes never met.

Lang was unnerved by Fox's anger. "The Articles of Incorporation documents for Bartlett are what we need to be concerned about. That's why I wanted to talk to you both. But according to you two, we got the documents out and they're safe. Right, Denny?"

Fitch gave a tentative nod. "Yes. I told you that when you asked the first time."

"Hey, and just as a gesture to show you how much I trust you, I'm not even going to ask you where you put them. I'm sure they're in a safe place."

"How gracious of you," Fitch said with a stone-faced expression.

"However, permit me to offer this one caveat." Lang sat back and crossed his legs. "If those documents fall into the wrong hands, you and I both know that it is going to have some very real and extensive implications for some very powerful and prominent people. And once it reaches that point, we're all in trouble. It's every man for himself after that."

Fitch said nothing, nor did Fox.

Lang stood from the table. "Now, if you'll excuse me, gentlemen," he began, as he peeled his coat off the chairback. "I have a train to catch."

The other two men remained seated while Harry Lang immersed himself in the commuter traffic of Union Station.

Chapter 24

▼

Amber had been sitting in the lounge, nestled in the oversized armchair, for almost two hours. She had left her seat only twice—once to request the front desk to assign her to a new room and have her belongings moved, and another to use the ladies room, and that was only because she had been drinking cappuccinos without interruption since she sat down.

The lobby was becoming crowded as a tour group of elderly Americans filed in from a day of sightseeing. They talked loudly and moved in every direction across the lobby floor. The cyclone of activity distracted Amber from concentrating on the front desk. As far as she could determine, the envelope that she had left up there had not been touched. She had been eyeing the three clerks who were on duty, and none of them had picked it up yet.

After half of the tour group had cleared the lobby area and retired to their rooms, the lounge waiter approached Amber to ask if she wanted a refill on her cappuccino. However, the constant tapping of her feet and the fidgeting of her hands were signals to her that she needed to cut off the caffeine stream. The waiter nodded and walked away. As he did, Amber turned toward the front desk and saw one of the clerks standing at the end. For some reason, he didn't seem to fit the clean image of the rest of the employees of the hotel. Despite the uniform, he wore an earring and was unshaven. She noticed a short ponytail when he turned his head to the side. What was even odder was that among the chaos created by the elderly tourists occupying the other clerks, he appeared to be the only one who wasn't particularly busy.

Amber eyed him intensely as he casually meandered toward the end of the desk. She watched as he glanced around him before quickly disappearing through the rear door behind the desk. She left her seat and walked quickly toward the front desk, weaving through the geriatric convention. The polished top of the counter was clean. The envelope was gone. The manager was watching Amber's movements, filled with concern that she might initiate another outburst like the one she had earlier. Amber noticed his concern and quietly slid away from the desk.

From behind her, she heard a familiar voice.

"Yes, are there any messages for me?"

It was Kaitlyn. She was leaning against the front desk, on the other side of the crowd of tourists. She appeared exhausted for the first time since their trip began.

"Kaitlyn," Amber called out as she pressed her way through the group.

"Amber, I thought you'd gone to bed." Kaitlyn accepted a short stack of pages from the clerk.

"I had. But, unfortunately, my bed was covered with my clothes and all my other belongings."

Kaitlyn raised one eyebrow in confusion.

"Someone broke into my room tonight. Turned it upside down."

"What?" Kaitlyn was wide awake now. "Are you OK?"

"I think so. The shock has worn off for the most part. I asked them to…"

Kaitlyn put her hand up. "Hang on." She looked around the desk until her eyes stopped on their target. "Marcelo," she called out and beckoned the manager toward her.

Marcelo dutifully approached them. It was evident by his demeanor just how valuable a client Kaitlyn McBride was to the hotel.

"Si," he said, trepidation filling his voice.

"What happened here tonight?" she asked.

"Signorina calls us this morning and tells us to expect her husband to arrive and to allow him into her room. A gentleman arrives today and says that he is signorina's husband. So, we allow him to her room."

"It wasn't me who called this morning," Amber clarified.

"Well, that's quite clear," Kaitlyn said. "Did they take anything of value?"

"Nothing important. Just my passport. That's all."

"I suppose we should be thankful that you weren't hurt."

Amber felt a light laugh tickling inside her as she thought about the numerous close calls she had managed to elude during the previous month.

"I've asked them to move me to a different room."

"Nonsense, Amber. You'll stay in the suite with me tonight." Kaitlyn turned to the manager, who hadn't dared to move until he was excused. "Marcelo, can you please ensure that Miss Wakefield's belongings are transferred to my room?"

"Yes, at once, signora," he replied, dropping his head slightly in what appeared to be a half bow. He snapped his fingers in the direction of the bell captain and called out an order in Italian. He then turned to Amber. "Please do accept my apologies for the inconvenience."

Amber offered a quick smile, although she felt somewhat guilty about accepting an apology from him. After all, she knew that the invasion of her room had not been the result of inadequate hotel security.

"Thanks, Kaitlyn," Amber said, as they watched Marcelo return to his post behind the desk.

Kaitlyn didn't look directly at Amber when she spoke. "Amber, what's going on?"

"How do you mean?"

Kaitlyn cocked her head to one side. "Your room was the only one that was broken into. And apparently, by someone who knew you were here. This wasn't just a random intrusion, was it?"

"Kaitlyn, I don't know what you're talk—"

"I don't like being lied to, Amber. So, if you're in some kind of trouble, it's probably best that you tell me now."

Amber looked down at the floor. Kaitlyn could see that a tremendous weight was pulling her head down. She put her hand on Amber's arm.

"Let's go upstairs."

The two women walked toward the elevators that led to the suite.

Kaitlyn McBride sat in the Presidential Suite with an astonished look on her face as she listened to Amber tell her story. She hadn't spoken more than three words since Amber had entered her room, bearing the burden of desperation, fear, and exhaustion. Amber kept the details sparse, partly because there were far too many to list but more because of her desire to protect anyone else who might be associated with her. She apologized repeatedly for having taken advantage of Kaitlyn's offer to get herself out of the States and into Europe. But Kaitlyn wouldn't accept the apologies, as they were unnecessary, according to her.

At the mention of Bartlett Enterprises, Kaitlyn showed no reaction. Unfortunately, the name apparently didn't ring a bell for her, despite Amber's explanation that she had seen the Bartlett documents in a file labeled *Ensight* when she was probing Harper Phillips's storage boxes at Jackson Winthrop. If the CEO herself was unaware of any association with Bartlett, there wasn't much hope for Amber to link the two companies.

Kaitlyn remained stoic as she listened, trying to keep the chronology of events in order. Several times she resisted the urge to inquire why Amber felt the compulsion to insert herself further into this dangerous situation. But it was when Amber explained the suspected connection to Marty's death that Kaitlyn's demeanor turned from that of a mentor to that of a mother.

Throughout their conversation, Kaitlyn offered whatever assistance she could provide to Amber, the most vital of which was security. Kaitlyn, not unlike many high-profile CEOs, often traveled with an entourage primarily comprised of highly trained bodyguards. Kaitlyn pledged to Amber that as long as she traveled with her, she would have the benefit of being guarded. She agreed that the most important thing was for Amber to get out of Italy, and out of Europe, for that matter. Although her pursuers could have killed her at any time, they seemed to prefer to instill terror in her, almost teasing her. But as unpredictable as a trained tiger in a circus, these people could decide to finish the job at any moment. So, staying where she was could not be an option. Therefore, they would cut the trip short and fly out the next morning.

Unfortunately, they both knew that without her passport, Amber would not be permitted to leave. Over the years, Kaitlyn had become a regular visitor to Milan and had come to know a number of people in the U.S. Embassy. She dialed a number and listened, while Amber sat patiently on the sofa. She asked for someone whose name Amber didn't catch. After some pleasantries and a few giggles, Kaitlyn placed the receiver back into its cradle.

"It's all set," she told Amber. "First thing tomorrow morning, we'll go the Embassy and pick up your new passport."

Amber exhaled in relief. However, Kaitlyn could detect a sense of apprehension still.

"Don't worry, dear. I'll be with you the whole time, and my security team will be close by as well."

"It's not that, Kaitlyn. I just worry about dragging more people into this."

"Well, don't." Kaitlyn placed her hand on Amber's shoulder. "It sounds like if anyone got dragged into this, it was you. And don't worry about me or anyone else. The team who traveled here with us has been with me for years. Two of them are ex-Secret Service, who served on the president's protection team eight years ago. They're the best."

"If you say so," Amber said with more than a shade of doubt.

Kaitlyn seemed satisfied for the moment that she had restored at least some confidence into her new protégé. But she did not once envy the young woman's situation.

The next morning, Amber awoke to the scents of warm pastries and freshly brewed coffee. She hadn't even stirred at the sound of the room service staff wheeling the cart of breakfast fare into the Presidential Suite. Kaitlyn was on her cell phone talking business with someone. Amber peeked at the clock. 8:45.

"I thought I'd let you sleep in," Kaitlyn said, holding her hand against the phone. She returned to her call and after a few seconds, it ended. She closed the phone and tossed it onto the sofa. Despite the fact that her hair was still damp from the shower, the dressy slacks and blouse she wore were indicators that she had been up for quite some time. People as wealthy and as powerful as Kaitlyn McBride could neither afford nor require much sleep.

"Have something to eat," Kaitlyn told her. "The car is picking us up at 9:30 sharp. Hopefully we can get everything done quickly at the Embassy this morning so we can be in the air before noon."

Amber sat up and rubbed her eyes. She ran her hands through her hair.

"I'm really sorry about all this, Kaitlyn. I feel horrible that you're cutting your trip short on account of me."

"Amber, my travel schedule is usually fraught with unexpected surprises and detours. This is not new to me."

"Well, I'd venture to guess that the surprises that usually interrupt your schedule are the result of different circumstances than mine."

Kaitlyn laughed. "You've certainly got me there. This is a first."

Amber pulled herself off the sofa and poured a cup of coffee. Kaitlyn's phone began to vibrate again, and she promptly picked it up. It was Jamie back in San Francisco with some questions about the quarterly budget. As Kaitlyn walked around the room chatting into the receiver, Amber stacked some fruit and a croissant on a plate and devoured all of it in less than two minutes.

Soon afterwards, Amber stepped into the shower and let the warm water run down her face and her back. She leaned her head against the shower wall and closed her eyes. In her head, a dozen different images from her memory came swirling like a kaleidoscope. She thought about her high school prom, recalling the details of the dress her mother had spent hours at the sewing machine for that night. She remembered the sounds of giggles and the aroma of potpourri and candles in the house in which she lived with her girlfriends while attending St. Mary's College in Moraga. Next was the job interview at Ensight with Marty

Callahan. They met once, and Marty made her an offer the next day. The last image was of her sitting alone, comfortably and calmly in the plush leather seat inside the Gulfstream jet, as it flew over crystal blue waters with no evidence of land anywhere on the horizon. With a smile on her face while the shower continued to run over her, Amber Wakefield stood still with her eyes closed.

Chapter 25

▼

The Reuters newswire broke the story. Of course, the insiders within both companies dismissed it as a mere rumor. According to unnamed sources, the giant Maguire Solutions was reportedly making a bid for the technology company Ensight, Inc. The market responded in the most positive way. The NASDAQ opened that morning up another twenty points. The ticker at the bottom of the CNBC broadcast was lit up with green figures. As was customary, economists and analysts from the top investment banks debated the merits of the deal.

Jack Bennett stepped out of the Westin Palace's business center, a quiet room equipped with internet-ready computers, telephones, and fax machines. He had been waiting for the phone call from Washington, but it hadn't come yet. As he gradually got lost in his thoughts, his heart skipped a beat at the vibrating sensation in his shirt pocket. He pulled out his ringing cell phone and flipped it open, recognizing the number on the display.

"Yeah," he said, barely moving his lips.

"What happened?" asked the voice on the other end.

"She's gone."

"Who's gone?"

"Amber." Jack pinched the bridge of his nose in order to suppress the raging inferno building within him. He took a deep breath and spoke quietly and calmly.

"What happened?" asked the voice.

"Well, I spotted her in the hotel last night. I watched her for quite some time, in fact. And then she disappeared into the elevators with her boss, the Ensight CEO. She must have spent the night in the suite with Ms. McBride. I've been hanging around the hotel since then. But about fifteen minutes ago, I slipped some waiter a hundred euros to go up to the presidential suite. You know, to see if the two ladies looked like they were getting ready to leave."

"And?"

"Well, he just came back down and told me that the room is empty. They're gone."

"Shit," the voice said. "Now what?"

"I'll find her. I think I know how to do it. I'm going to have to dig deep, but it's my last alternative."

He hung up his phone and walked to the front doors of the hotel, where a taxicab was waiting to take him to the airport.

Amber followed Kaitlyn across the tarmac, shielded by a dense curtain of security staff. The trip to the U.S. Embassy had taken less than thirty minutes, after which Amber, Kaitlyn, and her team were whisked away through the rear of the building.

The Gulfstream was waiting for them with the hatch open. The engines were running as they ascended the steps. Before stepping into the aircraft, Amber stopped to turn around. Her eyes slid from side to side, not sure what she was searching for. The only thing competing with her intense paranoia was the uneasy feeling that she hadn't the first idea of what to do when she disembarked from this jet. She turned back toward the doorway and stepped inside.

Amber plopped into her seat and stared out the window. As Kaitlyn gave instructions to her staff and spoke briefly with the crew, Amber silently chastised herself for having pulled another innocent person into the mix. She had made nothing but poor choices over the last few weeks, she acknowledged. She shouldn't have followed Jack to Europe. She shouldn't have lied to Kaitlyn. She shouldn't have followed that courier, a rash choice that eventually got him killed. Her curiosity had evolved into an obsession, she admitted. But she didn't believe that the price of being obsessive should be her own life, or anyone else's for that matter.

She wanted so badly to instruct the pilot to take her back home. Her first home. Her real home. The home where her mother still lived by herself, far from the bustle and backstabbing of the cities. It was a place where families who lived within a five-block radius from one another knew each other by name, and where front doors were left unlocked at night and children played in their front yards and rode their bicycles to and from the park. A lone tear rolled down Amber's cheek as she realized that no such place actually existed anymore, even for her.

Kaitlyn held a tissue in front of Amber's face and sat in the seat next to her. She remained silent for a few minutes, noting that Amber had drifted off somewhere outside the present time and place.

"You're safe now, Amber," she finally said.

Those words had become hollow to Amber over the last few weeks, despite the fact that she wanted so desperately for it to be true.

"But you have to tell someone in authority. I can protect you only in the short term. But for God's sake, you don't even know what you're running from. I want to help you, dear, but I cannot afford to risk the safety of my own staff unless you promise me that you'll take steps to report this."

Amber stared down at her lap. "I don't know who to tell or who to trust."

"Start with the police. Or the FBI. I'll vouch for you. Whatever you tell them, I'll stand behind it. After all, if what you say about this Bartlett organization is true—the fact that it's somehow affiliated with Ensight—well, I think I have a vested interest." Kaitlyn put her hand on Amber's. "But you have to let someone know."

"Do you know anybody at the FBI?"

Kaitlyn shook her head. "The contacts I've accumulated over the years have come primarily as the result of my business dealings. I'm proud to say that the FBI is not on that list. Knock on wood." She chuckled delicately, a futile effort to lighten the mood.

"I'll tell you what," she continued. "I'll have a talk with these guys during the flight." She was referring to the members of her security staff. "I'm certain that more than one of them have friends at the Bureau."

Amber continued to stare forward. "Don't take this the wrong way. But how much do you trust these guys?"

Kaitlyn leaned forward so that her face was only inches from Amber's. "I trust them with my life. I don't think one can trust another any more than that. Wouldn't you agree?"

Amber nodded slowly. "Thanks, Kaitlyn." A hint of a smile touched her face. "For everything."

Kaitlyn smiled back with a maternal expression. "Get some rest." She patted Amber lightly on the knee and stood from her seat.

In five minutes, Amber could hear Kaitlyn jabbering on the phone, setting up her next round of meetings. Back to business. She was right, Amber agreed. She needed help. After all, if Jack Bennett really did work at the FBI at one point, it would not take long for them to find him and put an end to all of this. She finally felt her breathing begin to ease and her heart rate mellowing out. Her eyelids fell heavily, only to be opened abruptly by every rumble in the engine or jostle of the fuselage. Before she was aware that she was falling asleep, they were in the air.

Chapter 26

The hotel desk clerk peeled off the pants and coat of the uniform that he had stolen from the hotel's laundry services and put on over his own clothes. Then he dropped them into a garbage bin near the rear exit. He folded the envelope and deposited it into his own coat pocket before walking out the back of the hotel. Before he reached the train station, he peeled it open and peered inside. He wondered why Amber would have hidden the Bartlett documents inside a folded newspaper. He slowly slid the newspaper out of the envelope and began unfolding it, peeling off layer after layer, only to find more pages of that day's edition. When he reached the last page, he stood motionless in the center of the sidewalk, biting his upper lip. He dropped the newspaper and envelope into a trash bin and glanced down at his fingers, which were blackened by the ink.

He was scheduled to call his boss in Washington in fifteen minutes and would have to tell him that he, a professional, had been taken for a ride by this young woman. He could sense his boss's diminishing faith in his abilities to execute the plan, and it worried him. It wasn't merely the possibility that he might have forfeited his compensation, but that his employer might wish to remove him from the job. Permanently.

"This is not what I signed on for," he muttered to himself.

He yearned for the day that this job would be completed so he could return to being his own boss and to calling all the shots himself. Of course, with respect to this particular job, if he was able to pull off everything he had been hired to do, he'd be able to use the paycheck for a long sabbatical from his profession. He might even be able to live for a little while as himself. And that was far too appealing a prospect to walk away from at this point.

The man took a cab to a small building, where he walked up the steps to a small studio apartment. Quickly stepping to a small table where a laptop computer was cabled into the wall, he tapped in a few commands and soon found himself staring at the log-on screen for the Ensight system administrators. Entering the password and navigating to the employee account section, where all the Ensight employees log-on IDs were stored, he scrolled down until he found the name he was searching for: *Jamie Atwater, Executive Assistant to the CEO*. Tightening the rubber band on his ponytail, he typed her log-on ID, entered the skeleton password reserved exclusively for system administrators, and moved the cursor to Jamie's calendar, aware that all executive assistants maintained the calendars of the officers they supported. He pulled down the menu and found the item labeled *Kaitlyn's Calendar*.

As he had anticipated, the CEO's schedule was filled most days with appointments and meetings from seven in the morning until nine in the evening. Including weekends. Some time slots had up to four entries in them. He slid his cursor to the current day. It showed a relatively clean slate, which he found surprising. He closed the calendar but inadvertently clicked on the link to Jamie's e-mail inbox. He immediately went to exit but stopped as he noticed a number of recent messages from Kaitlyn. All of them had been sent that morning, and none were more eye-catching than the one entitled *AGENDA CHANGE*. It had been sent only hours ago. He opened it and read to himself.

> *Jamie—as I told you on the phone this morning, we are cutting our trip a bit short. Please move my staff meeting up to tomorrow morning, since we will be arriving back in SF tonight.*
>
> *Rgds,*
> *KM*

He smiled broadly. "Gotcha," he said.

He pulled out his phone and after inserting the ear bud in his ear, he hit a single digit on the keypad. Harry Lang picked up on the other end.

"Did you get it?" he asked, disregarding any need to exchange greetings.

"Well…"

"You fucked it up, didn't you?" Lang asked with certainty in his voice.

"I wouldn't say that," he tried to explain.

"Really? I would. You would have no other reason to call me."

"True. I didn't get the documents you were looking for. She duped me."

"Oh, *she* duped *you*? Well, that's comforting to know that a professional identity thief got schooled by a young girl," Lang mocked.

"It wasn't quite like that. She did leave the package as we instructed her to. Only she stuffed a newspaper into the envelope instead."

"Clever gal. She's got bigger balls than you. Maybe I should ask her to finish this job for me, since she seems to be better at this than you."

"Fuck you!"

"Pay mind to who you're talking to," Lang shot back. "You work for me. Remember? And I've been less than impressed thus far. If you don't like the way I talk to you, then we can put an end to this right now. You can go back to your old life. Of course, that will mean that I may have to carry out my duties as a federal investigator against you."

"OK, I get the message. But just so you know, she'll be in San Francisco tonight."

"And just how the hell do you know that?"

The man reached back with one hand to adjust the rubber band holding his ponytail. "Well, I knew she was out here traveling with her boss on business. So, I checked her boss's schedule through the company's network. She has a meeting in San Fran tomorrow morning."

"Impressive, I suppose," Lang said, hiding his admiration.

"I was planning to get on the next flight out there."

"Not so fast," Lang cut in. "You have more important things to accomplish out there. In case you're forgetting, there is still money to be retrieved. That was your original mission. Don't lose sight of your priorities."

"Then what about the girl? She could still cause problems."

"That's my concern. You're not being paid to speculate. You're being paid to follow my instructions."

The man gritted his teeth, trapping the words in his mouth which he was so tempted to say.

"You're the boss," he said.

On the next morning, he left the apartment and walked back in the direction of the train station. As he strolled through the plaza, he passed two men holding a map and pointing in opposite directions. The cameras hanging around their necks spelled *tourists*. He didn't notice them watching him as he picked up his pace and dialed numbers into his cell phone.

Special Agent Griffin removed the sunglasses from his face and spoke to his partner.

"That's him, for sure," he said.

"Should we pick him up?" asked his younger partner.

Griffin shook his head. "We need to get the green light from Lang."

The two men watched as their subject continued walking with his phone to his ear. The younger man pulled off his hat and scratched his head.

"What do you think he was doing at the Westin?" he asked.

"What can I say, the guy likes to stay in nice places. After all, it's not his money, right?"

"I don't think he's in Milan to pull out any money, Griff."

"Why do you say that?"

"We canvassed every bank in this city. None of them show any evidence of an account belonging to any Harper Phillips."

Griffin shrugged. "So, maybe he's taking a little break. Even thieves deserve a vacation in a luxury hotel," he said with a smile.

"And do they generally leave through the rear employee exit?"

The corners of Griffin's mouth flattened, as his smile faded. "*Touché.*"

The two FBI agents began walking through the plaza, maintaining a safe distance behind their target. The younger man dialed, and then handed the phone to Griffin.

"Yes, sir, it's Griffin. We're in Frankfurt right now," he said into the receiver.

The younger man turned to him quickly, his face contorted in confusion. Griffin noticed and held an index finger up to his partner with the universal signal that he would explain later.

"We think he's in Italy somewhere, but we're not sure."

He listened into the phone some more.

"Yes, sir. We'll find him." He ended the call.

He looked at his partner, who stood in front of him with his palms facing the sky. "What the hell was that?"

"Something's not right. I want to know why this fella is in this city. We're not leaving until we find out."

"But why did you lie to the big man?" asked the younger agent, who would never have thought about deceiving Harry Lang.

"If he knows we're this close to nabbing our guy, he won't hesitate to send out a team of reinforcements."

"So?"

"I want more time. You and I are going to blow this investigation open. Whatever this guy is doing in Milan, I can guarantee you that it's not legal, but I'll bet you it's spicy. I can also promise you that Deputy Director Lang will be pleasantly surprised if we bring him more dirt to nail this guy on. We're not sharing the glory on this one."

The young agent smiled in agreement.

"You keep an eye on that guy," Griffin instructed, pointing toward the moving ponytail. "Don't lose him, but more importantly, keep your distance. If he looks like he's relocating, ping me immediately."

"Got it. What are you going to do?"

"I'm going back to the hotel to do some of that detective stuff we always read about," Griffin replied, smiling giddily. "We'll meet back here in the plaza at six o'clock sharp."

"Six o'clock," his young partner confirmed.

"Now go."

The two men parted ways, and in less than a minute, they were no longer within sight of one another.

Special Agent Griffin walked through the lobby of the Westin Palace and approached the reception desk. Still clad in his tourist attire, he blended in nicely with another tour group, this time from Amsterdam, who was boarding a luxury bus in front of the hotel.

"Yes signor, how may I assist you?" asked the young brunette behind the desk.

"I'm looking for the hotel manager," Griffin said in a quiet voice.

"May I ask what this is regarding?"

"It's an official matter," he replied, displaying his badge.

The young woman backed away from the desk, not sure what the badge represented. She turned to her fellow clerk and mumbled something in Italian. In a few seconds, the other clerk returned from the back, with the manager closely in tow.

"Yes, I am Marcelo, signor." He reached his hand out. "How may I help you, Mr...," he began, looking at the badge that Griffin still held in front of him, "Griffin."

"I'm a special agent with the United States Federal Bureau of Investigation," Griffin replied, shaking the manager's hand.

"The FBI?" Marcelo asked.

"That's correct. I'm looking for a guest at this hotel."

"I'm terribly sorry, Mr. Griffin. I cannot provide that information to anyone."

"I'm not just anyone. I told you that I'm with the FBI, and this is part of an investigation."

"But you are in Italy. Not inside the United States. So, you are a bit outside of your jurisdiction, no? Therefore, you are the same as anyone," Marcelo said proudly.

"Listen, there is a man staying here by the name of Harper Phillips. His crimes are…"

Marcelo held up a hand to interrupt. "I'm sorry. Harper Phillips, you say?"

"Yes, you know the man?" Griffin noticed the recognition in the manager's tone.

"Si. He came yesterday afternoon. He told us that his wife was staying here."

Griffin looked at Marcelo strangely. "His wife?"

"Well, we learned that it was not in fact his wife. He stole some items from the woman's room," Marcelo explained, still embarrassed by the incident.

"What woman?" Griffin's head was spinning.

"The young woman traveling with Signora McBride," Marcelo explained matter-of-factly.

"McBride," Griffin repeated quietly to himself, shaking his head at the lack of recognition.

"Si, they departed this morning."

"Can you describe this man?" Griffin asked.

Marcelo shrugged. "I don't remember his face well. All that I recall is his hair."

Griffin nodded slowly. The most distinguishing characteristic of the man he had been tailing was his hair.

"Short. Like a military man," Marcelo continued with his description.

At that, Griffin stopped nodding. "Are you certain that he had short hair?"

"Si. Very short."

As the two men continued to talk, Griffin pictured the ponytail swinging behind the head of the man whom he and his partner had just seen a short while earlier in the plaza. He was on his cell phone in seconds.

"Yeah," answered his young partner.

"He broke into some girl's room here," Griffin explained.

"What girl?"

"That's what we need to find out. It's bad enough that this guy's stealing someone's money, but if there are innocent bystanders in danger, we'll need to step up our efforts."

"Are there witnesses?"

"Yes," Griffin began. "Well, actually, no one really saw the break-in occur. But apparently it was a pretty big deal. I guess the girl was traveling with the CEO of Ensight, Kaitlyn McBride."

"Don't know her," the younger man said. "But it doesn't sound like a random robbery."

"Hell, no. The hotel manager said that a man by the name of Harper Phillips came to the hotel yesterday in search of this girl. It wasn't a random incident. He knew who she was."

There was silence on the line, which indicated to Griffin that his young partner was awaiting instructions. Griffin broke the silence abruptly.

"There's something else that's a little off."

Another brief silence. "Yeah?" asked the young man.

"The hotel manager insists that the guy he saw had short hair. Like a crew cut. Doesn't exactly sound like our guy."

"I'm sure he was confused. He probably sees hundreds of people come in and out of there each day."

"I don't know," Griffin replied with a doubtful tone. "With as much of a ruckus as this thing created yesterday, I would think he'd remember the details pretty well."

"Do you know anything about this girl?"

"Yes. She's the assistant to Kaitlyn McBride. That's about it," Griffin said, recalling the manager's account of the previous day's events.

"So, what next?"

"We'll need to split up. The boss won't like it, but we'll cover more ground this way. I'll hang back here and follow our ponytailed friend," Griffin said. "The boss will be calling me, so I should stay with the subject."

"And what do you want me to do?" his partner asked.

"You find her. She clearly has something or knows something that's very valuable. Something about this fella with the crew cut." Griffin cleared his throat. "We'll start with Kaitlyn McBride. My guess is that she's pretty prominent since she stayed in the presidential suite. Find out where she is now." Griffin paused for another few seconds. "We find her, we find the girl."

Chapter 27

The afternoon in San Francisco was warm, and the sky was clear—a perfect climate for a Gulfstream jet to land. As they made their approach, the city looked gigantic with its recognizable skyline in full view from the cockpit. However, from Amber's seat, the city seemed smaller than she remembered, with fewer corners to hide in. She felt more like a visitor with an uncertain agenda rather than a resident returning home.

Kaitlyn already had the phone to her ear by the time the aircraft touched down. She was talking to Jamie and issuing orders at a rapid pace. It may just have been her subconscious, but Amber swore she had heard Kaitlyn's voice chatting away throughout the entire flight. As she watched the CEO of Ensight on the phone, it didn't seem so farfetched an idea that Kaitlyn hadn't slept a wink during the flight.

The women crawled into the back seat of the black limousine, and as the doors shut, the noise and daylight from the outside world were sucked dry as a vacuum. Kaitlyn finished her phone call and tossed the phone onto the leather seat in front of her.

"So," she said, taking a deep breath as she turned toward Amber.

"So," Amber repeated.

"Do you have somewhere to stay tonight?"

"Maybe I'll just sleep under my desk in the office."

"I'll pay you overtime."

The two women laughed.

"Now, about what we discussed before we left Milan," Kaitlyn began, quickly altering the relaxed atmosphere within the limo. She handed a slip of paper to Amber. "Here is a list of names of people in the San Francisco office of the FBI."

Amber took the paper and studied.

"Talk to these people," Kaitlyn continued. "They can help you."

Amber nodded. "I will. I promise."

The limousine pulled up in front of the Ensight offices. As the two women rode the elevator to the top floor where the executive offices were located, Kaitlyn told Amber to wait for her in her office. When they emerged from the elevator, Kaitlyn quickly disappeared, wasting no time to catch up with each of her lieutenants.

Amber sat in Kaitlyn's corner office, staring out the large window overlooking the bay. Kaitlyn's office exuded an image that mirrored her own. The glass desk and black leather chair emitted an aura of power and influence. However, the softer undertones of the floral arrangements and framed, colored prints on the walls reminded those who entered that a woman occupied the office. The stark contrast and her ability to balance the two perceptions impressed Amber. But the office was also a reminder of what an enigma Kaitlyn was.

Kaitlyn's voice could be heard faintly down the hall as she exchanged updates with her staff. Amber's eyes wandered aimlessly around the office. The desk was neatly organized with numerous stacks of papers across the top. She focused her eyes on a few of the pages and skimmed what was legible. Her eyes stopped moving when they fell across the name *Maguire Solutions* on one of the pages. She looked to the doorway, which was still empty, and she could still hear Kaitlyn's voice down the hall. Before she knew it, her fingers were flipping through the stack.

"Eh-hem," came a clearing of the throat. Amber immediately looked up and saw Jamie standing in the doorway with her hands on her hips.

"Hey, Amber," she said as she walked into the office. "What are you doing?"

"I know what this looks like, Jamie," Amber replied. "I was just being nosy."

"Obviously," Jamie said smugly. Apparently, she was aware that Kaitlyn had taken Amber under her wing, a position that Jamie had hoped to occupy instead. She made her way toward the desk, and specifically to the stack of papers that she had seen Amber thumbing through.

"This is highly confidential stuff," she said as she collected the papers and moved them to a separate section of the desk.

"I know. I really didn't see much, anyway."

"Uh-huh," Jamie said bitterly.

Amber watched her movements and sensed the animosity. "Listen, Jamie, I hope there are no hard feelings about my coming to work for Kaitlyn."

Jamie shrugged in an effort to communicate her disappointment.

"Besides, I'll need you to help me out. I'm sure there are a lot of things about Kaityln that you'll have to coach me on."

Jamie smiled slightly. She hadn't thought of it that way. "That's true, I suppose." As she turned to exit the office, she stopped. "Kaitlyn told me to tell you to wait here for her."

After she left, Amber took a seat in one of the large chairs in front of the desks. She breathed a sigh of relief that Jamie hadn't known or asked how many of those pages she had actually read. According to the few sentences she had been able to scan, Maguire and Ensight were getting very serious about their merger plans. There was the mention of a due diligence of Ensight's financials in the coming days. She also saw a term sheet in the pile. The last thing she saw were two words written in the margins in pencil: *Damage control.* She knew the comment wasn't meant for her eyes nor for anyone else's who wasn't in the upper stratum of the company. This was probably considered to be insider information, although she admitted that she wouldn't know what to do with it even if she wanted to profit from it. But it sounded like whoever wrote the phrase in the margin was urging something unethical. Amber wasn't naïve enough to believe that the company was run by noble do-gooders. But she was quickly reminded of the explosion of corporate scandals like those at Enron and WorldCom, and a sudden rush went through her. It wasn't fear or disdain. It was sheer excitement. *How shameless of me*, she thought.

Amber picked up the telephone on Kaitlyn's desk—the type with dozens of buttons on it—and dialed her own voice mail service. There were no messages, which surprised her, considering that she had been away for several days. She wanted to call her mother because weeks had passed since Amber had talked to her. She didn't want the older woman to completely forget about her as her condition declined. What had become an all too familiar sense of loneliness for Amber was gradually becoming more than just a feeling. It had become a reality.

From her chair, she perused the walls of Kaitlyn's office. There was her diploma from New York University. She had graduated with an art history major, which Amber would never have guessed. To the right, was her MBA diploma from Northwestern's Kellogg School of Business. There were a number of photographs in decorative frames on the desk and in the bookcase against the wall. They were all snapshots of Kaitlyn standing next to or among a group of men. Probably foreign diplomats and politicians, Amber imagined. And the fact that Kaitlyn was the only woman in all of these photographs almost appeared to be the result of a conscious effort. Amber suddenly realized how different she was from Kaitlyn. Despite the fun they had enjoyed at their dinner on the first night in Milan, they had come from very different worlds, and Amber knew that there was a limit to how close they could ever become. But at least she trusted Kaitlyn, which was more than she could say about most of the people to whom she had allowed herself to get close recently. And that included Marty. Kaitlyn had offered her opportunity and safety, and she had delivered on both of those promises.

With the hum of executive voices in the hallway, Amber looked out of the large window that surrounded the doorway, from the floor to the ceiling in a single piece of glass. She could see Jamie typing away at her desk and answering phone calls, no doubt taking messages from the throngs of people who tried to reach the CEO on a daily basis. She estimated Jamie to be in her mid-twenties, maybe only a couple of years younger than herself. During her time at Ensight, Amber had never said more than a few words to Jamie, in the halls, in the elevator, at the Christmas parties.

She walked out of the office and approached Jamie's desk. Jamie held her index finger up to wait, chatting on the phone while scrolling through Kaitlyn's calendar on her computer screen. She hit a button on the phone and pulled her headset off.

"What's up?" she asked, looking up at Amber.

"What are you doing tomorrow night?"

Jamie shrugged. "I don't know. I was planning to go to the gym tomorrow after work."

"Can I join you? I thought it might give us a chance to catch up. You can bring me up to speed on all I need to know about our mutual boss."

"Sure," replied Jamie, with an air of indifference.

It was eight o'clock by the time Jamie and Amber left the gym located on the basement floor of their office building. All Ensight employees were given substantial discounts at the gym, and it was usually crowded during the week. Jamie and Amber had spent twenty minutes on the treadmill before calling it quits. They showered and walked out of the gym together and agreed to get a bite to eat at Chaya. On their way out of the building, Jamie stopped in front of the elevators.

"I need to run upstairs to get my laptop. I forgot to pack it."

"I'll just wait for you down here," Amber said.

"OK, I'll be only a minute," Jamie called back as she entered the elevator.

Amber sat patiently in the lobby, considering the conversation she had just had with Jamie in the gym. In that brief time, Jamie rattled off a list of likes and dislikes of the CEO, in an effort to coach Amber. Contrary to Jamie's initial chilliness toward Amber's new role, she seemed to be willing to help. Amber reminded herself to thank Jamie when she returned.

While waiting, Amber did her best to make small talk with the security guard, a short African-American woman whose uniform was stretched to its maximum potential around her ample body. Amber listened to the woman's complaints about everything that was wrong in her life. She bitched incessantly about her lazy replacement who had been scheduled to relieve her a half hour before. The shift change never occurred on time. At least not while she was on duty, she insisted. The bastard had gone upstairs to get a cup of coffee from one of the break rooms before his shift began.

"Lazy fucker," she hissed over and over.

Thirty-four floors above the lobby where Amber stood talking to the guard, Jamie emerged from the elevator. She walked toward her desk quickly. Only the emergency lights were on, which always freaked her out. There was no one home on the floor that housed the company's top executives. And why would there be? It was after six o'clock, and virtually everyone who worked on this floor had likely left not long after that time. She unlocked the security cable to her laptop and undocked the machine. She shoved it into the leather carrying case and began walking toward the elevators. The sound of something crashing loudly in the break room made her jump. Jamie looked down the hallway and the fluorescent light of the break room cast a spotlight on the dark gray carpet.

"Hello?" she called out.

"Hello?" came a man's voice in the break room.

A head peered around the corner, and as he stepped out, she could see the security guard's blue uniform. He was clearly off duty, as was evidenced by the fact that he had already removed the necktie which was part of the uniform.

"Sorry, I dropped the coffee pot. I didn't mean to scare you there," he said, holding his hands up.

"Not a problem," Jamie replied. "I just get a little freaked out up here when the lights go down."

"Well, that's why we're here," he said, as he patted himself dry with a paper towel. "For whatever that's worth," he added.

Jamie laughed. "A pretty long trip for a cup of coffee, isn't it? I mean, there's a break room on the third floor too."

"Yeah, I tried. They were out."

After an awkward second, Jamie turned toward the elevators. "Well, have a nice night."

"Same to you."

As she waited for the elevator to climb to the top floor, she could hear the jangling of keys coming down the hall. The security guard appeared in the elevator foyer.

"Thought I'd ride down with you, if that's okay," he said.

Jamie's lips curled into a half smile. "Sure."

The two entered the elevator and the doors closed.

"So you work on this floor?" he asked.

"Uh-huh." Jamie loathed small talk.

"You're Ms. McBride's assistant, aren't you?"

Jamie looked at the guard. "Yes, how did you—"

He pulled the emergency stop button on the panel. The elevator jolted as it suspended itself between the twenty-sixth and twenty-seventh floors. "So sorry to hear that," he cut her off.

Jamie shrieked. "What the—'"

Before she knew it, a cold, silver blade was being held against the bottom of her chin.

"Where are the documents?" he said into her ear. His breath smelled of day-old coffee.

"What documents?" Jamie pleaded. "Please, I don't know what you want." Tears dangled from her bottom eyelashes.

"You know what I'm talking about, you little bitch!" He pressed the knife deeper into her flesh, resisting with difficulty the urge to cut her skin. "I saw you in Switzerland with that little faggoty courier. He gave you something, and now I want it."

Jamie's eyes darted from left to right. "Switzerland? Is this about the Maguire deal?"

"Now we're speaking the same language," he said, taking a sip from the Styrofoam cup.

Jamie found it difficult to speak without taking a breath between syllables.

"It's up-stairs. In Kait-lyn's of-fice. On the desk." She was bawling now.

The guard stroked her hair lightly, then suddenly tugged her head back. She screamed again. He moved close to her so that his lips touched her ear with each word.

"Thank you, Amber. Thank you," he whispered.

Jamie stopped her crying as he shifted so that they were now eye to eye. She shook her head.

"But I'm not…" she started to say, but her voice box had already been compromised.

He slid the knife laterally across her neck in a single motion, as though he was underlining a sentence on a chalkboard. Jamie fell to her knees, her hands clutching the open wound, as dark blood leaked between her slim fingers. He watched her struggle on the floor of the elevator.

The guard dipped the blade into his coffee cup. The light brown tint of the coffee immediately showed swirls of dark crimson. Leaving the cup beside Jamie's body, he climbed through the emergency hatch in the ceiling of the elevator car, pried open the doors to the twenty sixth floor, and hoisted himself into the elevator foyer. Another elevator with open doors was empty across the way, and he entered it. As he rode up toward the thirty-fourth floor again, Jamie Atwater lay still in the opposite elevator. With her eyes still eerily open, one last tear dropped into the pool of blood expanding around her.

Chapter 28

Amber looked at her watch for the fourth time in three minutes. Jamie had been upstairs for what seemed like an eternity. Of course, listening to the bitter security guard spew complaints was making the time go by even more slowly. As she listened to the woman talk about her hellish bus ride to work that morning, the bell from the elevator rang out. *Thank God*, Amber mouthed to herself.

The guard immediately rose from her seat behind the desk.

"Somfabitch, it's about time," she muttered as she walked toward the elevators. "Hey, where'd you go to get yo' damn coffee? Colombia? I was supposed to be home by now. I ain't gettin' paid no overtime in this joint," she shouted.

A second went by, and then Amber heard it—a scream so loud and high-pitched that the grout between the marble tiles on the floor practically buckled. Amber walked, but didn't run, toward the elevators. She saw the security guard standing in front of the service elevator, her hands covering her open mouth.

"What is it?" Amber asked, moving forward as the woman's finger remained pointed at the open elevator car.

The woman couldn't speak but only pointed her finger toward the inside of the elevator. Amber finally arrived next to her and looked into the elevator. She pushed the woman's arm down slowly as a cascade of hot blood rushed through her body. The slender man sitting in the corner, clad in only a white undershirt and blue boxer shorts, with his head slumped forward, could not have been older than twenty-five. The black necktie of his uniform was tied tightly around his thin neck, and pink bruises were already beginning to show. His assailant had probably killed him with a single jerk of the necktie around the poor kid's windpipe.

"Where the hell is his clothes?" the woman asked.

"Call the police," Amber told her. The woman was still standing motionless, obviously in shock. "Right now!"

The woman ran off in the direction of the front desk. Amber tilted her head back and watched the numbers above all of the elevators.

"Jamie," she whispered to herself.

Within six minutes, five police cars had arrived at the front of the Ensight building. As the officers entered the lobby, Amber could overhear one of them talking to the others.

"This is the same location as that car blast last month. Remember?" he said. The others acknowledged his observation.

Amber stood by the elevators, gnawing on her thumbnail. She noted that one of the elevators had been stuck on the twenty-sixth floor for quite some time. At this hour, with as few employees as there were still in the building, all the elevators were either on the lobby level or moving. An uneasy sensation filled her stomach.

One of the officers who had been talking to the still-shaken security guard walked past Amber and spoke in a low voice to the lieutenant in charge.

"We're pretty sure he's still in the building," he said.

The other one waved the rest of the group over. "The subject is in the building. Seal the exits. Now," he ordered. The other officers sprinted off in separate directions, each barking commands into their radios, as the sounds of sirens became louder outside.

Amber stopped the officer who had just issued the order.

"My friend is upstairs somewhere. I think something might have happened to her."

"We're going to check every floor, ma'am," he said, placing a reassuring hand on her shoulder. "But we are going to ask you to step out of the building at this moment. This is now a crime scene. We'll handle it from here on."

Amber walked reluctantly out the front doors of the lobby, with the security guard in tow. An officer standing outside the building escorted the two women across the street. During the next few minutes, small groups of people emerged from the building in response to the police efforts to evacuate the premises. Amber eyed the people closely, searching desperately for Jamie, but couldn't find her.

As her eyes moved upward toward the top floor of the building, where the Ensight executive offices were located, her attention was immediately drawn to the screaming sirens and screeching rubber tires on the pavement. At the precise moment the ambulance came to a halt in front of the entrance, a black Mercedes SL 500 pulled up to the front of the building and stopped in the red fire zone. Kaitlyn stepped out of the driver's seat and walked rapidly toward the building entrance, buttoning the jacket of her Armani suit as she moved. Apparently, style and appearance were not to be forfeited in any situation. She was alone, without her customary blanket of security.

From Amber's vantage point, she could see Kaitlyn immediately gathering information from the police officers who had all gravitated toward her as she entered the doors. Amber ran across the street and reentered the office building.

"Kaitlyn!" she called out.

Kaitlyn turned and excused herself from the group of police officers.

"Amber, what are you doing here?"

"I was working out at the gym with Jamie."

"Where is Jamie?" she asked.

"She went upstairs about twenty minutes ago to get her computer. But she never came back down."

Kaitlyn stared forward, her eyes concerned. "Did you see anything? I mean, anything out of the ordinary."

Amber shook her head. "No. Nothing."

The two women watched as one of the police officers who had come from the direction of the elevators approached his superior. They spoke in whispers and pointed in different directions as they talked. The older officer nodded and turned toward them.

"Miss McBride, would you mind coming with me?" he asked politely.

Kaitlyn followed him, and Amber stayed on her boss's heels. As they turned the corner, Kaitlyn moved forward toward a crowd of paramedics and police officers, while Amber hung back and watched anxiously. Kaitlyn stood in front of the open elevator car, stunned. It wasn't the same car that had held the strangled security guard. It was the car that she had seen stopped on the twenty-sixth floor. The crime scene investigators were snapping pictures and taking prints. Amidst the flashes popping from the cameras and the constant hum of conversations, Amber could vaguely make out what the police lieutenant was saying to Kaitlyn.

"You know her?" he asked.

Kaitlyn nodded. "Yes. Her name is Jamie Atwater."

"And she works in this building?"

"She's my assistant." Her voice faded a bit with these last few words.

The lieutenant stared at his shoes, not quite sure how long he should respect the silence. Finally, he cleared his throat. "Does she have any family we can call?"

Kaitlyn shook her head. "I'm not sure. I mean, I don't know if they're in this area." She put her hand on her forehead and the other on her hip. "How could something like this happen?"

The lieutenant glanced around in the hope that someone or something might pull him away from this woman and her rhetorical question. "Miss McBride, given the recent history of incidents that have occurred on these premises during the past several weeks, I'm going to advise that additional security be posted in and outside the building on a twenty-four hour basis. I realize it's a bit intrusive to your business environment, but we'd prefer to err on the side of caution. Do you have any objections to this?"

Kaitlyn shook her head again. "None."

After the lieutenant stepped away, Amber placed her hand on Kaitlyn's arm. "Kaitlyn, I am so sorry."

"It's not your fault, Amber," Kaitlyn answered as she walked away.

Amber watched her from behind. "Right," she said to herself.

The news broke that evening and early the next morning about the tragic deaths of a security guard and a young executive assistant at Ensight, Inc. It was the second such incident in as many months at the company. The stock opened the next morning down twelve points and continued to slide throughout late morning trading, as a frenzy of short selling ensued among hedge fund managers and other investors. At the request of the CEO, the company shut down operations in its San Francisco headquarters the day after the incident so that employees could seek grievance counseling throughout the weekend.

By the time Monday rolled around, the Ensight building had been converted into a forensic laboratory. Despite the beefed-up armed security around the building that morning, less than a third of the employees showed up for work, and those that did, trickled in throughout the morning. Even Kaitlyn herself canceled her early morning meetings and arrived at work shortly after nine o'clock. Her eyes were red and swollen, no doubt from lack of sleep.

Amber, who had spent the night at the Park Hyatt, had managed only two uninterrupted hours of sleep. She slept with the lights on inside the room and with the television on. At six o'clock that morning, she took a taxicab to the office. There was yellow caution tape around two of the elevators, with two armed officers standing in front to protect the crime scene. Amber sat in Kaitlyn's office for the next few hours, facing the large window. The morning fog was still dense and hung low under the dark sky of the city. Ironically, sitting there in the large executive office felt like the safest place to be.

Lost in her thoughts, she didn't know Kaitlyn had entered the office, and Kaitlyn made no attempt to call her attention away from the window. Amber spun around in her chair when she heard the thud of Kaitlyn's briefcase on her desk.

"Kaitlyn," she said.

"Amber," Kaitlyn acknowledged. "I'm surprised to see you here."

"Why's that?"

"Thursday night's events apparently scared everyone else off from coming in today. I can't say I blame any of them. I considered staying away myself." Her voice was hoarse and exhausted.

Amber watched as Kaitlyn fumbled around her desk, her eyes wandering the surface. She stood behind the desk with her hands on her hips, her eyes still moving side to side.

"Are you looking for something?" Amber asked.

"There were some documents here last week that I needed to review. Jamie said that she had left them for me," she said, with her hand on an empty area on the corner of the desk.

Amber recognized immediately that the area was the same one that had been occupied by the pages she had thumbed through the day before. Something about the Maguire deal. *Damage control*, she recalled.

"What was it?" she asked.

"Just some information regarding the merger."

"Am I to take it that the merger with Maguire is going through as planned?"

Kaitlyn looked up from her desk. "That information doesn't leave this floor. Is that understood?"

"Absolutely," Amber assured her.

"There's enough speculation going on out there as it is. I don't want to be responsible for leaking any information prematurely. I shouldn't be telling you this much, but now that Jamie's gone, I need someone to pick up where she…" Her voice drifted off.

"I understand, Kaitlyn. You don't need to say any more." Amber watched as Kaitlyn attempted to maintain a businesslike demeanor, but it was obvious that the woman was distracted.

"By the way, have you called those contacts at the FBI that I provided to you?" she asked.

"Not yet. I haven't had time. We just got back a few days ago, and with all the stuff that's been going on…"

Kaitlyn exhaled loudly, almost obnoxiously. "I thought I told you not to wait." Her tone was firm, with a touch of disapproval. "I wasn't going to bring it up, but what happened here last week was no random murder. It was clearly premeditated."

"Do you think it had something to do with my situation?"

"Yes, I do. And I think you think so as well."

"Kaitlyn, I don't want you to blame me for what happened."

"I don't. But when I asked you to talk to someone, I meant immediately. I promised to help you, but I have a greater obligation to this company, its board of directors, the shareholders, many of whom have run for the hills recently. The Maguire deal is going to be in jeopardy, no doubt."

Amber took all the words in. "I guess I never considered how many people would be affected by this. But I didn't ask to be in this mess."

"I'm not suggesting that, Amber. But the fact is that you are. And despite what you think, it's not a hopeless situation. Get some help. I don't want to see anyone else get hurt. Especially you." Kaitlyn managed a quick smile to let her young protégé know that she was still on her side.

"I just know that if I could find out what this Bartlett organization is all about, it might clear things up."

"Amber, I'm serious about this. Stop trying to play detective. You're risking a tremendous amount. Call those people," Kaitlyn demanded.

"I will. I'll take care of it today."

"Good." Kaitlyn sat in her chair and picked up her phone. "Now, if you don't mind, I have a million calls I have to return, and even more people to try and calm."

Amber turned and walked out of the office. She took the elevator down to the floor where her desk was located, since she hadn't yet moved to the executive floor. She flipped through her day planner and found the slip of paper that Kaitlyn had given to her upon their return. There were two names that Kaitlyn's security personnel had referred her to at the FBI. Amber picked up her phone and dialed the number beside the first name. She listened to it ring four times before a woman picked up. Amber asked to speak to the first name that appeared on the piece of paper, which happened to be the special agent in charge of the San Francisco field division. Her conversation with him was brief, but pleasant, and he seemed willing to help her, largely due to her association with Kaitlyn McBride and more importantly, with her security staff. Evidently, there was a fraternal bond among former and current Secret Service personnel, which fortunately worked to Amber's advantage, as she was able to get through directly to the head of the field division. He invited Amber to come to the FBI offices in San Francisco on the following morning.

She hung up the phone and stood up from her desk. She opened the glass door to Marty's office and stepped in, leaving the lights off. There was still a slight hint of his cologne in the air. She sat in his chair and reclined backwards, much in the way Marty used to do when he was talking on the phone. She ran her hands across the top of his desk and noticed a couple of coffee ring stains in the corner. At the front edge of the desk was a business card holder, with a few cards in the cradle. She pinched the card between her fingers and read the black letters: *Martin Callahan, Senior Vice President, Human Resources.* Her lips trembled. She missed him. She missed him terribly. And she needed him now more than ever.

Chapter 29

Bruce Fox stepped into the lobby of the St. Regis and removed his sunglasses. He walked toward the lounge and found Harry Lang sitting on one of the sofas, with *The Wall Street Journal* held up so that his vision was obstructed. A sweaty glass of scotch rested on the small table in front of him, and Fox held strong doubts that it was the first of the day. There was a small rolling suitcase resting on the floor next to Lang.

Fox made his way slowly toward the deputy director, almost feeling the dense layer of arrogance and self-importance that Lang wore proudly.

"Want a drink?" Lang asked from behind the newspaper.

Fox rested his finger atop the paper so that it folded in the middle. Lang's eyes watched as whatever he was reading crumpled from view. "No, thanks."

"Sit down."

Fox sank slowly into the chair adjacent to the sofa. "Why are we meeting down here and not in the suite?"

"I don't have much time. I'm headed out West for a week, and my flight leaves in a couple of hours."

"Where are you going?" Fox asked, looking down at the suitcase.

"Well, not that it's any of your concern, but I have some meetings in LA and Denver. Official FBI business."

"So, what do you have to tell me?"

"The Maguire-Ensight deal is stalled. Serves us well, don't you think?"

"Why is it on hold?" Fox asked, his voice falling quieter.

"After what happened last week at the Ensight headquarters, the folks on both sides of the deal are in somewhat of a fluster." Lang took a long swig from his glass.

"And you swear that you had nothing to do with what happened?"

"I already told you so. I'm not going to say it again." Lang shifted in his seat and crossed his legs. "Besides, why would I go after the CEO's assistant? I didn't even know this Jamie gal or this CEO chick."

Fox considered this and acknowledged that his question did seem illogical. Lang sat forward and held the *Journal* in front of him.

"Have you seen this?" he asked, tapping his finger on one of the columns on the front page.

"What am I looking at here?" Fox asked.

"There's a rumor going around that someone connected to the Maguire camp orchestrated the murder."

"What? That's absurd." Fox said, shaking his head.

"I'm sure it was the brainchild of some eager beaver in the media trying to make a name for himself," said Lang. "In any case, it suggests that this incident, coupled with Marty Callahan's limousine cookout, will scare a lot of folks into questioning the security and stability of Ensight. Particularly shareholders."

"And why would Maguire want to sabotage its own deal?"

"It wouldn't be sabotage. If you paid any attention, you'd notice that Ensight's stock price has been on a downward tumble recently. Well, this latest event sent it into a vertical nosedive."

Fox finally got it as he listened to Lang's explanation and scanned the article in the paper.

Lang verbalized it into simple terms. "With shareholders freaking out, Ensight starts to show real signs of distress. All the decision makers at Ensight—the executives, the board of directors—all those who were looking to cash out on this deal are getting spooked. And so…"

"And so," Fox finished the thought, "Maguire can now lowball their offer because the market value of Ensight is well below what it was several months ago."

"You got it."

"And why do you think this works to our advantage?"

"Oh, come on, Bruce. Do I have to draw a portrait for you? This is just the type of distraction I've been waiting for. It gives us more time to find the cash and move it. You and Denny have the documents in your possession, so that phase of the plan is complete. Things are looking up now."

"Right," Fox replied, wondering how long he could keep Lang believing that the Bartlett documents were safe. "And what about Jack Bennett? Until we have a handle on him, he's still a problem, isn't he?"

"Absolutely. But whatever Jack Bennett is up to, I have no doubt it's directed only at me. He's got a personal vendetta against me. You just focus on the Committee's objective. Let me worry about Jack."

"If he's fucking with those accounts, then it's a problem for all of us," Fox reminded him.

"Bruce, I've got it covered. I'll find him. And when I do, we'll never have to worry about him again."

"OK, Harry."

At that moment, a young, uniformed clerk from the bell desk approached.

"Mr. Lang, your limousine is waiting for you outside," he said politely.

Lang glanced at his watch and immediately popped up from his seat. "Thank you, young man."

As the clerk walked back to his post, Lang held his hand out in front of Fox.

"Wish me a good trip, Bruce."

Fox shook his hand. "Have a good trip," he said with a stale tone.

Fox watched as the deputy director walked out the front doors of the St. Regis and slid into the back of the limousine. Inside the limo, Lang sat back and looked straight ahead.

"Well, I gave that son of a bitch a chance to come clean. A chance to tell me that he and that asshole Fitch lied to me about having those documents. He chose not to take it. That says a lot," he said as he loosened his tie.

Watts sat in the opposite seat, listening but saying nothing.

"I need to get my hands on those docs," Lang continued. "That dumb fuck that I sent to the Ensight offices not only killed the wrong girl but picked up the wrong documents. He brings me some shit about the Maguire deal. Serves me right for sending a boy to do a man's job." He laid his head back. "And I think Fox still believes that I ordered that girl to get killed, but I denied it."

"Well, you did order her to be killed, didn't you?" Watts asked.

"No! I wanted Amber Wakefield! The same girl I wanted you to take care of awhile back. What's worse, he goes and kills her before he gets his hands on the right documents. I mean, shit, I should just take care of this myself."

"You want me to take care of it?"

"No. Absolutely not. The situation is different now. She has something I want, and I need her alive until I get it." Lang realized that he might as well have been talking to himself. "Why I am telling you this stuff? It's like giving a bulldog a trigonometry problem."

Watts sat in the seat opposite, sneering. "What do you want me to do?"

"I'm giving you another chance. This is your third shot. You screw this one up, and that's it. You're out."

"Thanks, Mr. Lang," Watts managed to say.

"Don't thank me. Just follow my instructions. Keep an eye on Mr. Fox and Mr. Fitch. That's your job for now. I still need them at this point." Lang looked out the window at the DC afternoon. "But there will come a point soon when I'll have to disassociate myself from them. I'll call when that time comes. I trust that you'll know what to do then?" he asked.

Watts smiled and nodded.

Chapter 30

▼

At eight o'clock the next morning, Amber climbed into a cab on the corner of Spear and Howard. She sat in the backseat, turning her head throughout the ride to look out the rear window. If they were following her, they would have to be pretty bold to try something, especially to where she was headed. Of course, she had already known them to murder a person in a hotel and two others in an office building, so perhaps that kind of bravado wasn't so far-fetched after all.

At her request, the driver stopped on the corner of Grove and Larkin. The FBI office was located three blocks away, but she wanted to have no shortage of escape routes in case her paranoia turned out to be real. Besides, she would have to pass by City Hall along the way, and at the first sign of danger, she was prepared to sprint through the front doors screaming, which would no doubt attract every security guard in the vicinity.

After passing City Hall, she stopped briefly on the corner to look around one more time before crossing the street. There was an afternoon crowd milling around the Civic Center Plaza and the homeless fixtures populated the sidewalks, pushing their shopping carts and holding their cardboard signs. Just a typical afternoon in that part of town. She walked onto Golden Gate Avenue and entered the building with the number given to her earlier by the special agent in charge. She squeezed her way into the elevator among a group of other people, whose collective perspiration odor was difficult to stomach. The elevator finally arrived on the thirteenth floor, where she stepped out into the lobby.

"I'm here to see Mr. Dalton," she told the woman at the front desk.

The woman looked at her quizzically. "Did you have an appointment with him?"

"Yes. In fact, I spoke with him yesterday. My name is Amber Wakefield."

"Please have a seat," the woman said, pointing to a row of chairs against the wall.

Amber found a seat at the end of the row. She watched as the receptionist spoke in a muffled tone into her headset. With each sound of the elevator doors opening, Amber whipped her head around to see who would emerge. She closely watched each person who passed by, but none seemed particularly interested in her. After fifteen minutes, she heard the clattering of heels approaching from the nearby hall. A woman in her mid-forties, dressed in a black pants suit, appeared.

"Miss Wakefield?" she asked.

"Yes, that's correct. Amber." Amber extended her hand.

"I'm Gloria. I'll take you back to Mr. Dalton." She beckoned Amber to walk with her.

Amber stood and, with one more look around her, followed the woman to meet the special agent in charge of the San Francisco field division of the FBI.

Gloria left her in a modest-looking conference room with a paper cup of coffee and a promise that Mr. Dalton would be joining her shortly. Amber gazed out the window, watching an airplane flying somewhere toward the east. She thought of her mother in Providence.

"Miss Wakefield," he said as he entered the room, closing the door behind him.

"Yes. And please call me Amber," she replied as she shook his hand.

"Please take a seat," he said, showing her an uncomfortable looking chair with a torn vinyl upholstery.

She sat and crossed her legs.

Amber noticed that he was younger than he sounded on the phone, likely in his late forties. He looked like he probably kept in shape at one point but had let himself go a bit in recent years. The tight jacket to his suit was hugging his shoulders snugly, an indicator of self denial. He took a seat in the chair opposite the table from Amber and folded his hands in front of him. Other than a travel mug, presumably filled with coffee, he had nothing else with him.

"Well, it sounds like you've gotten yourself into quite a situation here," he started.

"You could say that," she replied.

"I know we didn't talk too much about it over the phone yesterday, but given what you say happened at your offices last week and the incident with the car bomb last month, I thought we should meet face to face."

"I appreciate that, Mr. Dalton. I've just run out of people I can trust. As you can see, the company I work for is becoming an increasingly more dangerous environment. And the men who work for Ms. McBride recommended that I talk to you."

"Well, I've known a couple of those guys for years. And I'll do what I can. But I can't make any promises. What happened there with that young woman last week is a local investigation at this point, and the San Francisco Police Department has jurisdiction over it. It's not a federal matter. But it sounds like your situation *is* separate and of a broader nature."

"Well, that's probably fair to say. Of course, I wouldn't eliminate the idea that my situation and Jamie's murder are mutually exclusive."

"You're saying there's a connection?" Dalton asked, his attention more focused.

"I'm not sure. But it seems a little too coincidental that something like that would hit that close to me and not be related to my issue."

Special Agent Dalton leaned forward, placing his elbows on the table.

"Amber, why don't you start from the beginning? Let's see if we can put some of these pieces together." He pulled a tiny recording device from his coat pocket and placed it between them on the table. "Do you mind?"

Amber looked at the recorder for a few seconds, and then slowly shook her head.

"OK," he said, pressing the red record button on the device. "Whenever you're ready."

For the next three hours, Amber reviewed the details of the past several weeks. She tried her best to relate the events chronologically, but she was sure that she had swapped the sequences of more than a couple of the occurrences. At one point, she had to stop to recover from her own surprise at how much had actually happened to her during that period. She discussed Harper Phillips, the men from the IRS, a man named Jack Bennett who had tried to have her killed by another man. She described how she had posed as Priscilla Phillips in order to get into the Jackson Winthrop offices and noted that Priscilla had been murdered in the park. She told Dalton about the murders of Marty and the Italian courier, the Bartlett documents, the break-in that occurred in her hotel room in Milan. At the end of the hour, Amber sat back and took a deep breath. Agent Dalton sat with his hand over his mouth, almost like a victim of information overload.

"Well, that's it," she concluded. "There's just one problem remaining."

"And what's that?" he asked, almost afraid to hear anymore.

"I have no idea how any of these events tie into one another. Like I'm the single common denominator here. And that's impossible because I haven't done anything wrong."

"Well, let me give you both sides of it from where I sit. Do you want the good news or the bad news first?" he asked.

She chuckled lightly. "Gee, let's see. Considering the fact that it's been a while since I've received any good news, and since I'd like to end this meeting on a high note, why don't we start with the bad news."

"Very well," Dalton said. "The bad news is that what you told me doesn't paint an awfully flattering portrait of you. After all, you could have forgotten easily about this Harper Phillips person after that initial meeting with the IRS. But you chose to be nosy, and you kept probing. You lied about your identity in order to trespass and investigate a law firm's confidential records. That's two wrongs. A double whammy." He stopped for a second to note her reaction, and then continued.

"You used your boss to hitch a ride to Europe so that you could follow some guy who you say tried to have you killed. And two of your close work associates have been murdered in your office. And from what you say, you were the last person to see each of them alive." He sat back and looked across the table. "So from the standpoint of most people who hear this story, your credibility isn't exactly stellar."

Amber took it all in, dejection and discouragement spreading across her face. No one had put it to her that way before. The fact that she had had more than a single opportunity to put an end to this nightmare made her stomach queasy. *How dare you ask for other people to help you when you practically inserted yourself into this chaos*, she chastised herself silently.

After almost ten seconds of deafening silence, Amber finally spoke.

"So, what the hell could possibly be the good news out of all this?" she asked, nearly on the verge of tears.

Special Agent Dalton leaned forward and turned off the recording device. He looked at her and smiled. "The good news is that I believe you, Amber."

It was eleven o'clock in the morning, and Amber was sure that by this time Kaitlyn would be wondering where she was and why she had not yet come in to the office. But she also knew that she was in the FBI office at Kaitlyn's behest. Together with Dalton, she reviewed the recorded session they had just conducted. Amber added a few details and some supplemental context that she had neglected to mention earlier. Then they organized the events so that they fell into sequence.

"OK, it sounds like we finally have everything in order here," Dalton said, as he pulled together the numerous pages containing the scribbled history of the previous two months of Amber's life. "I couldn't tell you how any of it fits together yet, so we'll have to start from the beginning."

He pulled out the page that recounted Amber's first meeting with Bruce Fox and the other men from the IRS.

"I'm going to find out what I can on this Harper Phillips fellow. I'll start at the law firm where he worked." He looked at another sheet of paper and read off of it. "Jackson Winthrop. If necessary, I can get a subpoena to confiscate all of his records from there."

"Well, you can start right here, I would think," Amber said.

"How do you mean?"

"You guys were investigating him out of this office, weren't you?"

"Not that I'm aware."

"Well, actually, I don't believe he was investigating Harper himself, but rather the man who was posing as him."

"Wait a minute. Who was investigating him?"

"Jack Bennett. I told you that he used to work for the FBI out here."

Dalton fumbled through the pages on the table, in search of the notes where they discussed Jack. "All you said was that he was fired by the FBI at one time. You didn't mention that he worked out of the West Coast office."

"Sorry, I thought I had."

"I've never heard of the man until now. And I know there's no one in this division by that name." He pulled out his cell phone and hit a digit.

After a second, someone picked up. "Yes, Gloria. I need you to run a check across the global database for an agent by the name of Jack Bennett." He put the phone back into his pocket. "We're going to find out who the hell this guy is."

Amber felt an overwhelming rush of ease and comfort, as if someone was holding her securely in the air so that she wouldn't plummet to the earth.

Dalton stood from his chair. "OK, Amber. While I get to work on this stuff, I need you to stay in close contact. So, don't wander too far. Do you have a place to stay tonight?"

"I've sort of been bouncing around to different hotels in the city."

"OK. Just tell me where you'll be, and I'll make sure we put a man on the premises for additional security. And don't worry, we'll be discreet."

Amber stood and held out her hand. "Thank you, Mr. Dalton. Thank you so much."

He took her hand and squeezed it gently. "You're welcome, Amber. And remember what I told you."

The two opened the door to the conference room and stepped out. On their way down the hall, a number of voices could be heard around the corner. As they neared the group of people that were source of the noise, they saw a man in a charcoal suit standing in the center of the group. When he saw Dalton approaching, he immediately excused himself and stepped forward.

"Special Agent Dalton," he said, extending his large hand. He was in his fifties and well built.

"Deputy Director Lang," Dalton acknowledged, shaking the hand of his superior. "Welcome back to San Francisco."

"Thank you. You about ready for me?"

"I will be in just one minute," Dalton replied, walking to the front desk.

Amber stood there for a moment. The man looked familiar, but she couldn't place him. Given his title and the respect he seemed to command in that office, she was fairly sure she had seen him in the newspaper or on CNN at some time. In turn, Lang leered at the young woman who stood by Dalton's side. He wished he was twenty years younger and unmarried, so it wouldn't be so shameful for him to drool over the attractive woman, as he was at that moment.

Dalton leaned over the front desk to the receptionist. "Would you please call Miss Wakefield a cab?"

Lang's expression changed, as he stood still and stared at Amber. Dalton walked up behind him to escort him down the hall, and then turned one last time. "We'll talk soon, Amber," he called out. She smiled and walked toward the elevators.

As the two men walked away Lang turned subtly and looked again at Amber Wakefield, up close and personal.

Chapter 31

▼

The sky was dark and the rain was falling when Jack's plane landed at Dulles International Airport. He stepped out of the terminal and climbed into the back of the Toyota Sienna parked in the fire lane. As the minivan pulled away from the curb, he hit the window button, and the window slid down.

"Ah, that feels nice," he said, closing his eyes as the raindrops tickled his face.

"Hey, what are you doing? You're getting the seat wet," said Watts, as he steered the vehicle out of the terminal.

"Relax." Jack rested his head against the headrest.

"How was Europe?"

"Peachy. I took a bus tour around town and brought you a Swiss Army knife." His sarcasm never went over well with Watts.

"You know what I mean, smart-ass. Did you get everything done?"

"I hope so."

"You hope so? How do you mean?" Watts asked, alternating his view between Jack and the road in front of him.

"Well, I got the docs and shipped them off. But I haven't heard back from our friends down in the Caribbean as to whether they got them or not. So, I'm getting a little nervous."

"I suppose you heard about that courier," Watts added.

Jack lifted his head off the seat and turned to Watts. "Yeah, that was unfortunate. I feel like I got him killed."

"This is no time to find your conscience," Watts reminded him. "Lang's sadistic. You knew he might pull something like this."

"Yes, I suppose I did."

"He's even got his own guys afraid of him."

"How's that?"

"Word is that Bruce Fox and Dennis Fitch told him they already got the documents. But he knows they're lying to him."

"Since when is Lang confiding in you all of a sudden?" Jack asked.

"The guy thinks I'm some ogre with only two brain cells competing for space in my head. When he talks to me, it's like he's talking to a lamppost."

Jack resisted the temptation to tell Watts that he agreed with Lang's assessment but thought better of it.

"We can't let that bastard get his hands on those documents. If he finds them, it's over" Watts said.

"Where is he now?"

"He left today for the West Coast. Some official business in Denver and LA.

"What kind of business could he have out there?"

Watts shrugged. "What do I know? I'm just some dumb ogre."

"Let's find out. I can't imagine he would allow himself to get distracted by real FBI business at this point. He knows the clock is ticking on him."

Watts merged onto the highway, adjusting his windshield wipers so that they were on the highest speed. "And what about the girl?"

Jack rolled his eyes. "That's a whole other problem. She's all over the map. For someone who doesn't know how much information she has, she sure is doing a phenomenal job of keeping it concealed."

"Where is she now?"

"If I had to guess, she's in San Francisco, no further than a few inches from Kaitlyn McBride's side."

"Then what are you doing here?

"I can't go out there. What I mean is I won't be able to get close to her. Kaitlyn's her only friend at this point, so Amber needs her. I just wish someone could tell the unwitting Ms. McBride what kind of a time bomb she has walking around with her. I'm sure she'd cut Amber loose in a second."

Watts continued to drive, periodically checking his rearview mirror.

"I need her to come to me," Jack continued.

"And just how are you going to do that?"

"She's got a mom who lives in Providence. She's pretty sick."

"How do you know that?"

"Give me some credit, will you? I've still got friends at the Bureau. They did some checking for me."

"So…," Watts began.

"I know she's close to her mom. She'll do anything to protect her."

"Geez, I didn't think you had it in you."

"What's that?" Jack asked, his eyes remaining forward.

"I didn't think you'd stoop to that level."

"Well, I underestimated Amber Wakefield. And up until now, I've never been desperate enough to resort to something like this."

"So, I take it you'll be paying a visit to Providence while you're out here?"

Jack paused for a moment. "I'll let you know everything once I have a plan. But not right now." He glanced at the green numerals of the clock illuminated on the dash. "I have a meeting I'm almost late for, so could you please do your best to get me there?"

Watts pressed his foot on the accelerator, and the minivan glided along the sleek highway. After a few more minutes of utter silence, he pulled the vehicle toward the off-ramp, and in a matter of seconds, it drifted into the darkness of a Virginia suburb.

Chapter 32

The cell phone rang out like a siren in the hotel room. Amber jerked her head off the pillow, wrenching a muscle in her neck. She rolled across the queen-size bed and grabbed the flashing phone from the nightstand.

"Hello?" She massaged the back of her neck with her free hand.

"Amber, did I wake you?" asked a man's voice.

"Who is this?"

"It's Dalton." After a pause, he expanded his answer. "Special Agent Dalton."

Amber finally stepped completely into the world of consciousness. "Yes, of course, Mr. Dalton."

"Sorry to have awakened you."

"No, it's all right," she said, looking at the clock on the nightstand. 7:15.

Special Agent Dalton had spent the previous evening reviewing the audiotapes and handwritten notes from his meeting with Amber Wakefield. Unfortunately, the rest of the day after their meeting had been consumed by the deputy director, who needed updates on the field office's investigations. Then it turned social toward the evening, complete with dinner at The Red Herring and then cocktails at The Clift. Dalton had two drinks compared to Lang's six. He recalled how Lang had badgered him about the young woman he saw Dalton escorting to the reception desk when he arrived that afternoon. The deputy director had appeared much less interested about whatever business she had with the FBI and more interested in what she might look like without her clothes on. In fact, Dalton distinctly remembered the phrase "piece of ass" coming out of Lang's mouth several times in reference to the girl.

"Amber, I spent most of last night going over my notes from our discussion. I've got some folks checking into Harper Phillips. But I was curious about one thing."

"And what is that?" she asked, rubbing her eyes.

"I did some checking on his law firm."

"Jackson Winthrop."

"Yes. Well, first of all, I couldn't find much. Their Web site doesn't tell much."

"I know. I should have told you that."

"I was thinking of paying a visit to their office downtown. You know, ask some questions about Harper Phillips."

"That's a good idea." She was standing up now, running her hand through her hair.

"Who did you talk to when you were there?"

"No one. Well, just the receptionist. But she didn't know anything."

"OK. I guess I'll have to start from scratch."

"Sorry I couldn't be more help," she said.

"Don't worry about it. I'll let you know what I find out."

"Thanks, Mr. Dalton."

"You're welcome, Amber."

The line went dead, and Amber stood in the middle of the room. It was the day of Jamie Atwater's memorial service. Amber couldn't bear the thought of going to another funeral. As the executive assistant to the CEO, Jamie had been a very popular person at the company, so there would be no doubt that most of the Ensight employees would be in attendance. Kaitlyn would deliver a eulogy and then push through the frenzy of people wishing to get close to the powerful executive. It was too much of a scene for her to bear, so she decided to stay away from the service. It was disrespectful to Jamie, she knew, but it wouldn't be safe for her to go. After all, she hadn't been as close to Jamie as she'd been to Marty.

Amber left the room and took the elevator down. As she crossed through the lobby, she saw two men in dark suits, with no ties, sitting in the lounge. As she passed by them, they nodded in acknowledgment as they had done on the previous evening when they escorted her to her room. Dalton had been true to his word that they would not be in her way. But knowing that they were close by was enough to allow Amber to get a good night's sleep.

The cab dropped her off in front of the office. As she walked toward the elevators, she passed several fellow employees who had stopped by the office before heading to Jamie's memorial service. It was easy to spot them as they were all wearing dark mourning attire rather than the borderline casual dress that they usually wore to the office. All of them noticed her dressed in her normal business clothes, clearly not appropriate for a funeral, and offered disdainful glances. *Whatever*, she thought to herself. *If only they knew my reasons.*

Amber stepped out of the elevator on the thirty-fourth floor. It was quiet, except for a few assistants shutting down their computers and walking quickly to the elevators to go to the memorial service. She approached Jamie's desk and saw that her headset was still plugged into the computer and resting across the top of the keyboard. A few paces away, Kaitlyn's office was dark and undisturbed. Amber's cell phone began squawking again, echoing through the empty office space.

"Hello?"

"Amber? It's Dalton here."

"Yes, Mr. Dalton."

"I'm down here at the Jackson Winthrop offices," he said. "At the address you gave to me yesterday."

"Did you find anything? I mean, have you spoken to anyone there who knew Mr. Phillips?"

"Not exactly."

"What do you mean?"

"I think you should come down here," he said. "You'll know what I mean when you get here."

She could hear him talking with some other people in the background but couldn't make out what they were saying.

"Mr. Dalton, I don't understand…,"

"Just get down here," he interrupted. "Now, please." And he hung up.

His tone sounded much different from that of the man she'd met the day before at the FBI office. She couldn't imagine what he would need her to come down there for, since she had told him everything she knew, which wasn't much to begin with.

She took the elevator down to the lobby and caught a cab on the corner. In seven minutes, she exited the cab at Bush Street and entered the black building. The elevator stopped on the floor where the law office's reception area was located, and she stepped out. She immediately recognized the scent of paint fumes and heard faint voices in the distance. She stopped in the middle of the floor leading to the reception desk as she saw what was in front of her. It had become very clear to her why Agent Dalton wanted her to see it.

The large mahogany desk where Gina was supposed to be sitting was gone. Also missing were the large brass letters which only weeks ago had proudly borne the name of the firm behind the desk. Everything was gone, even the birds of paradise that had hovered in the corners of the waiting area.

Amber stepped through the reception area toward the offices that lined the halls—those same offices she'd seen on her first visit, with desks and bookcases stacked with law books and now all were empty spaces with telephone wires hanging from the wall jacks. She stepped into one of the vacant offices and stood with her hand over her open mouth.

"Is this how you remembered it?" asked a voice outside the door.

Amber spun around to find Special Agent Dalton standing there. Beside him were two men whom she suspected to be fellow FBI agents. Behind them was another, shorter man.

"Mr. Dalton, I don't get it. What happened here?"

"I might ask you that same question," he replied.

"Excuse me?"

"Amber, who exactly did you talk to when you were here last?"

"Some girl named Gina. She was the receptionist."

Dalton looked at the other men, then back to Amber. "And did you see anyone else? Like a lawyer, for instance?"

She shook her head no. "No. You see it was the Labor Day weekend, so everyone had gone for the day when I got here."

"How do you know that?"

"Gina told me."

"Oh, Gina told you. This same girl who happily let you into the storage room where the firm housed all the confidential records," he went on sarcastically.

"Don't you believe me?"

"Amber, this is Mr. Cameron," he said, making room for the short man standing in the back. "He works for the property management company for this building."

She looked back and forth between him and Dalton.

"He tells me that this floor and the three floors below it have not been leased for the last five months."

Mr. Cameron stepped forward. "With the way things are in the economy, there aren't many businesses willing to pay for high-rise building space."

"Mr. Dalton, I swear to you there was a law firm here. I saw a large reception desk out there," she insisted, pointing toward the reception area. "All of these offices had desks and computers and bookshelves. You have to believe me. Please. Why would I lie to you?"

"I don't know, Amber. I just don't appreciate having my valuable time wasted."

"But don't you see what's going on? They obviously knew that someone would come back here looking for answers."

"*They* who?" Dalton asked, annoyed.

"Whoever the hell is trying to kill me!" she shouted.

Dalton put his hands on his hips, exasperated. "OK, Amber," he said, struggling to maintain a calm tone. "But put yourself in my position. You have to admit that it seems implausible that an entire law firm could close shop without leaving a trace of itself behind."

"But...," she began, but he held his hand up to silence her.

"Furthermore, they managed to clear out what you describe as a pretty extensive setup here without one witness."

Amber folded her arms across her chest, not trying to hide her frustration at Dalton, who had claimed only a day ago to believe her story and was now finding doubt all over the place. And then she remembered.

"The storage room," she muttered to herself.

"What was that?" Dalton asked, leaning his ear toward her.

"The storage room," she repeated more loudly. "Downstairs. Gina let me in there to look at Harper Phillips's files. That's where that man tried to shoot me."

Mr. Cameron rolled his eyes, finding it impossible for something so outrageous to have occurred in his building. "This is ridiculous," he said.

But it evidently struck a nerve with Dalton, whose expression had changed to the look he had had the previous day in the FBI offices.

"Mr. Cameron, would you mind escorting us downstairs?" he asked.

"Are you serious?" Cameron asked.

Dalton stared down at the smaller man, who recognized the answer to his question immediately. "Follow me," he said sheepishly.

The group proceeded down the emergency staircase to the floor where Amber recalled the storage room to be located. The door opened into another stark hallway, with empty cardboard boxes and strips of packing tape littered across the carpet. By this time, Amber had passed Cameron and was leading the expedition. She stopped in front of the doorway to the storage room. The door was open, and to no one's surprise, the room was empty. Even the brass plate that had hung on the wall outside the doorway was gone; its space painted over.

"He shot his gun at me here," she said, standing two steps inside the doorway. "The bullet hit this door as I was trying to get out of the room." She pointed to the large oak door, but as was consistent with everything else, the surface of the door was entirely unmarred. "I started a small fire that caused the sprinklers to go off. It was the only way to create a distraction so I could escape."

"Are we done here yet?" asked Mr. Cameron. "As you can see, there's nothing on this door indicating that it has been damaged. Not by a bullet, not by anything. And this business about a fire? I certainly haven't received a report about the fire system being triggered in this building in the last two years."

Dalton ran his hand gently over the surface of the door, a gesture that suggested he desperately wanted to find something to support Amber's story. Despite his reaction upstairs, he still wanted to believe her.

"How many times did you say he shot at you?" he asked. He was suddenly an investigator again.

Amber shrugged. "It all happened so fast. Three, maybe four times."

Dalton instructed his men to enter the room and examine the empty space.

"He tried to shoot me in the hallway, too."

She led Dalton down the hall, back toward the emergency door, leaving his two lieutenants with Cameron. She pointed to the areas she recalled hearing the bullets piercing the wall. Again, as he had with the door to the storage room, Dalton ran his hand over the wall. The white paint appeared unscathed, other than a few scratches and blemishes. As Amber attempted to trace her path of escape for Dalton, he began walking in the opposite direction.

"Where are you going?" she asked.

He stopped about midway between the emergency exit and the door to the storage room. She watched as he gazed up at the fluorescent lights lining the ceiling. His eyes moved from the ceiling to the wall on his right, then back to the ceiling.

"Mr. Dalton?" she called out, trying to get his attention. But he was not listening.

He stood close to the wall and rested his cheek against it, facing in the direction of Amber. She could see his eyes moving wildly as he slowly moved his head, attempting to view various angles of the wall.

"What exactly are you doing?" she finally asked.

"These white walls tend to reflect the fluorescent lights if the paint's sheen is glossy enough. These seem to be painted with some type of semigloss."

Amber said nothing as he continued to examine the wall. He moved closer toward her, his shoulder hugging the surface of the wall, his eyes fixed on a single spot closer to her. When he came within two feet of her, he raised his hand to an area on the wall, approximately six feet up from the floor.

"Right here," he said.

Amber moved closer to see what he was pointing at. He pulled her to where he was standing and turned her body so that it was facing the direction of the emergency exit.

"You see that spot?" he asked her.

"No."

She followed his finger as it came to rest on an area about two inches wide. And there she saw it. A slight discoloration in the paint.

"This one area here has been painted over with a flat sheen. Like it was repaired."

Dalton reached into his pocket and found a keychain with a small nail file attached. He pulled out the blade and scratched the small area of the wall he had just pointed to. As small chips of paint snowed on to the carpet, he began digging into the surface.

"Now what are you doing?" she asked.

"See this stuff?" he asked, as he peeled off the layer beneath the paint he had just etched off. "It's putty. The kind used to spackle divots and dents in the wall to smooth it out."

He blew the dust from the wall and rubbed the area with his hand. "The horizontal angle and size of this patched area looks pretty consistent with a bullet. I couldn't tell you by looking at it what type of gun it came from, but that probably isn't important."

Amber breathed a sigh of relief, knowing that Special Agent Dalton was starting to question his own doubts. At that moment, one of his lieutenants peered around the corner of the doorway to the storage room.

"Sir, I think you should come in here and take a look at this."

Dalton walked toward the room, with Amber closely behind. When they entered, they moved toward the center of the large room where the three other men stood in a triangle.

"What is it?" Dalton asked.

"Up there," the other lieutenant said, pointing to a sprinkler head hanging from the ceiling.

"What is that?" Dalton asked, noticing the dark patches against the white ceiling.

"It's mold, sir. From water damage."

"That's just from the humidity," said Cameron.

"Or from the sprinkler system," Dalton offered.

From the expression on his face, Amber could see the pieces of her story finding cohesion in Dalton's mind. "Do you believe me now? That there was indeed a law firm here at one time?"

Dalton continued to stare at the ceiling. "I believe there was something here." He shifted his gaze to look at her. "I'm just not convinced it was a law firm."

Chapter 33

After leaving the empty offices of what she once thought was the headquarters of Jackson Winthrop, LLP, Amber walked back to the Ensight office. She made her way quickly through the crowd on Market Street, careful to glance occasionally behind herself to ensure that Dalton's men were still in sight. She felt a bit absurd behaving as though she didn't know they were there, but that's how Dalton had insisted it be done.

Some of the employees had returned from Jamie's memorial service by the time Amber reached the office. The rest had probably attended the wake or had decided to knock off for the day, likely citing emotional anguish as the reason. Amber was not surprised to find Kaitlyn sitting in her office, talking on the phone. There were throngs of reporters and associates of the top institutional investors calling her, all inquiring about the fate of Ensight. Amber had read some of the recent articles in the *Wall Street Journal* and *Business Week* commenting on Ensight, and their tone was discouraging.

Amber walked past the glass doors of Kaitlyn's office, only to see the CEO waving her in. Pushing open the door, Amber stuck just her head into the office.

"Amber, I need a favor," Kaitlyn whispered, with her hand over the speaker on the phone handset.

"Sure. What is it?" Amber asked as she walked in.

"I need you to take these down to accounts payable." She handed Amber a short stack of invoices and expense reports.

Amber took them and nodded. As she was about to leave, she turned around. She wanted to tell Kaitlyn that she was sorry for not having attended the funeral and that she had found someone at the FBI to help her. But Kaitlyn was already back to her phone conversation and had probably forgotten that Amber was there.

She walked down the emergency staircase to the floor where the accounting department was located. The floor appeared completely deserted except for the hum of computers and fax machines receiving pages. She found the row of desks where the accounts payable staff sat and dropped the pages into a tray on one of the desks. As she looked at the volumes of invoices in the tray, it occurred to her how many bills and debts a company that large must pay on a monthly basis—from the building lease and the capital equipment to the telephone bills and the employee expense reports, many of which were inflated to at least some degree. It was at that very moment that an idea leapt into Amber's brain, an idea she had not considered ever since her ordeal began.

With the office as quiet as it was, Amber found that it presented the perfect opportunity to poke around. She recalled the billing invoices she had seen at the Jackson Winthrop offices during her first visit. If her memory served her correctly, the invoices were issued to Bartlett for services rendered but were filed in the Ensight folder. At the back of the row of desks in the accounts payable section of the floor, there was a large black file cabinet. It was the only one of that size in the vicinity. Amber glanced around the floor, listening for any hint of life. There was none. She walked to the cabinet and opened the top drawer. She figured there might be something related to Jackson Winthrop in there. She flipped through the plastic tabs above the folders. They were not organized in any particular order, or at least none that seemed logical to her.

In the drawer below that one, she found a number of tabs in alphabetical order. She peered into the first folder and found a number of invoices. Then she looked into the file behind it and found more invoices. The same held true for the next few. She pulled the drawer out further until she reached the "J" section. But unfortunately, there was nothing in it related to Jackson Winthrop. *At least it was a good theory*, she thought to herself.

When she arrived back at the thirty-fourth floor, Kaitlyn's office was once again empty. A few more executive assistants had returned from the service and were now either on the phones or chatting in small circles. Since joining Kaitlyn's team, Amber had not yet penetrated this sorority. Although she couldn't pinpoint any one instance to support her instincts, Amber felt a sense of disapproval from them, as though they viewed her as moving in on their beloved Jamie's territory. Maybe one day they'd lower the barrier. Amber turned away from them. At any rate, Kaitlyn was gone and from the looks of her office, she wasn't returning that day, so Amber stepped inside.

She decided to check her home voice mail service. There were only five messages—three hang-ups, one from a sweepstakes company claiming that she had won something, and one from her mother. She hadn't heard from her mother in an unusually long while, so it was both reassuring and comforting to hear her voice again, exactly what Amber had been longing for.

The message from her mother was recent, only a day old. She sounded happier than she had in the past, despite her Alzheimer's. For some time, her mother had been urging Amber to come back to Providence, but her daughter was insistent on having a life in the city. Amber considered New York and Boston too close to home, so she decided to remain in San Francisco, only twenty miles from her alma mater.

At first Amber was confused by her mother's message, but after listening to all of it, she understood the source of her mother's elation The message started out by saying how happy her mother was that her daughter was safe, since she hadn't heard from her in a while. But Amber wondered how her mother could have known how she was doing and that she was safe. She hadn't called her mother and hadn't spoken to any family or close friends who could have relayed the message. Her mother went on to thank her for the beautiful roses she had sent. *What roses?* Amber asked herself. And then she heard it. The words were chilling. Her mother said that one of Amber's friends from California, a nice man named Jack, had contacted her. Evidently, he had told her that he was visiting Providence for the first time on business, and that Amber had requested that he do her a favor by making a delivery to her mother. The last thing her mother said on the message was something about sitting with Jack in her living room, sipping tea and looking at baby and childhood pictures of Amber.

She sat down unable to move or to think, paralyzed by panic. Amber lowered her shaking hand and placed the receiver into its cradle. She wanted to scream. She immediately grabbed the phone again and quickly dialed the number to her mother's Rhode Island home. She allowed the phone to ring fifteen times, but there was no answer. Despite Amber's constant pleas, her mother had refused to invest in an answering service. After slamming down the phone, Amber flung open the office doors and sprinted toward the elevators. She jammed her arm in between the closing doors of one of the elevator cars so that the doors violently reopened, much to the dismay of the three occupants, who all looked at Amber disapprovingly.

In less than a minute, she was back out of the elevator and on the human resources floor, where her desk was still located. She found her address book and rapidly flipped through the pages in search of a number. When she finally found it, she dialed the number to her mother's neighbor. The woman who answered told Amber that she had not heard from her mother since the day before and then attempted to engage in catch-up talk with the young lady whom she had seen grow up next door, but Amber had already hung up the phone and was in the process of dialing another number.

"Mr. Dalton," she gasped into the phone, each syllable separated by a heavy breath.

"Amber? What's wrong?"

"It's my mom," she said, nearly unintelligibly.

Until now, Amber had never made mention of her mother, so it took a second for Dalton to understand what she was saying.

"Your mom? What about her?"

"He's going to hurt her. He's going to do something to her."

"Calm down, Amber," Dalton pleaded. "Take a breath." He could now hear her breathing at a normal rate. "OK, now who are you talking about? Who is going to hurt her?"

"Jack! Jack Bennett!" she yelled through the phone.

Dalton held the receiver out at arm's length while she yelled. "How do you know this?"

"She called me. He told her that he was a friend of mine. That he was visiting Providence and I had asked him to drop some flowers off at her home." She was crying again. "He was in her goddamn house!" she sobbed.

"Oh, Jesus," Dalton said under his breath. "This guy is like a damn virus."

Through her tears, Amber managed to talk. "What do you mean?"

"Well, according to our background check, he didn't work out of the West Coast office. However, he did have a brief stint with the Bureau, doing some work in Washington DC."

"Well, I suppose I shouldn't be surprised that he lied to me about that."

"The circumstances of his termination with the Bureau are supposedly classified."

"Wonderful. I guess that works out well for him."

"Don't you worry, Amber. We'll start moving on this at once."

"Well, whatever you're planning to do, can you please do it faster?" Amber pleaded. "She's the only family I have."

"I understand. But you have to…"

"I don't think you do understand, Mr. Dalton," she interrupted. "This is not a game. People are dying around me because of whatever Jack wants from me. But now it's very personal."

Dalton remained silent for a moment, perhaps embarrassed by his apparently insensitive approach to the problem. "You're absolutely right, Amber."

"I don't care what you have to do, Mr. Dalton. You find him. You find that bastard. If he so much as touches one hair on her head," she began, but didn't finish the thought.

Dalton sat still, stunned by this side of Amber Wakefield that he had not seen before. Despite the fact that he had known her for only a short while, the surprise he felt was likely not too far off from whatever her closest family or friends would have felt. Then it struck him.

"Amber, I have an idea. Can you get to my office? My guys should be waiting for you outside your building. I'll call them now to tell them to drive you here. Meet them downstairs in five minutes."

The confidence in his voice was encouraging enough for Amber.

"OK, Mr. Dalton. Five minutes." They hung up simultaneously.

In two minutes, Amber dashed out the elevator doors and through the lobby. She looked to her left and saw the black Oldsmobile parked in a blue handicapped zone. One of Dalton's men was leaning against the car with his cell phone to his ear, taking instructions from his boss. He waved to Amber as she emerged from the office building and held open the rear door to the car as his partner started the ignition. The car was moving before the doors were closed. She sat in the backseat, gnawing on her thumbnail and staring out the window, her eyes still moist.

She jumped out of the car as it stopped in front of the FBI building. Special Agent Dalton was standing outside waiting. He led her upstairs, neither saying anything to the other. When they arrived on the thirteenth floor, they walked directly to the back toward the same conference room where the two had met on their first encounter.

Dalton opened the door, allowing Amber to enter first. She stopped when she noticed that they were not alone. Seated at the conference table was a man with his back turned to them. When he swung his chair around, she recognized him as the man she had seen in that same office a few days ago as she was leaving.

Dalton put a hand on Amber's back and nudged her forward slightly. "Amber Wakefield, meet Deputy Director Harrison Lang."

Lang stood from his seat and held his hand out courteously, with a quick glance below her neck. "Amber, it's a pleasure."

She shook his hand, still unsure of what they were all doing there. "Likewise."

"I wish this could have been under different circumstances," he said.

Dalton stepped forward and pulled a chair out for Amber to sit in. He walked around the table and sat in the opposite chair, while Lang resumed his seat.

"Deputy Director Lang is out here from Washington, visiting a number of field offices on the West Coast. He was scheduled to leave today, but I've asked that he stick around to meet you."

She glanced over at Lang, who was sitting cross-legged, smiling. "Why?"

Dalton looked toward Lang and nodded, the cue for Lang to start his explanation.

"Amber, I understand that you had a run-in with Jack Bennett."

"That's right. He told me he was investigating a man named Harper Phillips, who…"

Lang stopped her. "That's OK, dear, you don't have to go into the whole thing. Mr. Dalton was kind enough to bring me up to speed on your situation. But I'm curious to know what Mr. Bennett told you about his involvement with the FBI."

"Well, that he used to lead a team investigating identity theft. He said he worked out of the West Coast office. But Mr. Dalton here tells me that wasn't the case."

Lang nodded in agreement.

"Anyway, Jack told me that he'd been fired for no apparent reason and that he was on a quest to find out why," she continued. "As a matter of fact, I think he may have mentioned your name, Mr. Lang." To this point, Lang's name hadn't registered with her as being the same one Jack had mentioned in their initial meeting.

Lang recrossed his legs. "I can't say I'm shocked by that."

"He said you fired him and that you didn't really offer him a good reason." The details of that meeting across from the ballpark were beginning to come back to her.

"Well, that's partly true. I did ask for his resignation. But that was due to my dissatisfaction with that entire division. He was merely a casualty. There were a number of others who were let go as well."

Amber shifted her gaze to Dalton, who sat in his chair quietly, then back to Lang. "I guess you should also know that he seemed pretty sure that you were involved in something," she said, struggling to find the appropriate word. "Something fishy, let's just say."

Lang laughed, and Dalton joined in. "Sounds like Jack, all right." Lang chuckled a few more times. "He has something personal against me, although I can't say I blame him. His termination was a rather humiliating ordeal. And now he's bitter. You can understand that, can't you?" His laughter faded. "Besides, from my post at the Bureau, I'm two degrees separated from the president himself. It would be pretty difficult for me to engage in the type of impropriety that Jack is accusing me of."

"I guess," Amber replied. "But then why would he try to hurt *me*? Why on earth would he go after my mom?"

"That's what we intend to find out. There's something that you know or have that he wants very badly."

"But people are dying," Amber reminded them.

"I know, and it's reprehensible," Lang said. "It frightens me just to get inside the head of someone who's willing to perpetrate such a grisly crime. But he's obviously desperate."

"Listen, I appreciate everything you're telling me," Amber said. "But we still haven't gotten around to talking about my mother. I feel that the clock is ticking."

Lang sat forward and leaned closer to Amber. "OK, first things first. We don't know that he's taken her anywhere."

The sound of hearing the word *taken* pertaining to her mother caused Amber to shiver. "She hasn't answered her phone, and she rarely goes out. She's not well, so she spends most of her time at home."

"OK, I'll tell you what. I'll order some folks to head out to her home and check it. But, in the meantime, I need you to remain in close contact with either me or Mr. Dalton here."

She nodded.

He placed his hand over hers. "Amber, I know this man. I know him well. Is he dangerous? Yes. I think we've seen that. But he's extremely rational. He doesn't do things unless there's a purpose."

"Even murder," she said.

"We'll find your mother. And when we do, we'll take every step possible to protect her," he offered reassuringly. "And you."

"And for how long do you think you can protect us?" she asked, doubting Lang's promise.

"Until we find Jack Bennett," he said. "And we will find him."

Chapter 34

The man with the ponytail stepped off the train at Atocha Station, the main railway hub in Madrid. Agent Griffin had been following him ever since he and his young partner had parted ways two days before. It was against the orders of the deputy director and contrary to general protocol to separate from his partner, but he felt that he was onto something. Telling Lang about it would have to wait. This was the closest he had managed to get in weeks, and he wanted the glory to himself. His young partner was smart and eager. But he would have his day. On the other hand, Agent Griffin was forty-five years old and had been stuck in a rut with the Bureau for fifteen years. He had been told in the past that the reason for his inability to ascend in the ranks was his lack of initiative. One superior had told him that he was a member of the "yes-man club." He needed his big break, his chance to stand out. This was it.

He had watched the man with a ponytail walk out of two small banks in Barcelona in the past two days. After brief interrogations with the bank staff, all of whom testified that a man named Harper Phillips had been there to withdraw all the funds in the respective accounts, he felt that he now had sufficient evidence to close in. *The deputy director will be proud*, he thought.

He walked about fifty feet behind the ponytailed man, as the man made his way through the train station and out into the overcast skies of the Madrid afternoon. As his quarry moved northward among the crowds, Griffin picked up his gait so as not to lose sight of him. Once through the gates of the picturesque Jardin Botanico, he kept his eye on the ponytail as the man moved at a quicker pace along the gravel-surfaced paths of the park. Sliding between groups of tourists snapping photographs and dope dealers sitting on benches, Griffin sensed that his man was definitely moving at a faster clip. The arches in his feet began to ache as he stepped increasingly faster over the uneven ground, trying to keep up with the man who he thought was the ticket to his future with the FBI.

Rounding a corner behind a row of dense trees, Griffin's trot developed into a jog as the ponytail briefly disappeared from sight. Griffin stopped running when he saw the man standing toward the opposite end of the park, near the gates leading back into the busy street. The man turned slightly to face Griffin, who stood still, exposed. Even from that distance, he could detect a subtle curl in the man's lips, challenging him. Then, as if a starter gun had been fired, the ponytail spun around and took off through the gates.

"Shit," Griffin said, as the soles of his shoes slipped and slid over the gravel while he attempted to run after him.

He saw the end of the ponytail fly upwards as the man descended the steps to the underground crosswalk beneath the street. Griffin ran his sleeve across his forehead. The sweat dripping from his brow was on the verge of flooding his eyes. He made it to the top of the stairs, only to hear the clatter of footsteps echoing through the tunnel below. He took three steps at a time to reach the bottom. Running through the tunnel flanked by its graffiti-laden walls, he coughed loudly as he inhaled the acute odor of day-old urine and other signs of civic disrespect and abuse.

The sound of the steps ahead was becoming fainter, so Griffin pushed into a higher gear. He rounded a slight bend in the tunnel, knowing he wasn't far behind his man. His focus on the ponytail was so sharp that he barely saw the dark figure that slid into his path as he emerged around the blind spot.

"What!" he barked. But as he was about to push aside the obstruction, he stopped, holding the man by both shoulders. "What the hell are you doing here?"

His young partner freed himself from Griffin's hold. "Griff," he started to say but the elder agent cut him off.

"What are you doing? He's getting away," he said, pointing toward the daylight coming through the open exit of the tunnel.

But the younger man stood still, saying nothing. The expression on his face told nothing. It was not the cockeyed countenance of inexperience that Griffin had been accustomed to ever since the two had been partnered up.

"Did you hear me?" Griffin asked. "You just let him get away."

Again, nothing from his partner.

"What the hell are you doing here, anyway? I thought I told you to stay in San Francisco until I said otherwise."

"I was called back," the young man mumbled.

"By whom? You follow my lead. You follow my instructions. Remember?"

"That's a bit hypocritical, don't you think?" The young man's voice was deeper and sounded hollower than Griffin ever remembered it.

"What is that supposed to mean?" Griffin asked, well past the point of total annoyance.

"It means that you should have followed Lang's instructions."

"What? Fuck him! And fuck you!" Griffin shouted.

The young FBI agent shook his head. "I'm sorry you feel that way, Griff."

The confusion on Griffin's face was short-lived, immediately turning to surprise when his partner stepped forward and hugged him. His body fell against the young man as the bullet punctured his chest. The sound of the gunshot would go completely unheard beneath the deafening noise of the traffic overhead. A heavy gasp escaped Griffin's mouth as his eyes met those of his young protégé. He would not get his chance to impress the higher-ups within the FBI. He would remain in that dreaded rut infinitely.

Letting Griffin's body slump to the ground, the young man slid the pistol back into his coat pocket and ran his hands over his own clothes, smoothing any wrinkles that could indicate he'd been in a hand-to-hand struggle. After a brief glance around, he walked quickly toward the steps leading back up to the street. Halfway up the staircase, he pulled out a mobile phone and dialed several digits.

"Sir," he said, acknowledging the authority on the other end. "It's done."

There was no reply, which was what he'd expected.

He continued ascending, and toward the top of the stairs, he turned his head to see the ponytail standing on the opposite sidewalk, peering directly at him. Three seconds elapsed with both of them motionless, facing one another, and like the strangers who passed by each other in the nearby botanical gardens, the two men began walking away in opposite directions.

Chapter 35

Following her meeting with Deputy Director Lang and Special Agent Dalton, Amber worked the phones in the FBI office for the next day, contacting every one of the few relatives and friends who might have a clue to the whereabouts of her mother. Unfortunately, her mother's secluded lifestyle had turned many of the people who were once close to her into distant acquaintances. As a result, none were able to help Amber.

The guilt was overwhelming. Had she moved back to Providence as her mother had wished, Amber could have protected her. In fact, she wouldn't have been a part of this mess she found herself in. She wouldn't know anything about Harper Phillips or Jack Bennett. She would never have been introduced to Jackson Winthrop or Bartlett Enterprises.

Kaitlyn would not miss Amber on this day. She was reportedly in Chicago, trying to salvage the Maguire deal that had gone south since Jamie's murder. She had instructed Amber to stay in San Francisco and to remain in safe contact with the FBI. She had even called her from the corporate jet to offer her prayers for Amber's mother.

It was three o'clock in the afternoon, nearly twenty-four hours after Amber had first heard her mother's strange message. She was wearing the same clothes she had worn the day before, and her eyes were red. Her mouth felt cottony and reeked of coffee. By this time, Lang's men would certainly have made it to her home in Providence and searched it. Amber hoped that she would hear something soon. Anything.

At that moment, there was a knock on the conference room door, and the deputy director entered. Apparently, he had taken the time to go back to his hotel and shower, shave, and change his suit.

"Well, Amber, our men did search your mother's house in Providence," he said, pouring himself a cup of coffee.

"And?" Amber urged him to finish his sentence.

"Well, the good news is that there didn't appear to be any sign of struggle or forced entry."

"Is that necessarily good news?"

"Sorry, I just meant that it rules out the worst case scenario."

"And what would that be?" she asked, although she had a fairly clear idea of what he meant.

He started to respond, but she held her hand up to his face. "You know what, never mind. Don't tell me. I don't think I want to hear the words."

"I understand," he said.

"So, now what, Mr. Lang?" she asked, her voice sounding less confident with each syllable.

"Well, we're checking all of the local car rental agencies and service stations, as well as all airports in a one-hundred mile radius, and scanning the passenger lists."

"And how long does that take?"

"Don't worry. We do it all the time. We can cover a lot of area in a short period."

"A short period? Mr. Lang, a short period might be all it takes for Jack Bennett to carry out what you call the worst case scenario, if I understood you correctly. So, don't tell me not to worry."

"I apologize. That came out wrong." He fought back his growing impatience with this girl.

"I want to know everything that's happening, *as* it's happening, Mr. Lang."

"You have my guarantee on that, Amber."

The door to the conference room opened, and Special Agent Dalton entered, dressed in the same suit as the day before, although he had managed to change his tie.

"Any progress?" he asked, closing the door behind him.

Lang shook his head. "I was just explaining to Amber what we found at her mother's house and going over our next steps."

"Excellent," Dalton replied, less concerned about his insensitive choice of words and more about his need to impress his superior.

"I was also explaining to her that we have a tremendous level of confidence in handling these kinds of issues."

"Absolutely," Dalton said, continuing his acquiescent behavior. "Amber, the deputy director here is the finest investigator you'll find."

Amber did everything to keep from rolling her eyes. Even Lang experienced a brief temptation to stuff a cork into Dalton's mouth.

"Did you pop in here for a particular reason, Dalton?" Lang asked.

"I came to jog your memory some more, Amber," he said. He pulled some papers containing a summary of Amber's testimony. "I know it's not the best time, but all of this will help us get to the bottom line. Believe me, we have your mom's best interests in mind."

"What is it?" Amber asked, her elbow on the table and her head resting against her hand. She was exasperated.

"Bartlett Enterprises," he said.

"What about it?"

"You mentioned that the courier in Switzerland handed you some documents just before he died," Dalton said, while reading.

"That's right."

"And these documents were the Articles of Incorporation for Bartlett. Is that correct?"

"That's what the documents said."

Lang gradually leaned forward. He had been waiting for the opportunity for this topic to arise.

Dalton continued scanning the report. "And the names on the document. The principals, I believe you said."

Amber nodded. "Correct."

"Were there any other names other than Harper Phillips listed on there?"

Lang slid down into his chair slightly. His pulse was increasing, nearly to an audible level.

Amber thought for a moment. "There were three or four names. I can't recall all of them. Of course, I do remember seeing Bruce Fox's name. I remember that one well since I met the man in person once."

"Is this really necessary, Dalton?" Lang interjected, realizing that the interrogation was going in a direction he didn't want.

Dalton and Amber looked at him with some surprise.

"I mean isn't it more important to focus on the whereabouts of the documents? Perhaps starting with who stole them out from her room?" Lang said.

"Well, I planned to get to that, sir. But I thought it might be helpful to paint as colorful a background to this as possible, rather than initiating a blind hunt. Besides, I'm not sure the location of the documents is the important issue here. It's what those documents represent that's going to get us what we need." Dalton could see that Lang was not happy that he had selected this moment to argue. "Wouldn't you agree, sir?" he added meekly, trying to win back the favor of the deputy director.

"I think they are equally important. But it's your investigation to manage, Mr. Dalton." Lang had made his point, and with some conviction, he hoped.

Dalton turned back to Amber, relieved that he had avoided what nearly could have been a public admonishment by the deputy director.

"Now, Amber," he started, clearing his throat, "is there anything, anything at all, that you can remember from that document? More names, a location, perhaps?"

Amber shook her head. "I'm sorry. I had it in my hands for only a few moments. I didn't even know what I was looking at, so I certainly didn't have my antennae up to detect anything."

Dalton watched the young woman with an intense stare, in hope that he might penetrate her memory. "I'm sorry, Mr. Dalton," she repeated, looking away from his gaze. "Besides, I barely understood most of the language on the few pages I saw."

"Yes, legal jargon is often like a foreign language."

"No, that's not what I meant. It was literally in a different language. Dutch, I believe," she said, recalling the memo that preceded the articles of incorporation.

Lang sat up again. "And how do you know that?"

"There was a small note attached to the front. It just said that the original Dutch version and an English translation were enclosed in the packet." She frowned as she herself wondered with some surprise how that particular detail had managed to remain embedded at the forefront of her mind.

"That could be an important detail," Dalton said, a hint of elation in his voice.

"Or it could be a red herring, Mr. Dalton," Lang offered indignantly.

Amber's eyes bounced between the two men, as even she was starting to sense the contention in the room.

"Excuse me, sir, but don't you think that we should discuss the merits of my assumptions in private?" he demanded.

Dalton had suddenly found his balls. He smelled something in what Amber was telling him and couldn't for the life of him understand why the deputy director was publicly challenging him on that point.

After a long ten seconds of silence, Lang glanced over at Amber after considering Dalton's latest remarks.

"You're right, Mr. Dalton," he said.

Dalton smiled at his triumph.

"Thank you, sir."

"And I apologize for that, Amber. I think we're all just a little anxious. After all, I've got a vested interest in this myself."

Amber shrugged, not really understanding why she was receiving an apology from the deputy director of the FBI.

"OK, Mr. Dalton," Lang continued, rising from his seat. "See what you can formulate from this latest information. But don't lose sight of the big picture. We promised this young lady we'd help her. Don't lose her mother in the shuffle." He sounded very sincere.

"I won't, sir," Dalton assured him, returning somewhat to the role of the dutiful underling.

"I'm giving you exactly forty-eight hours to find something on this Dutch lead. Then it's back to the manhunt for Jack Bennett and Mrs. Wakefield. Is that understood?"

"Absolutely, sir." Dalton reached to shake Lang's hand but didn't get the chance. The door closed behind Lang as he hurried from the conference room.

Outside the door, Lang leaned his back against it and wiped his forehead with a handkerchief he had retrieved from his pocket.

"Forty-eight hours," he muttered through an exhalation, staring straight up at the ceiling. "Jesus Christ."

And with that, he walked down the hallway, holding his cell phone to his ear.

Chapter 36

Amber had managed to escape the FBI office long enough to return to her hotel room to shower and lie down. As usual, her two escorts were close the entire time. She called her home message service twice during that time, in the desperate hope that she might hear from her mother. A part of her even hoped that she might hear from Jack himself. She checked her messages at work. Kaitlyn had called her to say that she was planning to remain in Chicago with the other executives. Apparently, the Maguire deal was not as dead as the media was depicting it.

When Amber arrived back at the FBI office three hours later, she found Special Agent Dalton seated in the conference room with the door wide open. He looked up behind the mountain of papers that had been growing each day.

"Amber, good morning," he said. He nodded toward the open door. "I decided to ventilate the room a bit. It was starting to take on that stale coffee and body odor scent." He laughed lightly. "Did you manage any sleep?"

"Not much. Too much noise in the hallway of a hotel during the day." She glanced around. "Where's Mr. Lang?"

"He left this morning. He had to complete his rotation around the West Coast offices. He'd already delayed his trip a couple of days to stay behind."

Amber sensed a hint of satisfaction in Dalton's tone. Based on the manner in which their last meeting had ended, she could understand why Dalton might be happy that Lang had moved on.

"But, if you couldn't tell, he'll be checking in once my forty-eight hours are up," he said.

Amber sat in the chair across from him. "Mr. Dalton, I know you have a process to follow here, but I feel like that's taking a very long time. I feel that we should be doing something now."

"I understand, Amber. And we are moving as quickly as possible. I've got an exclusive core team of men looking at this. We're already making strides."

He noted the subtle wave of encouragement shudder through her. She was hungry for more information.

"That's all I can tell you right now."

He watched as the illumination in her face faded slightly. He was about to speak again, to offer some sort of consolation. But he was interrupted by a knock on the door. They both looked up and saw a young man with a pad of paper in his hand. He was probably in his late twenties and was wearing glasses. The rolled-up sleeves and loosened tie, along with his five o'clock shadow, were indicators that he had worked throughout the day and into the evening.

"Yes," said Dalton.

"Sir, I'm sorry to interrupt you, but I thought you might like to hear this." The eager young man pulled out the pen that had been tucked behind his ear and stepped inside the conference room.

"Not at all. By the way, meet Amber Wakefield," Dalton said, holding his hand out toward her.

"Ma'am," he said, nodding at her in acknowledgment.

"Amber, Gil here is one of the men I was just talking about." He turned back toward Gil. "What do you have for me?"

"Well, sir, after our briefing this morning, I did some checking on Dutch companies. We ran a search for all entities incorporated in the last five years within the Netherlands's territories and provinces. Then, we…"

Dalton stopped him. "Gil, get to the end please."

Gil nodded dutifully. "Sir, we found it."

"It?"

"Bartlett Enterprises," Gil said.

"Where?" Dalton asked, sitting up in his chair.

"Aruba, sir."

"Aruba? Are you sure?"

"Positive. We checked with the Ministry of Justice as well as the Chamber of Commerce and Industry down there. Bartlett appears on their registrar."

Dalton smiled and glanced toward Amber. Her face contained that glint of hope he had seen earlier.

"What kind of company is it?" Dalton asked.

"Well, we spoke with the trust company that incorporated them. Apparently, on the application they stated that Bartlett is some type of consultant agency. Pretty vague stuff, sir."

"Big surprise," Dalton said sarcastically.

"What would you like me to do, sir?"

"Find out everything you can. Talk to whomever you need to down there." Dalton was issuing orders in rapid fire. He could feel the momentum building and could hardly wait to impress Lang with his results.

"I want to know all the details," he continued. "I want a complete list of the company's officers. I want to know who pays the registration fees. I want to know who completed the application process. All of it. Is that understood?"

"Completely, sir," Gil replied, his eyes dancing in anticipation.

"Well done, young man," Dalton said.

"Thank you, sir."

And with that, Gil was gone.

Dalton looked over to Amber, who he had nearly forgotten was sitting in the room listening.

"So, what does this all mean?" she finally asked.

"I'm not exactly sure yet. You know that the reasons for setting up an organization in the Caribbean can be numerous. But clearly, whoever stole those documents from you in Italy is intent on keeping it concealed."

"I can't believe all this fuss can be over a bunch of papers. For all we know, whoever took them could have stashed them into a file drawer in any corner of the earth," she said.

"Frankly, I could really care less where those documents are," said Dalton. "I just want to why they are so valuable. Whatever is worth hiding is obviously worth something."

Six hours had passed since young Gil had shared his findings with Special Agent Dalton regarding Bartlett Enterprises. Amber continued to leap from her seat at the sound of every ringing phone, even if it was coming from several doors down. She hoped that someone would run into the office to tell her that her mother had been found. That she was safe and had simply gone out of town for some personal time. But Amber knew that would never happen, not to the woman who, in recent years, had become more and more of a stranger to her.

Between the waves of panic for her mother's well-being and her anger toward Jack Bennett, Amber experienced brief moments of calm as she considered the FBI's logical theories. Jack was apparently doing all of this to get to Amber. He needed something from her. It didn't seem rational that he would harm her mother out of spite. Besides, he was a smart man. He would know that any harm to any of her loved ones would remove him further from her and whatever he was ultimately after. She felt consoled to think about it that way. And at this point, she needed all the consolation she could get.

She sat in the conference room, which had now taken on the appearance of a full-fledged war room. Diagrams and matrices covered the white board, and an enlarged image of Jack Bennett's complete dossier was pinned on the walls around the room. For some reason Amber couldn't explain, she shamefully recalled their night together in the motel. She didn't think about the staged scuffle in the motel room with the tattooed man, or about the next morning when she had seen Jack and that man eating doughnuts and drinking coffee together. Instead, she thought about how she had held the icepack to his bruised eye. How he placed his strong hands over hers. How they kissed. She hadn't kissed many men in her life, but this one felt like no other. It felt gentle, real, safe. *Safe.* How strange for her to feel safe when she thought about Jack. Now she thought sadly that perhaps she didn't know what it meant to be loved after all.

The conference room door suddenly opened, startling her. Special Agent Dalton stepped in with Gil on his heels. Dalton was in mid-sentence when they entered.

"And you're sure about this?" he said to Gil.

"I'd say 95 percent certain," Gil replied. "We're going off the testimony of an eyewitness down there."

"How long ago did she see him?"

"Only yesterday, sir. That's why we're pretty confident that what she saw is still fresh in her memory."

Amber walked toward them. "What's going on?"

Dalton and Gil turned toward her as if they had forgotten she was still in the room.

"We found an eyewitness who saw Jack Bennett," Gil answered, immediately looking as though he wished he could recall the words. Dalton shot a look at Gil that reminded the young rookie that he had violated the Bureau's protocol by speaking ahead of the Special Agent in Charge. What was worse, he was sharing uncorroborated evidence with a civilian. It was obvious even to Amber that Gil's information was not meant for her ears.

"You found him?" she asked.

"We don't know anything yet, Amber," Dalton said, attempting to undo the young man's blunder.

"But wait, he just said that someone saw Jack," she said, pointing a long finger at Gil.

Gil took a couple of steps backwards, hoping to disappear into the darkness of the doorway.

"It's just one eyewitness, Amber," Dalton said. "We haven't confirmed anything. We still need to talk to her more extensively."

"Where? How long ago?" Amber pressed. She was not going to let Dalton convince her that it was nothing.

"Down in the Caribbean. An employee at the trust company that managed the incorporation process for Bartlett said she saw a man who matched Jack's description in there. But," Dalton added emphatically, "this doesn't mean anything yet."

"So we're going down there to check it out, right?"

Dalton cracked a smile and shook his head gently. "Not we, my dear."

"Excuse me?" she asked.

"You heard me, Amber. You're a civilian. I can't take you with me."

"I don't think you understand, Mr. Dalton. I'm not going to sit here and not worry my pretty little self while you casually look into this thing." Her voice was fiery.

"Amber, look...," he started.

"No, Mr. Dalton. This is the first solid lead you've had since I brought this to you. And if you're not going to go after it with the vigor I need, then I want to be there to make sure you do. Besides, you said it yourself. Jack wants *me*. Now what better way is there to get close to him than to bring him what he wants?"

Even Gil was shocked by her taking charge and speaking to Special Agent Dalton in such a manner.

"Amber," Dalton said again.

"I'm going with you," she interrupted, her arms now folded.

"I'm sorry, Amber. But I can't. You shouldn't know even this much," he said, shifting his eyes in Gil's direction. "We don't bring civilians with us into the field. And what's more, we most certainly don't use them as bait."

Amber dropped into one of the chairs, realizing the futility of her efforts to win a battle against one of the most powerful agencies in the world.

Dalton leaned forward and placed a gentle hand on her arm. "But I promise you, Amber. We're going to turn over every stone on this thing. Believe me, when we get down there, and if Jack Bennett is as close as we think he is, we'll find him. And when we do, we'll find your mother. But you need to wait while we do our job."

Amber continued to stare down at the surface of the table. He was right, and she knew it. Even though it had come from her own mouth, the thought of using herself to lure Jack frightened her. Then an idea abruptly entered her mind. As though she had been convinced by Dalton's wisdom and reassurance, she looked up at him.

"OK, Mr. Dalton."

As Dalton reveled in his ability to coax her, Amber turned toward the window. She needed to get back to the Ensight office. The clock was ticking.

Chapter 37

Harry Lang closed the door to the Royal Suite of the St. Regis Hotel and walked toward the sitting room. Already seated on the ornate chairs were the surviving members of the Committee.

"Welcome back, gentlemen," he said. He looked in the direction of the oldest member. "Terry, nice to have you join us for a change."

"Sorry, Harry. I've been a bit busy trying to help thwart terrorist attacks against our country. What the hell have you been doing with your time?" Terence Hammond didn't allow his age to erode his sharp tongue.

Bruce Fox scratched his goatee, fighting hard to hold back a smile. He loved the old man for taking it straight to the rack when it came to Lang.

Dennis Fitch, who wore his customary scowl, stood at his assumed position by the window. He pointed his pipe at Lang. "Are you going to tell us what the hell you brought us here for?"

"There's been a new development," Lang announced. He preferred to omit details from his opening statements. It facilitated his ability to control the pace of the discussion.

"Good or bad development?" Fox inquired.

"Both." Lang smiled as he looked at the other three, holding them in suspense.

"For Christ's sake, spit it out," Fitch demanded.

Lang took a sip from his water bottle and set it down on the lacquered table beside the sofa.

"During my visit to the West Coast field offices last week, I had the unexpected fortune of meeting Amber Wakefield."

Fox swallowed the little saliva in his mouth.

"Whoa, you were right about her, Bruce," Lang continued. "She is one smoking piece of ass. I would love to get between those…"

"Will you shut the fuck up about that! Tell us why we're here, goddamnit!" Fitch shouted.

Lang held his index finger to his mouth. "Inside voice, Denny. Remember?"

Fitch extended his middle finger skyward at the deputy director, to which Lang smiled, having evoked the precise reaction he wanted.

"It turns out that our good friend Jack Bennett has sunk to levels even I would never go." He had their attention now.

"Apparently, young Amber has a sick mother who lives in Rhode Island," Lang continued. "Jack made contact with her, claiming to be a friend of Amber's, and now the elder Mrs. Wakefield has gone missing."

He went on to explain how Amber had enlisted the aid of the San Francisco field office, specifically the Special Agent in Charge. He recounted how Dalton was following up on the Bartlett angle.

"Dalton is obsessed with the why and the how of the whole thing. Under normal circumstances, I'd applaud that. But I can't allow him to get sidetracked. I gave him forty-eight hours to find something on the Bartlett deal. But we all know he's barking up the wrong tree. As long as Fitch here keeps those documents safe, we have no worries."

He looked directly at Fitch, who was not looking back.

"As soon as the forty-eight hour period expires, I've ordered Dalton to get back to directly finding Jack."

"And what if he finds something before his time is up?" Fitch asked.

"Well, that depends first on what that 'something' is. But either way, it's going to lead us to Jack. We need to find him, too. He's got our money."

"Speaking of the money, where are we on all of that?" Hammond asked. "I've been a bit out of the loop for a while, so would you oblige me by catching me up?"

"My guy recently left Milan, having cleared out the last of the accounts. Or at least the last of the ones that Jack's man hadn't gotten to first. My man is now headed to Curaçao to move the funds to the account in Belize."

"And how long are you going to keep up the charade with your agents who've been following him?" Fox asked.

"Until it's all done and the funds are secure," Lang said curtly, trying to avoid any more details about the two FBI agents, one of whom he knew was permanently off the case. It was time for a deterrent, he felt.

"Denny," he said, turning toward the venture capitalist, "the rumor out there is that Maguire is pressing Ensight to resume moving forward on the acquisition deal. So, I need for you to transfer the Bartlett documents to the account in Belize. I've trusted you this long to keep them safe, but nothing is entirely secure if it's kept in the same place for too long."

Fitch glanced quickly at Fox, who looked back. This exchange did not go unnoticed by Lang, who was suddenly fuming inside. He hated being lied to. But he was confident that neither wanted to tell him the truth because deep down, they feared him. Besides, he had his own agenda. Once the documents were in his hands and all was secure, he would make that call to Watts to take care of his colleagues. The whole plan would fall together rhythmically like a string of dominoes.

Outside the suite, Fitch and Fox walked with Hammond in silence toward the elevators. As the men rode down, the elevator stopped on several floors as more people crammed into the space, almost leaning on one another. The crowd only added to the suffocation of the moment as the Committee members held their tongues. The burning urge to speak felt like trying to inhale underwater. But they knew they had to be alone before they talked.

Fox and Fitch helped Hammond into his waiting car, and it was only when they were two blocks from the hotel that they spoke.

"We've got some work to do," Fox said. "If we don't find those docs, it will spell the end for us."

"Don't worry, Foxy," Fitch replied. He reached into his coat pocket and pulled out an envelope, which he handed to Fox.

"What's this?" Fox asked, opening the envelope.

"Read it."

Fitch watched as Fox read intently, then looked up. "When did you get this?"

"It arrived this morning," Fitch replied. "What do you think?"

"It's like having a guardian angel looking after us," Fox said, rereading the letter. "I've always wanted to go to Belize," he added, in a playful attempt to calm his friend.

"Me, too. But you better book me a one-way ticket. I don't think I'll be returning."

"That makes two of us."

Fox looked across the street and for a moment, his eyes steady, then just as quickly looked away. He held his hand out, which Fitch shook firmly, nodded, and walked off.

Seated in the driver's seat of the Toyota Sienna across from the St. Regis, his dark sunglasses shading his eyes, Watts removed the earpiece and grinned. Following Lang's explicit instructions, he had managed to affix a tiny microphone tablet onto the sleeve of Denny Fitch's topcoat as he pressed against him in the elevator as they rode down to the hotel lobby only minutes before. He knew that Lang would review the tapes later.

He pulled away from the curb, driving the minivan past Dennis Fitch as he strolled down 16th Street. Fitch looked up and glanced at the van as it went by. Watts continued past on his way to a drugstore to pick up some sunscreen. He knew the sun in the Caribbean this time of year would be sweltering.

Chapter 38

Amber stepped into the Ensight offices at six-thirty on Thursday. It had been two days since she had left the FBI offices. Special Agent Dalton had already departed for Aruba on the evening after their meeting.

The office was nearly deserted. Ever since Jamie's tragic death, the employees' desire to work past normal business hours had all but disappeared. Most left the office or rode the elevators in groups. Most of the women carried pepper spray on their key chains. The company had even sponsored self-defense courses in the gym downstairs.

From the moment she entered through the lobby doors, Amber knew precisely where she was headed. She walked out of the elevator onto the ninth floor, the home of the information security department. It was virtually the only department in the company that still had more than half of its occupants working at this hour.

She weaved in between the cubicles until she reached the east side of the floor. She stopped in front of one of the corner cubicles and rapped her hand on the makeshift wall.

"Miss Wakefield, you startled me," said Sanjay Mehta, clearing the empty Dr. Pepper cans from his desk, much in the manner one would if he were surprised by a special visitor in his home.

"I'm sorry, Sanjay. I didn't mean to scare you," she said.

"Not to apologize, Miss Wakefield."

As he had done many times before, he looked around to see if any of his cronies could see him talking to Amber. This time, a few of the other engineers who were walking the floor caught sight of her talking to their Indian friend.

He turned back to her. "I was so sorry to hear about Marty." He said Marty's name by emphasizing the 'T' more than any other letter. "He was a fine man."

"Yes, he was."

"Now, what may I do for you?" he asked, doing all he could to distract himself from ogling her.

"I need to have some technical questions answered, and you were the first person who came to mind."

"I'm flattered," he said, blushing. "I would be pleased to assist you in whatever manner I am able."

"I need access to one of the privileged systems here."

Sanjay looked at her, regretting that he had offered his help so willingly.

"Which system would that be?" he asked.

"Cyclops," she replied.

The engineer cocked his head back. "I'm sorry, Miss Wakefield, but I cannot do that."

Cyclops was a proprietary system used to store the records of all corporate expenses that exceeded $200,000 and those not related to Ensight's day-to-day business operations. Access to Cyclops was exclusively reserved for a few privileged people in the company, namely the CEO, the CFO, the controller, and the chairman of the internal audit committee. The special system had been developed at the behest of the former CEO as a way to have a financial checks and balances system among the top executives and to discourage collusion among them. The former CEO had believed in that type of trailblazing, and as a result, won public accolades from the Securities and Exchange Commission and the New York Attorney General. Most employees didn't even know that Cyclops existed, but Amber had learned of it because it was designed by the same engineer who had built her personnel database in human resources.

"Please, Sanjay," she pleaded.

"I'm very sorry," he repeated. "But that is an exclusive system for privileged eyes only."

"I realize that, which is why I need your help. This is extremely important to me."

"But it is password protected," he explained.

"You could get in if you really had to, couldn't you?"

She placed a gentle hand on his arm, sending butterflies up his torso.

"I'm terribly sorry, Miss Wakefield. But I'm afraid this is one thing for which I can provide no assistance to you." His head fell, his chin touching the top of his chest. "I have to say no."

Amber stood from his desk, which she had been leaning on. "I understand, Sanjay. I won't ask again. Sorry to have bothered you." And she was gone.

As she walked down the hallway, Sanjay sat at his desk, chastising himself. The sweetest, most beautiful woman in the office had just asked him for a personal favor. She had selected him from the entire pool of engineers, any of whom would probably have sold their mothers at auction to get near Amber. But he couldn't bring himself to surrender his integrity. Of course, he couldn't imagine a person with any more integrity than Amber Wakefield. Her request must have been of exceptional importance to her. He turned back toward his computer screen and continued to busy himself with work. It was all he could do to stop thinking about her.

Amber rode up to the thirty-fourth floor. She heard a number of voices down the hall, coming from the direction of the CFO's office. As she walked toward it, she could see three of the executive assistants talking with one another. By the tone and the demeanor of the group, obviously they were not discussing the latest Hollywood gossip. It was business.

She approached them with caution, weary that she had yet to be adopted into this order of office women. But when they saw her, they all seemed relieved.

"Amber, there you are," one of them said.

"What's going on?" she asked.

"Have you heard from Kaitlyn?"

"Not a peep. Why?"

The eldest and clearly the most experienced of the three stepped forward. She was the assistant to Dick Hale, the CFO.

"It's the Maguire deal. It's going south."

"Wasn't it already going south?" Amber asked. She immediately realized that these women were far more engaged in the business than she was.

"Well, now it's in big trouble. I just got a call from Dick. He says that Kaitlyn is resisting the latest Maguire offer."

Amber decided to make an attempt at sounding intelligent. "Well, if they're lowballing us, then she's probably just negotiating, don't you think?"

"I don't know," said Dick's assistant. "He said that Maguire was offering a 12 percent premium on the current stock price. All things considered, I think that's a pretty good offer. But evidently, our fearless CEO doesn't seem to agree." Her sarcasm in referring to Kaitlyn was unmistakable.

It was the first time Amber had the sense that these women were not exactly flag-waving fans of the chief executive. Perhaps it was the old theory about women being threatened by other powerful women. Then, as quickly as they had beckoned her over, the other women closed the circle and continued talking among themselves. Apparently, Amber's defense of Kaitlyn was not what they were hoping for.

As she walked away, Amber heard some of the other women discussing how much they anticipated exercising their stock options following the acquisition and taking vacations with their husbands and families. Escaping their voices, Amber stepped into Kaitlyn's dark office. It seemed like weeks since she had seen Kaitlyn, even though it had been only a matter of days. Ever since she had met Special Agent Dalton, her life seemed to be measured in the equivalent of dog years, Amber thought pensively.

She looked around the executive's office with its neatly piled papers atop the large wooden desk. The palm tree in the corner was badly in need of watering, and despite its lifeless appearance, Amber felt that it was watching her.

She sat in the large leather, high-back chair and scooted it toward the desk. It was a slim shot, but Amber hoped that Kaitlyn might have had a careless moment in her haste to leave the office for her meeting in Chicago. She hoped that perhaps Kaitlyn might have left her log-on ID and password to the Cyclops system in plain view. But she stopped looking when she tried to open the desk drawer. It was locked. Apparently, Kaitlyn hadn't been that careless.

Amber felt guilty for doing this. After all, Kaitlyn had been kind to her over the last few weeks. *Shame on you*, she told herself. She pushed the chair back in and walked out of the office, but not before stopping and looking at the surveillance palm tree in the corner.

"Not a word," she said to it, holding her finger to her lips.

Outside the office, she walked to Jamie's desk. Perhaps the former executive assistant might have had access to Kaitlyn's Cyclops account and might have the password stored somewhere. As she pulled the chair out, she spotted a blue interoffice envelope lying in it. The envelope had never been used, as all the lines on the front were blank except for the first line. It had Amber's name on it. She quickly opened it and found a single sheet of paper. In scrawled handwriting were two words—*sys_admin* and *PYRAMID*.

She glanced around the office and saw the black hair that covered the back of Sanjay Mehta's head as he walked quickly back toward the elevators. She was about to run after him to thank him but thought better of it. The clandestine nature of the delivery made it clear that he wanted nothing more to do with whatever she was up to.

Unfortunately, there were only four workstations within the company with the Cyclops application installed on their computers. In addition, certain members of the IT department had access for system development and testing purposes, but Amber was not about to impose on Sanjay again. He had already put himself at great risk of losing his job. She wouldn't do that to him again.

Recalling that Kaitlyn's laptop was removed from its docking station, Amber knew she couldn't access the system from that office. She walked down the hallway at a casual pace, careful not to appear openly anxious. Her heart was beating faster and her feet felt heavy as she approached the doors of Dick Hale's office. Looking behind her, she could see that his assistant was gone, her computer shut down and her chair pushed in. She was likely sipping Chardonnay at this point, commiserating with her two fellow assistants about their Ensight jobs.

She stepped into the CFO's office. The complete opposite of Kaitlyn's office, it smelled musty and was cluttered, with papers scattered across the desk. An unwashed coffee cup with the company logo on it sat on the edge of the desk, and a dead houseplant remained in its final resting place on the windowsill.

As she had expected, Hale's computer was there. He apparently did not use a laptop, from what she could see—probably because of his staunch refusal to perform any work when he was not physically in that office. Amber was reminded of Marty Callahan's similar philosophy.

With the lights still off, Amber sat in Hale's chair and pulled it close to the desk. The chair had been adjusted to recline fully, and she could feel the massive indentation in the center of the seat that told her its owner spent more time on his ass than on his feet. She turned on the computer, and it hummed to life. She squinted in the dark office as the bright screen illuminated her face.

Searching the window for her target, she finally found it at the bottom left corner. She clicked the mouse on an icon with the image of a single eye with the word Cyclops printed across it. At the log-on screen, she unfolded the paper she had received minutes earlier. Typing in the logon ID and the password, she glanced through the glass doors to be sure she was still alone. Other than the flickering of a dying fluorescent light tube in the hallway ceiling, there were no other signs of movement out there.

From the images appearing on the computer screen Amber realized that the access granted to system administrators was far more transparent than any of the other profiles. She was accustomed to this, as a similar principle applied to her personnel database. There was a small window at the bottom left corner of the screen which displayed the log-on IDs of those who were currently logged into Cyclops. The log-ons were reported in real time, with perhaps a one or two second lag. As she watched the screen, she could see the words *system_admin LOGGED ON 19:13.*

Even though she had been unable to locate the invoice from Jackson Winthrop anywhere in the files of the accounts payable department, she wasn't convinced that it had never existed. After all, she had seen a paper copy of it when she was browsing the files in the storage room of the law office downtown.

Amber wasn't exactly sure how to go about her search, so she decided that a rudimentary search would have to suffice for the moment. She entered the words *Jackson Winthrop* into the search field and waited. As it scanned the database, Amber tapped her fingers nervously on the desk while her knees bounced up and down off the balls of her feet. She stopped when she heard a pinging tone from the computer as her database search was completed.

She watched as row after row of text appeared on the screen, each row containing almost identical information. On every row was the name *Jackson Winthrop*, a U.S. dollar amount, a date, and a ten-digit reference number. As the rows continued to appear down the page, she read closely. The piece of information that caught her attention immediately was the dollar amount. There appeared to be repetitive payments to the law firm, ranging from three hundred thousand dollars to two and a half million dollars. The payments were also very near each other in date, some as close as two days apart.

Amber took a pen and began transcribing bits of information as she read from the screen. But as luck would have it, the pen that was on top of the CFO's desk was soon out of ink. She opened his desk drawer and fumbled among the loose Tic Tacs and old packets of Taco Bell hot sauce to find a working writing utensil. Finally she found a small golf pencil and began to copy what she could see on the computer's monitor.

Suddenly, Amber stopped her note-taking. The rows of information, one by one, had begun disappearing from the screen, vanishing from the top of the screen downward, and from right to left, much in the manner it would appear if one were resting one's finger on the backspace key. Her eyes slid from the rapidly disappearing lines to the small window on the bottom corner, where she could see that another user had logged on. She read it closely as the letters appeared from left to right across the row. Her eyes froze. *phillips_h LOGGED ON 19:18.*

"Oh, my God," she whispered behind her hands, which were now cupped over her mouth.

She looked back up and saw the rows continuing to disintegrate from view, even faster than before. With the dull tip of the pencil, it was impossible for her to write anything down fast enough before it was gone. Without hesitation, she dropped the pencil and grabbed the mouse. With a steady hand, surprising even herself, she clicked the *Print* icon. She watched as the print job was sent off, but it didn't appear to be processing quicker than the rate at which the text on the screen was being deleted.

Without bothering to shut down the computer, Amber pushed herself from the desk and ran out of the CFO's office. The laser printer set on a table behind Hale's assistant's cubicle was humming. A single page fell into the tray, and she grabbed it. There were two rows of information printed on it, one of which had been cut off halfway. Fortunately, whoever was on the system had not managed to delete it completely before the print job was sent. There was nothing telling on the paper, but considering that all the rows on the screen looked similar, she figured that just one complete row was enough.

Although it was only a virtual experience, this was the closest Amber had ever come to Harper Phillips. Real or not, he was the reason all of this was happening to her. And now she held in her hand at least one part of what he was trying to conceal. Questions began to whirl through her head. *Why would he decide to delete the information now? And where the hell was he?* He could have logged on from anywhere in the world, she thought. Or he could have deleted the material from a few floors beneath her. At that thought, she moved quickly to the elevators.

As she waited, she could see that one of the other elevators was ascending. As it passed the twenty-eighth floor, she felt panic set in again. A bell rang out and she looked up. The elevator car directly in front of her opened its doors, and she stepped in. She poked repeatedly at the button to the lobby, and then slapped the *Close Door* button. As the doors began to shut, a similar bell rang out across the hall. Through the sliver of the closing steel doors, she could make out the image of a man stepping out of the opposite car. She leapt out of view toward the side of the elevator car, and the doors closed shut.

Chapter 39

▼

"Ladies and gentlemen, welcome to Phillip SW Goldson International Airport. The local time in Belize is 3:18 PM." The voice of the American Airlines flight attendant had a Texas twang. It was her accent and not the bump of the wheels touching down on the tarmac that awoke him from his deep slumber. Her accent seemed appropriate, considering he had departed from Dallas only a few hours before.

"The temperature here is eighty-one degrees Fahrenheit," the flight attendant concluded.

Despite the safety warnings, one could hear the clapping of seat belt buckles unfastening, like a row of tap shoes in an Irish folk dance performance. Watts removed the headset and stuffed it into the seat pocket in front of him. He flexed the muscles in his neck and stretched his long frame, cracking every joint from his shoulders to his toes.

As he descended the steps toward the tarmac, he immediately felt beads of sweat forming on the top of his head. The neutral air inside the fuselage was suddenly stripped away, replaced by a blanket of heat and humidity from the Belizean sky. He followed the other passengers into the air-conditioned terminal, negotiating his way toward the front of the pack. Having cruised through customs, he stood outside the terminal. A line of independent taxi drivers approached, making attempts to take his bag and lead him to their cars. But he ignored them, his eyes looking over their shoulders toward the street in front of him, until he at last recognized his ride.

He crawled into the passenger seat of the dusty blue Jeep with no doors. As it drove away toward the town of San Ignacio, Watts turned toward the driver of the vehicle. Jack Bennett sat calmly, wearing a pair of aviator sunglasses and a Boston Red Sox cap backwards. Heavy stubble covered his face and neck.

"You look nice and tan," Watts commented, noticing the light brown tint to Jack's face.

Jack smiled. "It's hard to stay out of the sun here."

"How much time do we have?" Watts asked, avoiding any more pleasantries.

"You tell me."

"Dennis Fitch and Bruce Fox will be here soon."

"And Lang?"

"He won't show his face here. No way. He's expecting me to be his eyes and ears down here." Watts mopped his forehead some more.

"And what about Amber?"

"That's your department, compadre. All I've been able to hear is that she's freaked out to all hell about her mother."

The Jeep passed two trucks on the bumpy road, as Jack kicked it up to sixty-five.

"Then, it's working."

"Let's hope. Although she's put a whole lot of faith in this Dalton guy. He could foul up everything for us."

"I'm not concerned about him. I don't know him personally, but I know his type. He's textbook. He won't go outside the lines on this investigation. I'm sure he's seated comfortably at his desk in San Francisco as we speak, waiting for one of his little boy scouts to feed him leads piecemeal." Jack looked into his rearview mirror, careful to control his speed so as not to appear conspicuous.

"Where is her mom now anyway?" Watts inquired.

"Don't worry. She's safe."

Watts chuckled playfully. "You don't trust me by now?"

"When all is said and done, I'll trust you."

The two men laughed as the Jeep sped past the grassy terrain. The strong breeze created by the forward motion of the Jeep whipped at the canvas canopy above their heads. They rode in silence for the next two and a half hours, trading positions halfway to town.

It was nearly seven by the time they pulled into San Ignacio. Watts steered the Jeep slowly over potholes and around rocks in the dusty road as they passed local residents stumbling or riding their bicycles to and from one of the local bars. He parked the Jeep in a dirt parking lot on the corner of Burns Avenue and Mission Street. The two men walked one block up the hill to Martha's Guest House, an eight-room villa with wooden doors and stone floors. The Mayan art lining the staircase qualified Martha's as the nicest hotel in town, relatively speaking.

They entered a room on the second floor, where Watts tossed his bag onto one of the two beds. He opened the bag and began to remove the contents.

"Don't bother unpacking," Jack said. "We're here for just one thing. We're leaving tomorrow morning."

Other than bars and restaurants, all of the merchants and other businesses were closed by this time. The two men walked downstairs and ordered T-bone steaks and a couple of Belikin beers. They made meaningless, hollow chitchat with each other. Only a few other people were sitting at the outdoor tables around them, but the place was not isolated enough for them to discuss business. The next morning, they were awakened by the sounds of merchants spraying down the floors to their storefront entrances, all talking loudly in their Spanish-Creole dialect. Jackhammers and cement trucks could be heard a mile away through the open window of their room. Jack and Watts took turns showering and shaving in the common bathroom down the hall, and within an hour they were out of the room.

They dropped their bags in the Jeep, which had three beer bottles resting atop the hood when they approached it, no doubt the site of some local drinkers the night before. The tiny branch of the Belize Bank was only two short blocks up the hill, so they walked to it. When they arrived, the door on the front was locked, and a sign indicated that it didn't open until ten o'clock, which was two and a half hours away.

Jack leaned toward the window, cupping his hands at the sides of his head to shield the reflection from the glass. He jumped back when he saw the whites of two eyes peer back from the other side. A young black woman in her late teens opened the door.

"Buenas," she said, looking at the two men.

"Good morning," Jack replied.

"What may I do for you?" she asked in her Caribbean accent.

"I'm here to make a deposit," he said slowly, reciting the coded dialogue his superiors had coached him on.

She eyed him carefully. "U.S. dollars?" she asked.

"That's correct."

She opened the door wider and let the two men inside, then immediately locked it behind them.

"Please wait here," she instructed them as she walked to the back behind a curtain.

The rest of the office was small and confined. There were two chairs against the far wall. Posters advertising local expeditions to the nearby caves and rivers were attached to the wall by pieces of clear tape. A small fan rested atop the counter, but was turned off at the moment.

The young girl returned holding a black, leatherette suitcase. Jack glanced at Watts, who was still standing only a foot inside the front door. He took the case and set it on top of the counter. He adeptly rolled the numbers with his thumb until he had the combination. Opening the case only slightly, he peeked inside and then quickly shut it again. Nodding at the young girl, he handed her a U.S. hundred-dollar bill. The two men walked out of the bank branch without saying anything more to her. They heard the door lock behind them.

Jack placed the suitcase snugly behind the driver's seat of the Jeep and hopped in, and Watts took the passenger seat. As they rolled away in the direction of Belize City, a cloud of dust kicked up behind them.

Special Agent Dalton, who sat a block ahead of them in the back seat of a parked brown Mazda station wagon, watched the Jeep roll past him. He wore army green cargo shorts and a black T-shirt. Behind the fake Oakley sunglasses he had purchased in a gift shop down the street, no one would have guessed that this apparently goofy tourist was the field agent in charge of the San Francisco field division of the FBI.

After a moment, Dalton's hired driver pulled away from his parking spot and followed the blue Jeep. According to his instructions, he would follow the Jeep as far it went.

Having arrived from Aruba the night before, Dalton was tired, but his adrenaline was running at top level. He had caught sight of Jack three days ago, only hours after arriving in Aruba. Although he was certain that Jack did not know him and would not recognize him, he remained out of Jack's view. Following Jack through Aruba and onto Belize had been a challenge, since Jack flew to Miami first and then to Belize. The additional leg to the trip created some nervousness for Dalton, who was sure that it would increase the chances that Jack would detect that he was being followed. But it soon came clear that Jack was completely focused on getting to his destination and that he was confident that nothing would prevent him from reaching it.

Dalton sat up in his seat, making sure that he could keep the Jeep in view. He knew that the deputy director would soon learn of his unauthorized trip to the Caribbean. He also knew he had to get to Jack soon. If he didn't, he would have to answer to Lang, a thought that scared the hell out of him. He dropped another hundred-dollar bill on the driver's seat and told him to step on it.

Chapter 40

▼

Amber sat at the far end of the busy bar at the Cosmopolitan Café, still clutching the printed page she had taken from the office. An untouched glass of sparkling water was on the table in front as she remained quiet among the growing Thursday night crowd.

The list of payments to Jackson Winthrop in the Cyclops system, coupled with the fact that those same law offices had since vanished from sight, sent a spine-chilling feeling through her. She needed to tell someone. She couldn't reach Kaitlyn in Chicago because she knew that the CEO had far more pressing matters to deal with there. Agent Dalton was somewhere in the Caribbean, but he had told her to call Gil if she needed to reach him.

She walked out of the bar and into the neighboring Rincon Center, a large building near the bay, that housed restaurants, a post office, and office and living space. Immediately inside the doors, she stepped into one of the phone booths and closed its door. She dialed the FBI office, her eyes pinned to the booth's window, surveying everything that moved into or out of the building.

A woman's voice picked up.

"Yes, this is Amber Wakefield," she said. "I need to speak to Gil…" She paused, realizing that she had never learned the young man's last name. "He'll know who I am," she assured the receptionist.

Five seconds later, Gil was on the phone.

"Miss Wakefield, how can I help you?"

"Gil, I need you to get me in touch with Mr. Dalton."

"What's wrong?"

"I just need to speak with him."

"I'm sorry, but I can't reach him right now. I've been trying, but he must be on the road or in the air because he's not picking up."

Amber closed her eyes tightly and held her fingers to her temples. She could feel the onset of a migraine headache.

"Is there something I can do?" Gil asked.

She was about to say no and hang up, but stopped herself.

"As a matter of fact, there might be." She unfolded the page she had printed out. "Is there a way for you to check on what I'm guessing is a wire reference number?"

"Sure." She could practically hear the cap being removed from the pen and could imagine Gil waiting eagerly with his notebook.

Amber read off the ten-digit reference number from the page and added, "The payment should have been made from Ensight's account to Jackson Winthrop." She could hear Gil parroting back the numbers and letters as he wrote them down.

"Got it," he said. "I'll take a look now. It shouldn't take me long. Where can I reach you?"

"Can you meet me? I'd rather not wait near this phone. I don't feel safe." She flinched as the door to the street opened but relaxed when she saw a couple walk in.

"Where should I meet you?"

"I'll be in front of Boulevard. There are a lot of people standing out there right now, so I'll look for you."

"Give me twenty minutes. I'll be there."

She hung up without saying good-bye. The cold air outside was biting, and the wind from the bay howled loudly, so much so that she could hear only her own breathing. She reached the corner of Steuart and Mission and stood among the groups of restaurant patrons handing their parking tickets to the valets. She peered inside one of the windows and spotted a foursome enjoying their dinners and wine at the very table where she and Marty had enjoyed their last lunch together. It seemed like only a week ago.

Eight cars had pulled to the curb during the time she waited for Gil. She glanced at her watch. It had been only twenty-two minutes since she had hung up the phone. She pulled the collar of her coat up around her neck and tried to keep warm. Finally, she caught sight of the young man jogging across Mission Street. She held her hand up from her position under the building's awning.

"Sorry I'm late, Miss Wakefield," he said, as plumes of his breath escaped his mouth.

"It's OK," she said, looking around.

She took his arm and pulled him to the corner of the street.

"Well, I did a search on that reference number you gave me," he started, still trying to catch his breath. "It turns out that it's not a Fed reference ID, which means that it's not a U.S. bank transfer," he continued. "It's actually a SWIFT code."

"What does that mean?"

"SWIFT is the standard used by financial institutions to exchange messages and transfer payments on a cross border level," he explained. "It's used by brokerages to settle securities transactions and…"

Amber stopped him, not needing the entire history of SWIFT. "So, what are you telling me?"

"On that particular reference number you gave to me, the recipient is a bank in Aruba."

"Aruba? Isn't that where Mr. Dalton is?"

"Yes."

"We need to alert him. He's close. This could be a key piece to what he's looking for down there."

"Or it could be a coincidence," Gil offered.

"No," she shot back. "I'm through believing in coincidences. How do we get in touch with him, Gil?"

"Well, he's scheduled to call me for an update tomorrow morning and…"

"That's too long to wait," she interrupted. "Gil, I need your help in getting down there."

Gil shook his head. "No way, Miss Wakefield. Dalton was adamant about you staying here. We can't guarantee your safety if you go to Aruba."

"Dammit, I'm already in danger! And now my family is in danger. Do you get that? Does anyone fucking get that?"

The restaurant patrons and a few of the valets turned as Amber raised her voice. Gil noticed and tried to calm her. He spoke softly.

"Miss Wakefield, I have an obligation to keep you from interfering with this investigation. Dalton will have my head."

Amber's eyes softened for a moment. "Please, Gil. Please."

He tried to look away but could do so for only a few seconds before looking back at her.

"Even if, and I say if, I wanted to help you, I don't have the authority to OK this. Dalton doesn't even have the authority, technically."

"Who does?" Amber pressed on.

"There's really only one person."

"Who?"

"The deputy director."

"Mr. Lang," she said.

Gil nodded.

"How do I reach him?"

"I suppose you can call headquarters," Gil said, slowly surrendering. "But it's really late over there. I doubt he's available."

"I'll take my chances. Please don't mention any of this to Mr. Dalton if he asks. I'm doing this for my own reasons."

Gil nodded reluctantly. "I'm sorry I couldn't be of more help to you, Miss Wakefield."

She placed her hand on his arm. "Gil, you've been more help than you can imagine. Thank you."

"You're welcome, Miss Wakefield."

And she was gone.

* * * *

Amber negotiated and pleaded with the woman at the FBI headquarters to allow her to speak with the deputy director. He was traveling, the woman said, and could not be reached. Furthermore, the deputy director did not receive calls directly from the public. After fifteen minutes more of pleading that bordered on slight verbal abuse uncharacteristic of Amber, the woman on the phone asked her to hold. She remained on hold for the next eight minutes, listening to the hold music and certain that the woman would not be returning, until finally the hold music was interrupted.

"OK, ma'am, I have your name and your number. The best I can do is to leave him a message that you called," the woman said coldly and hung up before Amber could express her thanks.

Not even ten minutes had passed before Amber's cell phone began chirping. The number on the display started with the area code 310. Los Angeles, she recognized.

"Amber?" asked a man's voice.

"Mr. Lang?"

"Yes, dear. What is it?"

"I'm so sorry to have called you."

"Not at all. It must be important."

"It is. I found some information today that I think the FBI should know about. I can't say if it has anything to do with my mom's disappearance or Jack Bennett, but at this point, I'm willing to try anything."

"Absolutely. What did you find out?" His tone was more interested than she had thought it would be. After all, here she was, talking to the second man in command at the FBI, and he was apparently all ears.

"I learned that Ensight has been paying large sums of money to the law firm of Jackson Winthrop over the last few years."

"Jackson Winthrop," he repeated. "Isn't that the law firm that you told Special Agent Dalton about?"

She was pleasantly surprised to hear him recall such specific details in the midst of everything else he must be handling at his level.

"Yes, sir. Only I found out that the bank that the money was transferred to is in Aruba, of all places."

There was a long pause on the phone.

"Mr. Lang? Are you still there?"

"Yes, Amber. I'm still here. How did you find out this information?"

Amber thought for a moment. She didn't want to tell him that she had coerced someone in Ensight to reveal the password to a privileged system. She envisioned all of this getting back to Sanjay, resulting in his humiliating termination.

"Let's just say that I found out," she said.

"And have you told Special Agent Dalton about this?"

"No. That's why I'm calling you. I can't reach him right now. He left for Aruba two days ago."

"He's in Aruba?" Lang asked.

Amber realized at that moment that Dalton had left without authorization. But she didn't care much that she might have created a shakeup in the FBI chain of command.

"Yes, Aruba. I don't think he knows about these payments, so I think someone should alert him to them while he's down there. I think he's really close to finding something, and this information may be helpful."

"It certainly sounds that way, doesn't it?" Lang said, trying to maintain a moderate tone to his voice.

"Mr. Lang, I need to get down there. I know it's against protocol, and it's dangerous, and you think I'll get in the way, but…"

"I can do better than that, Amber," he cut in. "I'll escort you down there myself."

The surprise Amber had felt at the deputy director's attention to this matter now turned to shock. But she was not about to turn him down. Not now.

"When can we leave?"

"We leave tomorrow morning. I'm in LA. I'll fly up early tomorrow, and we'll fuel the jet in San Francisco. Be at the airport by 6:15. No later."

She listened to his tone. He sounded determined. Perhaps he was more intent on getting down there to admonish Special Agent Dalton, she guessed. But that was Dalton's problem, not hers. She just needed to get down there.

"6:15, Mr. Lang. No later. I'll be there."

After ending the call, Lang dialed his phone again. His face was expressionless, concealing the blood rising to his scalp.

"What the fuck happened?" he said into the phone. "I thought I told you to delete the payment details from the company's system."

"I did. About an hour ago." The man ran his hands through his ponytail.

"Well, young Amber beat you to the punch. She knows when the payments were sent. She knows who they were sent to. She even knows where the fucking bank is!"

"Mr. Lang, you asked me to extinguish any record of those payments. I did that. No one knows that those payments existed."

"Correction. One person knows. And I'm personally going to make sure that it doesn't go any further than her."

"What do you want me to do?"

"Get your ass down to Belize. Now. We need to take a shortcut to the finish line. It's time to fast-track this thing."

Chapter 41

▼

With Watts asleep in the passenger seat, Jack rolled the Jeep steadily along the Western Highway toward Belize City. It had been a long journey since his last days as an official employee of the FBI. Harry Lang was close. He could smell him. He couldn't quite remember how Amber Wakefield had even become caught in the middle. It generally wasn't his style to use uncivilized tactics as he had used with her mother. But he had instructions, and they were explicit. There was no time to allow emotions or personal attachments to influence his decisions. He had a job to do.

Watts stirred in his seat as the Jeep's engine rumbled on. The morning sun was rising quickly behind them, toward the sky's apex. Along the two-lane road, they passed three dusty buses, coughing black smoke, with handwritten destination signs in their front windows. Jack pressed his foot on the accelerator as the Jeep went by and then quickly swung the steering wheel back into the lane. After he had passed the third bus, he heard the driver lay on his horn, as another car, a small taxicab, performed the same passing maneuver. The only difference was that the taxicab nearly lost a game of chicken with an oncoming truck approaching in the opposite lane, causing him to swerve back close in front of the bus.

Jack noted the incident in his rearview mirror and shook his head. That was all he needed—to be involved in a wreck on a remote highway in Belize. He shifted gears on the Jeep and sped away as the taxicab and the buses became smaller and smaller in his mirror. By the time they entered the town, there was no one behind them.

Jack coasted the Jeep through the town's dusty roads until they were in front of Novelo Bus Terminal, the main bus hub in and out of Belize City. Watts opened his eyes as he inhaled a breath of exhaust coming from the line of buses lumbering in and out. Scores of tourists and locals alike made their way through the narrow doorway toward the boarding area. One after another, old converted tour buses coming from as far north as Chetumal in southern Mexico, and from as far south as Punta Gorda on the southern tip bordering Guatemala, unloaded sweaty passengers, only to leave fifteen minutes later with a new group.

The two men jumped out of the Jeep, leaving it parked in front of a line of taxicabs. Jack left the keys in the ignition. Some lucky person would assume ownership before lunchtime. Clutching the suitcase tightly, Jack followed Watts away from the terminal and toward the town. The car traffic was heavy as they walked through the streets, past the local merchants standing outside their storefronts chatting with loiterers and mopping the perspiration from their faces as the scorching sun beat cruelly upon the town.

Five blocks later, Jack and Watts arrived at the swing bridge, the site of the water taxi launch. Their shirts were soaked through as they stood in line to purchase their tickets. Tourists with gargantuan suitcases and sunburned skin waited in the open-air lobby, some hovering around the giant oscillating fan suspended in the ceiling corner. Watts bought two tickets to Ambergris Caye and handed one of them to Jack.

After twenty minutes, a short man called out that the next water taxi was departing. Without any organization, all the passengers stood and formed a makeshift queue as the man accepted their tickets and tossed their bags to another man standing just inside the boat. Jack watched as the passengers' luggage was ruthlessly tossed into a large storage compartment toward the bow. As he and Watts found the front of the line, the short man accepting the tickets grabbed the handle of the suitcase. Jack pulled it back, an act that the young man did not appreciate.

"I'm sorry," Jack said. "It's fragile, so is it OK if I carry it on my lap?"

The short man looked at his partner, who nodded, but not before shooting a look at Jack to let him know he was not pleased.

As the other passengers filed into the boat, it became clear that this was going to be a tight fit. No one was permitted to stand during the ride, so that each person had to tolerate the sweat and stickiness of the person sitting beside him for the next seventy-five minutes.

Jack and Watts did not sit immediately next to one another but instead were separated by an overweight American wearing a white, sweat-drenched tank top with the words *Don't Mess With Texas* inscribed across the front. Jack closed his eyes. Seventy-five minutes, he thought to himself. 4,500 seconds. He let out three quick breaths, like a pregnant woman experiencing labor pains.

The young man who had collected the tickets had untied the rope from the dock, and the taxi operator had fired up the engine, when a voice called out.

"Wait! Wait! Hold the boat!"

All the heads on the boat turned toward the dock, where they saw a Caucasian man running toward them. By his accent, he was clearly American. He was dripping in sweat. His pale white arms and legs made it clear that he was a new arrival.

The taxi operator shook his hand from his position behind the wheel.

"No! You wait for next one."

"No, please. I have to get on this one," the man pleaded.

There were groans from the other passengers, who were anxious to get to their next destination. At last, the operator waved him on, shaking his head to make sure the man knew he was expecting a fat tip when he got off his boat. The late-arriving passenger had only one small bag with him, which the operator snatched from his hand and tossed toward the front.

"Sit," he told the late arrival.

The man immediately wedged himself between two dark-skinned women on the back bench of the boat. They each gave him sharp sneers, but he refused to look at either of them. Jack watched him get comfortable, and for a split second, the man looked up and their eyes met. The man quickly looked away. In a minute, they were out in the open water, the water taxi moving at a rapid clip, spitting up seawater fore and aft.

The boat ride was refreshing, as the lapping breeze dried the collective perspiration of the passengers. With no clouds in the open sky and with the open sea in front of them, Jack closed his eyes and enjoyed the setting. He knew that this would be his only opportunity to relax. Once he stepped off that boat, he'd be back to work. And this was the most critical stage of his mission. It would require all the precision and attention he could muster.

Jack was nearly immersed in his dream state when he heard a change in the rumble of the boat's engine below him, signifying that the vessel was decelerating. The water taxi had already made one brief stop in Caye Caulker, about twenty minutes earlier, which he hadn't even noticed. Half of the passengers disembarked there before the taxi took off again.

The time before the next stop seemed short. "Ambergris Caye!" yelled the taxi operator as he spun the wheel and gently adjusted the throttle lever, inching the boat toward the nearby dock.

The remaining passengers rose and stretched as the boat slid laterally toward the wooden dock and the crew grabbed hold of the dock with their hands and pulled the water taxi toward it. Everyone could see the blue clapboard structure of Shark's Bar & Restaurant in front of them as they climbed out. The late arrival stepped off last from the taxi, and as Jack and Watts walked down toward the beach, a voice called out from the front of the boat.

"Dalton? Mr. Dalton?"

The man who had climbed out last spun around to see one of the crew, who had been sorting through the luggage, now holding up his small bag. He was reading off the luggage tag. Dalton leaned over the boat and accepted the bag from the young crew member. When he looked back up, he saw Jack and his companion walking between buildings toward the main street.

Dalton picked up his gait a bit so as not to lose sight of the two. He didn't recognize the man with Jack but was sure he would find out who he was very soon. As he made his way up to the sandy street known as Barrier Reef Drive, he saw the two men hop into a white golf cart, the primary mode of motorized transport on the barrier island. The cart drove south down the street, moving no faster than eight miles per hour. It was easy for Dalton to keep pace with them on foot.

He was close. So close. He thought about calling Lang and telling him that Jack Bennett was within arm's reach. But he also knew that if he could collar Bennett by himself, he would become a household name throughout the Bureau, even if for only a day. He could live with that.

Chapter 42

▼

Amber stood at the foot of the steps leading up to the private jet. It was 6:20, and the blue lights along the runway illuminated the darkness of the San Francisco morning. After waving good-bye to Gil, who had escorted her to the airstrip, she pulled the collar of her coat around her neck and shivered.

Deputy Director Lang finally stuck his head out from the open doorway, with a mobile phone to his ear. He waved his hand at Amber, signaling her to step aboard. As the jet was being fueled, she stood in the aisle, not certain where she was supposed to sit. Lang turned to the side and spoke into the phone in a muffled voice, a not-so-subtle hint that this was a confidential conversation. She tried to busy herself by finding a seat toward the rear and fumbling through her backpack.

After a few more brief exchanges, Lang finally put the phone down and walked back toward her.

"Sorry about that, Amber. It's a twenty-four hour per day job," he said, holding his hand out to her.

She shook his hand. "I can only imagine. Thank you again, Mr. Lang, for letting me tag along like this. I'm sure you're breaking all sorts of rules."

"Well, the luxury of my position is that I have to answer to only one person above me." He smiled. "Which reminds me, there's been a slight change. We're going to Belize, not Aruba."

"Belize? But what about the Aruba bank and all that?"

"I just received some new information."

"So you've spoken with Mr. Dalton?" she asked.

Lang's expression changed quickly as his smile faded. She knew that she probably shouldn't have reminded him that Dalton had gone to the Caribbean without authorization. But then again, the little she knew about Lang told her that he didn't need a reminder. She felt somewhat guilty for inadvertently blowing the whistle on Dalton, but that was his problem now. He's a big boy, she told herself. He can take care of himself.

"As a matter of fact, I have spoken to him," Lang lied. "He reported there's nothing in Aruba. He's got a lead in Belize now." He looked out the opposite window, trying not to look directly at her.

"And my mother?"

"No news yet on that front, I'm afraid. But Mr. Dalton is a very focused agent. He knows the primary goal is to reach your mother. So, we're not going off track." Lang stopped himself from saying any more from concern that his continuing lies would eventually contradict one another.

They fastened their seat belts as the compressor turbines beneath them increased their start-up whine. As the jet taxied down the runway, its engine thundering, Amber stared out the window. Once they were airborne, she watched as the San Francisco skyline grew smaller and more blurred behind the clouds and fog. She wondered when she would be seeing that view again.

"So tell me about your first encounter with Jack Bennett," Lang said thirty minutes into their flight.

"He asked me what I knew about Harper Phillips. He was particularly interested in Phillips's involvement with Ensight. Whoever was claiming to be Harper obviously wanted something from the company." She subtly put the back of her hand to her nose. Lang was wearing some inexpensive cologne he had probably picked up from a mail sample. It was nauseating.

Lang nodded, as though this was all new information to him.

"And then when I saw those payment records in our system," she continued, "it became clear that this person was intent on hiding them. For all I know, it could have been Jack deleting those records. Or it could have been that big lug with the tattoo who tried to kill me."

Lang sat forward. This was the first he had heard about an accomplice to Jack.

"What big lug?"

"Didn't Mr. Dalton tell you?"

Apparently, Dalton hadn't fully disclosed everything, a discovery that further fueled the deputy director's disdain.

"No. Why don't you tell me?"

Amber felt that she had told the story a dozen times already, as she probably had.

"This man tried to shoot me at the Jackson Winthrop offices, then again that evening in a downtown motel. The next morning I saw him and Jack drinking coffee together. That's when I knew that Jack was using me for something."

"What did he look like, this other man?" Lang pressed on.

"It was hard to tell. Both times, it happened fast and it was dark. But I remember only an unsightly tattoo on his neck." She pointed to her own neck to show where the tattoo had been. "It was like a Chinese symbol or something."

Lang pursed his lips tightly, trapping the series of curses that were steaming up in his mouth.

"Well, if he is working with Jack, it sounds like he'd stick out in a crowd."

"Please understand that I'm just spewing right now. So much has happened over the last couple of months. I couldn't even put the events into order if I had to. So, who knows if anything I tell you is relevant to your investigation or my mother's disappearance."

"Well, I, for one, am glad you told me all of this. What seem to you as random events are probably connected in some way. I don't know about you, but I'm not a big believer in coincidences."

Amber looked at him in the eye. She felt comfortable knowing that they shared the same philosophy on that topic.

"When it's all said and done, I suspect the Bureau is going to owe you a debt of gratitude, Amber."

"I'd trade all that in, Mr. Lang, if you could guarantee that my mother will be safe."

"Generally, I'm not one to make guarantees. But this much I can promise you. This will all be over soon."

They sat in silence for the next twenty minutes. Amber read the *New York Times*. The front page contained a series of profiles on the leading candidates to run against the president in the November election. It was accompanied by a detailed spread discussing how much money the candidates were raising in their campaigns. By the time Lang glanced back at her, she had drifted off to sleep. He stepped toward the front of the jet, well out of earshot of Amber. He picked up the phone and dialed.

"Where are you?" he asked softly, peeking over the seats to make sure Amber was unable to hear him.

The young man on the other end cleared his throat. "I'm at the airport in Miami, sir. Waiting for my flight to Aruba."

"Change of plans. Forget Aruba. Get down to Belize. There should be a direct flight on American in two hours. Make sure you're on it."

"Why? What's happening?"

"Things are coming apart. I just spoke with our guy. Dalton's in Belize. I don't know how he knew to go there, but he's down there. He's pulling a John Wayne act, trying to do this thing solo. Find him."

"Sir," the young man began, then paused.

"What is it?" Lang asked impatiently.

"After what happened with Griffin in Spain, I'm not sure how I feel about having the blood of my fellow FBI agents on my hands."

"Are you serious?" Lang said sternly, but without raising his volume. "I didn't hire you for your loyalty to the Bureau. Understood?"

"Yes, sir, but...," the young man replied, sounding defeated.

"Your orders are to find Dalton, not your conscience."

Other than the light static on the line, there was silence. The young man understood what Lang was conveying to him, and it was far more than the stated orders.

"I'll call you when it's appropriate. Do not call me under any circumstances. And watch your back. I don't need any more uninvited guests showing up at this party." With that, Lang hung up.

He dialed the phone again.

"Foxy," he said, "is Fitch with you?"

"No, of course not. We're not going to travel together."

"This little island is about to get crowded really quickly."

"Why? Who else is down there?" Fox asked.

"Don't worry about that. I'm taking care of it. The less you know about these petty details, the better."

"Bullshit. I'm not just a pawn in your scheme. I'm your partner, remember?"

"No, Foxy. Take a look at our names. You're Bruce Fox, IRS poster boy. I'm Harrison Lang, deputy director of the FBI. So, at the end of the day, you're nothing!" His voice was raised now. "If this thing goes to hell, who do you think people are going to believe? Me or you?"

Fox said nothing.

"Meet me at our agreed spot on the island tonight," Lang concluded. "We need to finish this thing."

Consistent with his usual telephone manner, Lang hung up without listening for a response to his last order. He rose from his seat and walked back to the rear of the jet to the restroom. At the sound of the door lock clicking, Amber stirred in her seat. She opened her eyes and recounted what she had just overheard. *Bruce Fox.* She couldn't believe it. *How did he know Lang?*

She heard the toilet flush and the door being unlatched again. She closed her eyes and turned her face toward the window to hide the rapid eye movement under her lids. Lang walked down the aisle and stopped in front of her. She knew he was looking at her. After what seemed like two minutes, he continued walking to his seat in the front of the jet. Amber eased her head around to watch him, from behind, as he leaned his seat back and rested his head on the cushion with his face toward the aisle, his eyes closed. He looked different now. She continued to watch him, but he remained motionless, a wry smile on his face. And in one minute, he was snoring.

Chapter 43

▼

Special Agent Dalton lay in a hammock under a palm tree at the Victoria House, a beautiful villa on the southernmost tip of Ambergris Caye. Had it not been for his pale skin and lack of island fashion, he would have projected the ideal image of Caribbean leisure.

Through his dark sunglasses, he eyed Jack Bennett as he entered the hotel premises from the beach. He also noticed the other eyes watching Jack, all of whom belonged to forty-something women under big umbrellas with even bigger diamonds on their ring fingers. Jack apparently was the perfect visual pastime while their potbellied husbands lay asleep next to them like beached whales.

Dalton had watched Jack for two days. Several times, he saw him emerge from his bungalow but hadn't had the opportunity to go inside it yet. The bungalow faced the pool and the rest of the hotel, so it was difficult to slide in without being seen. Besides, he had no idea who the other man with the tattoo was and needed to be wary of his presence as well.

On this day, Jack walked back in the direction of his bungalow and stepped inside. Dalton craned his neck to get a view of him. In thirty seconds, Jack was outside again, but this time he was clutching a suitcase. He walked quickly past the pool and disappeared around the hotel building toward the main street. Dalton rolled off the hammock and clumsily plodded through the white sand in the direction Jack had gone. He rounded the building and saw Jack's tall frame walking casually but quickly up the street. Dalton's strides weren't as long as Jack's, so he picked up his pace a bit to prevent any more distance being created between them.

Jack stopped at the corner of Buccaneer Street and entered a white building. Dalton arrived at the front door of the building and read the sign: *Belize Bank*. After a brief pause, he entered the building and nodded at the security guard standing just inside. He watched as Jack ascended the stairs, holding the suitcase close to his side. Dalton stepped toward one of the counters and pretended to fill out a deposit slip. In less than four minutes, Jack appeared again, but this time without the suitcase. He reached the bottom of the stairs and stepped toward the exit, only to stop and glance around the floor. His eyes moved right past Dalton, as if he were a houseplant in the corner. After surveying the room, he walked back out into the sunny street.

Dalton walked quickly to the door and watched, drawing suspicious looks from the security guard, who probably wasn't trained to prevent any serious security breach but rather had been placed there as window dressing. Dalton again followed Jack back in the direction of the hotel. He figured he would return to the bank later and find out what Jack had left there. It was the middle of the day now, and there were too many people coming in and out. So, he would wait until it was closer to closing time.

He was sweating profusely by the time he stepped into the open-air bar of the Victoria House. As he walked through, Dalton was immediately met by a young Caucasian man, clad in what appeared to be some type of uniform consisting of white pants and a colorful floral print shirt. He was short in stature but had the build of a middleweight wrestler. He introduced himself as a member of hotel security at Victoria House.

"Pardon me, Mr. Dalton. But I regret to tell you that someone has broken into your bungalow."

"Excuse me?"

"We don't believe anything was taken, but we're advising you to check your room nonetheless."

"Yes, absolutely."

"If you'd like, I can escort you back there."

"That will be fine. Thank you."

As the hotel staffer led the way, Dalton took note of something strange. The sleeves on the man's shirt were particularly short. It almost looked like he was wearing clothes that were not his own. What was even more odd to Dalton was that he could see a sharp tan line on the man's arm. Most of the locals and employees on the island wore close to nothing when they weren't in uniform and thus they had no visible tan lines on their bodies. This young man had the appearance of a tourist. Perhaps it was exhaustion or the natural instinct of a seasoned FBI agent to profile an individual quickly, but Dalton recognized something else interesting about this man. Glancing down, he saw the man's brown shoes. Virtually every employee wore white sneakers with their uniforms. This man was no employee, Dalton concluded.

He continued following the young man but slowed his pace a bit, gradually creating distance between them. The young man approached the door to his bungalow, which was slightly ajar.

"Please," he said, holding his hand out, indicating that Dalton was to enter first.

Dalton stepped in and walked toward the closet.

"Is there anything missing?" the young man asked.

"Let me see," Dalton replied, reaching behind the headboard. "I hid my passport back here."

He felt the cold metal of the Glock 23 that he had taped to the back of the bed. Through his peripheral vision, he could see the young man closing the door to the room. Dalton ripped the pistol off the headboard, creating a sharp tearing sound from the tape. The young man reacted immediately by reaching toward the back of his belt. Dalton released a single shot, which found the middle of the young man's chest. He dropped to the floor, screaming in pain. As he fell to the ground, the impact jarred his finger and unloaded a shot from his .357 revolver, piercing the ceiling. Dalton moved quickly toward the young man, his pistol poised. He kicked the man's gun away and knelt down, pulling the man up by his shirt collar.

"Who are you? Who sent you?" he demanded.

But the young man could only open his mouth, revealing the blood that now filled the spaces between his front teeth. Dalton couldn't determine whether he was smiling or grimacing from the hole in his chest. He gasped something incoherent, to which Dalton responded by pulling him closer.

"C'mon! Tell me who!"

"Lang," he whispered through his violent coughs.

"What did you say? Say it again!" Dalton persisted.

"Lang," he mouthed in near silence. His eyelids began to close.

"Lang? Harry Lang?"

The young man nodded, dark pink foam spilling out of the corners of his mouth.

"What about him?" Dalton pushed on.

A loud shriek escaped the man's mouth as an apparent sudden rush of pain stunned him.

But Dalton kept up the interrogation. "Did he send you? Harry Lang sent you down here to kill me?"

The young man looked up at Dalton. He was just a kid, from what Dalton could surmise. Unarmed and wounded, he now was controlled by fear. Tears streamed down each of his cheeks. His neck surrendered the fight to uphold his head, and his eyes rolled to one side, locking in on a single spot on the floor. He was gone.

Dalton ran to the door and locked it. His heart racing, his body drenched in perspiration, he dialed his cell phone.

"Gil," he said into the phone, his breathing labored. "It's Dalton."

"Sir, where have you been?" Gil asked.

"No time to explain. Listen to me very closely. Deputy Director Lang. Find out where he is. Call headquarters, whoever. I don't care. Just find out his present location."

Despite the desperation in Dalton's voice, Gil considered the promise he had made to Amber—that he wouldn't tell Dalton about her plans. But he had just received an order from his superior, and even a promise to the Pope himself was not to take precedence.

"Sir, where are you?"

"I'm in Belize. And so is Jack Bennett. Gil, pay close attention. Lang is dirty. I don't know what he's involved in, but he doesn't want me to find out. And I must be close, considering what I just went through."

The silence on the line made Dalton uncomfortable. "Are you there, Gil?"

"Yes, sir, I'm here."

There was tension on the line. "What's wrong, son?"

"Sir, I think there might be a problem."

"What kind of problem?"

More silence filled the line. "Gil?" Dalton called out.

"Deputy Director Lang took the jet early this morning. It was originally headed to Aruba. But I called in for an update, and just before departure the crew logged the destination as Belize instead."

"Shit," Dalton whispered under his breath. "What the hell is he doing coming down here? And how do you know that?"

"I saw his jet being fueled in San Francisco." Gil wanted to eat those last words because he knew what question it would prompt next.

"What? San Francisco?"

"Sir, I…"

"Gil! Goddamnit! What the fuck is going on?" Dalton yelled into the phone.

Gil could be heard swallowing his own saliva. "Sir, Amber Wakefield is on the jet with him."

Dalton stood in the dark hotel room, frozen. The evening sun was resting comfortably at his eye level, and as he and Gil listened to the silence over the phone line, the day's light source disappeared quickly below the horizon.

Chapter 44

Amber stepped off the jet after it had landed in Belize City. The sky was darkening, but the air was still thick with humidity. It felt good to be on the ground again, where she could move freely. Behind her, Deputy Director Lang stood in the door hatch of the jet, looking around. He wore his sunglasses despite the fact that there was little light in the sky. Amber guessed that it was a machismo thing shared among FBI agents.

A twin prop plane sat a hundred yards away, its engines growling. Amber and Lang hurried toward it. A dark-skinned man in a knit shirt displaying the Tropic Air logo held his hand out to assist Amber into the aircraft. She stepped in and the air conditioner was offering little relief from the sweltering heat inside. She found a seat at the front of the plane, behind the pilot.

Lang stepped in and sat across the aisle from her, mopping his forehead and wiping the sweat from his sunglasses with a handkerchief. Despite his slumped posture, his eyes were determined. He had a plan, the execution of which meant everything to him. His reputation. His career. Perhaps even his life.

When they touched down in San Pedro, a light drizzle was developing outside. A young man holding an umbrella stood outside and immediately held it over Amber's head as she stepped off. A minivan awaited them with the side door open. The rain began falling more heavily.

"Did you sleep well?" Lang asked as he climbed inside and found a seat next to Amber.

Amber turned to him with a questioning look.

"On the plane," he continued. "You looked like you were in a pretty deep slumber."

She wondered whether he had sensed that she was actually awake during his phone conversation.

"Yeah," she said. "It's been a while since I've been able to sit in one place in peace."

He talked for the next few minutes about Belize—the history, the people, the climate. It was like a hypnotist attempting to lull his patient to sleep. She heard none of it. She needed to separate herself from him, even if only for a few minutes. The minivan stopped in front of the Banyan Bay Beach Resort. As they entered the front doors, Lang guided Amber forward by placing his hand gently on her back. It was probably a mere male instinct, but it was enough to make her shudder.

The cool air blowing from the ceiling did not mix well with her soaking clothes and hair. She hugged herself while her teeth chattered.

"Let's get you into a room quickly. A warm shower should do you right," Lang told her.

In less than five minutes, he was holding a key in front of her. It was the quickest check-in she had ever experienced, almost as though the staff knew Lang.

"This is yours," he said, handing her the key. "The young man over there will show you to your room." He pointed to a smiling local to their side. "I have to take care of some things, but I'll be by your room in a couple of hours," he continued.

She nodded and began following the young man toward her room.

"Oh, and Amber, do me a favor."

She turned to him.

"Don't leave your room. It's risky enough that I brought you down here with me. I'd feel a lot more comfortable if I knew where you were at all times."

She managed a quick smirk and walked away.

When she entered the room, she closed the door behind her and locked it. She rested her head against the door and closed her eyes, exhaling several times to calm herself. Turning around, she saw that the room was beautifully decorated, not unlike the pictures she had seen in travel magazines of tropical vacation resorts. She only wished that she could enjoy it more. She was shivering wildly from the air-conditioned breeze. She peeled off her damp clothes and got into the shower. The shock of the hot water made her wince. She ran her hands over her arms to smooth out the goose bumps. Then she heard it: a door slamming. Her hands rose immediately to the shower knob, and she turned off the water.

She heard nothing more. Maybe it had been the door of the room next to hers. Only if her luck had changed, she thought. Still dripping, she wrapped the thick towel around her body. With careful steps, she moved toward the bathroom door and put her ear to it. With both hands, she grasped the ends of her wet hair over one shoulder. She heard light tappings, almost thumping sounds, in rhythmic succession. She quieted her breathing to isolate the noise, only to discover that the thumps were her own heart beating rapidly. She placed her palm over the left side of her chest as if to muffle the sound.

She picked up a glass atop the counter. Poising it over her shoulder in strike mode, she felt silly. But she was not about to open the door without some type of protection, and her naked body and towel weren't sufficient.

She turned the knob and cracked the door open. The only activity in the room was the floating curtain, caused by the light breeze from the balcony. She walked across the room, peering into each corner. As she stepped onto the balcony, she inhaled the sea air. The rain had stopped temporarily. The balcony overlooked a large swimming pool, lined with beach chairs and tables. In the darkness, a few honeymooning couples strolled around the perimeter, alternating between whispers and light kisses. It was an extremely romantic scene, and she was suddenly reminded of how lonely she was.

She walked back inside and slid the glass door shut. As she did, a dark form passed behind her in the reflection. She screamed and spun around, her hands to her mouth.

"It's OK, Amber. It's me."

She focused her eyes. "Mr. Dalton? What are you doing here?"

"Several hours ago, I would have been asking that same question of you."

"I'm sorry. I know you told me not to come down here, but I just had to. I called Mr. Lang and…"

"It's all right, Amber. I talked to Gil. He told me."

Nice going, Gil. So much for keeping your promise, she thought.

"How did you find me?"

"I followed you here from the airstrip."

"Have you found my mother? Or Jack?"

"I don't have time to go into it in great detail. Please trust me. I'll explain everything to you on the way. But right now, I need you to come with me, Amber," he said, holding out his hand. "It's not a good idea to talk here."

She clutched the towel around her, suddenly remembering that she wasn't wearing anything underneath.

"I can't. Mr. Lang is expecting me to stay by his side."

Dalton shook his head. "You don't understand. Lang is not who you think he is. He could put you in great danger."

"Why do you think that?" She wanted him to fill in the gaps for her.

"It's hard to say. But he tried to have me killed today. Obviously he thinks I'm close to learning something."

"And you think it has something to do with my mother and Jack and all the rest of that?"

"What was that you told me once about coincidences? That you don't believe in them?"

She couldn't believe he remembered that.

There was a loud knock on the front door, and she jumped. Dalton stepped to the side and slid into the darkness inside the closet. He held his index finger to his lips. Amber opened the door slightly and stuck her head out. Deputy Director Lang stood outside.

"Sorry, Amber. I didn't mean to catch you at the wrong time," he said, noticing that she was holding only a towel around her. He imagined what was behind that single layer of cotton.

"No problem," she responded.

"I just wanted to make sure you were settled, but it looks like you're adjusting quite nicely."

"Yes, thank you. It's very nice. I just wish I was down here under different circumstances."

"Of course. I understand. I feel the same way."

She noticed his eyes glance over her shoulder, in an attempt to inspect her room from his vantage point. But she kept the door opened only slightly.

"Well," he said with an exhalation. "Don't let me keep you. Get some rest. And please remember what I told you about staying put."

"Absolutely. Good night, Mr. Lang."

"Good night, Amber."

She shut the door and stood still, looking at Dalton, who had emerged from the closet. There was silence on the other side of the door. After a minute, they heard footsteps walking away.

"Now what?" she asked him.

"Get dressed. There's someone we need to talk to."

Amber slipped into a pair of white cotton pants and a pink sleeveless knit shirt from her backpack. A Nike cap held her damp hair in place. She walked casually downstairs, hoping Lang wouldn't see her. If he knew that she had left her room, he would certainly follow her. She found Dalton standing on the beach in the darkness, precisely in the spot he had told her he would be. Only the illumination from the moon's reflection on the water revealed his face.

They walked down the beach and made a sharp left turn toward the main street. It was ten o'clock, and there were still plenty of people walking. Most were happy to be outside, having been confined to their rooms during the downpour only hours before. The sand in the streets was dark and moist, and Amber's feet sank slightly with each step. Dalton walked quickly, and she had to double-time her steps to match his pace.

After a few more turns, they found themselves walking a few blocks from the main part of town. It was darker and quieter here, and Amber felt a bit of apprehension.

"Where exactly are we going?" she finally asked.

"It's just up here," he replied, pointing to a small yellow building that resembled a house.

They stepped through a labyrinth of clotheslines and bicycle parts until they reached an open door on the side of the building. Dalton stepped inside, but Amber hung back for a moment before following him.

Except for a few cracks in the paint, the house was pleasantly decorated inside. A sofa and a loveseat were set next to a wooden table. A television rested in the corner of the room. Amber could smell something delicious cooking in the back. A rustling came from an open doorway in the rear of the room, but it was too dark for them to see inside.

"What are we doing here?" Amber whispered.

Dalton held up a hand. "It's us," he called out toward the darkness.

A figure stepped out and approached them slowly. Amber began to backpedal, but Dalton held her arm, urging her to stop. As the figure stepped into the light, Amber gasped. Her eyes bulged, and then quickly narrowed.

It was Jack.

Chapter 45

Harry Lang sat on the edge of the wooden dock that led to Ramon's Village Dive Shop, with his cell phone to his ear. He was expecting the young FBI agent to pick up, but the phone continued to ring. He grew nervous. The younger man was supposed to have checked in over an hour ago. By this time, he should have taken care of Special Agent Dalton as instructed. Where the hell was he?

The wooden planks of the dock creaked, and he spun around. Bruce Fox approached him.

"Right on time, Foxy." Lang glanced at his watch.

"Where's the girl?" Fox asked.

"She's back at the hotel. She's pretty exhausted, so my guess is she'll be asleep until morning."

"Who were you talking to?" Fox asked, pointing to the cell phone in Lang's hand.

"No one. Just listening to my messages."

Fox didn't believe a word of it, nor did Lang expect him to.

"So, is the money all here?"

Lang looked around. "That's what I'm told. It's all in an account at the Belize Bank. I'm meeting our guy at Fido's in an hour."

"And the incorporation documents?"

"You tell me. Where's Denny?" asked Lang.

"He should be along soon. He got stuck back at the hotel."

"Where's that?"

"Victoria House. It's all the way on the other end of the island," Fox explained, pointing south. "They're checking everyone's rooms after the incident today."

"What incident?"

"You didn't hear? Geez, I figured everyone on this little island had heard by now."

"Heard what?"

"Apparently, some young staff member of the hotel got waxed there this afternoon. A Caucasian kid."

Lang's tired eyes suddenly awoke. "He was killed?"

"Yeah. Single shot to the chest."

"Any witnesses? Was there anyone with him?"

"How should I know? I'm not a detective."

"Dalton," he mumbled.

"What was that?" Fox asked.

"Nothing. I have to go." He began walking down the dock.

"Wait a minute. Where the hell are you going? There's still more to talk about."

But Lang was already walking through the sand, his back turned. Fox pulled out his phone and dialed.

As rain started falling again, Lang began running. It was quite a way to the Banyan Bay resort, but he had no other choice. He needed to get to Amber before Dalton did.

"Where the hell is my mother, you son of a bitch?" Amber demanded. She hadn't seen Jack in weeks. He appeared as though he had aged, but quite nicely, she had to admit. However, that didn't suppress her urge to lunge at him and tear his eyes out.

Dalton pulled her off as she clawed at Jack. The tears in her eyes were not so much for her mother, but more for herself and for the way Jack had betrayed her. Especially for the way he had charmed her heart and broken it, both within hours.

"Amber, let me explain," Jack started. "You have no idea how many times I've tried to say this to you, but it just never seemed like the right time or place."

"Don't ask me to feel sorry for you, you bastard!"

"I wouldn't think of it." He took a step toward her.

"Stay the hell away from me!" she shouted, backing away. She glanced over at Dalton. "And you were in on this the whole time?"

"Absolutely not," he said in defense. "Until late this afternoon, I was on a mission to find Jack here and take him down. After I was almost killed this afternoon, I finally caught up to him. He explained it all to me. He's on the right side. Trust him."

"There's a whole lot you don't know, Amber," Jack said.

"First things first. Where's my mother?" she demanded again.

Jack looked at Dalton, who nodded. "She's safe, Amber."

"Enough!" she yelled. "Where is she?"

Her eyes were burning into Jack's face, and she was prepared to lunge at him again when she heard a faint voice from the dark doorway.

"I'm right here, dear."

Sliding to the right, Amber saw the silhouette of a woman standing in the dim doorway. She looked old but strong. She wore an apron and held a wooden spoon in her hand.

"Mom!" she called out. She ran to the older woman, wrapped her arms around her, and held her tightly.

"Oh, my," said her mother, laughing as her daughter wept on her shoulder. "I can't recall such a warm welcome from you."

"Oh, Mom. You have no idea how happy I am to see you." She clutched her mother even tighter. "I'm never letting you go."

"Now, nonsense, young lady. How was school today, sweetheart?"

It was the first time that Amber realized that her mother's Alzheimer's had developed into a worse stage. She still saw her daughter as a young girl.

"Mom, is everything OK?" Amber offered a sharp look toward Jack.

"Why, of course, dear. Everything's perfect. I'm just making dinner for you and your friends. I hope everyone likes stew."

Her mother's thoughts were in another, earlier place, which was probably a good place to be, in Amber's opinion.

"Now, you kids sit down so you can eat. I don't want you and Jack to be late for the dance."

Amber shot another look at Jack. He shrugged, almost embarrassed.

She watched her mother disappear into the kitchen, humming a medley of show tunes as she cooked. Despite the anguish Amber had felt for her mother, it was practically a blessing to see her in the state she was. Her mother had no idea that she had been led away from her Rhode Island home by a complete stranger. And clearly, Jack had done a lot to make her feel comfortable with him. Of course, he had also managed to charm Amber when they first met.

While her mother was in the kitchen, Amber leaned toward the two men. "Any time you two want to fill me in on what the hell is going on, I'm ready."

Jack pulled out a chair, and she sat in it. "I'm not exactly sure where to start," he said.

"The beginning is always a nice place," she responded, making sure not to disguise the sarcasm in her tone. She was through playing games. If he harmed her, at least she could say that she saw her mother alive.

"Give him a chance to explain, Amber," said Dalton, trying to reassure her. "I had to be convinced as well."

She said nothing. Sitting back, she folded her arms across her chest and looked up at Jack.

"I never meant to frighten you, Amber. Things spun out of control so quickly, and I couldn't afford to compromise my assignment." Jack's blue eyes were still bright, even under the dim lights.

She looked away quickly. She was supposed to be mad at him, she reminded herself. "What are you talking about? What assignment?"

"What I'm going to tell you is highly confidential," he started to say.

"No," she cut him off. "You lost your right to hold me to confidentiality the moment you tried to have me killed."

Jack shifted his eyes toward Dalton, who was staring back. Amber noticed.

"What?" she asked.

Dalton sat down next to her. "Amber, Jack isn't trying to kill you or to have you killed. He's trying to protect you."

"Protect me? He hired some thug to try to shoot me. Or have you forgotten?"

"It was a setup, Amber," Jack explained. "I realized early on, when I first met you, that you were not simply going to excuse yourself from this whole mess. But I also knew that the deeper you dug, the more you'd uncover. And there is a group of people who are dedicated to preventing that from happening. I knew you trusted me at the time and that you didn't have anyone else to turn to. So, I orchestrated the events at the law offices and in the motel room to discourage you from investigating further."

Amber frowned. "First of all, I would have been more than happy to walk away from it all, but you dragged me back in. You asked me to go into that Jackson Winthrop office. Secondly, what kind of sick person are you to fake an assault like that just so you could come swooping in like the hero?"

"It worked at the time, didn't it?" As soon as the words were out of his mouth, he knew he shouldn't have said them—at least not now.

"You're right," he continued. "I did take advantage of an opportunity. But let me ask you this question: were you really prepared to walk away as you claim now? Remember that your boss and friend, Marty Callahan, had just been murdered. Were you ready to allow his death go unexplained?"

He was right, Amber admitted to herself after several minutes' thought. At the time Marty died, she was so emotionally charged that she would have done anything to understand why. Evidently, she hadn't disguised her emotions well enough. But none of that mattered now. It still didn't justify Jack's actions.

"So, who the hell are you, Jack Bennett?" Amber wanted to cut directly to the chase. "I can't promise to keep what you tell me confidential, nor do I think I should have to."

Jack again looked at Dalton, who nodded. "I was hired to investigate this group of people I referred to earlier."

"I thought you said you'd been fired by the FBI."

"I was. Immediately following my official termination, I was contacted by some people in Washington. They'd been following my progress on the Harper Phillips investigation and essentially asked me to continue my work after I left the FBI's doors. I had no idea at the time how high and how deep this thing ran."

"What people in Washington?"

"I can't say. Let's just say that they are not fans of Deputy Director Lang."

Amber felt a nervous sensation run through her body. "And why should I believe you now?"

"I can't tell you that. You have to make up your own mind about that. But consider this. If I meant to do you any harm, I would have done it by now. I had plenty of opportunities. During any one of our meetings in San Francisco or in Switzerland or in Milan."

The same rush of anxiety flowed through her again as she realized that Jack had known her whereabouts this entire time. In Europe, she had thought she was tailing him, but clearly, he had known she was there all along.

He leaned forward. "I could even have done it in our motel room that night in San Fran."

Dalton looked between both of them, realizing for the first time that they might have shared an intimate moment at one time. He couldn't resist smiling a little bit.

"So, who are these people you're investigating? Why can't you go in and arrest them?"

"Until now, our evidence has been primarily circumstantial. But we're close to getting our hands on some real, hard proof. Besides, these men are extremely powerful and dangerous."

Amber leaned back at the word *dangerous*. She thought about Marty. And Priscilla. And Jamie Atwater. And the bloody image of the Italian courier. Whoever had been responsible for those deaths was ruthless and omnipresent—a terrifying combination, to be sure. She swallowed hard.

Her mother's voice could still be heard in the kitchen. She was singing a number from *My Fair Lady*.

"What have these men done?" Amber asked.

"They're involved in a money laundering scheme."

"Money laundering? That sounds like a pretty common crime. What's so unique about this one case?"

"Well, other than the types of people involved, we believe there's a broader conspiracy."

"How broad a conspiracy?"

"As broad as you can imagine."

"You couldn't begin to know the lengths of my imagination," she said, raising an eyebrow almost flirtatiously.

"Is the White House far enough for you?" Jack's face was serious. He was not going to engage in her adolescent game.

"Oh, my God," she muttered beneath her breath.

"My sentiments precisely," Dalton said.

"You're telling me that these men are involved in a scheme with our president?"

It was the stuff movies were made of. It was incredible.

Jack shook his head. "No, rather a scheme targeted *at* the president."

Amber's mother peeked her head around the corner. "Is anyone here allergic to spicy foods?"

They all turned to her.

"I don't want these boys' mothers calling me later and telling me that I shouldn't have fed spices to them."

"No, ma'am," Jack replied. "It's fine."

She looked to Dalton for a response.

"No problem here," he said.

She smiled and disappeared again.

Amber looked back to Jack. "Tell me more." She wasn't yet prepared to trust him again, but the story he was telling was intriguing. She felt that nosy teenage gossip queen part of her emerging again.

"They've been using a company by the name of Bartlett Enterprises to move the money through. I'm sure you're familiar with that name by now." Jack walked around her chair.

She watched him from the corner of her eye. "Then it's not a real company?"

"Depends on who you ask."

"I'm asking you," she shot back.

Jack shook his head. "They've been using the company as a depository. So to speak."

"What does that mean?"

"It's a place to park their cash until they're ready."

"Ready? Ready for what?"

"To put it to use toward its primary purpose."

"And what would that be?"

Her questions were coming back to him faster than he could answer, almost as if she was anticipating his answers.

"They're collecting money to fund the president's reelection campaign."

She turned to Dalton, and then back to Jack. "That doesn't sound illegal."

"It's not. But their agenda is."

Amber's mom came back out of the kitchen, carrying a large ceramic pot with steam drifting from the top. It smelled delicious. But for Amber, the aroma of the cooked vegetables and spices was overshadowed by the scent of nostalgia. Her mother's stew was her specialty, reserved for special occasions and privileged guests. Her mother carefully set the pot in the middle of the table and urged them all to help themselves. Despite her Alzheimer's, she retained certain instincts that made her recognizable to those who loved her. Once she filled everyone's bowl, she walked back into the kitchen and was gone again.

For the next few minutes, they all shoveled spoonfuls of stew into their mouths, like college kids returning home for winter break.

"Jack," Dalton called out, reminding him where he had left off.

"Oh, right." Jack wiped his mouth with the napkin. "Sorry about that, but this is the best dish your mom has made."

The *best*? Amber didn't care much for the notion that Jack Bennett had taken her mother to Belize, but apparently he was having her cook for him as well. However, she suppressed her indignation in the interest of finding out more.

"This agenda you're talking about. What is it?" she asked.

"The money is coming from all over the place. Including the principals involved, there's money being contributed from…other parties."

"Other parties?"

"Colombian drug cartels, Islamic fundamentalist groups, Aryan nation leaders, to name a few," Dalton chimed in.

Jack looked to him sharply. He was hoping to be a bit more subtle about it.

Amber's eyes were huge, and her mouth fell open. She said nothing, but her countenance left no doubts about what she was thinking.

"It doesn't make any sense," she said finally. "Why would those groups contribute money to reelect an American president?"

"Imagine the political and national firestorm it will create if the news gets out that the president is accepting contributions from such groups."

"I suppose it would be a public embarrassment for the president."

"Worse. It would be a catastrophic character assassination. There's nothing worse for a man in that position. If they were plotting to kill him, it might be better. At least he wouldn't have to carry around an ugly stigma for the rest of his days."

"These men have no intention of supporting the president's reelection, do they? They're ambushing him by manufacturing a scandal?"

"Pretty big-league stuff, huh?" Dalton commented. He could still hardly believe it himself.

Amber began thinking about all the other pieces which, before then, had made absolutely no sense. "And Harper Phillips? How does he fit into this?"

"Evidently, he was in charge of setting up the phony corporation. That gave him control over where the funds were deposited. Once he was dead, the rest of the group embarked on a scavenger hunt for the money, which he had apparently spread around the world."

"So they hired some guy to pretend he was Harper," she concluded. She was starting to see the light.

"You got it," Jack said.

"But why would this person pretend to be an employee of Ensight?"

"We believe Ensight must have some type of business relationship with Bartlett. Legitimate or not, we're not sure."

Amber shook her head in disbelief again. "This is amazing. And Mr. Lang is involved in this?"

"He's running it, Amber. And he's willing to take out anyone in his path, if that's not already obvious."

Amber's heart skipped another beat, as she considered just how close she had been to Lang. She had sat with him on the plane. *Why had he agreed to allow her to accompany him down here?* The answer to that question made her shiver.

"And what about Bruce Fox? Is he involved in this as well?" she asked.

"It certainly seems that way. Along with a venture capitalist named Dennis Fitch. Even your old pal Marty Callahan," Dalton told her.

Again, Jack shot him a look. He was telling her information that she didn't need to know. It was all information vital to their investigation and could jeopardize everything if it fell into the wrong hands.

Amber looked sharply at Dalton. She could hardly believe what she was hearing. A conspiracy had unfolded beneath her nose, and she hadn't had a clue.

At that moment, her mother arrived back at the table. "C'mon, kids," she said, clapping her hands together. "Chop, chop. You'll be late for the dance." She collected the bowls, not recognizing that they had been only half-eaten. She was now humming *Memories*.

After her mother returned to the kitchen, Amber looked at Jack. "Tell me why you decided to bring my mother here. What does she have to do with this?"

"It was the only way to get you to come to me," Jack answered. "If I had tried to approach you, I knew you would run. I know involving your mother was low, Amber, but I also knew I couldn't just call you on the phone and ask you to come here. I didn't protect Priscilla Phillips well enough, and she's dead. I couldn't allow that to happen again. Especially because I...," he began, but decided to stop.

She considered this. He was right. She probably would have fled if he had come near her.

"Besides, it was probably just a matter of time before Lang learned that you had a sick mother living by herself," he added. "There's no telling what he would do to her to frighten you or control you."

The thought made Amber's stomach turn over. "Well, what now? Do you intend to keep my mother here until she thinks I've graduated from high school?"

"No. We need to get both of you off this island. There's too much happening here right now, and I have a feeling it's going to get a lot more eventful."

"Great," she said. "What are we waiting for? Let's go now."

"Not so fast, Amber." Jack looked to Dalton. "We need you to do one more thing."

Lang approached the front doors of the Banyan Bay resort. He was drenched by the rain, but his adrenaline was running high. He bounded up the steps toward Amber's room, knocked on the door, and tried to calm himself. If she was indeed still there, he didn't want to frighten her by appearing panicky. But after three minutes with no answer, he knew. Dalton had found her. Dalton had killed the young agent, which probably meant that he either knew the truth about the deputy director or was on a straight and narrow path toward discovering it.

"Shit," he said through his teeth.

His watch indicated that the time was close to eleven. It was too late for any flight to take off from the island, and no boat operator would have the poor judgment to take passengers out on the water under the bad weather conditions. The odds were that Dalton and Amber were still on the island somewhere. He had to find them before morning. He glanced at his watch. He needed to get to Fido's.

As he walked to the door, his phone began ringing.

"Yeah?"

"Sir, it's me."

Lang knew who *me* was. It was the way he had been introducing himself over the past several months.

"I need to put off our meeting for thirty minutes."

Lang ran his hand over his sweaty forehead. "And why is that?"

"I'd like to wait for the rain to settle down a bit."

"What are you? Some sort of pussy? It's rain for Christ's sake."

"If it's all the same to you, I'd…," he began.

"Actually, you know what? That's fine." Lang realized that he could use the extra thirty minutes.

"And I think we should meet at Shark's Bar instead of Fido's."

"What? Since when do you call the shots?"

"Fido's is a zoo right now. It'll be difficult to talk there."

Lang shook his head. "Fine, whatever. Shark's Bar it is. Thirty minutes." He hung up without waiting to hear an acknowledgment.

He exited the room and headed downstairs. He needed to get to his suite to find the phone number to the FBI's San Francisco field office.

Chapter 46

He wore a dark green cap with his ponytail hanging out the back. His instructions were to move the cash from the Curaçao account and into the Belize account. It had been a long journey since Harry Lang had first engaged him. He was anxious to collect his paycheck and move on. His stint as Harper Phillips was by far the longest run he had ever had under one assumed identity.

The open-air bar at Fido's was bustling with sunburned tourists, their red skin steaming under the colored flood lights in the rafters. A small group of women in their mid-thirties danced in a circle in front of the stage, as a tone-deaf fifty-year-old man with a balding head and a potbelly sang classic rock tunes into the microphone.

The ponytailed man smiled as he watched an indigenous drunk ricochet his way through the bar in search of a free drink. He himself couldn't wait until this was all over. He'd done his part. It was time to get paid. He held up his empty Belikin bottle at the bartender, a signal that he was ready for his next drink.

"Make that two," a voice called out from behind him.

The man climbed onto the stool next to him. He had never met the man in person, but he knew it was him. From what he had envisioned, Lang appeared a lot less fit than he had thought. Lang had told him during their first conversation that the next and only time they would see each other face to face would be when the assignment was near the end. If they didn't meet, it meant that his identity had been compromised or one or both of them were dead.

"Mr. Lang, I presume," he said through the noise.

"You look relaxed," he said without looking at him. "Nice mane," he commented, glancing quickly at the ponytail.

"Call it my trademark," he replied, stroking the ponytail with his hand.

"Well, it does make it easy to spot you."

"So, am I getting paid soon?"

"You remember what I told you when I first engaged you?"

"Yes. You told me that if and when we would ever meet in person, I could rest assured that the end was near."

"Right."

"So when do I get paid?" he asked again. He was anxious as well as nervous about being there in public.

"When I confirm that everything is in place."

"And when does that happen?"

"Soon. Very soon." He picked up the beer bottle and removed the paper napkin that all the bartenders placed around the top of it. He took a long swig and swallowed. "What do you plan to do once you're paid?"

"Well, not that it's any of your business, but I'll be getting the hell out of here. I don't want to stay any longer than I have to. This island's making me claustrophobic."

"I understand. Here's what I need. I want you to move the money from Belize Bank first thing tomorrow."

"What? You just asked me to put it in there. Why do you want it out so fast now?"

"Well, not that it's any of *your* business, but if you must know, I just wanted you to park the money there as a diversion tactic. In case anyone was watching."

The ponytailed man shook his head, dismissing the urge to comprehend Lang's logic. "And where do you want me to transfer it this time?"

"I'll provide that information to you before you get to the bank tomorrow," the older man replied.

"Are you kidding? What the hell is going on here? I just spent the last few years retrieving money around the world. Now, you want me to redistribute it? What exactly are you doing?"

"That's not for you to know. I'm paying you to do, not ask."

He held his hands up in defense. "You're the boss."

"Get it set up by end of day tomorrow. Instruct the bank to pull the trigger the following morning."

"Whatever you say," he said, shaking his head again. "And when do I get paid?" he repeated.

"Once I confirm that the Belize Bank account is depleted, and the money is in the right place, you'll be paid."

"So, I assume this is it, isn't it? I mean, you and I won't be seeing each other after tonight, will we?"

"No."

Ponytail swooping, he tipped his bottle back until the last drop of beer was gone. He climbed off the stool and held his hand out.

"Good luck, Mr. Lang."

"Good luck to you."

The two men walked out of opposite sides of the restaurant. He watched his ponytailed friend walk down to the beach and disappear behind a thick palm tree. As he stood at the entrance of Fido's, Bruce Fox walked up behind him.

"How'd it go?" he asked.

"He's in."

"Did he suspect anything?"

"Not that I could tell. Obviously, he's never seen Lang before."

"Well, at least Lang didn't lie to us about that fact. Nice work, Denny."

"Thanks. What now?"

Fox pulled out his phone and dialed Lang's number.

"What is it?" Lang asked as soon as he answered. He sounded anxious.

"Harry, what the hell is going on?" Fox demanded. "Why did you take off like that earlier?"

"I, uh, remembered that I had to make a phone call to Washington. Real FBI business. I do actually have a legitimate job there, you know" said Lang.

"Did you meet your guy at Fido's like you said?" Fox looked to Fitch after asking the question.

There was a brief pause. "No. He asked to move the meeting and the time. We're meeting in thirty minutes at Shark's Bar instead. The guy thinks he's running things now that we're down here, so I thought I'd indulge him."

Fox smiled and nodded to Fitch. "Fine. Just make sure he's not gaming you." He had to maintain an air of anxiety about the situation.

"Anything else, Bruce? I'm sort of busy right now."

"That's it. We'll talk after your meeting. I'll be at Banyan Bay at one o'clock. We're finally close to finishing this."

"Yes, we are," Lang said. "Indeed we are."

They hung up, and Fox turned to Dennis Fitch. "It's on."

"Excellent."

The two men smiled at one another and shook hands. Then they parted and walked away.

Chapter 47

▼

Jack and Amber left her mother back at the house with Special Agent Dalton. Amber didn't want to leave her again, but Jack was her ticket off the island, and she had to cooperate with him, even if she didn't especially want to help him. It felt strange, even absurd, that she would help him after what he had put her through. But, in the end, he had made a good point to her. If he had intended her harm, it would have occurred by now. She thought about the excitement of being next to him again. She wondered whether it was possible to be angry at him without hating him.

She and Jack sat inside his quiet bungalow at the Victoria House. He was on the bed wearing a headset attached to a device that was connected to the telephone. Amber held the telephone receiver to her ear while she dialed the number to the Jackson Winthrop office in Aruba. It was eleven o'clock at night, so they were sure that no one would be there. But they had run out of time, and desperate measures were in order.

A voice recorder came on, and Amber looked up at Jack. He nodded, indicating that she was to leave a message. After the greeting, she was about to speak when the line clicked and a woman's voice came on. It was live.

"*Goede avond.* Jackson Winthrop, may I help you?" The woman had an American accent. Amber assumed that the greeting was Dutch, one of the local languages on Aruba.

"Uh, yes," replied Amber, who was caught off guard.

She looked again at Jack, who made a circular motion with his hand. *Keep going.*

"Yes, I'm calling from one of the mainland offices. I had some questions about one of our clients." Her heart was racing. Despite extensive practice over the last several weeks, she still wasn't confident of her skill at lying.

"Which office?" The woman sounded annoyed. She was probably on her way out the door after having worked overtime.

"San Francisco," Amber replied.

"San Francisco? I thought we closed that office a few weeks ago," said the tired voice.

"Yes, we did. I'm just following up on some unfinished business."

"Who is this?"

Amber swallowed hard and took a deep breath. "This is Gina." She closed her eyes and prayed that the woman on the other end would not ask for a last name.

"Gina! Hi, it's Wendy." The woman's tone had suddenly changed. "We met a couple of months ago when I was up there. Right after you got hired. Do you remember me?"

"Oh, of course. Wendy. How could I forget?" Amber shrugged at Jack, who rolled his eyes.

"Do you remember that night at the Velvet Lounge? Who was that guy you went home with?"

Amber fought back a smile, and she could see that Jack was also trying to restrain his laughter. *Good ol' Gina.*

"I never caught his name."

Jack smiled and shook his head.

"I was really sorry to hear that they closed down that office. What are you doing these days?" Finally, the woman was getting back to the business at hand.

"I'm just helping to tie up all the loose ends. I'm sorry to be calling you so late."

"Oh, don't worry. This day was shot the minute I walked in this morning anyway. What can I do for you?"

Amber looked to Jack, who gave her a thumbs-up. This is what they wanted.

"I'm hoping to get some information on a company called Bartlett Enterprises. They're incorporated there in Aruba and evidently used us to get the documentation in place and manage the registration process."

Wendy could be heard typing on a keyboard. "Let's see. Bartlett, Bartlett," she said, clearly searching.

After a few seconds, she came back on. "Here it is. Bartlett Enterprises. What do you need to know?"

"When did we receive our last payment from them?"

"Mmm, looks like two days ago. But it doesn't appear that we'll be getting anything more from them."

Amber and Jack looked to one another quizzically.

"And why do you say that?" Amber asked.

"According to what I'm looking at now, they've communicated their intention to dissolve the corporation."

Jack sat up and held the headset tight around his ears.

"Dissolve it? When?" Amber pressed on.

"They've set an effective date for this Friday."

"That's only two days away."

"I suppose they didn't want to waste any time. It's not terribly uncommon. Lots of Western corporations set up entities here for temporary purposes."

Amber shot her eyes back at Jack for further instructions. He mouthed the word *who*.

"Who authorized it?"

"Unfortunately, it doesn't tell me on the system. But I can inquire with the person who took the call."

"Can you? That would be wonderful."

"Sure. But not tonight. It's really late and there's no one here."

"Are you sure there's no way to get in touch with them? This is really urgent."

"Sorry, Gina. I wish I could help you. The best I can do is to have someone call you first thing in the morning."

Jack nodded reluctantly. They had no other options.

"OK. That's fine." Amber rattled off the number to Jack's cell phone. "Thanks, Wendy. It was great to talk to you again."

"You too, Gina. Good night."

Amber hung up the phone and looked at Jack, who sat back in his chair, exasperated.

The heat inside the suite was intense. For some reason, the air conditioner had been turned off. Lang flipped the switch back on and mopped his forehead for the fifteenth time in three minutes. As he stood there, he recalled what the old man Terry Hammond had once said in one of their earlier meetings. *You're running a real three-ring circus.* This was not the way it was supposed to go.

He stepped into the middle of the room and stood in the path of cool air emanating from the vent. He looked around the room. *Where the hell was Amber?* She had disobeyed his instructions to stay in her room. Clearly, Dalton had gotten to her. Lang knew that she trusted Dalton. He had seen it back in San Francisco.

She obviously knew a lot, although she probably hadn't put the pieces together. It didn't matter. She was still a threat to the success of his plan. He needed to get to her before she and Dalton figured it all out.

He picked up his phone and dialed the number he had found in his address book. After a few rings, Gil picked up.

"Gil, this is Deputy Director Lang here."

There was silence on the other end. The young man had probably soiled himself at the sound of Lang's voice.

"Yes, sir. What can I do for you?" asked the quivering reply.

"Gil, this is extremely important. I need you to tell me where Special Agent Dalton is. Find him for me. It can't wait until morning. Do you understand me?"

"Yes, sir. I understand." Gil's heart was pounding almost out of his chest. He recalled Dalton's words when they had last spoken. *Lang is dirty.*

"You tell him to get in touch with me. That's a direct order. Is that clear?"

"Yes, sir."

"All right, young man. Go see to it."

He hung up the phone and dialed again. He called Washington and asked for Surveillance at the FBI.

"It's Lang," he said into the phone. "I need you to run a cell-track." The Bureau used a controversial system that could track the location of cellular phones. Its primary purpose was for the FBI to perform surveillance on criminals, not on their own.

"I'm pretty sure this cell phone is in Belize." He read off the numbers to Dalton's cell phone. "When you get the location, call me back." And he hung up again.

Gil would be calling Dalton by now. And Amber would surely be with him. He stepped out onto the balcony and watched as a wedding party enjoyed a rehearsal dinner poolside. The music was loud, but he was still able to hear his phone ring.

"Yeah," he said, holding the phone to one ear and plugging his finger into the other. He listened and committed the location to memory. "Got it. I want to know what numbers that phone calls and what numbers call that phone for the remainder of the evening." It was late in the evening and even later in Washington, so he knew that any calls at this hour would be important.

He replaced his phone in his pocket and stepped back inside. He was sweating profusely. His watch indicated that he had fifteen minutes before he had to meet his hired identity thief at Shark's Bar.

He pulled out two brochures from the desk—one for Tropic Air and the other for Maya Airways, the two local carriers that transported passengers to various locations within Belize. The earliest flight the next morning to Belize City was on Tropic Air, departing at six o'clock. He knew that the earliest water taxi left Ambergris at seven o'clock. Surely Dalton would try to get Amber off the island as early as possible. That gave Lang about six hours to find them. It was a small island, the length of which one could cover on foot in about two hours. But there were plenty of back streets and corridors for one to hide in. It wasn't going to be easy.

"Sounds like Harry Lang is covering his tracks pretty quickly," Jack said, removing the headset.

"You think it was he who dissolved Bartlett?" Amber queried.

"Who else would it be? After all, it makes perfect sense. He doesn't want there to be any audit trail that might reveal Bartlett's activities."

"Unbelievable," she muttered, shaking her head. "What do we do now?"

Jack peered out the window of his bungalow. The sky was bright with moonlight.

"I need to make sure I don't lose him. And you need to make sure to stay away from him."

Amber yawned and rubbed her eyes.

"You look tired," he told her.

She looked at him, and his eyes, despite some redness, still shined brightly. "I feel like I've been awake for a month. I suppose, in some ways, that's not totally inaccurate."

"You should stay here tonight."

She looked at him with surprise but couldn't decide if she was excited or offended. He took notice immediately before she could say anything.

"Relax," he clarified. "I meant that you should stay in the bed while I stay on the floor. Besides, I don't plan on sleeping much tonight."

"And what about my mother? I'm not comfortable leaving her at that place overnight. Besides, she'll start worrying if I'm not home by curfew." She smiled at this.

"All right," Jack replied, also smiling at her remark. "I'll call Dalton and have him escort her here. It will be easier if we're all in the same place, anyway. The moment your new friend Wendy calls back tomorrow morning, there won't be any reason for you to stick around any longer. We'll get you both on the first plane off the island."

Jack dialed Dalton's digits into his cell phone. As he listened, Amber walked into the bathroom and ran cold water on her face. The multilayered blend of sweat, tears, saltwater, sand, and rain felt heavy on her face. When she stepped out, Jack was still holding the phone to his ear but saying nothing.

"Huh," he mumbled.

"What is it?"

Jack lowered the phone to his side and glared at her. "He's not answering."

Amber stood in the doorway to the bathroom, and her shoulders slumped. She wasn't going to sleep after all. "Oh, my God," she whispered.

"Stay here," he said. "And lock the door."

"Wait, where are you going?"

"Where do you think? Back to the house." He started for the door.

"I'm coming with you." She started to put her shoes on.

"No, you're not."

"Well, I'm not staying here. I've come a long way. I'm not going to sit back and just wait for you to give me updates. Besides, I'm still not completely ready to trust you again."

"Amber, listen to me. No offense to you, but I can move a lot faster alone. Besides, you're far too emotionally invested at this point."

He turned the knob to the door and opened it. Amber pushed the door closed, nearly smashing his hand in the doorframe.

"I'm going with you!" she insisted.

Jack looked into her eyes, which were ablaze with conviction. He looked at his shoes for a few seconds, and then released an exhausted sigh.

"You stay beside me the whole time. I mean right beside me. Understood?" He had a finger pointed toward her like a father lecturing his young daughter to hold his hand when crossing the street.

He knew it was a bad idea to have her tag along, but he knew she wouldn't stay put. She was a fighter. It was what he both hated and loved about Amber Wakefield.

She nodded in agreement. "Let's go."

They opened the door and walked out.

Chapter 48

The lights outside Shark's Bar & Restaurant glistened brightly through the drizzle falling on the dock. Lang could hear loud reggae music from inside. He approached the front doors. Outside, a group of tall locals stood talking with three young Norwegian girls, each battling through the language barriers that were clearly evident. Stepping inside, Lang noticed a band on the immediate right, singing and playing before an unstructured line of American tourists, all dancing to a different rhythm than that of the music.

To the left was a small round bar where tourists and locals mixed and drank. At the far end of the bar, seated on a stool, was a Caucasian man. He wasn't talking with anyone, only drinking something colorful with an umbrella in it. Lang wasn't sure if this was his guy, particularly since the man wore a crew cut. He was certain that his guy had long hair—in fact, a ponytail, according to the surveillance reports he had received from Agent Griffin during the past several weeks.

"Buy you a drink?" he asked as Lang approached the bar next to him.

"Sure. Anything but what you're having there," Lang replied, pointing to the orangish concoction in front of him.

Lang ordered a beer from the bartender. "What happened to your hair? I was told you had a ponytail thing going on back there."

"I had to cut it. Getting ready for my next job." He rubbed his hand over his head.

"And what would that be?"

He laughed. "Nice try. Like I'm going to tell the deputy director of the FBI what my next scam is. The beauty of your job is that you get to play on both sides of the ball."

"Just testing you," Lang teased.

The crowd began roaring as the young black lead singer danced provocatively with one of the blonde Norwegians who had reentered from the dock outside.

"So, what happens next?"

Lang took a sip from his beer bottle and looked straight ahead. "A couple of things. We need to get the money out of that account for starters. I've got some unexpected visitors down here, and I can't afford to keep it there."

"And the second thing?"

"The documents. My associates are lying to me about having possession of them. I know that much. But you don't need to worry about that part. I'm taking care of it, because I think I know who has them."

"The same person who stole the rest of the money, I presume?"

"You catch on fast. I like that. Perhaps we can work together again in the future." Lang shot a quick glance at his employee.

"I don't think so. But thanks for the offer."

Lang handed a piece of paper to him. There were a series of digits on it.

"Read this. Commit it to memory. This is where I need to transfer the funds."

He read the account number to himself three times.

"Got it?" Lang asked after several seconds.

He nodded.

"Good." Lang took a matchbook from his pocket and lit a match. He touched it to the corner of the paper and watched it burn as he placed it in the glass ashtray in front of them.

"After the transfer is complete, take the water taxi to Caye Caulker. I'll meet you at the airstrip. Together, we'll take a flight to the mainland."

He listened carefully as Lang laid out his plan. "Why are we meeting there? Why can't I just go my own way after that?"

"Because I need confirmation. If you have the balls to show up, I'll know you followed my instructions. If you don't..." He held his hands with his palms facing up.

"Yeah?"

"If you don't, I'll know otherwise. And then, I plan to hunt your ass down."

He ran his hands through his short hair and stared at Lang.

"Once we're both in Belize City," Lang continued, "we go our separate ways."

The man nodded slowly in acknowledgment. Finishing off his tropical drink, he slid off the stool and held his hand out to Lang.

"It's been a pleasure, Mr. Lang."

"Likewise," Lang replied, shaking his hand.

After Lang watched him exit the bar, he took another long sip from his beer bottle. For some reason, he stopped suddenly. As the cold beer ran down his throat, he slowly removed the bottle from his lips. How strange, he thought to himself. How strange it was that this man, this professional identity thief, would have come all this way, would have trotted around the globe, all the while avoiding detection, all the while remaining focused on his mission. How strange that he would have reached the final destination of his assignment—and not once inquire about his compensation. Lang recalled that in his earliest conversations, this man would speak of nearly nothing else but his paycheck. His constant attempts to renegotiate the deal for more money had become a theme on which Lang had come to rely. But tonight, it was different. There had been no mention of how or when he would be paid.

Lang placed the bottle on the bar and quickly walked outside. He stood on the dock, looking from side to side. The rain had died down, and the sky and the air in front of him were clear and fresh. Despite the impeccable visibility, he was unable to see the shaven head of the man with whom he had just shaken hands. Lang felt the stirrings of uneasiness. He shuddered when he also felt a tingling sensation in his left leg. He tried to put it out of his mind, attributing the sensation to the countless emotions running in high gear throughout his body. But it kept tingling his thigh, in rhythmic waves. *Was he having a heart attack*? He reached into his pocket and relaxed. It was his cell phone vibrating.

"Yeah," he said, trying to steady his breathing.

It was his surveillance team in Washington. Dalton had received another call, but it went directly to his voice mail box. According to the tracking system, the call came from another cell phone. Its registrant was Jack Bennett. And what was more, it had come from Belize. Ambergris Caye, to be precise. Ten minutes ago.

Lang couldn't believe it. Jack was so close, he could practically smell his aftershave. *But why was he calling Dalton? And what about Amber?*

Until this moment, Lang hadn't worried much about what any of them knew. But together they posed a serious threat. They each had enough pieces of information which, assembled logically, could jeopardize the success of his entire plan. And what was worse, they each had a clear and justifiable incentive to ruin him. They had to be working together. But since the call went to Dalton's voice mail box, it was evident that Jack had not been successful at reaching him yet.

Lang called up from his memory the coordinates that his Washington team had given him as Dalton's last known location. There was a good chance that Jack would be on his way to that same spot if he was really that anxious to find Dalton. If Lang hurried, he might be able to intercept Jack on his way there.

He stepped off the slippery dock and trudged through the damp sand and up to the main street. He pushed his way through the throngs of tourists who were back outside again, enjoying what they could only guess was a temporary break in the weather. As he turned the corner to get to the back street where the address was located, he reached into his side pocket and felt for his gun. Still moving, he released the safety. If he needed to use it, he would have time only to point and shoot. His heart was racing again. He had not anticipated this. He glanced at his watch. Eleven forty-five. A little more than six hours before they could put Amber on the first flight off the island. He took a deep breath and began sprinting toward the house.

Chapter 49

Jack and Amber slipped between the houses, occasionally ducking behind a tree at the sound of people approaching or a bicyclist passing by. They reached the yellow house and entered through the same doorway as they had earlier. The lights were still on inside, and the aroma of Amber's mother's stew was still pungent in the air.

Jack pulled his gun from his pocket. Amber stepped back in an attempt to keep her distance from the weapon. It was probably just the natural ease of law enforcement officers, but the way Jack wrapped his forefinger around the trigger seemed to indicate that the situation was more dangerous than she would have imagined.

A phone began ringing, and Jack reached into his pocket. With the gun still poised, he answered. But there was no reply. And the ringing continued. He glanced at the display, only to see that it was not his phone that was ringing. They looked around the room, following the sound. Amber saw it first.

"There it is," she said, pointing to one of the chairs at the table where they had eaten earlier.

A small Motorola flip phone lay on the chair, its green backlit display flashing with each ring. Jack reached down and picked it up. The area code of the number calling was 415. San Francisco. He answered it.

"Who is this?" he asked.

"Who is *this*?" asked the voice on the other end. "Where's Special Agent Dalton?"

"Who is this?" Jack repeated.

"It's Gil."

"Gil?" Jack asked, looking at Amber.

She stepped forward. "It's OK. He's FBI. He works for Mr. Dalton." She took the phone from him.

"Gil, it's Amber. Do you know where Mr. Dalton is?"

"No, I'm looking for him, too. I think he's in danger. And I'm afraid you are, as well."

Jack took the phone back from her before she could form a sentence and hung up. She was about to protest when she realized what was the cause of Jack's interruption. She looked to the doorway and saw the rain-drenched silhouette of Harry Lang. He held a pistol in his right hand, which hung at his side. She put both hands to her mouth and managed a muffled scream.

"Hello, Amber." Lang stepped inside and ran his hands through his wet hair. "I thought I told you to stay in your room. I can hardly protect you if you don't obey my instructions."

"Protect me?" she asked incredulously.

Lang turned slightly to face Jack. "Jack Bennett. You're a hard man to find."

"Drop the gun, Harry. It's all over." Jack raised his own gun and pointed it at Lang.

"I'm the deputy director for the U.S. Federal Bureau of Investigation. I don't surrender my weapon to anyone. Not even the president himself."

"That's fitting, considering your goal is to destroy the man," Jack retorted.

Lang laughed loudly. "Who told you that? Dalton? I suppose it doesn't matter. There's no proof. I'm way ahead of you, Jack. As usual."

"You have no idea what I know," Jack said, with a wry smile.

"You're no angel, Jack. I know you pulled some of that money out of Harper's accounts just to fuck me up. Especially that one account in Spain that required my authorization. That was a nice touch."

"I don't have your money, Harry."

"Bullshit!" Lang's eyes were on fire. "You're the only person alive who'd be able to access my personal data. And the only one who hates me enough."

"You underestimate yourself. But I have no intention of taking your money."

"So, what are you going to do, Jackie? Arrest me? You don't have any jurisdiction here. In fact, you don't have any jurisdiction anywhere. You're not FBI. You're just a bitter kid with a chip on his shoulder."

"Put it down," Jack repeated. His eyes were focused on Lang. But he also heard the echoes of what Lang had just said to him. He was right. Jack was not FBI. Not even law enforcement of any kind. If he shot and killed the deputy director of the FBI, he'd better have an ironclad reason. And at this point, his evidence was still primarily circumstantial.

Jack swallowed, trying to remain subtle about it, but he was sure that Lang had noticed. He had just shown weakness in the face of the enemy—a sin within the law enforcement circle.

Meanwhile, Amber had moved to a position behind Jack. This confrontation was not going to end peacefully; she knew that much. But who would remain standing was an open question. She was in a room with two highly trained professionals, each of whom was perfectly capable of killing the other. If there was any silver lining, it was that her mother was not here. She only hoped that she was in safe hands. The idealist in her imagined Dalton escorting her mother onto a private plane, destined for somewhere far away. But she knew that there was no way off the island at this hour. Even the highest authority wouldn't be able to order an emergency departure, considering the unpredictable weather swings.

"You don't have it in you, Jack," Lang continued. "You were never very good in the field. That's why you were relegated to analyst duty." Lang wasn't completely convinced of his own words, but he felt the urge to say something, anything to hide the fear he was experiencing at the moment.

"I know now why you fired me, Harry. It was all a cover-up. I have everything I need to nail your ass." He was lying again, but he had to hold his ground.

"You don't have shit!" Lang shouted, raising his gun.

The two men stood ten feet apart, each staring down the gun barrel of the other. Lang's hand was shaking slightly, despite his attempts to steady himself. Amber slid further back until she stood in the dark doorway to the kitchen. From there, she could see clearly the pot that held her mother's stew, still on the stove burner. A faint blue flame flickered beneath it. In what she could only imagine had been a desperate departure by her mother and Dalton, no one would expect an Alzheimer's patient to remember to turn off the stove before leaving.

"Don't do anything stupid, Harry. There's no way off the island until morning. We both know that. You take me out here, and you'll be found before daylight."

Lang's eyes moved away slightly, as if he was thinking. Then he turned back to Jack, more focused than ever.

"Fuck it. I'll take my chances." Lang extended his arm and wrapped his finger tighter around the trigger.

Jack held his breath, but was momentarily distracted by a movement in the darkness behind Lang. Lang saw his eyes move and instinctively spun around. He took two steps to the side as he saw Dalton standing outside, his gun pointed at Lang's back.

"You can't kill both of us, Harry," Dalton said. "So, you need to decide if you're willing to die tonight."

For the first time, Lang saw a steely-eyed Dalton. A brave Dalton. Until this moment, there had been no circumstances under which someone like Dalton would refer to his superior by the first name. It meant only one thing—that Dalton no longer viewed Harry Lang as the deputy director of the FBI. Lang was now a criminal. And that changed everything.

Lang stood between the two men in a cross fire. While he had been committed to his mission from the start, he was not willing to die for it. This was not a jihad, but a personal war. He slowly lowered his arm to his side, defeated.

Dalton inched forward, both hands on his weapon. In a single rapid motion, Lang raised his arm again and aimed it across the room, nowhere close to either of the men. Both Jack and Dalton froze in shock, giving Lang just enough time to get off a single shot. The bullet shattered the lamp hanging over the table, the sole source of light in the house. The room suddenly went dark. The shot created a shower of glass over the tabletop and onto the floor. Amber screamed and ducked into the kitchen.

Dalton fired in the direction of Lang, missing badly as the bullet found the opposite wall, creating an explosion of dust and plaster. From Amber's point of view, with the moonlight outside serving as a backscreen, three silhouettes were moving quickly in different directions, accompanied by incoherent screams and curses. She stayed in the kitchen, the only other light coming from the blue flame on the stove.

The wrestling continued, and for a moment she considered running out the front door. But something held her in place. *What was it? Did she feel some sort of obligation to Agent Dalton? To Jack?* The chaos in the other room was probably her best opportunity to make a move. Quickly, she felt along the countertop until she found a dish towel and wrapped it around her hands. Then she inched closer to the stove, picked up the almost-boiling pot of stew from the stove, and tiptoed toward the doorway. She couldn't recognize one man from the other, but there was no time to take roll call. She had to act fast.

Just as she entered the room, one of the men raised up on his knee, only inches in front of her. The other two were on the floor somewhere. For all she knew, one or none of them could still be in possession of his gun. The man in front of her had no idea she was behind him, for his focus was exclusively on the other two on the floor. But who was it? As he raised his arm from his kneeling position, she saw the outline of his gun against the background of the window near the front door. He had a point blank shot at either or both of the other two. And then she smelled the cologne, that cheap cologne. The man was Lang.

She steeled herself as the perspiration in her palms began to compromise her grip on the pot. She raised it to shoulder height, but it was heavy. She grunted as she tried to heave it higher, but the sound was loud enough to catch Lang's attention. He had probably forgotten about her amid the melee. He swung around but didn't have enough time to react. Amber tipped the pot toward him, and the steaming contents poured over his face. He screamed in pain and put his hands to his face, still clutching his gun. He fell to the floor violently, crying out in agony.

Apparently Jack and Dalton recognized the opportunity, and both were on their feet in seconds. Neither had his gun in his hand, and there was no time to search around in the dark room. They ran out the front door.

"Amber, get out of there! Now! Move!" Jack yelled.

Amber stepped around Lang and moved quickly to the door. But Lang, his eyes squinted and tearing, clutched her by the ankle as she went past him. She screamed and tried to kick herself free. But his grip was strong, and she was no match for his power. Still holding the iron pot in her hand, she swung it as hard as she could downward, and connected cleanly with the top of his head. She again heard his loud shriek of pain, and he let go of her leg.

As Amber ran outside, Jack considered going back in and finishing off Lang. But he remembered that he was unarmed, and Lang, although blinded by the scalding stew, was still holding his own gun. It would require a lucky shot by Lang, but Jack wasn't prepared to take that risk. He turned and took Amber by the arm, leading her down the street. Dalton was already eight paces in front of them, blazing a path for them to follow as they weaved between the houses and toward the main street. They moved quickly, but in utter silence. They all knew that they had accomplished nothing back there other than to fuel Lang's fury. Despite the lack of conversation among them, they were all thinking the same thing. They now had a common agenda—to stay alive.

Chapter 50

Bruce Fox watched the water lap onto the sand in front of the Banyan Bay Resort. The moonlit sky had cleared completely, showing no sign of rain. Harry Lang approached him slowly. His steps were wobbly at best, and when he moved into the bright moonlight, Fox could see the nasty burns on his face. One of his eyes was swollen, and some skin had begun to peel from his forehead. It was ghastly to look at, especially because of the accompanying smells of perspiration and what seemed to be some type of soup or stew.

"What the hell happened to you?" Fox asked, bracing Lang as he nearly collapsed onto the beach.

"Jack, that son of a bitch. And Dalton. They're together." He was out of breath. It was quite a walk from the house, especially considering the trauma to his body.

"And what about Amber?"

Lang looked at him. *Why the hell did he care about her so much?* "She's with them. She did this to me," he said, pointing out his burns.

"Looks pretty bad. Maybe we should get a doctor to take a look."

"What are you, my mother? I'll be fine. Besides, there's no more time."

"Why? What do they know?"

"They know enough. But they don't know everything."

"How can you be so sure?"

"Because we planned this too long and too carefully for it not to go right."

"Sounds like it's really your confidence speaking, not any real hard proof."

"Why are you busting my balls? It wouldn't kill you to exhibit the same conviction, Bruce. After all, we're partners, aren't we?"

Fox smiled and shook his head slightly. It always amazed him how Lang would refer to them as friends or partners only when he needed him most. He glanced at his watch. It was close to two o'clock in the morning.

"Yes, we're partners," he said, his tone lacking fervor.

"The money will be moved out tomorrow. I've asked him to transfer the funds from the Belize Bank account directly to the campaign fund's account at Riggs Bank in DC."

Fox listened intently.

"Terry Hammond is on the other side, waiting for the money. He'll confirm to us when the funds are received."

"And what about the money that Jack took?"

Lang scoffed. "He claims he doesn't have it. But then, of course, why would he admit taking it? If he doesn't have it himself, he sure as hell knows who does. I'll find it by tomorrow. You just leave that part to me."

"If you say so. This better go off without any more hitches. I plan to be off this island before ten o'clock."

"You can count on that, Bruce."

Fox looked at Lang, wondering if there was a double meaning in that last remark.

"Now, if you don't mind, I need to get to my suite to rinse off. This stew is starting to set in."

"So, we all meet at our agreed-upon spot tomorrow morning. Correct?" Fox asked as Lang began walking toward the hotel.

Lang nodded without turning around. Once he had disappeared into the building, Dennis Fitch walked up behind Fox.

"What the hell happened to him?" Fitch asked.

Fox laughed. "He got his ass kicked."

"Well, that wasn't part of the plan," Fitch said, almost reveling in Lang's misfortune.

"Call it a bonus, I guess."

They laughed.

"Are we set for tomorrow?"

Fitch nodded. "Yeah, but we're going to have to move fast."

"And carefully," Fox reminded him. "Any hiccup could result in you and me ending up on the wrong side of this thing."

"Good luck, Foxy."

Fox nodded and slapped his friend on the back.

* * * *

Amber stopped for the fourth time as they made their way back through the town. Each of the previous times they had stopped to rest, they hid in a dark doorway in one of the many alleys connecting the main street to the beach. Lang was armed, and they were not. They were also easier to spot as a cluster of three, as opposed to one. So he clearly had an advantage.

"Where did you take my mother?" she finally asked Dalton. Her hands were on her knees as she caught her breath. She hadn't had time until now to ask this all-important question.

"When Gil called to tell me Lang was looking for me, I knew it was a matter of time before he came by the house," he explained. "I had to get your mother out of there. I also knew Lang would track my whereabouts by tracing my cell phone, so I left it at the house. I never expected you two to go there."

"Where is my mother?" Amber repeated, ignoring Dalton's reasons.

Dalton glanced at Jack. "We hadn't planned to do this until tomorrow morning, but given the circumstances, I decided to push it up a few hours."

Jack nodded, understanding what Dalton was referring to. Dalton pulled Amber closer to him, so they were facing the water. He pointed.

"You see that boat out there?" he said, turning her to face in the right direction.

She squinted. In the darkness, with the aid of the moonlight, she could discern an image floating on the surface of the water.

"Do you see it?" he repeated.

"Yes. Vaguely," she answered. Then she realized what he was showing her. "My mother is on that boat? Why?"

"It was the only way to keep her a safe distance from this place. This island is far too small."

"Is she waiting on that boat by herself?"

"No. Not exactly." Again, Dalton looked to Jack.

"Jack?" Her eyes were pleading him to tell her the truth. She was exhausted. "She's with my associate," Jack told her.

"Your assoc…," she started to say but suddenly interrupted herself. "Wait. The guy with the tattoo? Are you crazy?" Until now, she hadn't thought to ask about the man who had tried to shoot her at the law offices.

"Relax, Amber," Jack said, trying to calm her. "He's with me. Don't you remember what I told you earlier? I staged the shooting in the law offices and the motel. It was just a ruse to get you to trust me."

Amber put her hand on her forehead. "Oh, my God. I don't want to leave her there with that man. I don't care what you say."

Jack breathed a loud sigh. He looked to Dalton for affirmation, who nodded back.

"OK. Let's go." Jack pulled out his cell phone and dialed Watts's number.

The three of them made their way down toward the beach. As they stepped onto the dock of Patojo's Dive Shop, they looked out toward the boat where Amber's mother waited. Jack stepped off the edge of the dock and into a small boat used for diving excursions. He held his hand out and assisted Amber on board, where she took a seat toward the bow. Dalton untied the line and climbed in, pushing off against the dock so that the small boat drifted laterally. Jack fished in his pocket and pulled out a set of keys. Amber watched his moves closely but quizzically. Evidently, he had managed earlier to bribe the dive shop owner to take out one of the boats by himself. She was constantly amazed at how easily these FBI men could get what they wanted.

Jack inserted the key, and the engine rumbled to life. As the boat moved slowly through the shallow water away from the shore, Jack stepped forward to the bow and tilted a large headlamp so that it was facing directly ahead. Aiming at the larger boat where her mother was, he flashed the lamp three times. A few seconds afterward, the larger boat in the distance returned three flickers of a lamp on its bow. Jack returned to his post behind the wheel and pushed the throttle forward. The small boat took off through the open water. As it picked up speed, Amber closed her eyes. The light spray from the sea below them felt wonderfully refreshing on her face, and under the dark Caribbean sky full of stars and a bright moon, the ride was even more majestic.

With her eyes still closed, she imagined living a life where she could hop into her boat at her will and select a spot on the map as her destination. The image was colored by the companionship of loved ones. Friends and family. Even children, perhaps her own. Despite her incomplete family growing up, she still carried with her the ideal that her life would be meaningless if it couldn't be shared with someone else, someone whom she loved and who loved her without judgment. Someone who would go the ends of the earth to ensure that she was safe. More than just a spouse. More than a soul mate. It was indescribable but very real. She slowly opened her eyes, unsure of what had prompted her to pull herself out of her brief dream. She glanced back toward the island and caught sight of Jack, navigating the boat along the water. He was looking directly at her. But for how long had he been looking? And were his thoughts similar to hers? She felt a gush of excitement, and then quickly turned away.

As they approached the larger boat, she could see that it was actually a small yacht about sixty feet long. She could also see that it was well cared for. What's more, she recognized the name on the stern: NICOLETTE. It was the same as the name of the boat that she had seen in the picture on Jack's camera.

Jack cut the engine, and it snorted in the water before dying. He spun the wheel, angling the boat so that it slid slowly toward the yacht. Dalton leaned out and extended his arms against it so the two vessels didn't collide. He threw the line up to the deck, and a large man on board in a black T-shirt and shorts took hold of it. Amber stared up at him. Although his face and his clothes were not familiar to her, the tattoo on his neck, clearly visible under the moon's light, sent a chill through her body.

He hung a short ladder over the side of the yacht. Dalton took Amber's hand and helped her climb up. As she reached the top, Watts held his hand out to assist her. But she declined, falling onto the yacht's floor in the process. Watts took her arm and helped her up, but she shook him off.

"I suppose I owe you an apology, Amber," he said gently. "I had no intention of harming you."

She said nothing but stared at him, her lips pursed very tightly.

"Don't worry, Watts. It's going to take her a little while to warm up to you," Jack said as he climbed up the ladder.

Amber's eyes locked on Watts with a piercing stare. "Tell me where she is," she demanded through gritted teeth.

Watts took a step back. "She's down below," he said, indicating the cabins beneath the deck. "I think she's sleeping."

Amber looked at him again, this time slightly less vengeful. She descended into the cabin below while the men remained on deck. As she reached the bottom of the steps, she paused. A sitting room lay before her with beige carpet from wall to wall. A burgundy velvet bench sofa rested against one of the walls, flanked by two matching chairs. A lacquered wood entertainment center leaned against the opposite wall, with a forty-two inch plasma television screen inside. White Bose cube speakers were suspended from the corners of the ceiling. It was a page out of *Lifestyles of the Rich and Famous*, and she practically expected the show's host, Robin Leach, to step out one of the rooms at any moment.

Straight ahead were two open doors, and Amber could see that each of them led into a stateroom. She found her mother in one of them, lying comfortably in a queen-size bed, fast asleep. She was snoring slightly, which Amber recalled as being customary for her mother. It reminded her of when she used to sneak back into the house after curfew when she was in high school. She would kiss her sleeping mother goodnight, but her mother would never awaken.

Watching her slumber, Amber thought her mother appeared frail, but peaceful, and Amber envied her for that. She herself wanted to be in that state of bliss, where the heaviest burden on her mind was what to cook for dinner that evening. She bent down and kissed her on the forehead.

"I'm home, Mom," she whispered, stroking her mother's hair. "I love you."

Amber walked quietly out of the cabin and climbed back up to the deck. She found the others standing there, exchanging whispers. The only sound, other than their voices, was the water slapping against the side of the yacht. The men ceased their conversation when they saw Amber emerge.

"Is she OK?" Jack asked.

Amber nodded. "She seems OK. Of course, it's always hard to tell with an Alzheimer's patient."

"But I kept my promise, didn't I?"

She looked at Jack. Ever since she had been reunited with him, it seemed as though he was trying very hard to win back whatever trust he had managed to acquire after their first meeting. But in the end, his attempts were more endearing than pathetic to her. And she loved the fact that he was trying so hard.

"I suppose," she replied, refusing to agree with him so quickly.

"Jack?" It was Dalton, reminding him that there were others on the boat besides Amber. "We need to get going. Our business isn't finished."

"I know," Jack replied. He looked back at Amber. Neither wanted him to go, but they both knew that he couldn't stay there all night.

"Try not to get yourself killed," she said to him.

"I'll be back," he told her. There was a confidence in his tone that sent a wave of comfort through her.

She tried to behave normally, but she knew herself well enough to realize that her emotions were clear for the world to see. This time, she didn't care. For all she knew, this could be the last time they saw each other. All she could manage to do was smile.

Jack turned to Watts. "Make sure you're ready to take this boat out of here at a moment's notice. You know where to go. With luck, I'll be back here by that time. But don't wait for me under any circumstances." Once again, he looked at Amber. "And take care of these ladies, will you?"

He handed Watts his cell phone. "Keep this with you, and call me if there's trouble. Press number nine on that phone to reach me." He reached into a compartment beneath one of the benches, pulled out two extra phones, placed one into his pocket and handed the other one to Dalton.

Reaching into the compartment again, Jack pulled out two guns and tossed one to Dalton. They checked the clips to make sure they were loaded. Amber watched nervously.

Jack approached Amber and placed his hands firmly on her shoulders. She suddenly remembered how strong he was.

"Amber, you're safe here. I promise you." He tightened his grip on her shoulders.

She closed her eyes and dropped her head. She didn't want him to see her tears, but it was quite evident to all of them. She wanted to kiss him but couldn't find it within her to do it.

He backed away from her and joined Dalton, who had already climbed into the smaller dive boat. Watts untied the line and tossed it to Dalton. As they drifted away from the yacht, Jack looked back up to Amber who was leaning over the side. He nodded to her, and she smiled back. As they sped away, she watched the wake of the dive boat gradually smooth out, until the boat was a small speck shrinking and disappearing into the darkness of the island.

"Go ahead and take any one of the beds down below, Amber," Watts said. "I'm going to stay up on top tonight. I'll be awake the whole time, so if you need anything, just holler."

Amber said nothing and descended the steps to the cabins below. She opened the door to one of the staterooms and found her mother still snoring away. Inside the bathroom, Amber looked at her reflection in the mirror. Her clothes were dirty, and her hair was sticking out in every direction. But it was her face that shocked her most. Her eyes were swollen and bloodshot. She looked as if she was twenty years older than she was. She quickly ran warm water and splashed her face clean.

She entered through the other stateroom door and found a room not as large as the one her mother was sleeping in, but decorated just as elegantly. Instead of one large bed, there were two twin beds, with fresh linens on both. She peeled off her clothes and put on a T-shirt and a pair of shorts she found on one of the beds. They were a little big on her, but they were clean. She climbed into the other bed and lay staring at the ceiling. She wondered whether she had done the right thing by not saying more to Jack before he left. She hoped that she would see him again, though she knew that what he was doing was extremely dangerous. *Mom is safe, and that's all that matters right now*, she told herself. And in a few hours, they'd be gone from this place. She lay awake for some time, but soon the subtle rocking of the yacht and the sound of the water just outside the porthole next to her bed became too hypnotizing, and she was asleep.

The dream was a flurry of childhood memories. She was in her Rhode Island home, seated at the dinner table. She had just had her eighth birthday the day before. On either side of her were two empty chairs, with two plates of cold, untouched food. As a child, Amber often ate alone. For the few years her father lived with them, her parents were usually in another room in the house, arguing and fighting. Her father never hit either one of them, but he was selfish and neglectful, which to Amber was in some ways much worse.

In this particular dream, she heard her mother's voice. It was raised, which was uncharacteristic. It was also incoherent. Amber saw herself as a little girl, tilting her head toward the other room, trying to decipher the words being exchanged in another heated argument. Then she saw the image of her mother, a much younger mother, entering the kitchen. She was instructing young Amber to get up from the table. They were leaving.

"I don't want to go," the young Amber was saying. "Where are we going? Where are we going?"

Amber could hear this question repeated as she watched the young image of herself following her mother out the door and driving away. As the little girl looked out the back window of the family's station wagon, she could see her father standing in the doorway of their house. He reentered the house, and suddenly, *bang*! A gunshot pierced.

Amber jerked awake and sat up in bed, back to the present. She felt beads of sweat on her forehead. It had been a long time since she had had a nightmare, but this one was particularly realistic. The voices, the sound of the shot. All of it was very tangible.

She looked around the room. The sun was just rising out of the sea, allowing a hint of light to creep into the cabin. She peered out of the porthole and could see the water beneath the boat moving laterally. And then she felt the vibrations of the engine below her. They were moving. Watts was carrying out Jack's instructions. Something had happened.

She hopped out of the bed and wrapped herself in the robe that had been hanging on a hook near the door. She opened the stateroom door and walked out. There was no one in the sitting room, and she saw the door to her mother's stateroom room wide open and fastened by a hook on the wall. The sheets on the bed were still rumpled, but her mother was gone.

Amber was wide awake now as she spun around, her eyes darting from side to side. "Oh, God, no," she whispered.

She walked to the stairs leading up to the deck, but not without first grabbing a small kitchen knife from the galley. She didn't know why she needed it, but it felt good in her hand. She began climbing the stairs. Halfway up, she heard whistling. She couldn't make out the tune, and she didn't care either. Something didn't feel right.

At the top of the steps, she squinted from the daylight. When her eyes finally focused, she nearly fell back down the steps at what she saw. Her mother was sitting on one of the benches to the right, her hands tied in front of her with a thick rope. Her mouth had a rag in it. Her eyes were watery.

"No!" Amber yelled, running across the deck to her mother. "Mom, what happened?"

She pulled the rag carefully out of her mouth. Her mother winced in pain, unable to speak. She was obviously in shock. What was worse, she was very much in the present, with no mind disease or false illusion of time and place. In all the years watching her mother succumb slowly to the disease, Amber could always tell where the woman's mind was. She watched her mother closely, following her eyes. Her mother knew what was happening, and that did more than sadden Amber. It enraged her.

"Watts," she whispered to herself. She was afraid to turn around. Even more frightening was the prospect that Jack had betrayed her again. The whistling continued above her. Taking a deep breath, she stood up and turned to make her way to the pilothouse, where she was certain she would find Watts steering the yacht. But when she turned, she was met with another horrifying sight. Watts lay at the bottom of the steps leading up to the control area. He was clearly dead. The bloody hole in his chest left no doubt. Amber held her hands to her mouth and felt a rush of bile rising up to her throat. With intense effort, she fought it back.

Averting her eyes from Watts's body, she slowly climbed the steps, still clutching the small knife. As she reached the top, she could see the figure of a man at the helm. He wore a blue hat and sunglasses, but he wasn't Jack. She saw a gun next to him, lying on the control panel. As the breeze from the sea blew past her, she caught a whiff of something familiar. That cheap cologne again.

"Good morning, Amber," Lang called out, continuing to stare straight ahead. "Why don't you go ahead and put down that knife? This gun still has a full clip, and I'd hate to have to haul *two* dead bodies on this beautiful boat." He patted the gun with his hand.

Amber gripped the knife tightly and prepared to rush him and jam the blade as far as it would go into his back. But she looked at the gun and knew that someone of his training could probably fire it faster than she could blink. After a few more seconds of struggling with herself, she tossed the knife to the side.

"That's my girl," he said. "Why don't you come up here and join me? The view from this height is gorgeous." He was enjoying this, although the skin around his eye was bright red from the painful burns he had experienced the night before.

"Why are you doing this?" she asked, still standing on the steps. "At least let my mother go. She doesn't know anything."

"Yeah, I'm sorry. I realize that the rag in the mouth approach is a little barbaric. It's generally not my style, but she kept whining. She kept asking 'Where are we going? Where are we going?' I wanted a little peace and quiet."

Where are we going? Apparently, Amber hadn't completely dreamt hearing those words. And the gunshot sound had not been merely part of a subconscious nightmare after all. It had been very real. It was the sound of Watts's life ending.

"You didn't answer my question," she said sternly, despite her voice shaking.

"I let my guard down and underestimated too many people, like Watts down there. I hired him first, but I guess Jack was able to woo him the way he did you. I knew after Marty Callahan was killed—which, by the way, was supposed to be you, and he just kept screwing up every assignment I gave him—anyway, after that I got suspicious. After all, no one is that incompetent." He took a deep breath and inhaled the fresh air. "Ah, that feels good, doesn't it?"

"And what about me?" she asked.

"As for you, I think I underestimated you the most. I should have killed you myself a long time ago. I had plenty of chances. But I never anticipated that you would be this goddamn nosy. You could have done yourself a favor long ago by not getting involved with Jack and by not poking around Harper Phillips's records. I mean, what the hell were you hoping to accomplish?"

It was a good question, she had to admit. She had asked herself that question several times, but the answer had never come to her. Instead, she would find herself plunging deeper into the mystery.

"Amber, consider it a service I'm providing. I'll be doing you a favor by taking you away from this whole situation." He laughed to himself.

"Where are you taking us?"

"It's a surprise," he said, and chuckled aloud. He was really enjoying himself. "Besides, I need you with me long enough to get to Jack."

"And what makes you think Jack is going to come to you just because of me?"

"Wow, I am surprised at you, Amber. You must be the only person who doesn't see it. Jack won't sit idly and watch someone he cares about get harmed."

Someone he cares about. Those words would have meant so much more if the situation was different.

"Besides, he probably wants to get one last fuck in before it's all over." He turned briefly and removed his sunglasses. He looked at her, up and down. "I can't say I blame him."

"You're a bastard," she said.

Lang threw back his head and laughed again.

"Don't you have any shame for what you're doing?" Amber persisted. "I mean, betraying the president? Betraying your country?"

"I think it's sweet how naïve you are, Amber."

"Don't patronize me, Mr. Lang. Despite the culture that people like you have promoted in this country, some of us still believe in respecting the institution that the president represents."

"Oh, don't get me wrong. I have extreme respect for the institution itself. But most people don't even know what the institution represents anymore."

"And you think this is the way to change it? By aligning yourself with Islamic terrorists and neo-Nazis?" She was putting the full court press on him. She was going to get her licks in while she could.

"I don't subscribe to their ideals, if that's what you're thinking. Anyway, don't bother presenting a lecture to me, young lady. You have no idea what's going on here."

"I think I do. Jack told me everything. That you're creating a phony campaign fund, just so that you can later expose the president for accepting donations from those groups."

"That's what Jack told you? For a minute, I thought Jack had actually figured it all out. I guess this is going to be easier than I thought."

She listened to his words carefully. Perhaps Jack had been outsmarted. "And what do these groups get out of all this, anyway? I imagine they're not forking over their money merely to embarrass the president."

"They have their reasons."

"It's treasonous. He doesn't deserve this."

"This isn't entirely political," said Lang. "It's personal as well. There are big businesses and colossal investment funds that are being adversely affected by what they view as the president's intense paranoia." He stopped talking for a moment, realizing that he had said too much. "And where exactly did you get the pie-in-the-sky notion that the president is some symbol of morality?"

"Who cares? Who made you the authority to decide on behalf of the rest of us that he isn't?"

"Relax, Amber. It's not like we're planning to shoot him from a book depository as his motorcade passes by." He laughed.

"Why not? What's the difference? You've killed everyone else in your path to get there."

"Because once you murder a president, he immediately attains martyr status. His legacy ends up nurturing a culture of people who try to carry out his ideals as some kind of perpetual tribute to him. That's the complete opposite of the result we're trying to achieve." He leaned toward her. "As for the rest of you? Well, the rest of you are dispensable." He laughed again.

"You can't get away with this. Do you actually believe the public will believe that its own president would be in any way affiliated with terrorist groups and other people like that?"

"Amber, my dear, we live in a society that has been carefully trained to believe whatever they are told about the president's character. Partisan lines are split down the middle at best in this country. We're also the most litigious citizens in the world. We celebrate the prosecution of a public figure like it's street theater."

The yacht cruised south through the open water, past Caye Caulker. The sun was low in the sky now, but the hour was still early. Amber thought she had stalled long enough with her arguments. She had hoped that by this time, someone—namely Jack—would have noticed they were gone and have come after them. But other than their yacht, there were only a few boats on the water, none of which appeared to be moving fast.

"Let's say that Jack does come after me," Amber called out. "What then?"

"Well, it's simple. I'll no longer need you. I'll have Jack, and then…"

Amber leaned forward. "And then?"

Lang turned back to face her. "I'm going to kill your mother." He leaned in close to her again. "And then I'm going to kill you." He returned his eyes to the water and began whistling again.

Chapter 51

▼

Jack had fallen asleep on a plastic deck chair. From his spot on the pier, he had a perfect view of the shoreline. No one would be leaving by boat in the morning without Jack seeing it. He hadn't intended to fall asleep, but the events of the last forty-eight hours had drained his mind and his body. Nestled beneath the awning at the rear of Patojo's Dive Shop, he shielded his eyes from the rising sun directly in front of him. He looked to his left to see Dalton fast asleep in another chair. The sea was perfectly calm, and the sunlight cast a shimmering golden beam across the surface, like an illuminated runway. It was beautiful. The visibility was clear to the horizon.

"Damn!" Jack yelled and leapt from his seat.

Dalton nearly fell out of his chair at Jack's exclamation. In the process of absorbing a postcard image of a Caribbean sunrise, Jack had momentarily neglected to realize that when they sat down the night before, a sixty-foot yacht was easily visible straight ahead. But this morning, there was nothing.

"What is it?" Dalton asked, his eyes still not focused.

"The boat. It's gone," Jack said, pointing to the undisturbed water.

Dalton quickly got to his feet and held his hand to his forehead like a visor. "Where the hell is it?"

He looked to his right and made out the tiny white image on the surface of the water, moving rapidly away from them.

"There!" he called out, pointing in the boat's direction.

Jack looked where Dalton was pointing. "What is that son of a bitch doing? I told him to go only on my order."

Jack reached into his pocket and fished out the keys to the dive boat they had taken out the night before. By this time, the dive shop operator had opened the doors to his establishment. Jack held the keys up to him and pointed to the dive boat, as Dalton untied the line. The dive master nodded. He had two other boats he could take divers out in that morning. Besides, Jack had paid him handsomely for the inconvenience.

Dalton placed one foot inside the boat, but Jack stopped him.

"No, I need you to stay here. Lang is still on this island somewhere, and he'll try to get off as soon as he can. We can't let him get away."

Jack threw the throttle forward, probably prematurely in the shallow water, but he didn't care. He had to get to that yacht. He dialed Watts's number on his cell phone, but there was no answer. He tossed the phone onto the bench beside him and spun the wheel toward the open water.

As his eyes locked onto the yacht directly ahead of him, his cell phone rang. He reached down and held it up. It was Watts's number.

"Watts! What the hell are you doing? I told you not to go until I said so."

But there was no reply.

"Watts?" he yelled over the lapping breeze. "Watts? You there?" he repeated several times. But there was nothing.

He was about to hang up when he heard voices. One of them was Amber's, although she wasn't doing most of the talking. The other voice was a man's, but it wasn't Watts.

"Harry," he said to himself.

He glanced back toward Patojo's, but it had become a speck, and he was sure Dalton was gone by now.

Jack put the phone to his ear tightly and listened. All he could discern was Amber asking Lang where they were headed. Then he heard Lang's answer. They were going to Caye Caulker, one of the many cays off the coast of Belize. He was planning to take a plane from Caye Caulker to the main airport in Belize City. It was probably Lang's contingency plan in case anything went wrong on Ambergris, as it had. Jack listened for more but was interrupted by a loud beep. He glanced down at the display. He was losing the signal.

"Damn," he said, as the phone automatically hung up.

But he had heard enough. He pressed the throttle forward, even though the dive boat was not equipped to go that fast, and sped toward Caye Caulker. He thought about his assignment: to find Harry Lang and stop him from executing his plan. The compensation promised to him by the independent group in Washington was extremely attractive. But none of that meant anything at this point.

He found himself worrying about Amber. He had come to care for her. Perhaps he had always cared about her from their first encounter. She had never given up throughout this entire ordeal. And he was not about to give up on her now.

The doors to Belize Bank customarily opened at nine o'clock, but he had managed to convince the manager to make an exception and to open earlier for him. There was a bonus of ten thousand U.S. dollars in it for the manager, who was more than happy to oblige. At that early hour, the security guard assumed his post just inside the doorway, while the rest of the staff readied themselves for the customers who would be arriving in the next hour. The guard watched him intently. The ponytail and the earring constituted a distinctive look he had seen before among wealthy young Americans who frequented the island.

The ponytailed man walked directly to the stairs and ascended without hesitation. He knew exactly where he was going. When he got to the top, the staff members upstairs were still settling in for the morning. A man in a suit, clearly the manager, met him at the stairs and escorted him toward the back and into an office, closing the door behind them. The other staff members whispered among themselves, speculating as to the type of shady business being conducted.

Only fifteen minutes later, the manager emerged from the office and walked around a wall, behind which was housed a small bank of safe deposit boxes. He returned carrying a black briefcase, reentered his office, and handed the case to the man with the ponytail. Inside the case was a short stack of documents. The ponytailed man thumbed through them and nodded in agreement, then replaced the documents in the briefcase, shook the manager's hand, and walked out of the office. He proceeded down the steps toward the exit with the case in his hand. When he left the building, he stood in the street and took a deep breath. He had just moved ninety million dollars—to where, he didn't know, and he didn't care. In a matter of hours, he would be getting paid, and he would be putting Harper Phillips, Harry Lang, and the rest of them behind him.

By this hour, people were beginning to spill out into the streets as the warm Belizean sky shined brightly. The ponytailed man moved among the tourists and shop owners, clutching the briefcase so tightly that he had to switch hands several times to wipe the sweat from his palms. His instructions from his employer—the man he had met in Fido's—were to drop the briefcase at the front desk of the Banyan Bay Resort. He was told neither to leave an accompanying message nor any contact information. And most importantly, he was to do it quickly and leave the area even more quickly.

The hotel desk clerk accepted the briefcase from him without hesitation. In exchange for the case, the clerk handed him an unmarked envelope. With the envelope in his sweaty hand, the man walked out quickly. Once outside, he opened the envelope and read the piece of paper. The step-by-step instructions on the paper left no room for any miscues, any of which would throw the schedule completely off track.

In accordance with his orders, he headed in the direction of the Shark's Bar, where the water taxi to Caye Caulker was waiting. The Atlantic Bank was located a block and a half from the public pier where the water taxi would drop him off. His payment would be in the account by the time he arrived there. He looked at his watch. His Tropic Air flight out of Caye Caulker was leaving in two hours. He picked up his pace as the anticipation of getting off the island heightened.

The water taxi was half full at this early hour. He climbed in and found a seat toward the front of the boat. As it coasted toward the open sea, he pulled off the rubberband that held his ponytail and ran his hands through his hair so that it could fly freely in the wind once the boat picked up speed. It all felt refreshing—the spray and the scent of the water, the wide expanse of open sky, and the freedom of knowing that he could be anyone he wanted to be again. That was the lifestyle he had grown accustomed to, and he was anxious to get back to it.

After a little more than fifteen minutes, the main pier on Caye Caulker became visible. He could see a group of tourists waiting to board the boat on their way to Belize City. Other than a few small dive boats hauling snorkelers out to the nearby reef, the only other craft on the water was an elaborate white yacht, just past the reef. It had apparently just anchored, as he could see one of the men on board placing a smaller boat in the water. *What a life*, he thought to himself. Perhaps someday he would own something like that.

After disembarking from the water taxi, he retied his ponytail and made his way to the bank. Making no attempt to remain inconspicuous, he walked quickly and with purpose. This was it. This is what he had been working toward for the last few years. He couldn't bear the thought of prolonging it even a minute more. He wanted his money.

It was nine o'clock and the Atlantic Bank's doors were just opening. He walked up Back Street until he arrived at the front doors. With one quick look around him—more an occupational habit than an exercise in caution—he disappeared through the doors.

Harry Lang carefully lowered a smaller boat into the water. Amber hadn't noticed it attached to the stern in the darkness the night before. It was about twelve feet in length. The inflatable collar was decorated with two red stripes. The sea was beginning to show signs of activity as dive boats and recreational tour guides set out from the shore. With his gun pointed into Amber's back, he guided her into the smaller craft. She moved with obvious reluctance.

"C'mon, Mom," she called up to the yacht.

"No, no, Amber." Lang put his hand up. "Your mom stays on the yacht."

"Why?"

"Because I need to keep you apart from her. For now at least."

"Why?" she asked again, but this time with a firmer tone.

"I've come to know you well, Amber, and the one thing that was clear to me from the start is that you're a thinking gal. I normally like that sort of thing. However I tend to take caution when one's plotting against me. But I know if you try something clever, you won't go anywhere without your beloved mother. And with her on the boat, you have no chance of making it out here before I find you and kill both of you."

He smiled obnoxiously at her, to which she sneered in response. Unfortunately, he was absolutely correct. In fact, she had already concocted a rudimentary scheme to get away from him once they were on land, but her mother had to be with her in order for it to work.

Lang approached her mother and reached behind her, tightening the twine holding her wrists together. Her mother was still in shock, her eyes fixed on a single spot on the deck. Lang escorted her down to the cabin.

"We'll be back soon, Mom. Don't worry." Amber wasn't sure whether these words would mean anything to her mother but hoped that her mind would slip into another time and place until the ordeal was over.

She looked around, hoping to see Jack approaching to help her. He surely must have heard her conversation with Lang after she had taken Watts's cell phone and dialed Jack's number. She was fortunate that Lang hadn't seen her hide the phone under the captain's chair while he was steering the yacht.

Lang emerged from the cabin and climbed in. The engine on the small boat started, and Amber and Lang headed toward Caye Caulker's shoreline.

Jack had lost significant ground as the yacht in front of him sped further away. When the boat traffic from the shore gradually increased, he was forced to decrease his speed. He passed the Split, a narrow channel dividing the cay, and saw the yacht anchored in the distance offshore. He spun the wheel toward it and pushed forward on the throttle. He reached into the waistband of his pants and released the safety on his gun. He knew there was no way to approach the yacht stealthily, considering the bright daylight and the open water. He knew he was putting Amber at risk but no more so than if he simply left her alone with Lang.

He cut the engine, and the dive boat coasted gently toward the portside of the yacht. It was eerily quiet on the larger boat, and Jack pulled his gun out as he steadily climbed the ladder. When he reached the top, his eyes moved laterally across the deck. It was empty. He stepped aboard and pointed his weapon, supporting it with both hands. Moving quietly toward the helm, he noticed several drops of blood on the floor next to the ladder. *Please don't let it be Amber's*, he said to himself.

Holding his gun at knee height, he slowly descended the stairs to the cabin. When he reached the bottom, he saw Amber's mother tied up on the velvet sofa. He ran to her, surprised that Lang had not bothered to cover her mouth. But he realized soon enough why. The older woman's face was ashen. She appeared catatonic, probably the result of shock, he surmised.

"Where is Amber?" he asked her, untying her wrists.

But she said nothing.

"Ma'am, please tell me. Where did they go?" He was kneeling directly in front of her face, but her eyes were focused somewhere else.

He looked to his left and saw the two doorways to the staterooms. One of them was closed. He stood and walked toward it, ready to fire his gun. He placed his free hand on the knob to the closed door and turned it slowly. As the door opened, he jumped back and was prepared to shoot until he realized that the person facing him was not going to shoot back. It was Watts. He was propped up on the bed, facing the door. The wound in his chest was small, but the blood stains on his clothes were extensive.

Jack ran through the cabin and back up to the deck, and then bounded up the ladder to the helm and looked around. From this height, he noticed that the small boat that normally hung off the stern was missing. He grabbed a pair of binoculars on the console and peered through them, spinning around in a wide arc. He stopped when his vision crossed the pier. The small boat with the two red stripes was floating in the shallow water, tied to the dock. Among the many people who had gathered during the morning hours, he saw a man and a woman walking much more quickly than the others. They were headed in the direction of the main street. They walked close to one another, and the man's inside hand was stuffed into his pocket, as if he were concealing something.

"Shit." He jumped down to the deck and back into the cabin. He took Amber's mother by the hand and practically dragged her up top. She didn't resist but didn't move voluntarily, either. At one point, he considered slinging her over his back and hauling her up like a firefighter toting a rescue victim from a burning building but decided the maneuver might frighten her.

Once they both were finally inside the dive boat, he started the engine and pointed toward the pier. He wasn't sure what Lang was up to now, since it didn't make any sense. Jack momentarily lost sight of his assignment to locate and stop Lang. Amber had saved him back at the house, and he owed her. But he knew that wasn't the primary reason he wanted to help. He glanced back at her mother, who had her eyes closed as the wind whipped past them. He watched her briefly, wondering what she was thinking. Then she opened her eyes, looked directly at him, and spoke, softly but firmly.

"Jack, when you find Amber, you tell her to come home immediately. It's not like her not to call if she's going to be late. I'm worried about her."

Whatever place in her mind she had found refuge in earlier was now gone. He wasn't quite sure by her words whether she knew what was really going on, or if she actually believed that Amber had stayed out late after the school dance.

He nodded to her. "I will, Mrs. Wakefield. I promise."

He held up the binoculars and continued to follow Lang's and Amber's movements up the beach. They were walking quickly. Lang was obviously on a rigid timeline. Jack knew he had to catch up to them soon. He tossed the binoculars onto the bench and pushed the boat forward.

Chapter 52

Standing in the lobby of the Victoria House, Bruce Fox checked his watch for the fifth time in the last ten minutes. The money certainly should have been transferred out of the Belize Bank account by now. This was the critical moment. They had planned for three years, and the margin for error was paper-thin.

His phone began ringing, and he picked it up after half a ring.

"Harry?" he said into the receiver.

"I'm in Caye Caulker now. At the airstrip."

"Any word from Hammond in Washington?"

"Yes. He's confirmed it. The money's in the president's campaign account."

Fox sighed a breath of relief. "We did it."

"Yes, we did. That president is officially screwed."

"What about Jack Bennett? He can still cause problems."

"Not to worry. He'll show up."

"How can you be so sure?"

Lang glanced over to Amber, whose arm was firmly in his grasp. "I've got some insurance."

Fox closed his eyes. He knew precisely what Lang was referring to. "There's no need to do anything to her, Harry. If and when Jack shows himself, you let her go. There's nothing to be gained by harming her."

"I'll make that decision, Foxy."

"She has nothing to do with our business here."

"Bullshit. She's the only reason Jack is still on this island. He stole twenty-five million dollars of our money. I don't care whether that money makes it to the president's campaign fund or not. But I'm not going to let him take it and run."

"You know that any delay can jeopardize our entire plan," Fox insisted. "Fitch is pulling together our exit off the island as we speak. When we're ready to go, we're not going to have any time to wait for you or anyone else."

"Don't worry about me, Bruce. I can take care of myself from here on out. Your job is to meet me at our rendezvous location tomorrow morning."

"We'll be there."

The line went dead.

Fox immediately dialed several digits into his phone. As he walked toward the beach, someone answered on the other side of the line.

"He's at the airstrip at Caye Caulker. He's got the girl."

Lang stood near the Tropic Air office. He had already checked in and was clutching his boarding pass. There was really no point in his being there, since he already had confirmation that the money had been moved. Still, he felt some uneasiness about how the meeting at Shark's Bar had ended, with his man not exhibiting the least bit of interest in getting paid for the job. It made him nervous.

He pulled Amber close to him, under the awning, as a line of passengers boarded the next flight. As he watched them climb the steps into the small aircraft, he stepped forward and focused his attention on one of the passengers. A white man in his thirties. A distinctive ponytail hung down his back. Lang felt a rush of anxiety.

He cupped his hands over his mouth and called out. "Harper!"

The man with the ponytail spun around instinctively. He looked around, eyeing the handful of people near the terminal, any of whom could have called his name. After a couple of seconds, he clearly didn't recognize any of the faces out there. He ducked his head into the doorway and disappeared into the plane.

Lang stood motionless, watching the small plane turn around and begin its takeoff. As he watched it leave, his eyes narrowed. That was his guy. He knew it. His instincts had been correct the evening before. The man he had met in Shark's Bar was not the man he had hired three years ago. He had been conned. And he had no doubt that Jack was behind it.

Through all of this, he didn't notice that he had gradually loosened his grip and finally let go of Amber's arm. When he finally snapped out of his trance, he spun around. Amber was gone.

Jack tied the line to the dock and helped Amber's mother out of the dive boat. They walked quickly up the beach toward the main street. Her mother walked with surprising energy, considering the ordeal she had been through in the last twenty-four hours.

"Where are we going, Jack?" she asked.

He wasn't prepared for this question. "Uh, we're just going to pick up Amber."

"Oh, just wait until I get my hands on that young lady. How dare she miss her curfew without calling me!"

Her mind was back in another time, which suited the current situation perfectly. Jack wasn't sure what was about to happen, but he knew that Mrs. Wakefield was better off in another place and time than here, even if it was only in her mind.

They stepped onto the main street and headed in the direction of the airstrip. He remembered from the phone call he had eavesdropped on earlier that Lang was planning to fly off the island to Belize City. Jack picked up the pace with Amber's mother in tow.

When they arrived near the entrance of the airstrip, Jack slid quickly to the side, pulling Amber's mother close to him. He saw Lang running out of the area, his hand tucked into his pocket. He was alone. *Where was Amber?* Jack studied Lang and could see the desperation in his face. He had lost her. It didn't surprise Jack that she would eventually find a way to shake Lang loose. After all, she had done it to him in San Francisco several weeks before. But it also meant that she was alone and unprotected. Jack knew that Lang was one of the most talented investigators in the world. He would find her eventually. *Where the hell was she?*

His phone began ringing. He picked up immediately, nearly fumbling the phone onto the sand.

"Yeah?" he said.

"Jack, it's me." Amber's voice was shaking. She had managed to take Watts's phone back from the yacht before Lang pushed her into the smaller boat.

"Amber, are you OK?"

"I think so. But he's looking for me. I know he is."

"Yeah, I saw him walking out of the airstrip entrance. Tell me where you are." She was breathing loudly, he could tell. "Is my mom OK? Let me talk to her."

"She's fine. She's with me right now."

"He killed Mr. Watts."

With her free hand trapped in her hair, she was talking faster now, none of her thoughts in any logical order.

"I know, Amber. Where are you?" he repeated.

"I sneaked into a room of some hotel down by the pier. I think it's called Seaside Cabanas or something like that."

"Can you see the pier from where you are?"

"Yes. It's just to the left of the hotel."

"Great. You get to the pier as fast as you can. We'll be there in less than five minutes. There're a lot of people around now. Lang won't try anything there."

Jack was walking at a brisk rate, and Amber's mother was doing well to keep up.

"Five minutes. Don't let me down, Jack." Amber's voice was shaking.

"I'm going to get you and your mom off this island safely. I promise."

They hung up simultaneously. Amber sat on a chair in the small room and looked out the window. After four minutes, she walked to the door and eased it open. The sunlight sent a beam of light through the room. She took one deep breath, and then stepped outside. She walked to the gate that served as the beach entrance to the hotel. In a single motion, she swung open the gate and sprinted clumsily through the sand in the direction of the pier.

When she arrived at the edge of the pier, she saw her mother walking gingerly through the sand from the direction of the main street. Jack had her arm and was pulling her along. Amber ran up to meet them and hugged her mother.

"C'mon, Mom, we have to hurry," she said, grasping her mother by the hand and giving her a hug.

"You and I are going to have a talk about this, young lady. I've been worried sick about you. You know you're supposed to call if you're going to be late." Her mother waved a finger at her.

Amber looked up at Jack.

"She still thinks you went to a dance last night and didn't bother to come home," he explained.

"Lucky for her," said Amber.

They reached the pier at last and stood near the end of it.

"Now what?" Amber asked, swiveling her head, nervously in search of the gun-wielding deputy director.

"There," Jack said, pointing out to the water.

A white, twenty-foot fishing boat was approaching them. Special Agent Dalton was steering it carefully toward the pier. When he was close enough, he tossed a line, and a couple of local teenagers on the pier caught the line and pulled it in slowly. At last Dalton was close enough to step to the edge of the boat and hold out his hand. Amber got in first, then her mother, who had become increasingly proficient at boarding boats during the several hours.

"Get them to Belize City," Jack told Dalton. "And you personally escort them to the airport."

"Wait, you're not coming with us?" Amber asked.

He shook his head. "I can't let Lang get off this island. I already lost him once, and I'm not going to do it again."

The disappointment on her face was evident. He couldn't help but feel a little flattered that she worried about him as much as she did. He wanted badly to go with her, but he still had a job to do.

"I promised to get you both off this island. This is the only way to do it. And it's the only time."

Amber's mother held out her hand to Jack, who took it in his. She shook it.

"Thanks for bringing my baby home, Jack."

"You're welcome, ma'am."

Amber looked up at him, doing nothing to fight back the tears in her eyes.

"Jack, I don't know what to say. I…" Her voice drifted off. But the message was clear.

He knelt down and took her hand. "I know, Amber. I know." He squeezed her hand once more. Then he stood and looked at Dalton.

"Go on, get out of here," he said.

The boat pulled out of the shallow water and, in seconds, its engine rumbled and it sped off toward the main city.

Chapter 53

The fishing boat coasted toward the swing bridge in Belize City. A large group of people stood inside the terminal, waiting for the next departing water taxi. Dalton maneuvered the boat slowly toward the edge of the dock, and an older local man in a hat and a tank top grabbed the line and pulled them to the dock.

Outside the terminal a dusty green Datsun was waiting for them with its engine running, spitting out black smoke into the eighty-seven degree air. A large Belizean man with a shaggy beard sat in the driver's seat.

Dalton guided them into the car, and it slowly moved through the town and toward the highway. They headed west toward the international airport. As the car rumbled along, Amber leaned forward.

"You're not coming with us, are you, Mr. Dalton?" she asked.

Dalton shook his head. "Afraid not. I have to go back. But you need to do what Jack told you. Get off this island. There's an American Airlines flight leaving for Dallas in three hours. Here are your tickets," he said, handing an envelope to her. "When you arrive there, Gil will be waiting for you at the gate."

Amber looked out the window and placed her hand in her mother's hand. She felt a light squeeze in response and turned her head to face the older woman. Her mother now had a serene expression on her face. Despite her illness, Amber felt reassured to see that calm look on her face, as though she was telling Amber that everything was going to be all right.

Amber and her mother had both fallen asleep in the back of the Datsun by the time it pulled in front of Belize International Airport. Dalton escorted them into the terminal, constantly looking around him. Bypassing the long line of weary travelers who stood at the ticket counter, he walked to the edge of the counter and called one of the clerks. Moments later, a man in his mid-forties approached Dalton and exchanged a few words. Dalton returned to the women. "Let's go," he said.

They followed him and the man behind the counter toward the security checkpoint. Another word or two from Dalton to the clerk, and immediately all four of them stepped ahead the line and through the doors toward the boarding gates. Evidently, the FBI had its privileges everywhere.

The flight was boarding in two hours. Amber and her mom found a bench near the gate. Dalton stood with them for a few minutes, surveying the area. "I realize, Mr. Dalton, that you can't stay," said Amber. "I want to thank you for everything. I don't think I would be here if it weren't for you."

"I'm not sure I deserve thanks for that," he replied with a smile.

She held out her hand. "Good luck, Mr. Dalton."

"Likewise." He shook her hand.

She looked at the ground, unable to put her thoughts into words, but Dalton sensed what she was trying to say.

"Don't worry, Amber. He'll be fine."

Still staring down, she smiled and nodded slowly. There was so much she hadn't said to Jack. They had been rushed off the island so quickly, she had not had a chance to put together the words to express her feelings appropriately. And now, as she sat in the boarding area, it occurred to her that she might never have an opportunity to tell him how she felt. When she looked up again, Dalton and the desk clerk were disappearing through the security doors.

As her mother sat back and closed her eyes, Amber looked around at the other waiting passengers. A group of young women stood in a circle nearby. Through their laughter and incessant talking, she ascertained that they had visited Belize to celebrate a friend's wedding. Amber could see by the way they interacted that they were close, longtime friends. She knew this because it was the way she and her girlfriends acted when they were together. She missed it terribly. As she continued to watch them, she realized that theirs was the life she was supposed to be living at her age. One of the girls complained about the sunburn on her back, and the others sympathized. Amber laughed to herself. If only she could have their problems.

The cell phone ringing in her pocket woke her from the temporary trance. She looked at the display. The prefix indicated that it was an international call. *Please let it be Jack*, she thought to herself.

"Hello?" she answered.

"May I speak with Gina?" It was a woman's voice.

"I'm sorry, but…" She caught herself before finishing her sentence. "Uh, yes, this is Gina."

"Hi Gina. It's Wendy from the Jackson Winthrop office in Aruba."

Amber took a deep breath. With all that had occurred, she had completely forgotten about Wendy.

"Yes, Wendy. Sorry about that. I'm just really tired."

"No problem. I feel the same way."

"What can I do for you?"

"Well, you asked me to call you when I found out who was responsible for dissolving Bartlett Enterprises."

"What did you find?" Amber asked.

"It looks like the authorization came directly from Bartlett's parent company."

Amber spoke quietly into the phone. "And who would that be?"

"A company called Ensight, in San Francisco."

Amber stared forward. "Ensight?"

"That's right. They're a major software company."

Amber switched the phone to the other ear.

"There's something else here which I thought you might find interesting," Wendy continued.

"What is it?"

"Jackson Winthrop was named as Bartlett's blind trustee at the time of incorporation. So all the payments go into an account in name of Jackson Winthrop but for the benefit of Bartlett Enterprises."

"A blind trust?" Amber asked. "What exactly does that mean?"

"It basically means that Jackson Winthrop has full discretion over matters concerning Bartlett."

Amber's mind was spinning. What had been a series of sporadic details until this point were now colliding violently with one another.

"So, for example," Amber queried Wendy, "Jackson has discretion over where money is deposited. Things like that?"

"Exactly. Of course, in the case of Bartlett, it looks like our firm did a pretty good job of spreading their money around."

"How do you mean?" Amber wished Jack was there to hear all of this.

"About three years ago, we received a healthy chunk of money, nearly ninety million dollars that came in over a four-day period. The money was sent immediately after the corporation was established. The money was then distributed into at least twelve bank accounts around the world."

"Who distributed the money?"

"Let's see. One of our lawyers named Harper Phillips. He was named as trustee. He's actually based in your office. Do you know him?" For thirty seconds, the line went silent, and Amber could hear typing over the line. Wendy broke the silence. "Hmmm, that's weird."

"What?" Amber asked. She wished she could be looking at whatever Wendy was reviewing.

"Well, the records I'm reviewing show that after those initial deposits, there were virtually no deposits for the next two years. Then we received more wads of cash, almost eighty million in the last ten months."

"And where did those funds get distributed?"

"Nowhere. They're just sitting in the trustee account in Curaçao."

"So where does all that money go when Bartlett is dissolved tomorrow?"

"It says here, and I'm quoting, 'Upon the liquidation of Bartlett Enterprises, the trustee shall transfer in full all monetary assets to the Corporation's account at the following institution: Riggs Bank, Washington DC.' There's an account listed here. Do you want it?"

"No, that's OK. But tell me, how soon after Bartlett is dissolved does the money get transferred?"

"My understanding is that they want it to coincide with their acquisition. Therefore, as soon as that event becomes effective, it triggers the liquidation process, and the funds go out. It's pretty simple."

There was another pause. "Wendy, did you say acquisition?"

"Yes. Good grief, Gina, have you been living in a box since they shut down that office out there? The big Maguire-Ensight deal? It's all over the business newswires. The deal is officially on. It becomes effective tomorrow. I would have thought you'd be much closer to it than I am, since they're in San Francisco."

Amber realized for the first time that she had not picked up the newspaper or watched a news broadcast in days. Apparently the acquisition deal was going through now, since after months of squabbling, the parties had come to an agreement. It was an abrupt development, but she supposed these big deals moved quickly once the right price was named.

"Gina, do you need the number to Ensight?" Wendy asked.

"No, thank you. I'll find it." Amber hung up without saying good-bye.

Brief images from memory flashed through her mind. The file marked *Ensight* at the Jackson Winthrop office in San Francisco contained invoices made out to Bartlett. The payments she had viewed in the Cyclops system were paid directly to Jackson Winthrop. A phony employee had been set up in Ensight's personnel database. Only an hour ago, these were all questions swirling in front of her—but not anymore. They were now pieces of a convoluted puzzle.

Amber needed to call Jack. What she knew now was the missing link he needed to complete his case against the men. She dialed his number, but the call went directly to voice mail. *How was she going to tell him?*

At that moment, the public address system began declaring last call for all passengers boarding the flight to Dallas. Amber rustled her mother from her nap and walked with her to the boarding gate.

Chapter 54

It had been a few hours since Dalton had escorted Amber and her mother to the airport. There had been no sign of Lang during that time. Jack stood among a group of tourists awaiting the water taxi on the pier that he and Watts had arrived at the day before. It was becoming extremely warm by this hour, and he wished several times that he could jump into the water to refresh himself. He watched two young couples who were apparently vacationing together, laughing and exchanging kisses. Seeing them, he regretted sending Amber away so quickly without saying a proper good-bye. After what he had put her through, she deserved more than that.

His phone rang.

"Yeah," he said, and then listened intently, nodding and taking mental notes. After a few more seconds of listening, he nodded once more. "Got it." And he hung up.

Dalton approached, just back from Belize City.

"Who was that?" Dalton asked, noticing the abrupt end to the phone call.

"A personal call. Did they seem to get off OK?" Jack asked, changing the subject quickly.

"Yes. They were at the boarding gate when I left them. They'll be fine."

For what seemed like a long while, neither man said a word.

"She's worried about you, Jack," Dalton finally said.

"I know." It was what Jack wanted to hear him say. "But she's better off this way. She's not safe with me, no matter how much I try to convince her she is."

"Well, you shouldn't have to worry about that anymore. I have one of my best guys waiting for her and her mother on the ground in Dallas. He's supposed to call me when they touch down."

Jack looked at his watch. "I'll rest when I get that confirmation."

"In the meantime, I was planning to call down some reinforcements."

"Reinforcements? What are you talking about?"

"We are planning to apprehend Mr. Lang, aren't we?" asked Dalton.

"Well, first of all, there is no 'we.' I have neither authorization nor jurisdiction to involve anyone else, including you."

"Precisely, which is why we need to get some people down here who do. I do have authorization, but I can't do everything alone."

"Let's not get ahead of ourselves," said Jack. "We still don't have any concrete evidence. We have no witnesses. Nothing. We need to be patient."

"He tried to kill us last night. You and I can corroborate each other's accounts."

"No. I want to nab him for conspiracy, not for trying to shoot us. He's the deputy director of the FBI. If he's going down for anything, it's got to be something huge. He'll sidestep anything less."

Jack could sense Dalton's confusion and frustration. But it was all he could do to stall the eager FBI agent.

"Why are you being so shy about this? We can make a strong enough case with what we have," Dalton insisted.

"Listen, Dalton, this is my gig. The people who hired me to do this called me in because they wanted to keep a low profile. All this smells of scandal, and it could embarrass some very powerful people if it's not handled subtly."

"You mean the president."

"Among others," Jack told him.

"You want to take down the number two guy in the FBI and keep it low profile?"

"Those were my orders."

"This is highly unorthodox, Jack."

"Yes it is, which is all the more reason to be discreet. Trust me, please, I know what I'm doing."

Dalton continued to look skeptical, and Jack could see it.

"Dalton, you're welcome to leave at any time. I appreciate everything you've done thus far, but if you're not comfortable being here, then you should probably go home. But just know that if you follow my lead on this, I can guarantee you'll be acknowledged for it."

That was an appealing idea to Dalton. In fact, that was the primary reason he had come to the Caribbean unauthorized. He wanted to be recognized by the people in Washington. Jack noticed his change in expression. Dalton was convinced, at least for now.

"Don't forget that there are other people involved in this," Dalton said. "We don't necessarily have to dedicate our search to Lang. We can go after the others, too."

"No. Lang is the kingpin."

"Jack, are you sure this isn't personal? It's no secret that there's no love lost between you and Lang."

"If it was personal, I would have killed him by now. Now, are you in or out?"

Dalton took a deep breath, and then slowly nodded. "I'm in."

"Good," Jack said, slapping him on the back. "There are only two ways off this island—a puddle jumper from the airstrip or a boat from this pier. Lang has to choose one."

"So, we should each stake out one of the areas."

"Right. You stay here and watch the boats taking off. I'll go to the airstrip. You see anything, you call me. Don't try to be a hero and apprehend him yourself. Is that clear?"

Dalton nodded. His eyes were focused again.

Jack walked away releasing a sigh of relief. Convincing Dalton was the most difficult thing he had to do. He could hardly believe he had been successful, as strict adherence to FBI protocol was the mantra of a dutiful agent. But Dalton's arrival in Belize had been a completely unexpected event. Jack wondered whether he should have disclosed to Dalton as much about his assignment as he had. He turned around and saw the FBI agent standing by the pier, no doubt with his eyes darting around behind his dark sunglasses. He was the epitome of a Boy Scout. And Jack had done well to appeal to him by offering him a chance to earn his merit badge.

When he arrived at the airstrip, it was bustling with passengers. Two planes had just arrived, and a chaotic scene had developed as visitors and grounds crew sorted through dozens of luggage pieces. It was hard for Jack to see through the moving crowd and still remain invisible to Lang, if he was there.

He stood by the small terminal building and eyed the passengers as they filed past. He looked to his left and watched a line of passengers as they approached a Maya flight. They were mostly couples and a few children, but no one who looked remotely like the deputy director.

Three hours passed, and Jack had walked the entire length of Caye Caulker. There was a chance that Lang might have returned to Ambergris, but Jack knew the man well. Lang might be deranged, but he wasn't careless. He wouldn't run the risk of returning to a place where he had narrowly escaped capture. For all Jack knew, Lang could be hiding in the corner of a dark room inside any one of the countless hotels and inns around the island, contemplating his next step. But that notion didn't match what Jack knew about Lang. The man wasn't passive. He was like a championship chess player: he always had a next move.

As Jack stood in front of Sobre Las Olas toward the northern section of Caulker, he looked out at the water, which was now heavy with activity. He saw the yacht still anchored outside the reef. That was Lang's best chance of getting away on water, so Jack had kept a steady eye on it, making sure he didn't let it leave without his knowledge as he had earlier that morning.

With his eyes still alert and pinned on the yacht, he thought about Amber. He had a sense that she was thinking about him too, a realization that sent a rush of excitement through him. He vowed to find her after all this was done.

His thoughts were disrupted by his cell phone, which began chirping. "Yeah," he answered.

"Jack, it's me." Dalton's voice carried a tone of intensity that Jack hadn't heard before.

"What is it? Did you find him? Remember what I told you. Don't try to take him down yourself. I'm on my way to you now."

Jack began running south toward the pier.

"Stop talking, Jack. It's not that."

He stopped running and caught his breath. "What is it, then?"

"I just got a call from Gil, my guy in Dallas."

"Yeah? Did they get there OK? Make sure he stays with them until…"

"Jack!" Dalton yelled into the phone. "They never arrived in Dallas. They didn't get on the plane."

A deaf silence took control of the line, as Jack hung up and closed his eyes, tilting his head skyward. After another deep breath, he looked out to the sea.

"What are you *doing*, Amber?" he said to himself.

The gate agent at American Airlines was not especially pleased with Amber when she and her mother decided not to board the aircraft in Belize City. Amber's change of plans drew suspicious sneers not only from the other passengers in line, but also from the security personnel who were stationed nearby. Holding her mother by the arm, Amber walked through the terminal and toward the exit. She tried Jack's phone again, but this time she noticed that the battery on her phone was practically dead, with only a single bar of energy showing. Amber hurried toward the front of the terminal building, shepherding her mother along. When she was outside, she dialed the phone once more, but this time to San Francisco. It was midday there, and the Ensight office was probably in full swing at this hour.

"Sanjay Mehta," said the tired voice on the other end.

"Sanjay? It's Amber Wakefield here."

"Miss Wakefield?"

"Listen to me. I need your help again."

There was an audible sigh on the other end, one she had not heard before from the usually acquiescent engineer.

"I need some information," she continued.

"I'm sorry, Miss Wakefield, but this has become a far too frequent ritual."

"I understand. And I wish I could tell you why. But it's better that you don't know, at least not for now. I'm hoping that one day I can explain it all to you."

"Are you in some kind of trouble, Miss Wakefield?"

"You could say that."

"I can't make any promises to you."

She had heard that from him before, and he had come through. "Thank you, Sanjay. When I was looking in Cyclops a few days ago, I noticed there were a number of sizeable payments sent to a law firm, Jackson Winthrop."

"Yes?" he responded.

"Those payments appeared to have a peculiar pattern. For example, the dates seem to be clustered together. They spanned a number of years, but there are months at a time when absolutely no payments were made. Then suddenly, there were dozens of payments made during a three or four day period."

"What is your question, Miss Wakefield?" Sanjay asked. He was growing impatient.

"My question is whether there's a way to determine the source of those funds."

"I imagine they are funded from the company's treasury," he said matter-of-factly.

"No, I meant even before they hit the treasury."

"Well, I'm not on the business side, but logic would tell me that the majority of incoming monies, particularly those of significant size, would come from product sales."

Amber nodded. "That was my guess, too. I just needed to hear it from someone else."

"Miss Wakefield, I still don't know what you wish me to do."

"I need someone to confirm the original source of the payments."

"I don't see how that is possible," said Sanjay. "Once the revenue from sales is received, the funds get commingled in Ensight's corporate account. There's no way to attribute outgoing funds to their source."

"There has to be some way," she insisted.

"I am not an accountant. I'm sure there is a way to do it, but it requires intense financial analysis. I am not the person for that."

"Is there at least a way for you to access the e-Sales Ledger system?"

"That is for privileged members of the sales team only."

"I know. But I need to see a snapshot of one of those date ranges to determine if, by chance, any large sums were paid to Ensight. The data probably won't be very telling, but I'm desperate here."

"Last time you asked me to give you access to Cyclops. Miss Wakefield, I am not willing to jeopardize my own career for this."

"Sanjay, if I told you that your career may already be in jeopardy, as are the careers of every other employee at Ensight, would that make any difference to you?"

There was silence. She had effectively relayed the magnitude of the situation to him without saying anything specific.

"Is our company involved in something illegal?"

"I'm not sure. I'm hoping to find out, but it's a delicate situation. That's why I called you. Because I know I can trust you."

"I don't know," he said, exasperated. "Besides, Miss Wakefield, I'm not sure I have the time anyway. It's quite crazy here as you might imagine."

"The Maguire deal?" she guessed.

"Of course. What else? It's all anyone here is talking about. Unfortunately, everything is happening far too quickly. They're not giving us much lead time. It's like a circus here. For the last three days, we have been informing our subsidiaries and renegotiating all of our strategic partnerships. You've never seen people move so feverishly. It's obvious that Maguire has big changes in mind for us."

"And they want it all to happen in the next thirty-six hours, huh?"

"I wish we had that much time left."

"I thought the acquisition was effective on Friday. I figured that meant end of day."

"No, no! Miss Wakefield, the official date is Friday, which means midnight on that day—the *beginning* of the day. Today is Thursday. We have ten hours!"

"Ten hours!" she yelled, attracting the attention of the others standing around her. "Oh, no!"

"May I ask a question?" said Sanjay. "Why have you taken it upon yourself to investigate this? If there is something fishy going on, should it not be the responsibility of the legal authorities?" Sanjay always knew to ask logical questions. Ever the engineer.

"Under any other circumstances, yes. But let's just say that it's complicated."

"It sounds like you have something personal at stake other than just your job." Amber thought about his comment for a few seconds. "Yes, I do indeed."

"As I stated before, Miss Wakefield, I will not promise you anything."

"I understand. You've been a wonderful friend to me, Sanjay."

"Will I see you again sometime soon?"

"I hope so." She made no attempt to conceal the apprehension in her voice.

The call ended, and Amber glanced toward her mother, who was standing inside a gift shop, browsing through the dozens of wooden figurines of tropical animals. She wondered whether she had made the correct decision by not getting on that plane to Dallas. It had been her chance to get away. She had taken a great gamble by not leaving, and she had put her mother and her own life in the betting circle. Nonetheless, she now knew something that Jack did not. She was the only one could help him. She thought again about him standing on that pier as they drifted away on that boat earlier.

According to the posted schedule, a Taca Airlines flight was leaving for Miami in two hours. Amber and her mother went to the ticket counter and found the man who had escorted them to the gate earlier. Amber explained that they had missed the flight because her mother, an Alzheimer's sufferer, was having an episode and that it didn't seem fair or safe to subject the other passengers to it. It was a shallow excuse, she knew. But the man behind the counter expressed his sympathies for her mother's illness and his appreciation for her consideration for the other passengers. He worked quickly to get the two on the next flight to the United States and said he would personally fast-track them through the security area.

While the agent was typing into his computer, Amber's phone beeped twice. It was probably the final warning that her battery was dying. But when she picked it up, she was surprised to find that the display indicated one message received. What was even stranger was that it was a text message. She didn't recognize the number of the sender, only that the area code was from San Francisco. She opened the message and read:

GIVE ME A FAX NUMBER. SANJAY

He must have read the number of her cell phone from his caller ID display. She stopped the man behind the counter from typing.

"Pardon, senor?" she said politely.

He looked up.

"Do you have a fax machine nearby?"

"Yes, of course," he replied, pointing to an old, dusty Canon resting on top of a ream of papers.

"May I have something faxed here?"

"Of course." He wrote down the number for her.

Amber quickly replied to the text message on her phone, punching the numbers carefully. When she hit the *Send* button, the display on her phone disappeared. The battery had sucked its last breath. She only hoped that her reply had reached Sanjay in time.

In three minutes, the fax machine began humming and spit out two sheets of paper, on which were printed screen shots of the eSales Ledger system. It was evident from the last line of the second page that the transmission had been cut off prematurely. However, in handwriting in the margin, the top page read:

THOUGHT YOU WOULD FIND THIS INTERESTING—S.M.

The snapshots had been taken under the system administrator's log-in access. Similar to Cyclops, each user had access to only his own sales activity to guard against manipulation of data by competitive sales professionals. But the administrator's view displayed everything. In a series of rows and columns, the pages listed the sales person's name, the customer's name, the date of the sale, the amount, the product code, and the amount of eligible commission. The print was extremely small, rendering it nearly illegible.

Amber searched frantically for anything telling. In the center of the page, there were twelve lines, each representing a sales transaction. For each of these particular sales, the column marked *SALES PROFESSIONAL* contained a name that had come to be highly recognizable to her: *Phillips, H.*

"What a surprise," she said softly.

She looked at the clock on the opposite wall. She had to warn somebody. These recorded sales were obviously fabricated in order to get the money into the company. But she wondered whether Jack knew about this already. She concluded that if he had known, then he certainly would have acted upon the information by now. He would not have asked Amber to help him find out what this identity thief's interest was in Ensight. But Amber had no way to reach him, and no time to look for him.

She turned quickly to the man behind the counter. "I've changed my mind. We're not going to Miami."

"Then to what city shall I book your tickets?" he asked, his hands poised over the keyboard.

She took a deep breath. "The shortest route to San Francisco."

Chapter 55

▼

"Where is he?" Dennis Fitch asked impatiently, looking at his watch. "He was supposed to be here an hour ago."

"I know," Fox answered. "Relax Denny, he'll be here."

They stood on the veranda in front of the luxurious villa, isolated in the middle of the western Caribbean Sea. The sun was nearing the horizon, but the heat was still quite intense. This was the final stage of their plan, one they had concocted nearly three years before. It seemed almost surreal that they were already at the end of the line.

Through the French doors of the main house, and moving slower by the hour, Terry Hammond stepped out. He now walked with the assistance of an aluminum cane with a supporting brace on the forearm, a new accessory since they had last seen the older man. Fitch quickly ran up the adobe steps and held his arm out to help Hammond down toward the veranda.

"Terry," Fox greeted him, holding out his hand.

"Hello, Bruce." The older man extended his hand. "It's been a while. I didn't think I was going to make it to see this thing through." He patted his heart playfully.

The men laughed, even Fitch.

"Well, I don't think we could have pulled this off without your connections," Fox said.

"Yes, sir, I may not have a desk at Langley anymore, but you bet your ass I've got more intelligence stored in my back pocket than any of those young hotshots there." He coughed violently, his old age showing its ugly face.

Fitch walked to a table and poured a glass of water from a pitcher. He handed it to Hammond, who accepted it with a shaky hand.

"So, where's everyone else?" Hammond asked after clearing his throat. "I was sure I was going to be the last one to arrive."

Fox looked toward the house. "They'll be here."

"Good. I'm too far along in my life to waste precious minutes."

"At least you'll be able to see the election in November," Fox offered.

"Knock on wood," Hammond said, tapping the top of his head with his knuckles.

"And where is our fine president these days?" asked Fitch.

"Where else? On the campaign trail. California this week, I believe."

"And he doesn't have a clue."

"He wouldn't know if it hit him in the face," said Hammond, taking another sip from his water glass. Fox picked up the day's issue of the *New York Times* from the table. He handed it to Hammond.

"I assume you've seen this."

Hammond looked at the headline.

PRESIDENT BASHES PATRIOT ACT REFORM

"Yes. Of course, I usually know these things long before they hit the printing press."

"I've always wondered which party this writer was affiliated with," Fox said, reading the name of the journalist who had penned the article. "When the president stepped into office, this same guy criticized him for being a traitor for wanting to soften some of the provisions in the Patriot Act. Now, he gives the president shit for doing a 180 turn on his stance."

"He's a journalist, Bruce. His job is to stir debate, especially during an election year," said Fitch. "Besides, he's right. The president can't change his mind so drastically during the course of his term, especially on a topic as controversial and sensitive as the Patriot Act. Even his own party constituents are questioning his conviction."

"Well that's his problem to deal with. You know the old saying. He made his bed, now he has to die in it." Hammond was always surprisingly witty, despite his old age.

The sun dipped lower, and a bright blend of pink and orange hues painted the sky. Amid the postcard backdrop, the three men stood side by side and stared out to sea. The conversation had died down, but they were all thinking the same thing.

The serenity of the moment was broken by the sound of a door closing behind them. Although they were surrounded completely by water, the rustling leaves in the trees around them drowned out any noise, even that of an approaching boat on the other side. In unison, all three men walked toward the house and entered through the large double doors. As they approached the foyer, which was flanked by two Buddha statues resting against the adobe walls on either side of them, they looked at the short figure who had entered through the front door. Beneath the dim floodlights in the ceiling, he appeared almost as a phantom, which was somewhat fitting, as none of them had seen the man in more than three years.

"Welcome, gentlemen. It's been a long time," he said to them.

He looked at each of them, nodding in acknowledgment. But it was Fox who spoke first.

"It's good to see you again, Harper."

Chapter 56

With her cell phone rendered useless, Amber made a collect call from a pay phone to the San Francisco field office of the FBI. While her call was being transferred, she eyed virtually every person who walked past her, most of whom couldn't help but stare at this woman in a dirty T-shirt and shorts standing with an older woman who was humming show tunes.

"Gil here," said the voice on the other end.

"Gil, it's Amber Wakefield."

"Amber! Where are you? You were supposed to have landed in Dallas hours ago. Mr. Dalton is freaking out."

"I know. I'm in Houston right now. At the airport, about to board my flight to San Francisco."

"San Francisco? Amber, why are you going back there? I can't protect you if you go there. Let me come to you. I'm in Dallas, but I can get on a flight right now and be there in an hour. Just sit tight."

"Sorry, Gil, but I have to get back to San Francisco now."

An announcement came over the loudspeaker for final boarding to San Francisco.

"That's me, Gil. Listen, I need you to arrange a car to pick up my mother and me when we land in San Francisco. You can arrange that, can't you?"

"Amber, please. Let me at least go with you."

"I can't wait for you. My plane is leaving. I have to go. Please, Gil, just do that one thing for me."

There was a sigh on the other end. "What should I tell Mr. Dalton?"

"Tell him I'm sorry and that I'll be in touch."

"What are you up to, Amber?" he asked suspiciously.
She didn't answer him.
"Amber? Are you still there?" But she was gone.

Jack stood nervously at the airstrip in Caye Caulker, watching every passenger who stepped on or off a flight. The last flight of the evening had just landed, as darkness began to cover the sky above him. He was far behind schedule. Lang had managed to elude him thus far, and Jack cringed at the possibility that his assignment might have been compromised as a result. And then there was Amber. She had not shown up in Dallas as she was supposed to. He couldn't imagine what she could possibly be doing or thinking. Things were falling apart quickly. Nonetheless, he had to remain focused.

Dalton approached him, replacing his cell phone into his pocket.
"Jack, that was Gil."
Jack turned to him. "Is she OK?"
"For the moment. But she's on her way to San Francisco now."
"San Francisco? What the hell is she going back there for?"
"She wouldn't tell Gil. But he said she sounded different. He said she didn't sound scared."
"What does that mean?"
Dalton shrugged. "I don't know."
"Whatever, Dalton. I tried everything I could to protect her. If she wants to put herself in danger, that's her problem." He said this with a feigned conviction.
"You don't really believe that, do you, Jack?" Dalton's phone began ringing.
"Yes, Special Agent Dalton here." He listened intently.
Jack watched him, hoping it was Gil telling him that he had caught up to Amber and that she was safely in his company. "Gracias, senor." Dalton hung up.
"Who was that?" Jack asked.
"The manager at the ticket counter at the Belize City airport. He said he helped Amber arrange her flights back to San Francisco. According to him, she's scheduled to touch down there tonight just before eleven local time."
Jack looked at his watch. "That's only three hours from now."
"The manager also says he just watched an American male get on a charter jet. I knew that Lang wouldn't risk using Bureau resources to get off this island, and he's not dumb enough to fly commercial. So, before I left, I had asked the manager to keep his eye open for any private aircraft. There aren't many here, so it was easy for him to spot."
"And he's sure it was Lang he saw?"

"He wouldn't know him if he saw him, but I'd bet my firstborn that it was him."

"Where's the jet going?"

"Cancun."

Jack ran his hand over the stubble that had developed over the last day. "Call whoever you have to and arrange another jet."

Dalton nodded and began dialing his phone. When he reached Gloria in the San Francisco FBI office, he said, "I need you to arrange a jet for me and my colleague out of Belize City to Cancun, Mexico."

"No," Jack stopped him and shook his head. "You're going to Cancun alone."

"What do you mean? Where are you going?"

"I'm going to San Francisco."

Chapter 57

▼

The four men stood in the foyer of the villa's main house, each silent. None of them had anticipated three years ago what they might say when they eventually reunited. The plan had been blueprinted to the most minute detail, and here they were, at the end of the process, almost speechless.

"I like what you've done to the place, Harper," Fitch finally commented.

"Oh, I knew you would," he replied. "I figured it would fit in nicely with your opulent tastes, Denny."

"Not very inconspicuous for a man who's supposed to be dead," Hammond said, looking at the careful detail in the ceiling's crown molding.

Harper laughed heartily. "Yeah, I tried to keep it modest. But in the course of three years, one has to occupy himself."

"You didn't have enough to keep you busy during that time, so you took up interior decorating?" Hammond joked.

Harper smiled at the older man.

At five foot five, Harper stood like a dwarf among these men, even Terry Hammond, who had once been tall, but his posture and height had suffered as the years went on. Harper's small stature did not diminish his ability to influence people or control situations. He was motivated by more than a Napoleonic complex. He was driven to excel, to be the best and to have the best. That trait had inspired some people to follow him easily. However, that same trait also made others like Harry Lang loathe him.

"I trust that the accommodations are to your liking?"

"The rooms are unbelievable, Harper. And what a view!" Fox said, replacing on one of the side tables the hand-carved jade piece he had been examining.

"So," Harper said with emphasis. "Shall we get down to business?"

The men moved to the adjacent living room. Beneath the eighteen-foot ceiling were four oversized rattan chairs with thick, white cushions. An ivory-colored stone table, which looked like it weighed a ton, rested in the center. A light breeze blew through the large double doors through which they had just entered. To the right was a large open kitchen with stainless steel appliances and granite countertops. A hallway on the other side of a wall ran between the kitchen and the foyer. It was hard not to be impressed, but they all knew there were more important things to deal with at the moment.

They each took a seat and waited for Harper to begin the discussion.

"OK, the most important topic first. Where is my good friend Harry Lang?" he said with a wry smile.

They all looked to one another nervously. Harper sensed their concern immediately.

"What is it?" he asked.

Fox sat forward, having been silently nominated to speak for the group. "He was in Belize as of this morning. Caye Caulker, to be exact. He should be here tomorrow morning."

"Should or will? There's a major distinction," Hammond remarked. "You don't think he suspects anything, do you?"

"Don't worry, Terry," Harper said. "He'll be here. I've known Harry for a lot of years now. His one redeeming quality is that he doesn't stop short. He always sees things through to the end."

Fox shot a quick glance at Fitch. The word *end* had so many interpretations that it made both of them nervous.

"What about the money?" Harper continued.

"Are you asking where it is or where Harry thinks it is?" Hammond said with pleasure.

"I'm guessing from that gloating reaction that it's where it should be," Harper said, nodding enthusiastically.

"And the documents?" Fox asked.

"I have them," Harper answered.

Fox leaned forward in his chair. "You know, it would have been nice if you had told us right after you received them. Before we got your letter in Washington a couple of days ago, Denny and I had been a little nervous."

"Sorry about that. It was hard to get word to you. Besides, I had to make sure they were secure before telling you."

"Three years of planning. I can't believe it," Fitch murmured. It sounded more like a quiet thought that happened to escape his lips. "Is this really going to work?"

"Yes," Harper said without hesitation. "You said it yourself. Three years went into this. We cannot afford for it not to go off as planned."

"I just want it to be over so I can get the hell out of here."

"We all want the same thing, Denny," Fox told him.

Harper stood up from his chair and walked toward the double doors leading to the veranda.

"I would tell you guys to get a good night's sleep," he began to say, but knew he didn't need to finish his sentence.

Through the doorframe, the glow from the sun was still visible along the horizon. The others joined Harper, each losing himself in his thoughts. Over the next ten minutes, they watched the sun's light fade quickly away. The day was over. And while they knew that it had been a long day, they knew that it would not compare to what the next morning would bring.

Amber pushed her way up the aisle, pulling her mother behind her. Before boarding, she tried to get two seats toward the door, but the best she could get was the sixteenth row. The other passengers expressed their disapproval of these two women who rudely pushed their way to the door immediately after the plane had landed and the seat belt sign had been turned off.

When they reached the arrival area outside the baggage claim carousel, Amber looked from side to side. She knew Gil wouldn't disappoint her by not carrying out her request for a car. Amid the horns honking and traffic police whistling and yelling, Amber noticed a black GMC Yukon parked in the red zone. It was the only vehicle that was not being shooed away by the airport police. A closer examination revealed that the license plate was government-issued. That was her ride.

A tall black male wearing a dark suit and even darker sunglasses stepped around the car from the driver's side. Amber took her mother's arm and began walking quickly toward the SUV. She gently pushed her mother into the backseat and slid in next to her.

"Spear and Mission please. As fast as you can," she told the driver.

As the SUV pulled onto the freeway toward San Francisco, Amber stared out the window, eyeing every car they happened to pass. The traffic at that hour was light, and the driver did not hesitate to cut across all four lanes to the left. Her mother clutched the door handle tightly. Amber leaned forward and looked at the speedometer. The driver was pushing the Yukon up to ninety miles per hour. She hoped that he would get them there in one piece.

As his wheels squealed around the corner of Mission Street onto Spear, Amber wrapped her hand around the door handle, ready to pull it open. The digital clock on the radio read 11:33. She prayed that she could reach Kaitlyn in time, even though she realized Ensight's CEO was probably in Chicago celebrating with the Maguire team or in New York preparing for her photo op at the stock exchange. But at this point, Kaitlyn was the only person who could halt the Maguire deal, and Amber knew she needed to provide more time for Jack and Dalton to complete their investigation. A faint voice in her head pleaded with her to walk away, to accept that it was none of her business. But she quickly shut out that voice. Men had tried to kill her, and they had killed people she knew, her friends. She couldn't bring herself to allow those deaths to go in vain.

The SUV stopped abruptly in front of the Ensight building, lurching them forward.

"Can you wait here while I run up?" she asked the driver, as she and her mother stood on the sidewalk.

"Yes, of course" the driver said.

The two women stepped inside the office building and walked to the elevators. Once inside, Amber pressed the button to the thirty-fourth floor, and the elevator ascended slowly toward the executive office.

Chapter 58

▼

Special Agent Dalton climbed the steps to the jet and offered a nod of acknowledgment to Jack before disappearing through the hatch. He had created quite a disruption to Jack's assignment, but as luck would have it, his presence ended up serving Jack well.

As he watched the jet taxi down the runway, Jack pulled out his phone and dialed. It was nearly 2:30 in the morning in Washington, and whoever was answering his call would no doubt be expecting him.

Jack listened intently as the phone continued to ring. Finally, someone picked up.

"I finally shook Dalton," Jack said. "It was like removing a barnacle off a humpback. Unfortunately, the only way to get away from him was to put him on a jet to Cancun."

He listened again, nodding. "We got confirmation from an airport employee that Lang got on a jet earlier. It'll take a while for Dalton to catch up to him. But you need to get down there now. He can cause problems. We're way behind schedule. By the time morning arrives, this thing will be over."

As he listened further, Jack placed his free finger into his other ear to plug out the noise from the jet engines roaring nearby. He then spoke with a raised voice. "Don't worry about me. I know what I'm doing. I've got another problem to deal with right now."

He again nodded emphatically, obviously listening to instructions. "I know, I will. I'll take care of it." And he hung up the phone.

Jack looked around him one last time and stepped back into the terminal. He walked briskly through the building, as if walking fast would get him to San

Francisco any sooner. He began doubting whether the assignment would succeed. It had been planned for so long and with such great care. But now, as he wiped beads of sweat from his forehead, he was improvising each minute along the way. Dalton's presence was a temporary setback. But Amber was stirring up much more trouble. *What could she possibly be thinking by returning to San Francisco?* She was up to something. *But what?*

There was no one in the elevator with them as they rode to the top floor. Her mother had barely uttered a word since they entered the SUV, and despite all the activity in the last several hours, she appeared surprisingly relaxed. Amber wasn't sure if her mind was in the present or not, but her silence and her content expression were enough for Amber not to ask any questions.

The doors opened, and they stepped out. The executive floor was dark, with only the emergency lights buzzing above. The door to Kaitlyn's office was closed. Through the large window, Amber could see her neatly organized desk undisturbed. She walked to Jamie's desk and searched for Kaitlyn's cell phone number. The small clock on her desk read 11:41. She called Kaitlyn's number, but there was no answer. She left a brief message, knowing full well that Kaitlyn wouldn't receive it in the next nineteen minutes. But it was all she could do.

Then Amber had one more idea. It was crazy, but she didn't care. She looked through Jamie's Rolodex but couldn't find what she was looking for. As she opened the door to Kaitlyn's office, the motion detectors on the lighting system responded immediately by flickering to life. Surely Kaitlyn would have what she was searching for. But Kaitlyn didn't keep a desk file of business phone numbers, storing them instead on her PC. Amber looked at the docking station on the desk, which was empty. Kaitlyn had taken her computer with her. There was only one other way, and Amber couldn't believe that she was about to tap into this resource one last time.

Dialing Sanjay's extension, she smiled nervously at her mother, who was beginning to show real signs of fatigue. The older woman sat in the large leather chair in the corner of Kaitlyn's office. There was no answer at Sanjay's desk. Perhaps someone else in the IT group could help hack into Kaitlyn's system and find her contact list. Amber ran to the door, stopping to speak to her mother, who was thumbing through an issue of *Architectural Digest*.

"Mom?" she said. Her mother looked up. "I'll be right back. Will you please stay here? It'll be only about ten minutes."

"Why, of course, sweetheart. I don't need you to entertain me." She turned back to the magazine.

Amber ran to the elevators. The clock on the wall facing the elevators—all the clocks in the office were synchronized to official world time—read eleven forty-nine. An elevator car was stopped on her floor, and she stepped inside, pressing the button to the IT department.

When the doors opened, the floor seemed uncharacteristically quiet. Amber heard a few voices in the distance, but for the most part, the area appeared deserted. It was ten minutes to midnight, and these employees had likely been working for the last seventy-two hours straight, so it wasn't inconceivable that nearly all had left at the first opportunity.

Making her way toward Sanjay's desk, she saw papers littered across the floor, many more than usual. The IT floor was the picture of chaos, and Amber could only imagine the rollercoaster that this company's staff had endured since the acquisition was announced days before. When she reached Sanjay's desk, it was unoccupied. In fact, it was all but cleaned out. She was about to follow the other voices on the floor to ask for their help, but she stopped when she noticed a small stack of pages on his chair. There was a fax confirmation page on top. On the line marked *STATUS*, it read *Transmission Incomplete*. She recognized the country code on the page as that of Belize. These were the pages he had faxed to her earlier that day. Apparently, Sanjay had not bothered to ensure that the pages were faxed successfully.

She picked up the stack and thumbed through them. She turned past the page that had been cut off during the transmission and fanned quickly through the rest of them. Toward the end of the stack, she saw a series of lines that caught her attention. What was visually obvious was that one of the columns had a number of cells populated only with zeroes. The corresponding dates of the sales were clustered together, much in the same way the payments to Jackson Winthrop were clustered. When she glanced at the top of the column, she was surprised to find that it was the column marked *COMMISSION*. It seemed peculiar that there would be so many sales with no commission earned on them. When she held the page closer, she was stunned at what she saw. In the column marked *SALES PROFESSIONAL*, a name appeared, one Amber was not prepared to see: McBride, K.

"Oh, God. Kaitlyn," she muttered. "What have you done?"

She checked the solar-powered digital clock on Sanjay's desk. It was 11:53 . She felt like she was holding a time bomb in her hands, and time had run out on her. For the next thirty seconds, she stared at Kaitlyn's name on the sales ledger. *How could she not have seen it?* It was no wonder Kaitlyn had pressed her so hard to go to the FBI. She was hoping to lead her right to Harry Lang.

As the clock changed to 11:55, Amber's mind suddenly cleared. She held the screen shots tightly and ran to the emergency stairs. Bursting through the doors, she bounded up the steps toward the human resources department. When she last saw it, Marty's desk was still intact. She hoped nothing had changed. This was her last option.

Chapter 59

Harry Lang watched the replay of the president's press conference from his hotel room. Although most of the news networks were broadcasting it, he preferred to watch the *CNN International* channel, with its anti-presidential comments and opinions. It fueled his animosity toward the president, making his own motives more justifiable.

The key topic of discussion was the president's much-publicized reversal of position on the Patriot Act. The president deflected the questions gracefully but with obvious caution, by reiterating his message about national security. The campaign rhetoric didn't fool many, especially not Harry Lang. He had known the man who held the highest seat in the land for many years, as had the rest of the Committee. In fact, they had been partners. One might even venture to call them friends. But in the last few years, everything had changed. It was far beyond just bad blood among old pals resulting from a difference of opinion. It was a complex, moneymaking venture that had been cut short by the betrayal of one person. That's how Lang and the others saw it, at least.

It was drawing close to midnight in San Francisco. The starry sky in Cancun was perfectly clear, and from the balcony of his Ritz Carlton suite, Lang watched the white foam collecting on the sand. By this time, Fox, Fitch, and Hammond should have been at the rendezvous location just south. They were probably wondering where he was at this moment and whether he would show up the following morning as they had planned.

He knew that chartering a jet might draw the attention of Jack Bennett and his new sidekick, Special Agent Dalton. But he had no other choice. There were only two convenient launch areas to get to the rendezvous site, and Cancun was the more appealing. The other was Belize, and he was not about to return there.

He had been careful, watching his back from the moment he stepped off the jet. Taking on Dalton would be a cinch; since the man had been stuck in administrative duty for so long he thought that his field instincts were rusty. But Jack was a completely different story. He was fueled by a personal motive.

Lang's phone began ringing. He flipped it open.

"Yes?" he said calmly.

He listened and nodded.

"I'll see you there in the morning." He hung up and replaced the phone in his coat pocket.

Returning inside, he turned up the volume on the television and picked up his briefcase. He pulled out a stack of papers, bound by a giant clip in the corner. The top page contained a list of addressees, among them *The Washington Post*, the *Associated Press*, the *Federal Election Commission*, and the *United States Senate Rules and Administration Committee*. It was a rich list, which thrived as a collective body on the public exposure of high-ranking officials in Washington DC. Across the page in red ink was stamped the word *Confidential*. The author of the report was anonymous, but the seal of the Justice Department was prominently displayed at the top of the cover page. Behind the cover page were twenty-five pages of text and graphs, illustrating three years of financial activity of a corporate entity based in the Caribbean. The name of the company was Bartlett Enterprises, and its primary purpose was to collect contributions from private investors and foreign nationals to finance the incumbent president in his bid for reelection.

As he read through the text for what seemed like the hundredth time, he reviewed the accusations, ranging from the campaign staff's failure to disclose such contributions to the FEC, to the numerous violations of the Federal Election Campaign Act, to the president's explicit knowledge of Bartlett's existence and purpose. It was an assassination on paper, but a pure work of art in the opinion of Lang and the others. On the last page, he read through the list of principals of Bartlett, which was without a doubt the most damaging component of the report. It listed two names of businesses that were known fronts for the Cali cocaine cartel in Colombia. Four individuals who were members of two different Islamic extremist groups were listed, along with one name reported to have ties to Hamas. It was an all-star list, and Lang felt a brief queasiness in his stomach.

The press conference was over, and several analysts debated their respective positions. Lang turned off the television and replaced the pages in the briefcase. He propped one of the pillow shams against the headboard and leaned back. The sun would be rising in a few hours, and the rest of the men would be expecting him. He set his alarm clock to wake him up in three hours. There was nothing left to do but wait.

After bursting through the emergency doors onto the human resources floor, Amber raced past her old desk and to Marty's desk, which to her relief had remained untouched since his tragic death. Although it took her only two minutes to find what she was searching for, it seemed like thirty. Fumbling through a stack of business cards he had always kept piled on his desk—Marty refused to organize his contacts into a file—she found the one with the name *Joseph DeMartini, Chairman and CEO of Maguire Solutions.*

Scribbled in Marty's chicken scratches, a mobile phone number was almost illegible in the bottom corner of the business card. With another frantic glance at the clock on the wall outside Marty's office, Amber dialed the number. As she listened to the phone ringing, her heart began beating wildly. She was surely going to awaken him, as it was nearing two o'clock in the morning in Chicago.

After several rings, her hope started to wane. But then the ringing stopped. Amber heard nothing for a few seconds. Then a slow, slightly groggy male grunt came through.

"This better be good," said the voice.

Amber paused. She hadn't rehearsed what to say, and she was also stunned to be on the phone past midnight with one of the most powerful and respected leaders in the corporate universe.

"Hello, is this Mr. DeMartini?" she asked meekly.

"Yeah, who is this?" he asked, clearing his throat. "If this is a reporter, I told all of you that I'm not making any announcements about the acquisition until the market opens in the morning."

"No, sir. I'm not a reporter." She steadied herself. "You don't know me. My name is Amber Wakefield."

There was no acknowledgment from him, but his irritation at having been disturbed was certainly palpable.

She held out the page from the sales ledger and took one last look at Kaitlyn's name beside the phony sales entries.

"Mr. DeMartini, there's something you need to know."

There was no answer.

Amber spoke for the next thirty seconds, unsure if he was hearing any of what she was telling him. When she stopped talking, she listened for a response.

"Mr. DeMartini?" she practically whispered. "Are you still there?" But it was silent on the other end.

As she uttered these last words, she looked up at the clock on the wall. It was midnight.

It took nearly two hours for the private jet to arrive in Belize. Dalton had managed to arrange a flight from the Dallas office to pick up Jack, who had checked his watch every ten minutes since Dalton left him. There were too many moving parts at this point, and he found it nearly impossible to keep track of them. He had managed to separate himself from Dalton, and while he had reiterated his point to the agent about not interfering in the assignment, Jack worried that the man might surrender to his zealous urge to be a hero. He hoped that his call to Washington a couple of hours earlier would prevent that from occurring. And of course, Jack himself still had a job to do. When he had first been hired for this assignment, it had been designed to be covert, but more importantly, it had been designed to be his to run. And then of course, there was Amber. He wasn't sure if he was going to San Francisco to stop her from jeopardizing his assignment or to save her. Unfortunately, he wouldn't know the answer to that until he arrived there.

With that thought, he climbed the steps into the jet while it was still being refueled. He said very little to the pilots, as their instructions were already clear. Sitting back in one of the leather upholstered chairs, he rested his chin on his fist and his elbow on the armrest. Before long, his eyes were closed.

When the doors to the jet shut, the fuselage began to shudder, and Jack was jolted. He would not sleep again for the entire flight, he knew that much. He was deviating severely from his carefully planned assignment, and that deviation could quite possibly be the reason his job would fail. It was highly uncharacteristic of him to lose his focus. But then again, he had never met anyone who could distract him in the way Amber did.

The jet reached its cruising altitude, and Jack fidgeted in his chair, even changing seats three times. He was suspended above the earth, entirely ineffective. He felt that time had frozen for him. Unfortunately, time was moving at full speed beneath him, and that fact scared him.

Amber walked quickly out of Marty's office. She had to get upstairs to her mother and get them both out of the building. It was creepy in there with its uninhabited desks and flickering fluorescent lights.

As she closed the door to Marty's office, she heard a clicking sound and saw a glow of light coming from behind her. She turned around slowly. Seated at her old desk, beneath the light of a small desk lamp, was Kaitlyn McBride. She sat comfortably, with her legs crossed, staring at Amber.

"Hello, Amber," she said in a low tone. She was dressed in a black business suit. Despite what Amber knew about her now, she still looked elegant.

Amber said nothing. She swallowed as many times as the moisture in her mouth would allow. Kaitlyn recrossed her legs in the chair, and Amber took two steps back.

"What are you doing here?" Kaitlyn asked. "Or better yet, where have you been? I generally don't approve of my assistants taking off for a week without extending the courtesy to inform me."

Amber didn't have a response, nor did she believe Kaitlyn was searching for one. "Let's just say that I had some personal matters to deal with," she managed. It was a weak reply, but it was the best she could do.

Kaitlyn stood from the chair. "You look nervous, Amber. Any reason for that?"

"You tell me," she said, retreating further.

Kaitlyn smiled at this. "It's OK, you don't owe me any explanations. I only put myself out there for you, endangered my staff, even myself, to make sure you were OK. But if you're not grateful for that, then…"

Amber cut her off. "Don't bullshit me, Kaitlyn. I know everything." Her voice was shaking.

"I have no idea what you're talking about. What do you think you *know*?" Kaitlyn replied with a condescending tone.

"I know that you've been using this company to funnel money through, and then to move it to the Caribbean. Let's start with that."

Kaitlyn laughed scornfully. "And who told you that?"

"Does it matter? How could you?"

"First of all, I don't know where you're getting your information, but it's preposterous. Secondly, even if what you're saying is true, it doesn't mean that I knew about it. This is a large, complicated organization. I may hold the highest seat here, but I'm so far removed from the business operations that I can guarantee you there are more than a few things I'm probably not aware of."

Amber reached into her pocket and unfolded the pages containing the screen shots from the sales ledger. She dropped them on the desk, directly underneath the light. Kaitlyn glanced down at them without picking them up. Her expression changed at the sight of her name, and her smile vanished. She looked back up at Amber, who was not making an attempt to conceal her nervousness.

Kaitlyn took a deep breath. It was the first time Amber had ever witnessed a hint of apprehension from the CEO.

"I think we should go somewhere to discuss this, Amber."

Amber scoffed. "There's nothing to discuss. I trusted you, and you knew all along what was going on. All of it."

Kaitlyn shook her head. "You are so naïve, Amber. I never thought you had what it takes to survive in big business."

"You call this business? People are dead because of what you did. Was it worth those people's lives? Marty? Jamie?" She found herself stepping toward Kaitlyn, but stopped as her pulse beat wildly.

"So, what are you planning to do, Amber? Do you have the guts to take the next step? Do you know how easily I can drag you down with me? Who wouldn't believe that my assistant knew all about this? Are you ready to go to jail? Think, Amber."

Amber looked away from her for a moment and stared at the carpet. With her hair twisting around her fingers at a frantic pace, she could sense that her eyebrows were furrowed, as she was deep in thought. In an instant, they relaxed and she took her hand out of her hair, and looked directly at Kaitlyn.

"I'll take my chances."

She picked up the phone from the desk next to her and pressed the number nine to get an outside line. Kaitlyn watched her intently. While Amber's eyes were on the keypad, Kaitlyn reached into her jacket pocket.

"Put the phone down, Amber."

Amber looked up with the phone receiver to her ear to see the end of a pistol staring directly at her. Amber dropped the phone onto the desk and stepped backwards. Kaitlyn, the sharpshooting biathlete, wrapped her free hand around the butt of the gun.

"Now, you and I are going to walk out of this building together." She reached down and picked up the incriminating pages. She inserted them into the shredder beneath the desk. As the pages came out the other end in confetti, Amber stopped retreating.

"What are you going to do, Kaitlyn?"

"I'm taking you on a trip. After all, we've done it before. We make good travel companions."

As Amber walked toward the elevators, with Kaitlyn pointing the gun at her back, she thought about her mother. The older woman was still sitting upstairs, reading her magazine. She would surely wonder where her daughter had disappeared to for so long. *Or would she?* Amber wondered to herself. She wasn't about to tell Kaitlyn that her mother was still up there. Right now, the safest place for her mother to be was away from her.

The two women rode the elevator down to the lobby. Kaitlyn walked beside Amber, with her hand in her inside pocket. She smiled at the security guard near the door and bid him a good evening. Outside, the wind was blowing wildly. Taking quick steps, Kaitlyn pressed her sharp fingers into the small of Amber's back and spurred her toward a black Town Car limousine. Amber looked up the street and saw the black SUV still parked but in a different spot than where it had dropped her off earlier. Kaitlyn nudged her again, and they crawled inside and shut the door. The limousine pulled away and headed toward the freeway.

Chapter 60

The alarm clock was screaming loudly. Lang picked his heavy head up from the pillow and opened one of his eyes. The digital display on the clock was nothing but a red blur. He focused hard, pounding the top of the device in a desperate attempt to find the snooze button. When he managed to kill the noise, the numbers on the clock came into clear view: *5:38*.

He rolled his sore body out of bed and lumbered to the window to peer around the thick curtain. It was still dark outside, no different than it appeared when he went to sleep a few hours before. Despite that, it was a new day.

He turned on the television and walked to the bathroom. After relieving himself and brushing his teeth, he ran a hot shower. Under the steaming water, his adrenaline began running high. He was a few hours away from meeting the rest of the Committee members, where they would follow their plan through to execution. Nonetheless, he was still cautious. It wasn't over yet. There was still work to do.

By the time he emerged from the bathroom, the president was back on the television, still on the campaign trail. Lang dressed quickly and packed his suitcase. The clock said five minutes after six. He called downstairs to have his rental car ready for him. Picking up his briefcase, he walked toward the door, pausing in front of the large vanity mirror and taking a long look at himself. This was it. He straightened a strand of hair with his hand and walked out of the room.

Amber's knuckles were white after having clutched both armrests on the Gulfstream for the last five hours. She had no idea where they were heading. Kaitlyn sat across the aisle from Amber, the gun resting at her side. She and Kaitlyn engaged in no communication during the flight, other than the occasional sneer at one another.

She allowed her eyes to wander around the luxurious interior of the jet. She had ridden in it once before, but the circumstances were quite different on that trip. Amber realized that she had flown more miles in the last two weeks than she had in her entire life. She had boarded a plane more times than she had showered in that same time frame. She wondered if Jack was thinking about her, or if he was even worried about her. She regretted having not followed his instructions to meet Gil in Dallas. Or perhaps she should at least have sent her mother there, where she would be safe. She hoped someone would find her mother still sitting in Kaitlyn's office, reading that *Architectural Digest*. She also hoped that her mother would be able to tell whoever it was that she was Amber Wakefield's mother, and that the person would have the kind heart and good sense to take her somewhere safe. It was a lot to hope.

Amber looked across the aisle at Kaitlyn, whose eyes were locked on that day's issue of *The Financial Times*. She looked no different than the commuters reading the paper on the train. The only thing that set her apart from them was that her hand was resting comfortably in her pocket, and inside was the gun that only hours ago was pointed at Amber's face. Perhaps Amber was underestimating Kaitlyn. Perhaps she just needed Amber as an insurance policy until she got to wherever she needed to go. Then she would let Amber go. After all, Kaitlyn wasn't a coldhearted killer. Of course, twenty-four hours ago, Amber hadn't known Kaitlyn was a corporate fraudster, either.

Outside the window, the brightness of the sunlight lit up the interior of the jet. Kaitlyn turned and closed the window shade.

"You know something, Amber?" Kaitlyn asked after a long silence.

"What?" Amber's annoyance was undisguised.

"We're not that different, you and I."

"Wrong. We are completely different."

Kaitlyn shook her head. "No. Think about it. We're both intelligent. We're inquisitive. We're resourceful. We're tenacious." She was beaming, as if she thought she was impressing Amber.

Amber frowned, unable to believe what she was hearing. "If you're any indication of what I have to look forward to, I think I'll pass."

Kaitlyn's smile disappeared. "I don't think you have to worry about that, my dear."

Her words were chilling to Amber, who turned away. She leaned her forehead against the window and let her eyes wander across the open sky. She wished she had simply walked out of the office rather than going down to Sanjay's desk. But there was no point in looking back. She was tired of regretting. She preferred hoping, as it was the only thing that might get her through the next hours.

Lang hopped off the cruiser and approached the front steps of the grand villa. It was only a two-hour ride from Cancun to this private island. He reached into his pocket, pulled out a brass key, and inserted it into the door lock. When he opened the door, a light breeze was blowing through the foyer, and he could see straight in front of him that the double French doors to the back terrace were wide open, permitting the sea air to travel in. His footsteps were loud against the stone floor tiles as he walked cautiously through the eerily quiet house.

It was nearly eight o'clock in the morning. Even though he was an hour early, the others should have been expecting him. But as he surveyed the property, he didn't see anyone. A sensation just short of panic began to consume him. Perhaps it was merely paranoia. Whatever it was, it made him uncomfortable. He felt like an intruder, even though this property was as much his as it was property of the other Committee members.

He walked to the edge of the terrace overlooking the rectangular swimming pool, which faced the blue Caribbean waters. *Where the hell are those guys?* he asked himself. There were no other boats docked on either side of the house. The others were supposed to have arrived there the night before.

Before he would allow himself to be completely hypnotized by the setting around him, he turned and walked quickly toward the house. When he entered, he saw something he had apparently missed on his way in. On the large, circular granite table in the middle of the entryway, a manila envelope was propped against an ornate vase filled with colorful tropical flowers. There was no label or writing on the front of the envelope, but it was far too tempting not to open.

Inside was a single sheet of paper. The letterhead on the page read *Riggs Bank*. It was dated the day before. He read it closely.

> *Dear Sir:*
>
> *Please accept this notification as confirmation of receipt of a funds transfer from the Belize Bank in the amount of sixty-five million U.S. Dollars (USD 65,000,000) into your account. Please contact us at your earliest convenience should you have any inquiries.*

We thank you for your continued business with our bank.

He held his hands together in front of him as if he was expressing gratitude to some divine entity. Slowly, he strolled toward the terrace and walked outside. Tilting his head back, he closed his eyes and felt a light mist from the sea upon his face. They had done it. He breathed a sigh of relief. As he opened his eyes and looked around him, he wondered why he was celebrating alone.

Chapter 61

Special Agent Dalton sat quietly in the brown Honda Accord. He had managed to get twenty minutes of sleep after getting off the jet from Belize. The forty-five minute drive from the Cancun airport had landed him in the town of Playa del Carmen. With a cup of coffee and a bagel, he relished his first hint of sustenance in forty-eight hours. Straight ahead, he could see the morning light enveloping the Caribbean waters.

He was unsure of what his next step was supposed to be, but he knew he needed help. Thus he was rather taken aback at his good fortune when he received a call from the FBI Legat office in Mexico City. Legats, or legal attaches, were FBI representatives stationed in foreign nations to help foster cooperation among international police partners. In his career, he'd had to work directly with them only twice on border control issues, and that was more as an observer. This was his first real encounter with them.

The call came as he was walking from the jet to the terminal building. It was from the Mexico City Legat office, by way of the Guadalajara subdivision. His instructions were to meet in the town of Playa del Carmen at sunrise. According to the message, the directive was being relayed to him from Washington. That detail perplexed him as well as worried him. *Who the hell knew he was even down there?* But he was not about to take the risk of not obeying an order from headquarters.

As agreed, he waited in front of the Banamex Bank branch on 10th Avenue. The armed security guard standing in front of the ATM vestibule had been watching him for ten minutes, perhaps suspicious of the Caucasian eating breakfast in his car.

Dalton was taking a long, careful sip from his hot coffee cup and nearly burned himself when a Hispanic man walked past the driver's side of his car and lightly tapped the window with his knuckle. The man did not break his stride, but rather continued walking along the avenue. Dalton watched him round the corner onto Calle 12, then opened the door to the Honda and made his way in the same direction. Still holding his coffee cup, he stepped around the corner and found the man leaning against the bright orange façade of the Hotel Costa del Mar.

"Are you DiRosa?" Dalton asked.

"Yes, sir." The man nodded, removing his sunglasses.

The men shook hands. The Hispanic, who was obviously an American, was in his mid-thirties, younger than Dalton but about three inches taller. Tucked tightly into his bottom lip was a wad of saliva-soaked tobacco. His demeanor and physique told Dalton that the man clearly was cut out to work in the field.

"How long have you been with the Bureau?" Dalton asked.

"Going on seven years, sir. Joined the Legat office in Mexico City two years ago." He had a strong New York accent.

"What's this all about?" Dalton asked.

"Sir, my only instructions were to meet you here and escort you."

"Escort me," Dalton repeated. "Where?"

"Up this way," DiRosa said, indicating with his chin.

The two men walked north along the avenue. After two blocks, DiRosa made a sharp turn into a small doorway. The red PADI flag hanging outside the small white building indicated that it was a dive shop. Dalton followed DiRosa toward the rear of the shop. They approached a green, weather-beaten door in the middle of the hall, and DiRosa knocked on it three times. The door opened, and they stepped inside.

Dalton looked around cautiously, making sure he had an open path to the exit in case this ended up being some kind of ambush. But when he walked into the brightly lit room, he was taken by surprise by what he saw. There were eight men inside, consisting of an even mix of whites, blacks, and Hispanics. Some had headsets on, while others were busy studying charts and surveillance screens on complex-looking equipment around the room. They spoke to each other in hushed voices, none paying much attention to Dalton.

He was just about to ask the young DiRosa what all of this was when one of the men, who was also the tallest, turned to face him. Dalton's eyes did not hide the intense awe he felt at that moment.

"Special Agent Dalton?" asked the man.

Dalton could do nothing but nod. DiRosa stepped between them.

"Mr. Dalton, I'm sure you know Director Lassiter."

A white cruiser was tied to the dock when they approached the north side of the villa in their Boston whaler. Fox looked at the others and nodded. They all stepped off the boat and walked to the house. The front doors were slightly ajar, and Fox pushed them open. Inside the foyer, they stopped when they saw four flutes of champagne standing at attention on the large center table. The envelope that they had leaned against the vase was still there, only it was open, and the bank letter was resting on top of it.

Fox moved carefully through the living room and toward the terrace, and Fitch helped Hammond along as they followed him.

"Where is he?" Fitch asked nervously.

"I don't know." Fox stepped outside and looked at his watch. Something wasn't right. Facing the terrace, they suddenly heard clapping. It wasn't the kind that signified applause, but was loud and sarcastic, with long pauses between each clap. They slowly turned around to see Lang sitting on the pearl-white sofa against the opposite wall. He wore a smirk that had become an all-too-familiar expression to them all.

Still clapping, Lang stood from the sofa and walked slowly toward the three men, who were all frozen in place. Resting heavily on the sofa was a stainless steel .32-caliber pistol.

"Well, allow me to be the first to congratulate all of you. Well done. Well done, indeed," he said loudly.

"Harry, you're already here," Fox commented.

"I'm eager, Foxy." He stepped forward and shook all their hands. "When you wake up to the greatest day of your life, you want it to start as soon as possible."

He looked at them closely but could detect no hint of the enthusiasm he expected.

"What the hell is the matter with all of you guys?" he asked, holding his hands out in disbelief at their stern faces. "We just wrote a page in history, gentlemen."

"You'll forgive me, Harry," said Hammond. "But I don't feel like celebrating the public sabotage of our president."

"Oh, come on, Terry," Lang said, wrapping his arm around the fragile older man. "You of all people should appreciate this. You've worked under more administrations than anyone in Washington. Getting that Patriot Act Reform legislation passed was the best way for us to restore our civil liberties. And the president backed out. This is our own way of letting him know how passionate we are about it."

Fitch scoffed. "Yeah, right. Our civil liberties? This was never about our civil liberties. This was about business, from beginning to end."

"Let's not debate this, guys. It's done, and that's all that matters." Lang walked back toward the entry. "Now, let's celebrate."

He picked up one of the glasses of champagne. When each man was holding a glass, Lang looked down at the table and was perplexed to see one flute remaining, full of champagne. He recalled pouring only four. They all saw the expression on his face.

"What's this?" he asked, looking at each of them.

They all looked at him, expressionless.

"Oh, that one's for me." The voice was immediately familiar.

Lang slowly looked up. He knew that distinctive voice. However, the last time he had heard it was over three years ago. He'd never expected to hear it again. He turned slowly and saw a short figure standing at the edge of the living room, against the backdrop of the blue waters behind him. The man appeared a bit older now, but the ambitious glint in his eyes left no doubt as to who he was.

The champagne flute fell from Lang's hands and shattered into a thousand glass pebbles across the stone floor.

"Try to be careful with those, Harry. They are expensive."

"Jesus!" he said, holding his hand to his chest. "Harper," he muttered, nearly inaudibly.

Harper stepped forward. Lang tried to step back, but his feet seemed glued to the floor. Despite their physical differences, the smaller man was the only person Lang had ever considered to be a worthy nemesis. It was largely for that reason that he had decided to partner with him when the scheme was originally planned. But as they stood there opposite one another, Lang realized that they were no longer partners.

"You look good, Harry." Harper always had a flair for subtle sarcasm.

Lang eyed Harper from head to toe. "You look a lot less dead than I would have imagined."

Harper laughed loudly in response. The other three men stepped further away from Lang, as if they were being repelled from him. Lang watched the space between them grow wider.

"I should have known." Lang saw it in his former partner's eyes. They were vengeful. "When I realized that someone other than my guy was taking our money, I should have guessed it was you."

Harper smiled back but said nothing.

"Well, what are you going to do, Harper?" he continued. There was unconcealed nervousness in his eyes. "Are you going to take out all of us here? There're four of us."

Harper looked at the others and each of them nodded. "It's over, Harry," said Harper. "It's all over."

"What the fuck are you talking about?" Lang asked.

"You've been outplayed, Harry," he said.

Lang eyed the men, briefly holding his gaze on each. "Outplayed? Sorry, but you missed the window, old friend," Lang said. "But I applaud your effort nonetheless." He began clapping in that sarcastic manner again.

"You have no idea what you're up against." Harper spoke in a slow, measured tone.

Lang turned and picked up the Riggs Bank letter and waved it at them. "You're a little late with the sanctimonious speech," he said. "As of yesterday, the president's campaign account received a large sum of money from the Belize Bank, in the name of Bartlett Enterprises." He looked to his partners for support, but there was none.

"Now that *is* all bullshit, and you know it, Harry," Harper said.

"Who cares? During an election year, where it's split down the middle, do you know how many voters are looking for anything to grab hold of? The general public is ready to believe the worst. Think of all the scandals that some of the highest officials in the land have had to endure recently. Speculation becomes fact very quickly. And very soon, the world is going to find out what Bartlett is. Just wait till they see the list of players involved. You're going to see some fireworks. It's all in the DOJ document I put together and in this letter." He tossed the letter to Harper, but it drifted slowly to the floor like a feather.

Harper reached down and picked it up. Looking at the other three men, he turned the page over. Lang hadn't bothered to look at the other side.

"The public does embrace scandal, almost to a shameful degree. But what they hate even more is betrayal," Harper said, glancing down at the page.

"What the hell is your point?"

Harper held up the paper. "Did you even wonder how the hell we even got our hands on a letter addressed to the president's campaign fund? Take a closer look, Harry."

Lang inched forward and stared at the page. His eyes stopped moving when he saw his own name listed as the account holder.

"What's wrong, Harry? Did we spell your name wrong or something?" Harper asked sarcastically, beaming with glory.

Lang's eyes moved from the page to each of the Committee members. They each stared back at him. There was a confidence in each of their glares which he had never seen before.

Fox cleared his throat. "Now you make sure to declare that whole amount on your tax return, Harry. We may be pals, but I'm still an IRS officer."

The others smiled at this jab. Lang remained motionless. He took the paper from Harper's hands and held it gently as he looked at it again. It was the first time he had ever hated seeing his own name in print. A sudden rush of images sped through his mind: the bank statements with the missing funds; the man with the ponytail boarding the plane in Belize; the man he had met in Shark's Bar. In retrospect, the red flags were all there. But he had been so focused on the prize that he had ignored them. Again, he looked at each of the men, but this time, realizing that he was no longer staring at his partners. He was alone.

The atmosphere in the room had changed dramatically. The rancorous taunts and the smirking had ended.

Harper stood in front of Lang. "What the world is about to find out is that someone embezzled sixty-five million dollars intended for the president's campaign fund. At least that's what it says right here in this letter. So, yes, the public may learn what Bartlett is, but they'll forget all about it when they learn that the FBI's deputy director is a thief."

Lang swallowed audibly. His eyes were wide, incredulous.

"You can proceed with this, Harry," Harper continued. "But it's going to cost you. Are you willing to pay that price? Your reputation? Your career?"

Lang's mouth twitched wildly. A small vein in his temple bulged as his face reddened. His voice came out high-pitched and tight. "You ungrateful bastards. You have no idea who you're fucking with." Lang reached into the back of his pants, but his holster was empty. He had forgotten that he had put his weapon on the sofa earlier.

"I think you dropped this," Harper said, pulling the gun from behind his back.

Lang stepped backwards. "You don't have the balls to use that thing, Harper. You're a lot of things, but a killer, you are not."

"Don't tempt me."

"What do you want?"

"You destroy the DOJ documents containing the accusations against the president, and we'll pull the money out of the Riggs account."

"And why should I believe you now?"

"What are your other options at this point, Harry? There's nowhere left to go."

Lang's eyes wandered briefly toward the sea behind them. "You took the words out of my mouth," he said with a smile. And with one motion, he dove away from the table and rolled along the floor.

They all stood dumbfounded as they watched him roll across the floor. They barely heard the gunshot echo through the open house. It was a single bullet that blew the champagne glass out of Terry Hammond's arthritic hand. Holding only the stem of the glass, Hammond turned around along with the others. Standing on the terrace, just outside the open French doors, Kaitlyn McBride stood with a semiautomatic pistol, a light wisp of smoke escaping the chamber. She had it poised, ready to fire her next shot if necessary. None of them had heard her boat approaching outside the doors. The rustling of the palm trees in the breeze outside drowned out most noise coming from the dock.

"Why don't you put that down?" she snapped at Harper.

He held up his hands and loosened his hold on the pistol. Lang crawled quickly to his feet and grabbed the gun from Harper's hand. He then took the shorter man by the collar and pushed him into the living room, while motioning the others to follow with his gun.

Pushing the four men onto the sofa, Lang walked around them, still pointing his gun at them. They sat silent, defeated.

"I thought we were expecting only three," she said, counting four people.

"Yes, we had an unexpected guest at our party," Lang replied, looking angrily at Harper.

"How appropriate," Kaitlyn said. "I happened to bring a guest of my own." She reached around the wall and pulled Amber close to her. "I didn't want to be the only girl."

Although Bruce Fox recognized her immediately, the others had never seen her. But they knew who she was. They looked with concern at the young woman, her hands in front of her, bound by a rope.

Lang approached the two women, with a lecherous grin on his face. "Nice to see you again, Amber."

Then he turned to Kaitlyn, wrapped his free hand around her waist, and pulled her close to his body. He leaned forward and pressed his lips against hers. Amber cringed. It was only at that moment that she finally recalled where she had seen Harry Lang. When she had first caught sight of him at the FBI office in San

Francisco, she hadn't been able place him. But watching them kiss, she realized that he was the man she had seen kissing Kaitlyn in the hotel lounge in Milan.

"What's she doing here?" Fox asked.

"I always take an assistant with me when I travel," Kaitlyn responded.

"That's my girl," Lang grunted.

Lang took Amber by the arm and pushed her toward the sofa. "I didn't think you would arrive in time," he said to Kaitlyn. "It was starting to get a little ugly here. I have so much to tell you, my love."

She sat down in one of the chairs and crossed her legs. She rested the gun on her lap, making sure that the barrel was pointed casually at the men on the sofa. She looked at Lang with bright, eager eyes, like a child ready to hear a story. "Ready when you are," she said.

Chapter 62

Special Agent Dalton spent nearly an hour, pouring out the details of his investigation. He left out little as he discussed how it had evolved from his meeting with Amber Wakefield, who had approached him. The story seemed incredible when he was relating it, but withholding information from the FBI director was unthinkable.

Director Lassiter only listened without writing anything down. He was known to be able to store information easily in his photographic memory. He nodded often, interrupting a few times to ask questions for clarification. Dalton was a bit surprised to note that the director's facial expression didn't change throughout the narrative. Nothing in his behavior indicated shock or surprise. Dalton surmised that the man had seen and heard so much during his career that very little surprised him anymore.

When he was done talking, Dalton sat back in his chair, relieved that he had at last unloaded everything he knew. At that point, it didn't matter to him that he had defied Jack's request to be discreet. It was too late for discretion, anyway. Besides, he didn't report to Jack and owed him little.

Lassiter informed Dalton in plain terms that he was displeased about Dalton's disregard for Bureau protocol by launching an unauthorized investigation. He also disapproved of Dalton's willingness to engage a civilian—Jack Bennett—in his investigation, as well as endangering the safety of another civilian, Amber Wakefield. But despite those errors, the director commended Dalton for aiding the Bureau to build a case against the deputy director and his colleagues.

Lassiter added that the Bureau had developed suspicions about Lang a while back, but had lacked anything concrete to move on. Evidently, Dalton's recent actions were the closest anyone in the Bureau had ever come to discovering what Lang was doing. And now it was time for the Bureau to take action.

At that moment, one of the surveillance legats turned to his supervisor and said something in Spanish. Dalton couldn't understand but could tell it was urgent. The young man in front of the screen pointed to a location on the map. His supervisor confirmed in Spanish and turned to Lassiter, who was staring back at him. He pulled off his headset and rested it around his neck. He stuck his thumb in the air and nodded at the director.

Lassiter stood from his chair and slapped DiRosa on the back. As if on queue, the rest of the men in the room began shutting down the equipment, unplugging wires, and packing everything into boxes and cases. In less than three minutes, the room was clear and the tables folded up. After all the men had exited the room, Lassiter put his hand on Dalton's shoulder.

"You ready to finish this?" he asked.

"Yes sir," Dalton replied, not sure whether there was another answer to give.

"Let's go."

The two men walked out and the room was suddenly dark and empty.

By this hour, the sun had completely disappeared from view, having been covered by a dark cumulus cloud above the private island. What had begun as a light drizzle had since developed into a violent downpour. The water spattering onto the terrace ricocheted off the glass of the French doors, which were still wide open. The view of the western Caribbean had become a blurry sheet of dull gray. The weather change was actually a refreshing change after the hot sun.

After offering Kaitlyn the unabridged version of the day's events, Lang stood in front of the group with his arms folded.

"So this is the infamous Harper Phillips," she said, staring at the short man on the sofa.

"One of them, at least," Lang joked.

Amber couldn't take her eyes off him. *Was this the real Harper Phillips?*

"I take it from the looks of things that we need to enact our contingency plan?" Kaitlyn asked Lang.

Lang nodded. "I was hoping we wouldn't have to, but my friends here seem to have taken some liberties of their own."

Kaitlyn looked at her watch. "We don't have much time. If we're going through with this, let's get on with it."

"What are you talking about? What contingency plan?" Fox asked.

"Ours," Lang replied, motioning between himself and Kaitlyn. "You didn't think I was going to exclude the CEO of the company that allowed us to move money through it, did you?"

"Why not? You killed the first one who did," Harper said, referring to Ensight's former CEO.

"That was only because he refused to cooperate. You know I did that to protect all of us. You could show a little gratitude."

"You killed him because he suddenly developed a conscience," Harper said. "Once you took it to the next level, Harry, and started engaging terrorists and drug cartels, none of us wanted to be involved anymore." Harper pointed at Kaitlyn. "Her predecessor was the only one who had the balls to walk away from the deal."

"And he paid the price for it, didn't he, Harper?"

"And what about my daughter, you prick? Did you just kill her for kicks?" His voice quivered slightly. It was the first time they had seen any real emotion from Harper.

"Oh, get over it, Harper. You were dead to her anyway."

Amber sat silently, listening to all the questions she had been asking for weeks being answered. She was sickened by the realization that she was sitting in a room full of conspirators and murderers.

"So, what's to stop you from doing the same to us now?" Fitch asked.

"Well, now that I know where all of you stand on this, there's absolutely nothing stopping me. Great point, Denny."

All of the men fidgeted in their seats as the rain continued to pour down in torrents.

"Tell us, what *is* this contingency plan, Harry?" Fox asked again. "You might as well share it with us. You know you're dying to."

Lang let out another of his patented obnoxious laughs. "You do know me well, don't you, Foxy?" He sat down in a chair, just inches from the other men. "While I must give you your proper dues for trying to frame me, nothing has changed. That president is still going down."

"How's that?" Harper asked. "The money's been transferred out already. There's none left. You said it yourself."

Lang waved a finger at them. "Not quite. What I said was that a large sum of money had been transferred to the campaign account. You never were a good listener, Harper."

As was customary, Lang watched their reactions. Then he continued. "Ms. McBride here was able to do some fancy footwork in that company of hers."

"What are you talking about?" Fitch asked.

"She's been booking phony sales at Ensight," Amber cut in, deciding that if she was going to die here, she was at least going to tell an unbiased version of the story. "She created a bunch of fake customer accounts—probably funded by those same terrorists and drug dealers—and passed them off as sales."

The others listened intently. Lang stared at Amber.

"Then the money was moved into the Bartlett account," Amber continued. "The Maguire deal was supposed to trigger the fund transfer to the president's campaign account."

They all looked at Kaitlyn and then at Lang, who smiled back.

"So you two were running a parallel scam," Fox said.

"I didn't think you had the attention span to pull something like that off," Fitch remarked.

"She is a clever one, gentlemen. I am impressed, Amber. I should have hired you instead of the Marx Brothers here."

The men on the sofa looked to one another, stunned. It wasn't a look of fear or anger. It was defeat. They had done everything to ambush Lang, and he had outsmarted them.

Kaitlyn walked to a telephone on one of the side tables, dialed several digits, and listened.

"Put it on speakerphone, dear, so we can all hear it."

Kaitlyn pressed a red button, and the ringing tone resonated throughout the room.

"Jackson Winthrop." It was Wendy's voice in Aruba.

"Hi there. To whom am I speaking?" Kaitlyn asked politely.

"This is Wendy. How can I help you?"

"Wendy, this is Kaitlyn McBride. I'm the chief executive officer of Ensight in San Francisco."

There was silence on the other end. "Will you please hold?"

Kaitlyn looked back at Lang, not smiling as widely as before. Amber leaned forward. She had no idea what DeMartini had done with the information she had given him the night before. After a few seconds, a man's voice came on the phone.

"Miss McBride, this is Mr. DeJong. I'm one of the partners here in the Aruba office. What may we do for you?"

Harper sat forward. He knew DeJong from his days at the firm but hadn't spoken to him in years.

"Well, I need to confirm something regarding our subsidiary, Bartlett Enterprises. As you know, we were scheduled to complete our acquisition by Maguire Solutions early this morning, and that event was to trigger the transfer of all monetary assets to an account here in the States."

"Yes, I'm aware of the instructions," he said.

"Can you confirm that the transfer was completed?"

There was another long pause. DeJong came back on, sounding confused. "Well, of course not, Miss McBride. The suspension of the acquisition would have deemed those instructions to be null and void."

Kaitlyn looked back at Lang, who had jumped to his feet. Their collective concern was felt by everyone else in the room.

"What are you talking about?" Kaitlyn demanded.

DeJong's voice paused briefly. "Miss McBride, when the morning's newswire broke the report that Maguire had called off its intention to acquire Ensight, we assumed that all standing instructions to transfer assets had been canceled as well. Was that not a logical assumption?"

There was silence now on Kaitlyn's end.

"Miss McBride, are you still there?"

Lang stepped forward and hit the button to end the call. He and Kaitlyn stared at one another, dumbfounded.

"What the hell happened?" he asked her.

Slowly, Kaitlyn's eyes narrowed, and she turned to Amber, who was staring back almost defiant. Lang picked up on it immediately.

Kaitlyn's eyes softened slightly. She wanted to kill her young assistant, but she knew her death would change nothing. With her arm hanging down at her side, she reached into her coat pocket and clutched her gun tightly.

The four other men sat without speaking, each trying to piece together what had just happened.

"I should have taken you out when I had the opportunity," Lang said to Amber.

He raised his arm and pointed his gun at Amber. She stepped backwards until she was pressed against the wall. Fox stood quickly.

"Harry, no!" he said, holding his hands up and lunging toward Lang. "Don't!"

Lang pulled his trigger finger back, and Amber closed her eyes tightly. The sound of the gunshot echoed through the house, and the others instinctively ducked in their seats on the sofa. The bullet found the wall behind them, having been sent off course by the impact of Fox's body against Lang.

When Amber opened her eyes, she found Fox on the ground wrestling with the deputy director. The gun had been jarred from Lang's hands and was now lying on the floor, far out of reach of either man. Amber's eyes moved quickly toward the terrace, where Kaitlyn stood in the doorway. The Ensight CEO watched the men struggle, almost entranced by the image. Kaitlyn was clearly growing desperate as the plan she and Lang had devised was spinning wildly off course. Suddenly, Kaitlyn's face changed. Her eyes took on a hollow expression, much in the manner she had looked at Amber back at the offices in San Francisco the night before. Amber watched that change, and she suddenly knew. As she watched Kaitlyn raise her arm, it was as if she was seeing it all in slow motion.

Dennis Fitch noticed the same thing and stood from the sofa. "Bruce! Look out!" he yelled.

Fox and Lang stopped momentarily and glanced up. The barrel of Kaitlyn's pistol was poised, and her hand was steady. Before Fox could roll out of the gun's path, another piercing shot rang out. Amber screamed and covered her head. Lang and Fox looked at one another, each realizing that he hadn't been hit, and wondering whether the bullet had found the other.

"Harry." It was Kaitlyn's voice. There was a subtle quiver in her tone.

Lang turned toward her. She was still grasping the gun, but her arm was back at her side. Lang sat up slowly and noticed something he had never seen before: a single tear ran down Kaitlyn's cheek. She collapsed to a knee, almost as if the weight of the tear had pulled her down. Her face was the first part of her body to hit the floor. Upon impact, she turned over, and they all got a clear view of her back and the moist red spot close to the center of her blouse. With three laborious heaves of breath, her legs twitched tightly. And then, as suddenly as she had fallen to the floor, she stopped moving.

Lang's eyes fell as he stared at her motionless body, then gradually moved upward to the spot where she had been standing, which was now an exposed view of the terrace through the double French doors. Lang's cheeks suddenly took on a white pallor.

Five men in soaking black uniforms stood with their guns raised and aimed in his direction. It didn't require a genius to know that one of those guns had fired the shot that left Kaitlyn McBride on the floor of the island villa. The man in the middle stepped through the doors, and Lang recognized Special Agent Dalton immediately. Behind him and the other men in the rain were six more men in the same attire. Lang identified the emblems on their jackets as those of FBI Legats.

Lang stood slowly, his mouth slightly open in an unmistakable expression of shock. The men in black stepped to the side, and the doorway darkened as a large figure stepped through. Dripping wet, the figure moved his hood and locked eyes with Lang, whose knees went weak for a moment and buckled beneath him. He managed to stay on his feet, but that gesture spoke volumes to everyone in the room.

"Gentlemen," Director Lassiter said, running his hand over his wet hair, while making eye contact with each person in the room.

"Art," Lang said, stepping forward. "Sir, I was just about to place these men under arrest for suspicion of…"

"Put a lid on it, Harry," Lassiter shut him up. The director was unarmed and unwavering.

Lang looked around and found himself staring down ten gun barrels. It wasn't worth trying to keep up the charade. The sight of Dalton standing there was a clear indicator of what the director knew.

Dalton stepped forward. "Amber," he said, beckoning her to come toward him.

Amber peeled herself off the wall and ran to his side, careful to steer away from Kaitlyn. One of the legats wrapped a windbreaker around her.

Lassiter took another step inside the room. "Harrison Lang, Harper Phillips, Bruce Fox, Dennis Fitch, and Terence Hammond. You are all under arrest on the charges of conspiracy, corporate fraud, money laundering, and a long list of other shit that I'm too cold and cranky to rattle off to you right now."

He then looked down at Kaitlyn's still body. "I was hoping it wouldn't have to come to *this*, Harry," he said, shaking his head.

The team of legats entered the room and placed cuffs on all of the conspirators. None put up a fight. After all, there was nowhere to go. They were surrounded by water, and there were ten highly trained men with guns on them.

The rain had subsided to a drizzle. As the Committee members were being escorted out of the house, Lassiter looked closely at each of them. The last to exit was Lang, who stopped in front of Lassiter.

"So this is how you treat your own?" Lang growled.

"I told you once before, Harry. I don't trust anyone, especially those who are on my team."

Lang sneered at him.

"Get him out of here," he told the young man who had his gun pointed at Lang.

They all walked down to the dock, where three police vessels awaited them. Lassiter approached Dalton.

"Well done, Special Agent Dalton. I'll make sure that the right people know about this. This is a big one for you."

Dalton shook the director's hand. "I appreciate that, sir."

"Now, with that being said, I think I'll grant you the assignment of escorting Mr. Lang back to the States. There's a security team in Cancun waiting. I've told them they are to follow your lead on this."

Dalton could barely contain his excitement. It was the opportunity he had been waiting for. This would no doubt put him on the map within the law enforcement circle.

"And what about Jack Bennett, sir?"

Amber heard this and tuned her ears so she could hear Lassiter's response.

Lassiter nodded. "He's out there somewhere. And he clearly has his own agenda. As soon as all of the people we've apprehended today are back in the States, I need you to find Jack. For starters, he interfered in a federal investigation. I don't know who he's working for, and I don't care. He's a civilian, and I have no tolerance for this kind of vigilante bullshit. I'm putting you in charge of finding him."

"Whatever you say, sir."

"I'll make sure these others are taken care of," Lassiter said, motioning toward the four men sitting in one of the police boats, their hands locked behind them.

In the second boat, Lang sat alone on one side, while three legats sat across from him. As it began to roll away, Amber caught sight of Lang, who was looking at her. She swore she saw a smile on his face.

Lassiter turned to Amber. "Miss Wakefield, we haven't been formally introduced. I'm Director Lassiter, head of the FBI. I understand you've undergone quite an ordeal."

"You could say that, sir."

"Well, I hate to do this, but we are going to ask for your cooperation. One of my men will be briefing you so that we can complete our case file against this group."

"Of course," she replied. "But Mr. Lassiter, I'm concerned about something else."

"Your mother," he said.

"Yes, how did you…?" she started to ask.

"Special Agent Dalton and one of his men, Gil, filled me in. The driver who transported you from the airport last night saw you come out of the building with Ms. McBride. He noticed that your mother wasn't with you, so he went inside to find out why. He said that when he found her, she was calmly reading a magazine."

Amber breathed a sigh of relief. "That's my mom."

"She's safe. He's escorting her to meet you."

"Meet me where?"

Lassiter smiled and called over DiRosa.

"Agent DiRosa here is going to take you to meet her."

"She's here?"

He put his hand on her back. "Just go with him."

"Mr. Lassiter, what's going to happen to Jack?"

"I don't know, Amber. Dalton was the last person to see him, and that was yesterday. If he knows we're looking for him, we may never catch him."

Amber sighed, disappointed.

"You're safe, Amber. Be happy for that."

Lassiter climbed into the other police boat along with the other members of the Committee. He nodded to Amber as the boat pulled away. As she watched it speed off, she caught Bruce Fox staring back at her. It was ironic to her that he would be the last person she would see after all of this, considering he was the first person who had brought this nightmare into her life.

Agent DiRosa led Amber to a smaller boat and helped her in. She couldn't wait to see her mother, but she was also nervous. She wasn't sure how much of these events would register with her mother's sense of the present time. She hoped that not much would. As the boat moved north toward Mexico, she glanced skyward. The dark clouds were fading, and the rays of the sun could be seen peeking out.

Chapter 63

Agent DiRosa offered nothing in the form of communication to Amber during their ride. He was a dutiful FBI agent, who spoke when spoken to. She didn't like the way her conversation had ended with Director Lassiter. The idea that Jack would never be found saddened her. She wanted one more chance to see him. Perhaps he would come looking for her someday.

The vivid image of those men being escorted in handcuffs was hard to shake. She had spent significant time with each of them, and now they were all going to jail. She envisioned the headlines and news stories that would come out in the following weeks. The country would be in shock when it learned that the deputy director of the FBI and the CEO of Ensight both could have orchestrated a money laundering scheme to ambush the president's reelection campaign. She would never tell anyone about her own involvement. It would invite too many questions. And besides, who would believe her?

DiRosa guided the boat through the open water. Amber had lost herself so far into her thoughts that she didn't notice the white yacht resting atop the ocean about three hundred yards in front of her boat. As they drew nearer, she leaned forward to get a better look. It looked identical to the yacht she had boarded two days before in Belize. The dimensions and shape resembled the same boat where Lang had taken her and her mother hostage. At about forty yards, she saw the ladder leading up to the helm. It was beside that ladder where she had seen Watts, dead against the cabin wall. When DiRosa turned the boat and made his way around the stern, she confirmed her assumptions. The name NICOLETTE in blue letters was dazzling under the now sunny sky.

DiRosa turned off the engine, and Amber held tight to her seat. The last time she boarded this yacht it had ended in horror. A young black man stood at the edge of the yacht, and when she looked up, he smiled at her. He secured the ladder and held out his hand to help her up.

"It's OK, Amber," DiRosa reassured her. "I'll be right here."

Amber stepped out of the smaller boat and slowly climbed the ladder. When she reached the top, she stopped and looked around. Everything seemed exactly the same as it had been when she had ascended that same ladder not long ago. Once on board, she glanced up and saw a man with a baseball cap sitting in the captain's chair. He was fiddling with the navigation device, his back turned to her. Still ready to jump back over the side in case this ended like the last time, Amber stretched her neck toward the cabin's interior. The plush décor had not changed, and there was music playing softly. On a table in the center, there was a tray with a dozen or so flutes of champagne filled about three-quarters each.

She inched forward, not letting go of the railing on the side. And then she heard it. It was singing. She recognized the show tune. It was some song from *Oklahoma* that Amber had never known the title of, despite having heard it almost every day growing up in her mother's house. She let go of the railing and stepped to the edge of the cabin. The older woman was in the galley, snapping the ends from a colander full of green beans.

Amber held her hands to her mouth, and through them, managed to speak. "Mom?"

Her mother spun around, startled, with her hand on her chest. "Amber! My baby's home." She wiped her hands with a dishrag and held her arms out to her daughter, who leapt down the steps to embrace her.

The two women held each other for a long while. Amber cried as she had so many times in the last several weeks.

"I'm so sorry, Mom. Can you ever forgive me? I'll never leave you like that again. I swear."

"I know, dear. I know. Hush now. I'm here for you." She patted Amber on the back as she had when Amber was a little girl.

It was so comforting to hear those words from her mother. It didn't really matter to Amber that she might be in a different time and place in her mind. The words still meant the same.

An hour passed as the two women sat on the sofa and talked and laughed. Amber never once brought up the events of the last few weeks. There was no point. She and her mother were together, safe. And that was all that mattered.

After helping her mother get into bed for a nap in one of the staterooms, Amber heard a boat engine nearby. Amber braced herself and stood on the sofa to get a look through the window. She hadn't noticed that DiRosa was long gone. A blue cruiser approached the yacht, and Amber ducked back down. She didn't have it in her to endure anything more. All she knew was that her mother would be within her sight the whole time. She sat still and listened.

Before long, she heard a number of voices. Male voices. They were all speaking over one another, separated by verses of laughter. She stood on the sofa and looked out the window. The cruiser outside was the same one she had seen remove Lassiter and the four men a few hours earlier. The sunlight reflected brightly on the silver sheen of the handcuffs, which were piled neatly on the boat's bench. She dropped back to the sofa when she saw two shoes move onto the first step leading down to the cabin. Then another set of feet followed the first. Slowly, more pairs of shoes appeared at the top of the steps.

The first face to appear in the cabin was that of Bruce Fox. Amber stood still and placed her hand against the door to the stateroom. There was nowhere else to go, but she felt that she needed to create as much distance as possible. After Fox, the short man who she now knew as Harper Phillips hopped down. The older man needed assistance getting down and was finally followed by the last man, Dennis Fitch. Not long ago, she had seen these four men in handcuffs. Once again, this yacht had become a dangerous trap, inside of which she and her mother were caught.

They all stood inside the cabin. Amber stood at the furthest point from the four men. For a moment, they looked at each other, none more sure than the other of what to say. The men smiled at her, almost in a paternal fashion.

"What the hell is this?" she asked nervously.

Finally, there were footsteps up top again, and two more feet appeared at the top of the steps. Before his face was visible, Amber recognized the physique. Director Lassiter could barely stand straight inside the cabin, but he managed to maneuver his way to the front of the group.

"Hello again, Amber," he said.

Amber was shaking her head. "What is going on here? I thought these men were going to jail."

"I suppose an explanation is warranted here," he offered.

She didn't respond for a moment. Then she sighed and said, "I'm not sure I can listen to any more. Every time I hear someone offer me a so-called explanation, I feel like I'm watching a bad film."

"I can understand that. But we feel like it's owed to you."

Amber folded her arms across her chest.

Lassiter didn't move forward but rather leaned against the counter in the galley.

"Amber, these men behind me are not going to jail. But I suppose you've figured that out already."

"I'm listening," she said, maintaining her distance.

"What I'm about to tell you is said in the strictest confidence," he warned.

"Mr. Lassiter, I don't owe anyone anything. So, whatever you tell me, you'll just have to trust me with. I'm done trusting. It's someone else's turn."

Fox smiled. He loved her defiance. He had seen it the first time he'd met her.

"We work for Art, or rather, Mr. Lassiter," Fox said.

"You work for him? You're with the FBI?"

"No, not quite," Fox said. He looked at the others, who offered nothing.

Fox continued. "You see, several years ago, we were each approached by Harry Lang individually to join him in what he termed an investment opportunity. He offered each of us a slice of a private investment fund he had started out of Aruba. There were about twelve investors, ranging from Saudi oil tycoons to South American government officials, and of course, our own president himself before he took office. All of it was clean money, but we chose to keep it quiet so we could shield ourselves from taxes and regulatory conflicts."

Amber sat on the edge of the sofa. This was going to be a long explanation, she could tell.

"But after Congress passed the Patriot Act in 2001, it was clear that our affiliation with some of these foreign groups was not going to be as simple to conceal as it had been in the past. It was just a matter of time before we were exposed for doing business with individuals who might be on the Patriot Act radar. In his position at the FBI, it was easy for Harry to manipulate the investigations outlined in the Act. He basically had discretion over who he thought was suspicious."

"But he also knew that he couldn't keep that up forever," Fitch added.

Amber was riveted. The others watched Fox as he told the story. It was almost as if this was the first time they had heard it as well.

"Anyway," Fox continued, "once the president took office, we convinced him to take a hard look at some of the proposed amendments to the Patriot Act. One of the proposals came from a Democratic congressman from Ohio. Its purpose was to place specific limits on U.S. federal law enforcement powers to scrutinize American offshore entities. It was a long shot to pass, but within the language, there was a provision that would have kept our business under wraps. Naturally, we were advocates for it. In return, we promised the president that he would get some hefty contributions for his reelection campaign."

"Are you going to tell me that our president was planning to pass a law allowing him and his buddies to make a bunch of money?" Amber asked.

They all looked at one another, forgetting that Amber was young and naïve enough to believe that someone like the president would never entertain such a thought.

"Well, he had the incentive to do it. After all, he had a lot to gain both personally and financially," Fitch said.

"I don't believe this," she said.

Fox waved off Fitch, as if to tell him that she needed to hear only the facts and nothing else. "The short version, Amber, is that the president ended up getting cold feet. He backed out of the deal and started shooting down the legislation reforms to the Act. What was worse, he began promoting more stringent provisions in the law. He basically told us to keep our campaign contributions and stick them where the sun didn't shine. That's a direct quote, by the way."

Amber was starting to see it. "What you're saying is that you guys decided to trash his campaign by collecting funds from these groups just to get back at him."

"There were millions of dollars at stake. We had come a long way, and he pulled the rug out. We took it personally."

"That's not a reason for doing what you did."

"You're right. And it was when Harry decided to take it to the next level that we started to get nervous."

"Why? What happened?"

"Even though our investment partners were all legal, their positions in their countries and governments gave them access to all sorts of people. For example, our Saudi investors had ties to some of the more extreme fundamentalist groups. Our Latin partners had friends in the cocaine trade. With their help and that of Mr. Hammond's CIA network, we were able to construct an entire system for collecting money from the least desirable groups imaginable."

"All of this to get back at one man? Didn't any of you have a conscience?" she asked.

"We all did, Amber. Except for Harry. He was completely focused on destroying the president. But when the first of us tried to leave, Harry had him killed. We took that as a warning that the price of betraying him was your life." Fox was out of breath. It was the first time he had told this story, and it sounded outrageous even to him.

Amber looked at all of them, disgusted, and then fixed her gaze on Harper. "Then you faked your own suicide to get away from Mr. Lang?"

Harper nodded. "Since I was the trustee for Bartlett, it made sense that I should be the one to disappear. My absence made it easier for us to execute our plan against him."

"So, I suppose that's where you, Mr. Lassiter, come in?" she asked, pointing to the director.

"Art found out about this whole thing a while ago, and he threatened to take us down." Fox told her. "In exchange for immunity, we agreed to set this whole thing in motion for him. It was dangerous, we all knew that much. But we weren't going to sit by and watch Harry succeed either."

"That's right," Lassiter said. "I knew what Harry's ultimate goal was. The president himself asked me to watch his back and told me he didn't trust Lang. It didn't take me long to find the rest of these guys and recruit them."

Amber frowned. "Recruit them? Then if these men aren't affiliated with the FBI, what exactly were you recruiting them for? What is their purpose?"

"In the simplest terms, our mission is to protect the presidency."

"Isn't that what the Secret Service's job is?" She wasn't sure what she was talking about but she was digging for more information.

Lassiter shook his head. "The Secret Service guards the president. We guard the presidency."

She shrugged. "What's the difference?"

"The Secret Service protects the man everywhere he goes. We look after the institution and everything it represents. That's the difference."

She wasn't quite sure what he meant, but it sounded impressive.

Lassiter went on to clarify his point. "I could care less who sits in the Oval Office. But I swore to safeguard the sanctity of the position."

"But in a situation like this, the president isn't exactly innocent. Don't you have to subscribe to his politics somewhat if you're going to look after him? Don't you want to care about who you're protecting?"

"It's the most powerful seat in the world. I know what I'm protecting," Lassiter said proudly. "And as for his politics, well, we're not permitted to think about that. That's why I haven't voted in the last twenty years."

Amber had never considered the president as an institution. He was always portrayed in the media as a human being.

"Anyway, what happens now?" she asked. "If these men aren't going to jail, then what? Do they go back to their normal lives?"

Fox shook his head. "No. But for all of us, that's probably for the best."

"Then what?" she repeated.

"When these gentlemen signed on to help me, it was for more than just one assignment. They signed on for life," Lassiter explained.

It sounded so infinite, almost like a prison sentence. But as she examined each of the men, none of them appeared to be regretful about their commitment. She turned back to the director.

"And how did you come to be a part of this guardian angel group, Mr. Lassiter?"

Lassiter smiled. He had never heard it referred to in that way. "I'm sorry, Amber, but that's classified."

"Well, how many people are involved in this?"

He shook his head again. "Classified."

"Can you tell me how long it's been around?"

"I'd say about thirty years. And they've managed to keep it secret all this time."

"Who are 'they'?" she continued to probe.

He looked at her with an exhausted expression. She held up her hands.

"Let me guess," she said. "It's classified."

"You're catching on," he said.

"So, then answer this. If all of this is classified, then how do you expect to charge Mr. Lang with anything? The story is going to get out with a scandal involving two high-profile people like Kaitlyn and Mr. Lang. Won't the media start asking questions about how they were brought down?"

"We'll likely charge him with fraud and obstruction of justice. Something generic like that."

"Wait a minute. I don't get it. That's not what happened. They tried to sabotage the president's campaign. They solicited money from terrorists and drug cartels. Isn't he getting off kind of easy?"

"That's not for anyone to know. A scandal like this can ruin the president, regardless of whether it's true or not. Our job is to stop it and make sure it doesn't get past us. The very notion that something like this is even possible is what we are trying to keep quiet. Once speculation begins, people start making up their own minds about its validity. That's when spin doctors come into play. But we're not in the business of damage control. We're in the business of prevention. Once the story is out, it's too late, and we've failed."

"Then what? He does a little jail time and that's it? It hardly sounds like he's paying for anything."

"He'll have to live the rest of his life under a cloud of suspicion. Believe me, that's the ultimate price to pay for people in positions of power, much worse than the fate that met his beloved Ms. McBride. He has nowhere else to go."

"But people died in the process. A lot of innocent people."

Lassiter nodded. "Unfortunately, the fight to keep the president guarded is a constant war. And like any war, there are casualties. It's a sad reality."

"Does the president himself authorize these assignments every time he anticipates something bad coming?"

"No way. I'd say that the president isn't aware of 50 percent of these efforts. Hundreds of schemes each year are targeted at marring him, and I'd say we catch close to 70 percent of them."

"I'm dealing with a real-life secret society here, aren't I?"

"We're only one of many independent groups in Washington whose task is to mold public image."

It sounded so textbook that Amber wondered whether that statement was engraved somewhere. *An independent group in Washington.* She had heard that phrase before.

After a long silence, Amber stood from her seat. She felt the vibrations of the engine below. The yacht was moving.

"Where are we going?" she asked, peering out the window.

The others began walking toward the steps leading to the deck. Lassiter stayed behind and waited for Amber.

"We're meeting some associates," he said, and invited her to join them up top.

While standing on the deck, none of them said anything. Amber stood the furthest away, consciously keeping her distance from all of them. Fifteen minutes later, the yacht slowed its pace.

"This is the spot," Harper called out to the boat captain.

The yacht's engine died in the open water. Amber held her hand up to her forehead to shield her eyes from the sunlight. She hadn't paid much attention to which direction they had been traveling, so she was completely disoriented.

All of the men gravitated to both sides of the yacht, leaning over the railings. They were searching for something.

"Why are we stopping here?" Amber asked. "We're in the middle of nowhere."

Lassiter had removed his watch from his wrist and was holding it in his hand, staring at its face. In his other hand, he held a compass, attached to his belt by a silver chain. It looked like a pocket watch.

"Which way?" Harper asked.

Lassiter looked for a second longer at his compass, and then pointed in the southeastern direction.

"There," he said.

The others followed his finger, as did Amber. From her view, there was nothing but calm blue waters on all sides around them.

"Over here, Art," Fox called out from the stern.

They all walked to the back of the boat. Amber tried to see what they were looking for. Then she saw it. A series of bubbles trickled to the top of the water's surface, and a head slowly appeared. Strapped into scuba gear and wearing a mask, it was hard to see who the person was. But when he removed the mask and cleared the water from his face, she felt a sudden rush of happiness. Jack's blue eyes looked up at her from the water.

"Hello, Amber," he said.

She said nothing, and then a smile came to her face.

Chapter 64

Once Jack was aboard, he put on a sweatshirt and warmed himself. He shook hands with the other men, exchanging embraces and smiles, as if they were old pals. All this time, he'd had Amber convinced that he was operating on the opposite side from these men. He had always been vague about the so-called assignment he had been hired for. He had managed to keep his lips tight about that supposedly independent group in Washington who had hired him. But after what she had just heard from Lassiter and the others, and after seeing them all slapping each other on the back, it all made perfect sense.

After rehydrating himself with a liter of bottled water, Jack parted from the group and approached Amber, who had been standing outside the circle.

The two remained motionless, each waiting for the other to step forward.

"I guess this is the independent group who hired you," she said to him.

"Part of it," he said.

"I didn't think I was going to see you again."

"I know. I don't know what to say. You deserved more than that."

Her gaze refused to leave him. Despite the disheveled hair, he was clean-shaven. She looked down at herself. She had been in the same clothes for days, and her hair felt like it was standing on end. She didn't feel attractive at all. But Jack continued to look at her nonetheless.

"I take it that Mr. Lassiter has explained this all to you?" he asked.

She nodded. "At least the part that isn't classified."

"Do you buy it?"

"It seems far too outrageous not to believe. If I hadn't seen it all unfold in front of my own eyes, I'd say you were all crazy."

"Well, I think we reached that status long before any of us met each other." He glanced toward the others who had overheard his remark.

Lassiter moved toward Jack and Amber.

"I don't mean to break up this reunion, but we still have one more piece of business, Jack."

Jack nodded. He glanced toward the starboard side of the yacht. "He should be up soon."

Ninety seconds of silence ensued. Jack stood close to Amber, a subtle sign that he was not going to abandon her again. At one moment, their hands grazed one another, and she was sure it wasn't completely unintentional.

"I see him," Fitch said, pointing to a spot approximately ten yards from the yacht.

Amber looked over and saw the dark figure of another diver ascending to the surface. As he swam toward the stern of the boat, Fitch and Fox walked over and held the ladder. After putting all his gear on board, the man climbed the ladder. He had his mask on top of his shaved head. She didn't recognize his face, but that all changed when he removed the mask. As he was greeted by the others, he smiled, and she knew for sure who he was. It was the same toothy smile she had seen in Milan.

Amber took a step back, but Jack clutched her arm.

"I think I owe you an apology, Miss Wakefield," the man said. "I never meant to frighten you back in Milan." He held his hand out to her.

"You were in my room, weren't you? You broke into the safe and stole those documents and my passport."

"That was a bit messy," Jack commented. "It was supposed to be a little more professional. But we had become desperate."

Harper stepped forward and placed his hand on the man's shoulder, which was at his eye level.

"Amber, this is Mr..." Harper started to say, but the man placed a hand on his shoulder and shook his head.

"Sorry," he continued, and then smiled. "I'm a freelancer." They all laughed.

"He's a personality for hire," Harper said with a wink.

"I was better at being you than you ever were," he told Harper.

"Tell me, why did you break into my room?" Amber asked, not yet sharing in the enjoyment of the moment.

"We needed to get our hands on those documents," Harper said. "They were the original articles of incorporation for Bartlett. I had stored them in a secure

Swiss bank three years ago, but once things were set in motion, particularly that Maguire-Ensight deal, we needed to conceal them before they got out."

"But how did you know that I would have them?"

"A desk clerk at the hotel in Bern saw you leave only minutes before they discovered the dead courier in the hall. Bruce had hired the courier to transport those documents back to the States. But Lang decided to take matters into his own hands and to try to intercept them. The documents were sort of an insurance policy for him, in case we turned on him."

"Talk about irony," Hammond said.

"So, he had that poor man killed?" She glanced over to Lassiter. "Another casualty of war, Mr. Lassiter?"

He looked at her and then quickly away.

She shook her head. "I just can't help but think that I was responsible for many of those people who died."

"Don't say that, Amber," Jack consoled her.

"I just wish I had walked away the moment Mr. Fox first came to our offices. I have to ask myself why I didn't ignore everything and go about my own business."

A long silence followed, as they watched her play out everything in her memory.

"Because you didn't take my advice to get out of town." The voice came from behind the circle of men. It was a familiar voice, but it was impossible for it to belong to the person Amber was thinking of.

She looked between the men in the direction of the pilothouse. The boat captain, still wearing the baseball cap, descended the ladder to join the rest of them on deck. Amber watched his movements closely. As he moved his large frame down the ladder, her heart began racing, although she had no idea why. It was only when he removed his cheap aviator sunglasses and his dirty hat that Amber's hands went directly to her gaping mouth.

"Oh, I don't believe this," she whispered.

"Hello, dear."

Although he had a full beard and his hair was virtually sheared off, she recognized the eyes. She shook her head in disbelief as she stood face to face with Marty Callahan.

Marty placed his hands on Amber's shoulders and squeezed them lightly. His reassuring smile immediately made her cry. She hugged him and kissed him on the cheek. Despite the flirtatious nature of their working relationship, he had always been the closest she'd ever had to a father figure.

She couldn't keep the tears from gushing from her eyes. But she finally managed to speak.

"I don't—I mean, what—." She was struggling to make a sentence. "I can't believe it's really you," she said, touching his face. "But I saw you die in that car."

"Actually, all you saw was a burning car. That was it. Harry had given Watts the green light to kill you. Luckily, Watts tipped us off in time. That's when we decided to make me disappear. Besides, Harry probably had plans to take me out eventually."

"So you staged the whole car explosion?" she said through sniffling.

"Not bad, huh?" Jack asked proudly.

Was there anything about the last several weeks that was real? she asked herself. She felt like the victim of a series of bad practical jokes.

"Then you lied to me, Marty. You knew everything from the start. I can't believe you, of all people, would be involved in something like this."

"I didn't want to be involved, believe me. But Bill Raleigh was one of my dearest friends. When he was CEO at Ensight years ago, he hired me on the spot and gave me every opportunity I could ask for. He also kept no secrets from me. When he started to get nervous about his involvement in this venture, he confided in me. And then when he was killed, I knew Harry had something to do with it. So I threatened to blow the whistle on all of them."

"That's when we approached him," Fox said. "We explained the situation and our work with Director Lassiter. In fact, that was the purpose of my visit to your office. It was sort of a final recruiting trip. From Harry's perspective, he thought he was cutting Marty into the deal in exchange for Marty keeping his mouth shut."

"I don't believe this," Amber repeated.

Lassiter pointed to a black box on the floor of the boat. It was soaking wet. "Is that it?"

They all turned toward it, digressing from their discussion.

"That's it," replied the man with the shaved head. "The thing weighs a ton on land, let alone underwater."

Lassiter fished in his pocket and pulled out a small brass key. He inserted it into the lock on the front of the box and opened it. Inside, wrapped in thick plastic, was a thick binder full of pages. He quickly unwrapped it and wiped beads of water from the surface. Amber could see clearly that the binder had a Department of Justice seal on the front.

Amber pointed to the thick binder. "What is that?"

He held it up. "This is an affidavit, signed by each of these men. It basically tells the same story you've just heard, but in much more detail. It's the only record of their participation in the investment fund, its purpose, and the other participants. It was an insurance policy to make certain that they would cooperate and follow through on their assignment. If they didn't, the information contained here would be sent directly to the U.S. Attorney General's office."

"That's blackmail, isn't it?" she asked.

"We call it effective persuasion," Lassiter said with a smile.

The others smiled and shook their heads.

"What was it doing underwater?" asked Amber.

"It was the safest place. I certainly couldn't keep it in the FBI office's files. We hid this box inside the cabin of a sunken wreck below us."

"So, why get it out now?"

"I'm keeping up my end of the bargain. If these guys completed their assignment, then this affidavit was never to see the light of day."

The men all looked at the binder. Lassiter was literally holding their fate in his hands.

The man with the shaved head and big teeth spoke up. "Well, since we're opening presents, I almost forgot to give you all of yours." He climbed the ladder to the cabin below and returned carrying a briefcase, which he set on the bench as the others gathered around. Thumbing through the dial for the combination, he opened the case. Inside there were papers bound by a clip. When Amber leaned forward, she recognized the title page: *Articles of Incorporation Bartlett Enterprises*. They were the same pages she had been handed by the courier before he died.

"Art, we trust that these incorporation docs will meet the same fate as the affidavit," Harper said.

"Consider them nonexistent," Lassiter replied, reaching out to accept the documents.

When Harper lifted the articles out of the briefcase, Amber's eyes grew large at what she saw beneath them. Stacks of hundred dollar bills bound in thick bands lined the case.

"How much is in there?" she muttered.

"Twenty million, if I'm not mistaken," Jack said. "I counted it after I picked it up in San Ignacio."

"That's about right," said the man who called himself a freelancer. "I hit about four different accounts in all. Harry's guy moved pretty quickly, so it was hard to get there before him."

They all watched Amber's reaction as she stared at the cash. Her face said it all.

"Amber, despite the impression I may have given you earlier, we don't do all of this for free," Lassiter said.

"But isn't this evidence? Wouldn't this be considered a kickback of sorts?"

Lassiter stood in front of her. "I can't tell you that."

She rolled her eyes. Exhausted and feeling the onset of a headache, Amber spoke. "I have one last question. If all of this is supposed to be classified, then why did you tell me?"

Lassiter turned and looked at each of the men, all of whom were staring back at him. It was the question all of them had been waiting for her to ask. She looked back at them and frowned. She wanted an answer to her question. Finally, Marty approached her and placed his arm around her shoulder.

"How do you feel about working together again, dear?" he asked, with raised eyebrows.

They spent the rest of that afternoon drinking champagne and talking. Amber took a shower and ate three plates of fresh halibut and assorted fruits. She managed to get at least half an hour with each of the men, acquainting herself with them. At one point, she felt like a prize on a reality dating TV show. She found each of them to be extremely interesting, and together they possessed a diverse set of backgrounds. She now understood why both Lang and Lassiter had found them to be such an effective team for their respective purposes.

By this hour, Amber's mother had woken up from her nap. She seemed not the least surprised to find all these men on board even though they had not been there when she went to sleep. She was in the kitchen, treating each of them as if they were her nephews and sons. They discussed everything they could, but not once did the subject of Harry Lang or their assignment arise. Amber remained relatively quiet throughout the discussion, not yet prepared to engage herself fully into any conversation. It was all so overwhelming, and she felt herself trying to catch her breath every few minutes.

Outside, the sun was low in the sky. Director Lassiter was the first to emerge from the cabin, followed by the others.

"All ready for you, sir," said the young black man on board, motioning to the cruiser waiting in the water next to the yacht. He climbed in and started the engine.

Lassiter turned to all of them, clutching the affidavit in his arm. "Gentlemen, I'll be in touch with each of you soon to schedule a debriefing. I also have a new assignment for all of you."

They all shook hands. Before he stepped onto the ladder to the cruiser, he turned to Amber.

"So, Miss Wakefield. Is this farewell?"

She looked up at him. "I hope you don't take this the wrong way, Mr. Lassiter, but I hardly think I fit the profile of what you're looking for."

Fox stepped forward. "I'd beg to differ, Amber. And I'm sure the rest of these men would as well. If it hadn't been for you, Harry and Kaitlyn would have succeeded. Don't forget that none of us even knew that Harry had developed a parallel plan to pad the president's campaign fund."

"One might even say that you're the one the president owes thanks to and not these guys," Lassiter said with a playful smile.

Hammond held his hand up. "Uh, you are still planning to destroy that affidavit, aren't you, Art?"

Lassiter waved his hand at the old man. "Don't worry yourself, Terry. It's as good as gone."

Until then, Amber hadn't thought about the magnitude of the situation when she decided to interfere in the Maguire deal. Two months earlier, she had been an assistant in the human resources department of a multinational corporation. For her, it would be an unprecedented career leap to enter the underground world of guarding the office of the president of the United States.

"I don't think this is for everyone, Mr. Lassiter," she said politely. "I wasn't trying to save the president or anything noble like that. I just don't like seeing powerful people bulldoze their way through life. I know a lot of people at Ensight, and I didn't want them to get caught in the path. I did what I did for them. And I did it for my mother." She glanced over at her mother, who smiled back. "And frankly, the notion of signing on for life, as you put it earlier, is a bit too suffocating for me. There are more important things for me to do."

"I understand, Amber. And you're right, this isn't for everyone. You should never be asked to abandon your life."

He turned and descended the ladder. As the cruiser sped away, Amber looked around. She began recalling some of the events in her life, particularly after her father left them, which had caused Amber to struggle to trust people. But throughout this ordeal, she had placed a tremendous amount of trust in a number of people. Some worked out for her, while others betrayed her. But she was safe, and that was what mattered the most.

Her thoughts were interrupted when her mother came to her side and put her arms around her daughter's waist. Next to her was Marty, smoking a cigar. He looked at Amber and offered that familiar wink which she'd thought she would never see again. And when she turned around, she saw Jack standing there, with his eyes locked on her. It was a brief snapshot of what she considered to be her life. As if on cue, Lassiter's parting words echoed in her head. He was right. She should not abandon her life.

Amber looked forward again and watched the cruiser shrink from view. The sky was growing a deep orange, and soon, the water around them was flat and calm again.

The others returned to the cabin below, as the sun was starting to dip to the horizon. As Amber sat on the back of the yacht with her bare feet hanging off, she took a deep breath and enjoyed the serenity of the moment, as the sound of water lapped against the side of the yacht. She didn't notice Jack standing behind her until he cleared his throat.

"May I?" he asked, pointing at the open seat next to her.

As they sat side by side, with the faint buzz of conversation beneath them in the cabin, a light breeze swept past. He looked over at her to see that she had tilted her head back, her eyes closed. She was smiling.

"Amber," he said, "I know there's a lot I should have told you. And there still is. The right time has never presented itself."

She opened her eyes slowly and brought her head forward.

"I'm not sure what you want me to say," he said.

Without looking at him, she inhaled deeply. "Nothing," she finally said. "At least not right now. It's too perfect."

He wasn't sure what she meant at first, but then, he followed her eyes that were fixed on the horizon and the open water. The view was boundless and unthreatening. The smile on her face indicated that she was reacting to the sound of her mother's laughter. It was at that moment that he realized what she meant.

She was clearly lost in her thoughts, and he felt like an intruder. He slowly raised his feet up and began to stand, until he noticed her inching toward him. He reassumed his position and gently placed his hand on her back. Still not looking at him, she leaned toward him and rested her head against his shoulder. For the next thirty minutes, they sat in silence. The residual daylight was starting to fade, and the pink sky was losing its luster. When the sun disappeared, he carefully leaned forward and looked at her. Her eyes were closed, and she was breathing calmly, asleep. He did not move for four hours.

EPILOGUE

The day's issue of *The Asian Wall Street Journal* contained a front-page column with highlighted excerpts from the U.S. president's address to the nation. He had been in office for one hundred days, and the election had yielded a dual victory for his party as they also managed to win back more seats in the House. As a result, the amendments to tighten enforcement laws in the Patriot Act were passed despite much resistance.

Amber sat reading the story in the Park Hyatt's Little Kitchen restaurant at a waterfront table with a view of the Opera House. It was a gorgeous April autumn day in Sydney. She had phoned her mother to tell her she was safe. The older woman was living in New England with a private nurse and spoke with Amber by phone every day.

As Amber read on, she noted a brief expose in the same paper about Kaitlyn McBride, and the still unsolved accident which had claimed the life of the former Ensight CEO. There was no mention of any criminal speculation on her part. There was no mention of Bartlett Enterprises, Harper Phillips, or Maguire's reasons for nixing the acquisition. The brief article was as bland and undetailed as the public announcement of the dismissal of Harrison W. Lang, the former deputy director of the FBI, which became public back in the beginning of October. The reasons for his dismissal remained undisclosed, but there were speculative accusations that he had been engaged in interfering with federal investigations. No specifics had been released as of that time. The public would soon forget all about it.

Amber had been with Lassiter and the others as they worked on formulating the appropriate stories about Harry Lang and Kaitlyn McBride. As long as this group knew the truth, Harry Lang would be walking on thin ice for the rest of his life, and Kaitlyn McBride's brief legacy would die as certainly and as quickly as she had. As Lassiter had said before, there was nowhere else for them to go.

The last she had heard, Dalton had been named assistant director of the Criminal Investigative Division in Washington. It was a multitiered career leap for him, which Lassiter himself had made possible. None of them knew what Lassiter had told him about Lang and Kaitlyn, and they had never asked. Something told her that Dalton would never ask either.

She folded up the paper and set it down on the chair beside her. She was not there to catch up on current events. She had a job to do. Her instructions had come directly from Director Lassiter when she had arrived at the hotel that morning. The others, with the exception of Terry Hammond, who was not in a condition to travel, should have arrived throughout the day, but they were not to contact each other until directed.

At that moment, a young waiter approached her table. "G'day, Miss."

"Hello," she replied.

"This was left for you moments ago." He handed her a slip of paper.

She looked around before opening it. It was an instinct but probably not advisable under the circumstances. Despite four months of training, she needed the practice. She read the note quickly, folded it, and left the table.

The lobby was relatively empty as she strolled across its marble floors. As the elevator ascended, her heart began racing. She had spent nearly half a year with them all, but they were still intimidating. She saw the reflection of herself inside the elevator, and quickly removed her fingers from her hair. Despite her training, she still had to remind herself on occasion to break that habit. She arrived at the door of the Premier Suite and took a deep breath. She ran her hands through her hair and knocked on the door.

Bruce Fox answered, and she entered. All the men were standing in the living room against the backdrop of the Sydney Harbor. Lassiter had just completed a phone call when she entered.

"OK, gentlemen," he said, and then looked at Amber. "And lady."

He handed Amber a photograph of a Caucasian man in his fifties. She examined it.

"Amber, this is our guy. He should be checking into the Four Seasons in an hour. He should be alone, but keep your eye out for anyone with him. Try to remain relaxed throughout. Are you ready for this?"

She nodded slowly. "I think so."

"Jack, you track her but not too close. This guy's a slick one."

Jack nodded.

"Don't panic when you're out there, whatever you do," Fitch reminded her.

"Denny, she doesn't need the additional pressure," Marty said, holding his hand up.

"It's OK, Marty. He's right," she told him.

"This is the last time we'll see each other until this is all over, just like the last time," Lassiter concluded. "Any questions?"

They all shook their heads.

"OK," he said. "Let's go to work."

They all exited the suite and stepped into different elevator cars. Jack joined Amber in the last car as the doors closed. He squeezed her hand on the way down, and she responded in kind. By the time they arrived at the lobby level, the other elevators had emptied, and the other men were nowhere to be seen. As they were about to exit the hotel to the back pier, Jack stopped and pulled her aside.

"Are you sure you're up for this?" he asked her.

"I'm nervous," she admitted. "You know, my first assignment and everything."

He stepped closer. "It'll be fine. Just know that I'll be close the whole time." He had his arm around her waist and spoke to her softly.

Looking up, she smiled and touched his face. "I know you will."

978-0-595-38245-3
0-595-38245-2

Printed in the United States
53222LVS00004B/322-357